THE HURRICANE LOVER

THE
HURRICANE
LOVER

JONI RODGERS
NEW YORK TIMES BESTSELLING AUTHOR

The Hurricane Lover

© 2022 Joni Rodgers

Published by Westport Lighthouse Books

jonirodgers.com

Westport, WA

Library of Congress Control Number: 2022900450

Paperback ISBN: 979-8-9855494-2-3

Ebook ISBN: 979-8-9855494-3-0

Cover design by Kapo Ng

Interior design by Liz Schreiter

Edited and produced by Reading List Editorial

ReadingListEditorial.com

Publisher's Cataloging-in-Publication Data

Names: Rodgers, Joni.

Title: The hurricane lover / Joni Rodgers.

Description: Westport, WA : Westport Lighthouse Books, 2022. | With a new foreword by the author. | Summary: Set during the time of Hurricane Katrina, a local news reporter draws in her ex—a Gulf Coast climatologist—to solve the case of a serial murderer using the storm-related chaos as cover.

Identifiers: LCCN 2022900450 | ISBN 9798985549423 (pbk.) | ISBN 9798985549430 (ebook)

Subjects: LCSH: Hurricane Katrina, 2005 -- Fiction. | Climatologists -- Fiction. | Natural disasters -- Fiction. | Serial murders -- Fiction. | Women journalists -- United States -- Fiction. | New Orleans (La.) -- Fiction. | Texas -- Fiction. | BISAC: FICTION / Disaster. | FICTION / Mystery & Detective / Amateur Sleuth. | FICTION / Thrillers / Historical.

Classification: LCC PS3568.O34816 H87 2022 | DDC 813 R63h—dc23

LC record available at https://lccn.loc.gov/2022900450

WESTPORT
LIGHTHOUSE BOOKS

THIS BOOK IS DEDICATED TO
MALACHI BLACKSTONE RODGERS

**A wonderful fact to reflect upon,
that every human creature is
constituted to be that profound
secret and mystery to every other.**

—**Charles Dickens,** *A Tale of Two Cities*

A NOTE FROM THE AUTHOR

I was storm-obsessed long before the epic hurricane season of 2005. I was born in the American Midwest, where summer storms brought green skies and the smell of tornados. For one wonderful year, my family lived in a rundown townhome on the beach in Florida. During the offseason, the Gulf of Mexico turned steely, wind whipped up blades of white sand, and skies blackened over the glorious chaos. Wrapped in a blanket on the balcony outside the room I shared with my three sisters, I hugged my knees and counted the seconds between thunder and lightning.

In 2005, my husband Gary and I were living in Houston, Texas, not far from the upscale area where Bob and Char Hoovestahl live in the book. New Orleans was an easy day-trip for music and great food, and it was a convenient stop just on the way to my sister's house in Lake Mary, Florida. I was familiar with the small towns, swamps, and fruit markets off the I-10 exits. In the early-morning hours of August 29, I worried for the people living close to the shore. I admit, I was among those who blew off warnings about the mass destruction of New Orleans. I didn't think about that. It was unthinkable.

Story vampire that I am, I watched the catastrophe evolve thinking I might have to find a way to use it in a book someday. I'd never written anything in the thriller genre, but I'd thought about it. One of my critique mates, Colleen Thompson, is a master of romantic suspense. I learned a lot about procedural structure from her standalone thrillers, *The Salt Maiden* and *Fatal Error*, specifically the core craft values of atmosphere, plot-driven character arcs, and blow-by-blow action scenes. I was ready to try my hand, just waiting for the right story to hit me.

In the wake of the storm, Gary and I volunteered with Operation Compassion, an interfaith effort to receive, assist, feed, and house hundreds of thousands of storm survivors who flooded into Houston. Downtown at Reliant Center, I cleaned bathrooms, served food, and hauled ice and beverages up and down the long lines of people deboarding buses and waiting for hours in the oppressive heat to fill out FEMA paperwork. It was a privilege to meet people in this extraordinary moment. The air was thick with humidity and stories, and I felt myself doing what a robin does when it's building a nest—gathering a thread here and a twig there, weaving it into a place where I might create something. When I heard a weary New Orleans police officer comment, "This is great for media people and con artists," the story hammer dropped.

I went home sunburned crawfish red and exhausted to the bone, but the characters had come for me. Corbin, Shay, and Queen Mab grabbed my hands and dragged me into the swampy mist. I sat up writing until dawn, napped for a few hours, and then went back to Reliant Center to keep doing whatever I could do to help. The skeleton of the story quickly took shape in my head, but I didn't have time to do more than sketch out a few scenes. Just four weeks after Hurricane Katrina, Hurricane Rita screamed into the Gulf, headed straight for Houston, and I realized a much larger story was yet to unfold.

Gary and I sheltered in place, following zoned recommendations, and we watched in horror as almost everyone else in our neighborhood panicked and bugged out. The hurricane veered off and lost a lot of spin before it landed, but the Houston metroplex was engulfed in a 200-mile-wide traffic jam—fact far crazier than any fiction I could have conjured—so, of course, that became a plot point that rewrote the ending I had planned. We experienced the remnants of Rita as a violent summer storm and sat without power for a few days. I recharged my laptop in my car and kept writing.

That winter, I was hip deep in a celebrity ghostwriting project, and the following year, my third novel went into the pipeline at HarperCollins, so I couldn't give *The Hurricane Lover* the undivided attention it takes to finish a novel, but this turned out to be a good thing. I hadn't yet wrapped my head around the true extent of the research that would be needed to give this book the depth I wanted it to have. I didn't even think about the documents that might later be released via the Freedom of Information Act, not the least of which turned out to be a thousand pages of email sent and received by Michael Brown in the days immediately before and after Hurricane Katrina.

For two years, while I wrote and published three other books, I continued gathering threads and twigs. I interviewed meteorologists, homicide detectives, an internist, an arborist, an architectural historian, plumbers, contractors, and many storm survivors from various walks of life. I watched with keen interest as New Orleans dragged herself out of the mud. I pored over thousands of weather bulletins, storm forecasts, government documents, and police reports and waded through a dense swamp of FEMA email and media releases.

The research was heartbreaking. Infuriating.

So much suffering could have been prevented, and so little had been learned from it in the years since. The blue-vs.-red ideological divide had cost thousands of lives. Rather than embrace unity and common sense, people trenched down into whichever *we the people* they identified with, and in the South, that boundary was starkly color coded. The story became more layered. I relished the idea of a book club uncorking a bottle of wine and taking on these issues, gloves off.

The book was still missing one pivotal character: the storm. I tried again and again to draft the passages in which Shay and Corbin make their way through the eyewall. It just felt like a lot of words describing what I thought it might be like. What did it smell like? What was the strata of sound beneath the screaming wind? How does a hurricane feel on your skin? I needed to know. In September 2008, I had the opportunity to find out.

Hurricane Ike fulfilled all the dire predictions made before Hurricane Rita (lacking the one dire prediction that mattered). When the call for evacuation came out, Gary and I made the decision to shelter in place. Gary, still an airline mechanic at the time, knew he'd be needed at the airport immediately after the storm, and we feared our elderly dogs wouldn't do well away from home. As Bonnie and Corbin do in the book, we filled the garage freezer with gallon jugs of water and stocked the pantry with batteries, protein bars, and other storm supplies. The eye of the hurricane made landfall in Galveston as a Cat 2 and moved inland along the east side of Houston. I watched CNN until the power went out, and then I sat in the garage on an Adirondack chair tucked in the back corner between my car and the chest freezer. Clutching a Maglite, I listened to the car radio and snacked on Sun Chips and homemade vegetable juice.

Beyond the open garage door, there was utter darkness cut by frequent lightning. I waited until the storm escalated to what I thought might be the eyewall. Then I strapped my son's bike helmet on my head and went out into the street. My plan was to walk through the park across the street, but the towering pine trees that surrounded the playground were casting off branches and cones. In the strobe effect of the lightning, I could see that the air above the playground was filled with projectiles. Best to stay in the street, I decided. Walk around the block and call it good. I pushed to the end of the driveway and sloshed through ankle-deep water gushing up from the gutter drains. I tried to turn my face away from the scouring rain, but it seemed to be coming from every direction. Bits of bark and God knows what drummed on the bike helmet. I felt weightless and weak, gasping for breath, pushing one step at a time against the force of the wind. Two or three houses down, I accepted the fact that this whole idea was incredibly stupid, and I turned back, fighting to keep my balance. The half block back to my house felt like a mile.

A few yards from the end of my driveway, I heard what sounded like the crack of a rifle. A large limb from a tall pecan tree smashed to the ground, and then another limb, and another until the whole tree gave in, like an umbrella closing. A towering oak that loomed over our front yard moaned and flailed. This tree brayed like a wounded animal, its wide trunk bending to an extent I wouldn't have believed possible. I scurried back to my Adirondack chair and sat, shivering and giddy, trying to find words for what I'd experienced.

The storm was everything I had imagined: razor-blade rain, pelting debris, body-slam wind, galactic noise, the peculiar smell of ozone and wet cement. What I hadn't anticipated was how deeply, viscerally frightening it would be. I expected to feel small; I did not expect to feel swallowed. I didn't know the storm would be as present within me as it was around me, in the ringing of my ears, the hammering of my heart, and a resounding pressure that seemed to push the plates of my skull apart. This was not the green-eyed summer storm of my childhood; this was the jackboot of a jealous god.

Hurricane Ike decimated Galveston. On the real-life beach where I'd placed Billy's bar and Shay's fictional sanctuary, only one home was left standing. Houston's infrastructure was crippled. In our neighborhood, far from the worst of the destruction, I'd say at least half of the big trees came down. The corner of our front porch was torn away, and our back deck and pergola were reduced to rubble. Miraculously, the old oak was still standing, but we lost three pecan trees. I hate the tall privacy fences that hash up every Houston neighborhood, so it gave me a modicum of mean pleasure to see 90 percent of them flattened, an apt metaphor for our common plight.

The postapocalyptic suburb was a ghost town. It was almost eight weeks before power was fully restored. Our generous neighbors, George and Toni, invited us to string a series of orange extension cords over to their generator so we could plug in the refrigerator and one lamp. By day, I conducted a guerrilla book mobile from the back of my yellow VW Bug, supplying books to the neighborhood kids and folks waiting in the long gas lines. By night, I unplugged the fridge and plugged in my computer, in the zone, fleshing out a finished draft of *The Hurricane Lover*.

I didn't rush to publish. I wasn't willing to make the compromises I knew I'd have to make if I put it into the mainstream publishing pipeline. Massive shifts in the publishing business model were making it possible to self-publish on a level we'd never seen in the industry. When I finally pulled the trigger on November 11, 2011, I had resources I couldn't have imagined in 2005 when I started writing this book. During its first year, the ebook was downloaded more than 90,000 times—more than the combined total sales of my first three novels.

In 2021, my thirty-third book, a celebrity ghostwriting project, debuted at #1 on the *New York Times* bestseller list, but I can honestly say that *The Hurricane Lover* still feels like the greatest success of my career thus far. It was a soul project that demanded a lot from me and asks a lot of the reader. The message beneath the mystery is more relevant than ever. Our political divide has deepened to a seemingly uncrossable chasm as disinformation and fascism find new footholds in our country. The warnings of climate scientists are still largely unheeded. Even those of us who are willing to accept the enormity of the situation are daunted by the mandate for significant changes in the average American consumer's voracious way of life.

In 2017, as Gary prepared to retire, we decided to move from Houston to our vacation place on the beach in Washington State. Gary's supervisor at the airline kept asking him to stay a little longer, so we put off the move again and again. I started having a strange recurring dream in which my mother, who had died a few years before, was jamming my things into big boxes, telling me, "Hurry! You need to go now." It was unsettling enough that I finally told Gary, "I'm going to Westport. You can catch up with me when you're ready." He agreed to put through the paperwork so we could leave together the first week of August.

I spent weeks downsizing, digitizing important papers and family photos, purging clutter. I packed up the furniture and belongings we really cared about, securing them for storage with plans to ship everything in a month or so. We took only a few things with us: a strongbox of important documents, my mother's ukulele, several pieces of art that we didn't want handled by movers, and two small suitcases with clothes for the road trip.

We arrived at our home on the Pacific Coast on August 19, 2017. On August 26, Hurricane Harvey, a catastrophic Cat 4 megastorm, swept the Gulf Coast. Our home in Houston was flooded to the ceiling.

I sat on the beach 2,500 miles away, looking out at the Pacific Ocean, weeping for our dear friends and neighbors who'd lost their homes and for the music venues, art galleries, and historic structures in this beautiful city we had loved and lived in for twenty-three years. I thought about the river of filth and debris that Shay waded through as the sun went down on the ruined city of New Orleans. That same river flowed through Houston now, and as far as I knew, all the belongings we'd so carefully put into storage were part of it.

But we were not.

We'd made the decision to step away from the city and lead a different kind of life. It was a big change, but people are capable of big changes when we choose to be. And change happens, whether we choose it or not. Change comes, catalyzed by decision or rained down by fate, an unstoppable force of nature that floats away the wooden chairs and garden gnomes, robbing us of our clutter, leaving us shaken but wiser.

Joni Rodgers
Westport, Washington
2021

I

KATRINA

NEW ORLEANS

FRIDAY EVENING
AUGUST 26, 2005

```
** WTNT42 EWA 270247 ***

TCDAT2 HURRICANE KATRINA DISCUSSION NUMBER 14

NWS TPC/ EARTHWEATHER ANALYTICS, NEW ORLEANS LA

7 PM EDT FRI AUG 26 2005


SATELLITE PRESENTATION CONSISTS OF PERFECT COMMA-SHAPED

CLOUD PATTERN OVER WESTERN CUBA WRAPPING AROUND LARGE

CLUSTER OF DEEP CONVECTION. EYE NOT CLEARLY VISIBLE ON

IR IMAGES BUT RADAR DATA INDICATE EYE EMBEDDED WITHIN

CIRCULAR AREA... KATRINA FORECAST TO MOVE DIRECTLY OVER

WARM LOOP CURRENT OF GULF OF MEXICO...LIKE ADDING HIGH

OCTANE FUEL TO FIRE... OFFICIAL FORECAST BRINGS KATRINA TO

115 KNOTS...CATEGORY FOUR ON THE SAFFIR-SIMPSON HURRICANE

SCALE.


$$

.


.
```

The Thibodeaux brothers stood side by side on the scrolled second-floor balcony of the flamingo-pink house in Algiers, drinking beer and looking a lot alike. Corbin Thibodeaux was older, a little taller, and somewhat better groomed, but only because he hadn't had time to change out of his press conference clothes. Guy was stockier, sporting the thick, ruddy neck of a biker, a full sleeve of tattoos, and unruly hair that cast him as Jesus for some people and Charles Manson for others.

Guy's grin was quicker, his easy laughter more from the belly. With a hawkish nose and straight-set mouth, Corbin came off as serious in a way that often put him at odds with the world in which he'd grown up. The Thibodeaux brothers shared their father's square Cajun bones and doglike urge to run. They each wore a sunburned version of their mother's fair freckled skin and studied the skyline with her exacting, hazel-eyed squint.

Corbin always thought of his mother, ached for her a little, whenever a good storm rolled up from the Gulf, but this evening, he was focused on the precise trim and trajectory of each breeze that lifted the Spanish moss and shuddered the whorled oak trees that shaded the street below. Keeping a quiet vigil between a loaded barbecue grill and solar-powered Remote Telemetry Unit, he checked the barometer on the wall, tapped a notation into his laptop, and trained his spotting scope on the crooked elbow of the Mississippi.

Beyond the rolling brown water, on the east bank of the river, lay the culture clash of scattered Marigny rooftops and the glassy angles of the Central Business District. Above the high-rise lights of the CBD, beyond a faint layer of cayenne-colored smog, the first thin swish of Katrina's dervish skirt could be seen in the evening sky over New Orleans.

Hurricanes were Corbin's bailiwick, industrial risk assessment being the core income of his one-man-band consulting firm, EarthWeather Analytics. Companies with oil rigs and mainframes in and along the Gulf of Mexico needed to know what each storm would do, where it would go, whom it would kill and how much it would cost. Over the years, Corbin had become very good at telling them. He'd been warning his clients all week that Katrina was going to cost a lot, and he was privately laden with the statistical probabilities of whom it was going to kill.

Corbin lived for events of this magnitude, but most storms were born and spun out their life cycles over the ocean. Never touched land. Never made news. The last several computer models he'd run before leaving his office in the CBD showed Katrina sucking in a deep, warm breath over the Gulf of Mexico and shrieking directly into New Orleans as a Cat 5 in approximately thirty-nine hours.

It was like seeing everything and everyone he loved tied to a railroad track.

"There's still time for you and Bonnie to get out," Corbin told his brother. "Leave tonight. Be in Houston by morning. I'll give you the hotel money if you need it."

Guy swiped at a trickle of sweat on the back of his neck and said, "We're fine, Doc. Give it a rest."

They both knew he wouldn't. Every year, Corbin preached the gospel of evacuation. Preached like John the Baptist.

Fat lot of good.

For most folks on the Coast, including Guy and his wife, the decision to "hunker down"—or in disaster bureaucracy parlance, "shelter in place"—was not unusual, particularly for residents of Algiers. Their French forebears had wisely chosen this fin of land on the west bank of the river for the very fact that it was above sea level, unlike much of the recumbent New Orleans metroplex, which came along later, a top-heavy madam who decided to take a load off her Saturday night heels and prop her feet up on the lakeshore.

For more than a hundred years, an easygoing population slid down into the mechanically drained bathtub of the lowlands, but heavy rains reawakened memories of the primordial back swamp. People had grown up with the roar of the aging pumping stations. Anyone who'd lived in New Orleans for any length of time had some high-water story to tell.

Guy would never voluntarily turn his back on a party. It was that simple. And Bonnie would never voluntarily turn her back on Guy. She was half white and a quarter Coushatta, but when she had to, she tapped into that remaining twenty-five percent, which was pure, empowered, mm-hmm black girl. She loved her husband and held her home ground with intimidating ferocity, and in deference to that, Corbin generally stayed out of their business, but this time, he was arguing hard for them to break with tradition and go.

"Best possible scenario leaves Algiers in hundred-degree heat without power and water for at least ten days," Corbin said. "At best, Guy, she'll be miserable. At worst—"

"Dude," Guy said sharply. "It's not your business."

Guy's truck pulled up to the curb below the balcony, and Bonnie struggled out of the driver's door, returning from a final sortie through the depleted grocery store. Eight months pregnant and weighted with canvas bags of dry goods, she waddled toward the gate at the side of the house.

"Hey, belle soeur," Corbin called to her. "Leave that stuff on the porch. Let Guy carry it up."

She smiled up at him and disappeared into the courtyard. Guy hastily dumped the last of his beer over the side rail, raked his fingers through his hair and sniffed under each arm. He lit up like a used car lot when Bonnie arrived on the balcony.

"Hey, ma femme." He kissed her and held her big belly between his hands. "How's Harley Davidson Thibodeaux doing in there?"

"Albert Schweitzer Thibodeaux." Bonnie gathered her wild, rust-colored hair into a kinky topknot. "Did you scrub those plastic garbage cans and fill them with water?"

"Sorry, baby, I got busy with something else. I'll do it tomorrow."

Bonnie had taken charge of storm preparations early on. Everything from the chest freezer was being thawed, barbecued, or braised for gumbo and dirty rice, making room to freeze gallon jugs of water. Downstairs, the wide shop windows and doors at Bonnie's Bloom & Grow were firmly boarded up. Upstairs, in Corbin's quarters on the third floor, the shutters were drawn and locked. Out back, Bonnie's brother Watts had secured the potting porch with tarps and bungee cords, plywood being as scarce as ghost orchids now.

"Guy, honey," she said, "after you haul in the groceries, I need you to scrub those cans."

"Later, baby. I gotta swing by the shop and make sure the insurance photos are backed up online."

"Be back in one hour, baby, okay? No jackassing around."

"Love you, Bon Bon." He bent to speak into her navel. "George Thorogood Thibodeaux, mind your mama."

She ruffled his hair and kissed him. "Isaac Newton Thibodeaux."

"Later, Doc," said Guy, and Corbin said, "See ya later," not really knowing if he would or not, because one never could tell with his little brother.

Bonnie consulted a list from her shirt pocket. "Were you able to get gas for the generator?"

Corbin nodded. "I made up a power rationing schedule for the first week. Hopefully, we'll locate some additional fuel before we run out. Watts and I did our best to secure your hydroponics project, but don't get your hopes up."

"Breaks my heart," she said wearily, "after all the work we put into building it."

"We did it once," said Corbin. "We can do it again."

He squeezed her shoulder and pushed open the French doors so he could see the TV in the living room, where Shay Ray, the *NOLA Now* Sunshine Girl, was effervescing on location.

"...a very special ice cream social benefitting the American Cancer Society."

The mask of television makeup was as unsettling as the phony name, but in the close-ups, Corbin could see Shay Hoovestahl, her eyes warm and alive, like they were when she used to laze in bed with him on Sunday mornings, arguing over op-eds, trading barbs, giving in.

"I'm here with 96-year-old breast cancer survivor Orofina Sampson and her great-great-great granddaughter—that's three greats, people—greatness cubed!" said Shay, cheek to cheek with the toddler in her arms. "Two-year-old Danisha Sampson is bravely battling leukemia."

"Greatness cubed?" Bonnie huffed, pushing one fist against the small of her back. "That would be touching if I didn't know she'd rather kiss a snake than a baby."

"Please, stop by my website," said Shay, "meet these two inspirational ladies, and support the important work of the American Cancer Society."

Shay's hallmark was indefatigable *joie de vivre*. There were moments when it felt like the antidote to Corbin's innate melancholy, but right now her Texas pep squad dynamism bordered on grating. Still, Shay was beautiful. Corbin noticed that she was wearing an easy light-brown ponytail now, which was more to his liking than her old bottle-blonde minesweeper helmet. It wouldn't be inappropriate, he decided, to give Shay a call. As a friend. He could give her a friendly call, encouraging her to evacuate.

Bonnie eyed him without pretense. "Don't even think it."

"Bonnie, is there anything on that list about you getting off your feet?"

"Guy," she called down to the curb, "don't you drive off without dealing with those groceries."

But he was already gone.

"I'll get them," said Corbin. "Bonnie, when Guy gets back, y'all two need to head for Houston. Or call your sisters and go without him. If Guy's too pigheaded—"

"Guy's a grown man," Bonnie cut in. "It's no longer your job to take care of him, and it never was your job to take care of me. Maybe if you weren't so busy minding our business, you'd find a nice girl to take care of you for a change." She trash-glanced the TV over her shoulder and enunciated, "A *nice* girl."

Corbin took the list from her hand, wrote GET OFF YOUR FEET, and handed it back.

Bonnie hugged him, her belly bulky and warm, a separate entity between them, and Corbin felt his nephew roll over inside her, pushing a fist or foot against his uncle's abdomen. The yet to be named Baby T would be the fourth generation of his family born into the flamingo-pink house on Powder Street.

The structure had weathered a good number of storms during the century or so that it stood among the Victorian ladies, shabby shotgun houses, and Creole cottages of Algiers Point. The Thibodeaux family history was a recitation of disturbances and depressions. Corbin and Guy's parents were married on this very balcony as tornados spawned by Hurricane Gladys spun out of the Gulf in 1968, and Corbin was conceived by candlelight in the back bedroom as Camille raged through in 1969.

His earliest memories were of towering clouds and the intoxicating smell of ozone, his mother sitting on a little iron ice cream parlor chair outside the shuttered doors, singing, "C'est la petite poule blanche, qui a pondu dans la branche, un petit coco pour mon bébé faire dodo …"

Long red hair streaming over her shoulders. Face tipped up to the rain.

"… dodiché, dodiché, dodiché, dodicho…"

She kept him pressed against her thigh and made him wear a red plastic fireman's helmet.

"To ward off lightning strikes," she said.

By the time his belief in that wore off, Corbin was consumed with the science of storms, studying the deep blue center of a satellite image in his favorite issue of *National Geographic* the way most red-blooded boys wear out their first pilfered Playboy.

"Guy just likes the noise," Corbin's mother said one rainy day when she was in a morphine haze. "For you, baby, storms are a soul-force."

She was an eccentric, a crazy lady, given to high winds and glory days, Southerly vapors, and dark bouts of overcast. Corbin's father was a jovial lush who downgraded to heartbroken drunk after the death of his wife and died under unseemly circumstances himself three years later, which is how Corbin, at eighteen, inherited the flaming-pink house, along with its burden of back taxes, and legal guardianship of thirteen-year-old Guy, all of which might be considered a sob story had the Thibodeaux boys lived anywhere other than Louisiana, where crazy ladies are revered for their beautiful bedtime stories and heartbroken drunks are accommodated with drive-through daiquiri stands.

When Guy turned seventeen, Corbin joined the Navy and went to Hawaii, then Japan. By the time he returned to New Orleans, Guy and Bonnie were married. Bonnie's Bloom & Grow had taken over the bottom floor of the house and the entire courtyard. Guy had been taken into a business restoring vintage motorcycles with Bonnie's big brother, Watts.

Corbin converted the third-floor attic rooms to a quiet hermitage for himself and started EarthWeather Analytics. There wasn't much money in it the first few years. A few nonprofits hired him to analyze climate trends and provide expert testimony against evil corporate leviathans. A few corporate leviathans hired him to parse their compliances, but hurricanes were Corbin's first great love.

"Risk assessment is where I'd like to focus," he told Shay on one of their lazy Sundays. "I know the science as well or better than the people who are getting big industry contracts. I just need to get in the room."

"I bet I could help you with that," she said.

"How?"

"Every time there's a hurricane in the Gulf, you should be the talking head," said Shay. "Let me make some calls and pageant-coach you through the first few appearances—Weather Channel, CNN, blah blah blah—and make sure they call you 'Hurricane Specialist Dr. Corbin Thibodeaux' instead of 'Paleoclimatologist Dr. Corbin Thibodeaux.' The average viewer is concept-resistant after three syllables."

"And I'd be doing all this…why?"

"Because saying something on TV makes it true. Establish that in the minds of the industry decision makers. You'll be hauling down serious meat and potatoes, doing what you love to do."

She was right, and Corbin was grateful. The business took off, and he moved up to a techno-friendly office space in an architecturally dramatic building in the CBD. Corbin's office featured a thunderhead-gray reception area, state of the art equipment room, an inner sanctum with austere, modern furnishings, and an airy conference room with a pool table and well-stocked wet bar.

In 2004, Corbin participated in Hurricane Pam, an eight-day table-top exercise that gathered 250 scientists and officials from fifty federal, state, and local agencies, including the Red Cross and the Army Corps of Engineers.

In the wake of 9/11, the new Department of Homeland Security had gobbled FEMA—the Federal Emergency Management Agency—into its budgetary belly, effectively washing it down with a drive-through daiquiri when President Bush appointed as the revamped agency's Undersecretary of Emergency Preparedness and Response a guy named Michael Brown, a lawyer by trade, who'd made an unsuccessful run for Congress and served as a commissioner with the International Arabian Horse Association before coming to FEMA. Corbin refrained from saying "Undersecretary of Horse Shit," but he knew he wasn't the only one thinking it.

It was time they all sat down to do the math. A Cat 3 or stronger hurricane made landfall somewhere on the Louisiana coastline every eight years. Sooner or later, New Orleans would take a direct hit. This was statistically inevitable.

The Hurricane Pam computer simulation projected that a Cat 3 hurricane would destroy 87% of the city's housing. Assuming a levee breach, surveyors charted water depth to the inch, block by city block, ranging from two to twenty feet. Floodwaters would be filled with organic and chemical pollutants: caskets, animal carcasses, sewage, thirty million cubic yards of destruction debris plus a quarter million cubic yards of hazardous household waste—all the toxic chemicals in garages and under kitchen sinks—every submerged vehicle giving off gas and oil, every snake washed out of its hidey hole, every rat drowning in a wall, every fire ant hill floating like an acid cloud.

Hurricane Pam left her audience with a healthy fear of God and a long list of imperative action items. A year later, little had been done to diminish either one.

It bothered Corbin, but there was a never-ending supply of cloud patterns and satellite images to be studied, a sturdy base of deep pockets to be invoiced, and after he and Shay parted ways, a surprisingly steady succession of women to sleep with. Those encounters were pleasant enough, and each one brought the necessary modicum of carnal solace with minimal distraction, the opposite of what he'd had with Shay.

Joie de vivre was frankly foreign to him, he concluded. He was better off without it.

For the most part, Dr. Corbin Thibodeaux liked the laboratory order of his life. He liked looking at vagaries and serendipity through a storm window of trigonometry and physics. He liked extrapolating with a fair certainty what would happen next. What one could not control, one could predict, and with judicious application of data, virtually any circumstance could be weathered.

NEW ORLEANS

SATURDAY AFTERNOON
AUGUST 27

From: Fugate, Craig

To: Michael D Brown

Sent: Sat Aug 27 15:45:14 2005

Subject: Mutual Aid

Let me know if we can help if we are spared the second landfall. Sometimes states don't ask for help through EMAC until late in the game.

craig

Craig Fugate, Director

Florida Division of Emergency Management

From: Brown, Michael D

Sent: Saturday, August 27, 2005 4:20 PM

To: Fugate, Craig

Subject: Re: Mutual Aid

Will do. This one has me really worried...look at this scenario compared to the cat planning we did for New Orleans and, well, you get the picture. I wish a certain governor was from Louisiana...and his emergency manager!

New Orleans wasn't Shay Hoovestahl's town. She was, in fact, a former Miss Texas, the daughter of Charlotte McKecknie Hoovestahl of the Dallas McKecknies and Robert Hoovestahl, a bona fide up-from-nuthin' Houston billionaire who'd married into a small oil company, parlayed it into a large oil company, merged that into a massive oil company and expanded his private holdings to Hoovestahl TransGlobal, a conglomerate that involved oil rigs, refineries, toxic waste storage in Mexico, Defense Department contracts in the Middle East, and Bob Hoovestahl's pet project, Hoovestahl Luxury Transport, a string of Mercedes dealerships with thirty-seven locations serving satisfied Gulf Coast customers and supporting President Bush and the US troops with a free yellow-ribbon magnet for every vehicle that came through the service bay.

Robert Hoovestahl cultivated his elder daughter with capitalist vigor, instilling in her a sharp awareness about the blessings and pitfalls of her station in life and training her up in the art of self-defense. This included kickboxing, boot camp, a concealed handgun permit, and an automatic skepticism about anyone who wanted to befriend or date her.

Shay's upbringing emphasized core values like self-discipline and strivership, shunning the murky "free to be you and me" claptrap that mollycoddled and stunted so many children of the '70s. She was inculcated with strong Christian values and a fire-in-the-belly work ethic, bumper-stickered with pithy winners-never-quit-quitters-never-win axioms.

Growing up, she slaved to get perfect grades and hone her charm-school skills, tutored by a debut trainer, a pageant coach, and a corps of funded academics. She hated herself whenever she failed to embody "the best" as defined by her father, but as a teenager, she tortured him almost compulsively with his worst fears for her private virtue and public facade.

Shay dominated the pageant circuit from Li'l Miss Houston Toddler to her Miss Texas victory, but in the final moments of Miss

USA, close enough to taste it, she was dubbed fourth runner-up. It was a bitter pill Shay had never been able to swallow, partly because she'd simply never learned to lose.

"You're better off," Corbin told her one day as they sat outside the Audubon Aquarium waiting for the Algiers Ferry. "If you'd been branded Miss USA, forget about your masters from Columbia, your thesis on human trafficking. You'd be taken even less seriously than you are now. That pageant crap is a joke."

It was one of many conversations that didn't end well between them, but Shay had eventually come to see his point and was now in the process of reauthoring her public image, starting with the Sunshine gig.

"Up next, on location in Metairie is our Sunshine Girl, Shay Ray."

Her attention came back to the mosquito voice in her earbud.

"That's right after these messages, as we continue round-the-clock coverage of Hurricane Katrina."

During the commercials, Shay checked her hair and makeup in the shiny microwave door and switched on her picture-in-picture smile as Christa Mullroy, anchor and managing editor of the morning news hour, capably steered to the shelter-in-place segment. The production assistant counted with the flat of her hand.

"Stand by, Shay. In four, three…" Silent two, one.

Fully engaged despite a short night's sleep, Shay opened her arms and said, "Good morning, everyone. Welcome to my home. No matter what the weather, it's a beautiful day when friends visit. At this point, officials are saying evacuation is 'recommended but optional,' so a lot of us will shelter in place due to pets, transportation issues, or just plain orneriness. Experts say to identify a safe core: look for adequate ventilation and load-bearing studs. Not that kind of stud, Christa, the boring kind."

She gave the camera a wink and a finger wag.

"We should remind everyone to stay inside," said Christa, "even during the eye of the storm."

"But if you must nip out in the rain," said Shay, "here's a little trick I do at the beach."

She dropped in her cell phone in a Ziploc sandwich bag and pressed the seal.

"Love my Ziplocs. Watertight. Cell doubles as a flashlight, and you can still talk." She held the baggie to her ear. "Hello? Anderson Cooper? C'mon down!"

"And of course, if a mandatory evacuation is ordered," Christa moved things along with the inflexible grace of a steel turnstile, "follow evacuation routes on our website."

"Absolutely, Christa. Safety first." Shay beckoned the camera to the patio door. "Notice how my hunky helpers from Grace Hardware secured my outdoor living accessories with zip ties. Strong, flexible, and they come in a variety of sizes—as do the zip ties! In the pantry, think healthy and nonperishable. Canned fruits and veggies, trail mix, protein bars. Don't forget to freeze several gallon jugs of refreshing Great Springs filtered drinking water. In the event of a power outage, move your icy jugs to the refrigerator, Christa. That'll cool things down in there, and you'll have plenty of cold, potable water as they melt. Very important to stay hydrated in this heat for good health and younger-looking skin, FYI."

"Thanks, Shay, thanks." Christa dropped a quick glance to her notes. Her penchant for saying everything twice set Shay's teeth on edge. "Next up—"

"Christa, on a personal note, I want folks to know that my mom's church in Houston is conducting a 24/7 prayer vigil for the people of New Orleans, asking God's hand on the levees." Shay pushed her fist against her heart and let her voice go a little emotional. "Like it says in Isaiah, 'Thou art strength to the needful, a refuge from the storm.' God bless, everyone."

"Coming up," said Christa, "Dr. Corbin Thibodeaux, a New Orleans hurricane specialist, flew over this massive storm early this morning on Navy reconnaissance aircraft..."

The PA waved Shay off. "We're out."

Shay loaded up the camera crew with trail mix and ice cream and hugged them all on their way out. A sense of camaraderie always blew in with these forming storms, and because Shay was lonely much of the time, she loved the "all in this together" vibe. It almost made her forget that the rest of the time, they called her Miss Cuntshine behind her back. The crew was gone in less than three minutes, and a minute later, her producer was on the phone.

"Shay, Christa didn't care for your tone in that segment, and she says you implied she looks old."

"Don't be silly, Renny. She looks fabulous for a woman her age."

"Look, the coquette for Christ thing—that's your shtick," he said. "Focus groups love it. Advertisers are happy. It works on an everyday basis. But given the situation, Christa felt you came off a little flippant, and you know she doesn't appreciate getting Bible belted on the air."

"Well, given the situation, I don't think an expression of faith is inappropriate."

"I don't care what you think," said Renny, "and neither does Christa."

"Note taken." Shay set the teakettle on, her mind already moving to her task list.

"Shay, you've been pushing me to let you tackle something with grit, develop your investigative chops. You think this helps your cause?"

"Renny, we both know that's never going to happen. It's been five years, and I'm still doing exactly what I was hired for: bright, banal, and busty."

"Your words, not mine."

"Then why am I not invited to the media staging area in Baton Rouge?"

"You're invited to go home to Houston for your own safety," said Renny. "This isn't a slumber party, Shay. It's a liability issue. You saw the memo. Management has gone on record telling all nonessential personnel to evacuate immediately after their last segment today."

Shay shook coffee beans into a little grinder. "Go ahead and tell Miss Christa you firmly chastised me and I apologized for the misunderstanding."

"Shay, you are appreciated," said Renny. "Okay, my angel? I appreciate you."

"Gosh. Thanks." She clicked off and buzzed the coffee grinder, congratulating her reflection in the microwave, "It's Miss Nonessential 2005, Shay Hooterstall of Tex-ass."

She speed-dialed her father's office, and his secretary answered with a leathery cigarette voice, "Hey birthday girl."

"Not till Monday, Millie. I'm not ready for thirty-something."

"Think of it as twenteleven," said Millie. "Your new .38 is ready at the engraver. Pick it up this afternoon. And send your father a proper thank-you note."

"I will. What's up with that charter jet Daddy sent over for me?"

"Keep your jeans up. I'll check."

Shay put the ground coffee and boiling water in a French press while Millie made a quick call and came back to report that the private jet had already landed safely back in Houston. Greatness Cubed was tucked in at M.D. Anderson Cancer Center's pediatric ward with the Sampson family in a hotel nearby, wondering about the identity of their anonymous benefactor.

"Thanks, Dixie diva," said Shay. "My freelance camera crew is on the way to Baton Rouge, mobile editing suite is online. I'll visit the good doctor first thing in the morning."

"Shay, I don't like what I'm hearing about this storm, and I worry that your history with this man is clouding your judgment."

"I'll be fine, Mills, and the history is history."

"I'm holding you to your promise," Millie said. "If it doesn't work out with Katrina, you'll tell this guy from the Tampa DA's office there's nothing more you can do to help."

"It'll work," said Shay. "I'll make it work."

"Come hell or high water," Millie coughed irritably. "Your father would like to speak to you."

"No, Millie, don't—"

Shay heard the telltale click. Millie knew better than to get between them.

"Shay," said Robert Hoovestahl, "I want you out of there. Now."

"Good morning, Daddy. I'm well, thanks, and you?"

"This ain't a drill, Blueberry. I'm pulling all my people out of the Gulf. I sent a jet for you this morning. Get your ass on it."

"I'm sorry, what?" Shay buzzed the empty grinder. "Daddy, you're breaking up."

"God damn it, Shay, stop playing."

"Sorry, Daddy—dang cell phone—love you, Daddy."

Shay clicked off and speed-dialed her cell again. A gruff, grandfatherly baritone answered.

"You've reached Detective Alberto Sykes, Hillsborough County DA's office. Please leave a detailed message, and I'll get back to you ASAP."

"Hey, Berto. It's Shay. From what we're seeing on TV right now, this is coming together exactly as we hoped it would, so keep me posted on the extradition paperwork and drive careful, sugar. See you when you get here."

She slid the cell in her hip pocket and carried her coffee to her bedroom, just in time to see the neighbor's cat dash in through the open patio door.

"Goddang it," Shay groaned. "She evacuated and left you here? Shoo! Go home. I keep telling you, I'm not a cat person."

The large gray tom glared up at her, pulling at the cashmere rug with its claws.

"If you piss on this rug again," said Shay, "I will feed you to the hurricane."

The cat sprang up on her bed and stretched out next to her leather messenger bag. Shay settled into a peach-colored easy chair with her coffee. Christa did the blah blah blah about Corbin's Navy recon flight and asked him to define "paleoclimatologist."

"He's a dang environmeddler," said Shay, imitating her father.

"It's a bit like archeology," said Corbin. "Looking at evidence of weather patterns over millions of years helps us understand how climate change will impact our planet in the future. Hurricane Katrina is a prime example of global warming getting harder to ignore. Just two weeks ago, a significant study was published, solid evidence that increases in hurricane intensity and duration on a global level—about fifty percent since the 1970s—corresponds directly with the rise in sea surface temperature. As polar ice caps continue to melt and ocean temperatures rise, we'll see more of these megastorms."

He was clean-shaven and properly manscaped, wearing his standard white dress shirt and Levis with a grey sport coat. Despite Shay's best effort to restyle him, that's all he had hanging in his closet: twenty identical white dress shirts from Target, twenty identical pairs of Levis, five grey sport coats. On the closet shelf were twenty white Hanes A-back T-shirts, ten Old Navy khaki cargo shorts and twenty BVD boxers, white with a thin blue stripe. He'd installed the exact same closet with the exact same contents at his office. Corbin was wearing a dark red necktie today, which was out of character, but looked very nice.

Christa gazed at him like he was made of pralines and lobbed a few softball questions about the evacuation, neatly avoiding how spectacularly off Corbin had been about Hurricane Ivan right about this time the previous year, until Corbin tented his fingers under his chin and said, "Christa, maybe we should have started with the elephant in the room."

He looked haunted and weary, but Shay promptly sandbagged a small surge of tenderness toward him.

"A year ago," said Corbin. "I sat here and told people to evacuate, and about 600,000 people did. It was costly and inconvenient and ultimately proved unnecessary."

"I'm sure you were happy to be proven wrong," said Christa.

"Of course, but I'm concerned that because of that, a lot of folks are clinging to a false sense of security now."

Shay moved onto her bed and curled up with the gray tomcat, absently stroking his ear.

"We learned a lot from that situation," said Corbin. "Traffic jams, special-needs folks being ineffectively warehoused at the Superdome, lack of transportation for low-income areas, the availability of ice and body bags—a lot of things we don't like to think about. We subsequently did a computer simulation called Hurricane Pam that reinforced what we already knew: fundamentally, Christa, hurricane preparedness in New Orleans is not what it should be, and only a third of the population will voluntarily evacuate. I can't urge viewers strongly enough. Don't wait for the mandatory evacuation order. You need to get out now."

Propping herself up with a mountain of lacy pillows against the headboard, Shay pulled a stack of files from her messenger bag. She'd already gone over the Thibodeaux material a hundred times: printouts, emails, the damning credit card receipts. She avoided looking at the chat room transcripts from HurricaneLovers.com. Too much information.

It was nothing personal, she reminded herself. Their history was history.

They'd met in 2001 at a holiday fundraiser for the family of a local musician killed in New York on 9/11. Shay had been a long time since getting laid and was wearing an emerald-green Versace cocktail dress that made that a crime. Corbin was finessing baby back ribs on a grill out behind the House of Blues, holding forth on the planet-raping policies of the Bush administration. She homed in on him like a smart bomb, informed him that her parents were longtime friends of "41" and Bar, and delivered a tart lecture on neocon ideals and the imperative of patriotism in times like these.

Predictably, he never dragged his gaze north of her clavicle.

From there, it was all very Big Easy. After a few boilermakers at a jazz joint down the street, he invited her up to his place to see his Blue Dog art. Shay liked how he kicked his bedroom door shut. He slid that elegant green zipper down her spine and told her she looked like Venus stepping out of her damn clamshell.

The next morning, she felt more like the disenfranchised clam; Corbin poured her into a taxi at 5:00 a.m. with raccoon mascara and panties in her purse and never even asked for her phone number.

Two months later, at a Historical Society fundraiser, Shay beckoned him into the empty coat check closet, knelt down and gave him about nine seconds of something to think about before she signed her autograph on his bony hip with a red Sharpie and left him mouth-breathing hard among the vacant hangers.

It would have been perfect if not for the flat tire on her Escalade when she got to the parking lot. Corbin came out and watched her wrestle with the lug nuts and ruin her Jimmy Choos changing the tire. Then he opened the passenger door, holding out his hand for the keys. She dangled them over his palm for a moment before she got in.

They were together almost every weekend for the next three years. Corbin was exactly the man Shay needed at the time: an intelligent drinking buddy, generous and inventive in the sack, able to leave things uncomplicated beyond that. It was unspoken but understood that he would never meet her parents.

Of course, being Corbin, he ruined it.

Shay hadn't seen him since Hurricane Ivan, and it hurt to think how he would see her now, in the gathering storm.

"With all due respect to Miss 'Ray' and the awesome power of Ziploc bags," said Corbin, "sheltering in place is not appropriate in this situation. And neither is her glib delivery."

Shay sat up, gripping a ruffled pillow. "Oh, blow me, you sanctimonious monkfish."

"About 100,000 households in the New Orleans metro area have no vehicle. Statistically, these are not people in well-constructed, high-ground homes. These are our poor, our elderly, our most vulnerable citizens. The Red Cross predicts up to twenty-five thousand casualties if these people attempt to stay in their homes."

"Talk to me about the Superdome," said Christa. "The shelter of last resort."

"Christa, they call it that for a reason. It's for those with no way out of the city when evacuation is mandated. FEMA sets minimum standards for that, and the Red Cross does the certification, but they never signed off on it, so we don't know if those standards have been met. Common sense would dictate, I think, that you can't stuff twenty-five thousand people into a facility with minimal food, sanitation, and security, expecting it to turn out like Woodstock."

Corbin drew circles with his finger on the electronic map.

"These areas," he said. "French Quarter, Warehouse District, Algiers Point. They aren't insulated from the hurricane itself—wind, rain, lightning strikes—but they'll be above the flooding. The levees will likely fail sometime during the storm, and here's what that looks like."

He tapped to an animated map. Shades of blue bled out from the Mississippi and Lake Pontchartrain until all but a sliver of the city had disappeared. Shay tucked her feet and hugged her knees, thinking about the gone charter jet.

"Alarming." Christa shook her head. "Very alarming."

"Hurricane Katrina will be talked about for generations, Christa, the way our parents and grandparents talk about Camille." Corbin leaned in, earnest, underscored with exhaustion and heartache. "The question is, will Katrina be an icon for a dysfunctional government's disaster management goat screw or an icon for common sense and science rising up with the better angels of the human spirit to survive one of nature's most powerful forces?"

It was part of Corbin's charm, this grandiloquent mix of profanity and poetry. Christa's expression pinched briefly when he said "goat screw" on live television, but the next moment, she was looking at him with Jell-O shots in her eyes.

Their history was history, Shay reminded herself, and tucked the Thibodeaux file into her leather messenger bag.

NEW ORLEANS

SATURDAY EVENING
AUGUST 27

Oil firms evacuate platforms for storm:
Katrina's shift west has Gulf on alert
New Orleans Times-Picayune
Saturday August 27, 2005

Energy companies were evacuating production platforms Friday as Hurricane Katrina shifted west, raising the possibility that Gulf of Mexico rigs would be affected by the storm.

A path toward New Orleans, farther to the west, "would be the worst type of path" for producers in the Gulf, said Fred Schuster, manager of the commodities trading desk at DRW Investments LLC in Chicago. Still, some remained hopeful that the storm would steer clear of many of the rigs.

"It is prudent to evacuate, but this is nothing like what happened with Hurricane Ivan last season where there were billions of dollars of direct damages to the offshore rigs, platforms and undersea pipelines," said Hemant Shah, chief executive of Risk Management Solutions Inc., which makes storm-damage estimates.

...Fears that Katrina would disrupt oil and natural gas production in the region were the main catalyst pushing crude futures to new highs earlier this week...The Gulf normally produces 547.5 million barrels of oil and 3.65 trillion cubic feet of gas per year.

The wind was beginning to whisper in Algiers as Tommy Odettes wrangled the cats into their crate, attempting to find room for them in the back of the Suburban on top of Georgie's bulging suitcases and a bin of scrapbooking supplies she vowed she couldn't live without for even a week. That was Georgie's latest thing. Scrapbooking. She was a sentimental saver of life's bits and byproducts, and as they weathered their seventies, all that miscellany began to add up and overwhelm. A sixth grade report card here, a ballet recital program there. A feather. A pebble. A cherry stem he'd tied in a knot with his tongue as they sat out on their front porch watching some bad weather move in. For whatever reason, Georgie had kept that stem in a plastic sandwich bag with a note that said, "Hurricane Agnes, June '72." Georgie sometimes couldn't lay hands on her heart pills, but, by God, she intended to keep that cherry stem properly archived.

For his own part, Tommy didn't pack much. He had every confidence they'd return to find this house and all its cluttered memories intact. They might lose a tree or two, but even if the dire predictions came true this time—if the levees finally failed for real—Algiers would be high and dry. Tommy's preference was always to ride out a storm, but Georgie had seen their back-of-the-block neighbor on CNN that morning, and somehow that meant he was no longer just the skinny punk kid who used to come begging at the porch door for Georgie to bake cookies for him and his punk brother or teach him how to make fried chicken or mend their ripped shirts. Now he was Dr. Corbin Thibodeaux, TV meteorologist, and he was telling everyone to evacuate.

"Tommy, he's a smart man," Georgie had said. "Probably could have been a real doctor if he'd had the opportunities."

So now they were going. She'd filled up a dozen Tupperware cubes with cookies and casserole and made Tommy tote the lot across the courtyard to the Thibodeaux place. They were having their traditional hurricane bash, providing all the lowlanders a place to ride out the night and wake up high and dry, if mightily hung over.

All down the block, people were on their way out. Heavy shutters or slapdash plywood covered every window and door. Trashcans and tricycles were stowed under porches. Bird baths and glider swings had been dismantled, tossed into garages and mud rooms. Folks drove by, piled up with luggage. Most dropped a quick honk and a wave, so thinking nothing of it, Tommy turned and raised his hand when a horn tapped lightly behind him.

A 1975 Chevy Caprice convertible swept up to the curb. Tommy whistled softly at its immaculate condition before he even noticed the pretty young woman. Jackie O sunglasses. Sleek ponytail. Bright red lipstick. Pretty summer dress. A pleasant sight on a Saturday. The whiteness of her smile. The flutter of her hand. He could tell she came from good people.

"Morning, sir." She waved, gay as the live blue sky. "Can you tell me where I am?"

"Right about here," Tommy grinned, crossing the yard.

She laughed brightly and unfolded a street map, fought the wind for it, smoothed it out in her lap. "Oh, this cockamamie thing. I can't make heads nor tails of it."

It was a bit awkward for Tommy, bending over the open window where a car hop would hang a tray, his arm just inches from her noticeably—well, hell, just to call it like he saw—this was some generous décolletage. Standing close enough to breathe in the scent of her clean floral perfume, Tommy wasn't too old to feel a little unbalanced by it.

"You, uh... let's see..." He touched his stubby finger to the map. "You're over here. Algiers Point. This here's the Pontchartrain Expressway that takes you over the river into downtown. Where you headed?"

"I'm supposed to meet my fiancé at one of those crazy fete de désastre parties somewhere around here. He emailed me this." She offered up the printout.

T-BROS HURRICANE BASH RULES
1) BYOB plus 1 gal water (frozen), 1 roll TP, 1 bag chips, dish to pass.
2) No fighting, fire-breathing, hard narcotics, lax hygiene.
3) Be respectful of female attendees.
4) You barf on it, you buy it.
5) Check your politics and religion at the door.

*Troublemakers will be ejected regardless of weather conditions.

**House NOT RESPONSIBLE for property loss or personal injury.

The girl said, "His friend has a motorcycle shop."

"Guy Thibodeaux," Tommy nodded. "Him and his brother-in-law Watts. They got Nawlins Chopper over in town. They make some noise, but they're good people. Party's on the other side of the block above the garden shop. Store's all boarded up, though. You'll have to go around back."

"Thank you so much, Mr. um…"

"Friends call me Tommy," he said, assuming anyone he saw on this street was a friend.

"Winnie Austin-Seybold." She offered a firm, graceful handshake.

"Pleasure." Tommy took her hand briefly, and the silky, arid feeling stayed with him.

"Such a beautiful day." She lowered her sunglasses on her nose and smiled up at him, her lashes as long as a doe's. "You'd never think a big ol' hurricane's on the way."

"Yup. We usually hunker down, but my wife got spooked. They say it could be as bad as Camille back in '69." Tommy winked and added, "That was a hell of a party."

The girl giggled, and for some reason, it reminded him of cherry cola.

"Same damn fuss with Ivan last year." Tommy shook his head. "Spent sixteen hundred dollars on rooms and room service for the whole famdamily, only to come home and find it didn't hardly tip over a flower pot."

"Better safe than sorry," the girl said primly. "How long do you expect to stay away?"

"Oh, three, four days. Up here, we take our tap water from aqueducts. Got the power lines underground. You can always figure on Algiers being first to bounce back."

"Still, I hope you got somebody watching the house. They talk about looters and all."

"Got the alarm set. And the Thibodeaux boys'll keep an eye on things." Tommy smiled and gave the side panel of the Caprice a gentle spank. "Nice setta wheels."

"I'll convey the compliment to my daddy. He is some kinda proud of this car."

"I can tell," Tommy grinned and nodded. Not like a dirty old man. Just the father of pretty daughters. "Now, listen, you can't leave your vehicle parked under these trees during a storm. Especially not a car like this. The Full Gospel Church three blocks up, they offered their parking lot for use of the neighborhood. It's clear of trees and fenced to keep out looters. They're locking it up Sunday evening, opening the gate first thing Tuesday morning."

"Thank you so much, Mr. Tommy." said the girl. "I'll be asking traveling mercies for you and Mrs. Tommy tonight in my prayers. B'bye now!"

As she drove off down the street, the doe-eyed girl fluttered her hand, her laughter floating back to him like a flock of soap bubbles. Tommy headed back to his task.

That scrapbooking bin, he decided, that would have to stay behind.

NEW ORLEANS

SUNDAY MORNING
AUGUST 28

From: Rhode, Patrick
Sent: Sunday, August 28, 2005 8:40 AM
To: Lowder, Michael
Cc: Brown, Michael D
Subject: Is New Orleans proper

Not under a mandatory evacuation order yet? I heard that an eastern parish is now under mandatory evac as well, but not New Orleans proper? Also, any word on evac via state or local transportation assets – for those that do not have transportation?

Thanks,

Patrick

From: Rhode, Patrick
Sent: Sunday, August 28, 2005 10:19 AM
To: Jones, Gary; Lowder, Michael; Buikema, Edward; Lokey, William; Wells, Scott; Robinson, Tony
Cc: Brown, Michael D; Burris, Ken; Altshuler, Brooks
Subject: need to know if the gov or Mayor is going to call for mandatory evacuations of NO asap!!!!

Importance: High

Very important –

Thank you,

Patrick

From: Worthy, Sharon

Sent: Sunday, August 28, 2005 10:47 PM

To: Brown, Michael D;

[--------------------------------------];James, Tillie

Subject: Monday media Schedule

All times Central. Location is Executive Board Room on 1st floor.

Please arrive at 5:10 am for makeup, etc.

5:20 am ABC – GMA pre-tape

Talent: Charlie Gibbons, Robin Roberts

5:30 am CBS – The Early Show pre-tape

Talent: Harry Smith

5:40 am NBC – The Today Show pre-tape

Talent: Matt Layer, Katie Curic

6 am MSNBC Live

Talent: Natalie Allen, Contessa Brewer

6:15 am Fox – Fox and Friends Live

Talent: Steve Doucy, Brian Kilmeade, Kenan Chatry

6:45 am CNN – American Morning

Talent: Miles O'Brien, Soledad O'Brien

The front door of Bonnie's Bloom & Grow was securely boarded for the storm, so Shay put two fingers in her mouth and sent up her New York cabbie whistle.

"Hey, Dr. Feel Good, you up there?"

Corbin looked down from the balcony, and his shoulders sagged when he saw the Escalade. He thumbed toward the back of the house.

"Go around."

Shay hefted her leather messenger bag and headed through the wrought-iron gate. Out back, in the heavily cultivated courtyard, a high-tech hydroponics system coexisted incongruently with the mossy old oaks and Victorian spiral fire escapes. Corbin's sister-in-law was out on the sagging potting porch, scrubbing plastic garbage cans and filling them with water. There was no love lost between Shay and Bonnie, but they were both descended from Junior Leaguers and knew how to comport themselves.

"Hey, Bonnie," Shay called with her sunniest smile.

"Shay!" Bonnie brightly smiled back. "Sorry, hon. Corbin's not home."

"I just saw him up there, sweetie."

"He's busy, darlin'."

"I'll wait. Sugar."

Corbin emerged at the bottom of the stairs and pulled his shirt-sleeve across his forehead, painfully conscious of how he must smell. He'd been sweating like an ox, scrubbing the greasy barbecue grill with a wire brush. Not how he'd envisioned meeting Shay again.

He cleared his throat and said, "Hello, Shay."

"Hey, Corbin. Good to see you." She paused long enough for him to return the pleasantry but not so long that it would be awkward when he didn't. "Pardon me for popping by. I know your week has been a whirlwind. So to speak."

"Yeah. Hell of a week," he said. "Maybe we could do this another time."

"Actually, Corbin, this is calendar-sensitive. It's not personal. Feel free to invoice me for an hour, but really, I just need five minutes." Shay glanced at Bonnie. "Privately."

He shrugged and said, "C'mon up."

She followed him up to the antiquated kitchen, past the narrow back stairs that led to his hermitage. At the far end of the wide living room, French doors opened onto the balcony, and a sixty-quart floor-mounted deep-fryer bubbled near the iron railing. There was a turkey on the table, and Corbin had used a wooden mallet and eight-penny nail to drive it full of holes.

He said, "You're not a blonde anymore."

"Turns out having more fun was vastly overrated."

She smiled up at him, her face clean and patted dry. Not a trace of makeup. She wore jeans and a scoop-necked T-shirt, instead of the usual Neiman Marcus advertorial.

"You look nice," he mumbled, giving the bird a few more healthy whacks. Hearing how weak the comment sounded, Corbin wanted to whack his own hand.

"Thank you," said Shay. "You did a fabulous job on the Today Show yesterday. In fact, you've had quite a week. CNN, Fox, MSNBC. You're a natural, Corbin. And you look great."

He trussed the turkey with twine and rubbed it thoroughly with his secret mélange: crab oil, butter, apple cider, honey, Jim Beam, and Creole spices. Shay leaned in and took a deep breath, offering a broad view of her décolletage.

"You're a man of many talents, Dr. Thibodeaux."

This was what she always did. Charm him. Disarm him. But she didn't usually work this hard at it. Corbin found it unsettling.

"What can I do ya for, Shay?"

"I need your help on a project that's about to come together in a big way. My agent is planning to pitch it as a pilot for a cable series."

"Shay, this is not a good time. Seriously."

"I understand, but—"

"No, I don't think you do," said Corbin, "or you wouldn't be on TV chirping about Ziploc bags."

"Oh, right, the great Ziploc heterodoxy. And didn't you feel big, thinking you spanked my bottom on the air."

"Next best thing to being there," he mumbled on his way to the RTU.

"I was doing my job, Corbin."

"So was I." He recorded the readings on his laptop. "Year after year, I and a lot of other people beg for funding to put something more substantial than a little Dutch boy between that bucket of people—" He stabbed his finger out over the railing. "—and those gigantic bodies of water. We conduct studies, do computer simulations, testify at congressional hearings. Meanwhile, robber barons like your father cut shipping channels and dump industrial waste and salt water into the wetlands that used to protect us from the tidal surge, and you tell the public to take another piss off the deck of the Titanic."

"Being an alarmist is equally dangerous," said Shay. "Recovering hall monitors like you demonstrated that during Hurricane Ivan."

"I was wondering how long it would take you to throw that in my face."

"You were just as certain then, Corbin, and you were wrong. That night, I found you drunk in a corner at French 75, sick on cigars and feeling like an idiot."

"A happy idiot," he said expansively. "I hope it happens again, but I can say with 100% certainty, it won't."

"One hundred percent certainty?" she tasked him. "As a scientist, you can say that?"

"Okay, 93.7% certainty." Corbin squared his jaw. "Want to stake your life on that last 6.3%, Shay? Or just someone else's life? Because I suspect your father has a private jet standing by, lest your feet get wet, and you'll take off without a thought for anybody south of Claiborne Avenue, including the little black cancer kid you accessorized with on your website."

Shay flinched, and he looked away from the sucker-punched hurt in her eyes.

"It's not my job to yell 'fire' in a crowded theater," she said. "If the people in authority don't order a mandatory evacuation—"

"Then it's your job to ask the hard questions and hold them accountable."

"My job is selling Dr. Pepper, Tampax, and diet pills, and every time you step in front of that camera with your adorably rumpled scientist-with-soul persona, that's exactly what you're doing. I know what all that media face time means for your business, Corbin, so the righteous indignation rings a tad hypocritical. You're riding this thing like a pony."

"Funny, that's not what you said four years ago when you talked me into all this media crap."

"Heavens, no," Shay scoffed. "Four years ago, I had the lofty ideals of a babbling twenty-something party girl. That's what attracted you, right, Corbin? My unshakable standards?"

"Both of them."

"Oh, bite me, you parsimonious ass."

Corbin bent a wire coat hanger and hooked it through the turkey.

"Are we about to turn some kind of corner, Shay? Because I really do have a lot going on, and candidly, I don't see myself jumping in to help you with your little project."

"Okay. Reboot." She made a finite gesture. "None of that happened."

Corbin rattled the top off the pot and said, "Step back. This'll spit when I put it in."

Shay stepped to the rail while he pulled on heavy work gloves, hoisted the turkey by the coat hanger, and lowered it into the hissing mist.

"Maybe we should have started with the elephant in the room," she said.

"Meaning what?"

"After Ivan." She traced her finger around an iron curlicue. "We didn't part well, and I never gave you a chance to apologize."

"Apologize for what? I said I loved you, and you cut me off at the knees."

"No, you said, and I quote: 'I'm almost drunk enough to say I love you.' And then you got angry at me for feeling hurt and insulted."

"I crossed your uncrossable Line of L-word Demarcation, and you burst into flame."

"Bottom line, Corbin, you couldn't expand your emotional vocabulary to satisfy me, and I couldn't rewrite my personality, politics, and religious beliefs to satisfy you." Shay shrugged and attempted a smile. "Fortunately, our mutual commitment phobia rendered all that moot."

"We had some good times, and we moved on," Corbin said stiffly. "I'm done discussing it."

"Good." She posted her messenger bag on the table. "Let's discuss my project."

"Make it the short version."

"There's an entire realm of geocentric fetishes. Tornados, blizzards, lunar and solar eclipses, auroras borealis. Naturally, fetish-feeding websites spring up."

"That has nothing to do with my work, Shay. That's like connecting the dots between MILF sites and orthopedic shoes."

"What do you know about the website HurricaneLovers.com?"

"Only that it exists," he said, dropping the grease-spattered gloves on a chair.

Shay closed the French doors and handed him a manila file folder from her bag.

"Basic membership on the HurricaneLovers forum starts at a thousand dollars per year. Premier level is ten thousand. Upscale individuals connect, exchange photos, and watch storm trends with the objective of hooking up for a major event. Some are thrill-seeking. Others think it's significant to conceive a baby during a hurricane. There's a BDSM sub-forum with a darker side, but the majority of these people are nice, average folks. I think sex has become so rote, so unceremonial in our culture, the only way they can reinvest it with ecstasy is to make it part of this death-defying, life-affirming, force-of-nature event."

"Shay. Short version."

"Someone started using this forum to steal information and exploit the credit of men who were understandably reluctant to come forward and press charges. At first, it was just ladylike larceny. Fifty or sixty grand. Damage the guy's dignity. I heard about it last year from a sorority sister whose marriage was affected. My interest was piqued—as a journalist—so I joined the forum as Dervish Dave: Seattle air traffic controller, father of three, enjoys parasailing, fine wine, blah blah blah, net worth a modest six million."

"And?" Corbin leaned against the door, curious despite himself.

"She was onto me almost immediately. As a warning shot, she opened several store cards in my name, enrolled me in Weight Watchers, and had three dozen pairs of plus-size Bella Abzug panties delivered to my apartment."

Corbin processed that with a rich, rolling belly laugh.

"I filed a complaint and was contacted by this guy." Shay handed him a copy of Alberto Sykes' official credentials. "He'd been investigating the same leads since a close friend of his died in a warehouse during a hurricane last August."

"Hurricane Charley," said Corbin.

"Before they even realized his identity had been stolen—"

"Ivan. A month later."

"Another man was found dead in a flooded parking garage in Pensacola. This guy drowned in his car, blood alcohol well above smashed. The coroner was swamped and ruled the death accidental, but according to the coroner's report, he also had Seconal in his system, and he was wearing one of these. Take a look."

Shay drew a little box of condoms from her bag and offered him one.

Corbin shrugged. "One's pretty much like another, in my experience."

"You haven't experienced this."

As soon as Corbin took it in his hand, he noticed the circle-in-a-square profile of the packet was somewhat off from standard. The weight didn't feel familiar. The wrapper had a radar-inspired logo on the front: "Get Twistered!" swirling from the eye of a storm. On the back, it said, "You don't have to play it safe to practice safer sex!" He tore the side of the packet and withdrew the contents.

"Looks like it's imbedded with one of those ionic electrolyte nano-batteries." Corbin held it up to the sun, peering at one side, then the other. "What does this little…oh. That's innovative."

"At least." Shay smiled at the self-conscious warmth in his face. "It's a promotional item they send when you pay for a year's subscription to the website. They can't be bought anywhere else. Definitive proof that links her to the site and ties her to at least six victims in the US, South America, and the Philippines."

She handed Corbin a spreadsheet showing dates, places, and names, cross referenced with a series of major storms he knew literally from the inside out.

"According to Detective Sykes," said Shay, "she has more than a hundred profiles right now. The most active one is Queen Mab."

"Like the evil fairy in—what was it—*Midsummer Night's Dream?*"

"*Romeo and Juliet.*"

"Ah. Makes sense."

"She's raised identity theft to an art. Zeroes in on a subject. Lures him somewhere for sex. Kills him. The power's out, infrastructure crippled, law enforcement gridlocked. Before the body's identified, she's on his bank accounts, home equity, life insurance—everything. A host of fresh credit cards instantly get cashed out. The death appears accidental, and it takes months for his family to clap on to what's happening. By that time, every line of credit is bled dry, jurisdiction is all over the map, and Queen Mab has vanished into thin air."

Corbin glanced at his watch. "How do I figure into this?"

"I've been following this thing for nine months, waiting for exactly the right moment to bring all the elements together."

"And this is it," said Corbin. "The perfect storm for the perfect crime."

Shay nodded. "She won't miss this opportunity, and neither will I. If half of what you're predicting comes true, this place will be crawling with national media in forty-eight hours. I have an independent camera crew on standby with a mobile editing suite. Sykes is on his way with the extradition paperwork. And I have solid information on the identity of the hookup. This is where you come in."

"Shay, I have my own—"

"It's Guy."

Corbin glanced at the French doors and said, "Come again?"

"Your brother has been corresponding with this woman. He's planning to meet her tonight when the storm hits."

Corbin's mouth froze slightly open, then widened to a grin. "You're jerking my chain. I call BS on that. How would you even be privy to something like that?"

"Sykes is limited by jurisdiction, warrants, admissibility. I'm not." Shay shrugged one shoulder. "As you know, I'm blessed with a variety of resources."

"And unhampered by scruples about using them."

"Good stewardship of one's resources," she said. "That's a Christian family value also preached by environmentalists."

"Cut to the chase."

"My source is able to access IP addresses, private messages, encrypted payment data. Short version: Guy's credit card came up, and for obvious reasons, the name got my attention."

"That doesn't prove a damn thing."

"For three years," said Shay, "the forum subscription has been charged to his Nawlins Chopper American Express card. Always paid immediately. Never disputed." She proffered a thick printout. "Here's a record of those transactions, along with private messages and chat transcripts from the last two years, all matching the IP address on his office computer, specifying dates, places, safewords, and every kind of gitcherfreakon this side of a circus tent."

Corbin flipped to the chat transcript. Portions had been boxed with pink highlighter.

> QUEEN_MAB: R we on 4 NOLA?
> LA_BLOWHARD: lezay lay bon tomps roolay
> LA_BLOWHARD: show me ur (*)(*)
> QUEEN_MAB: show me ur 3=e
> LA_BLOWHARD: 3=====e
> QUEEN_MAB: u got my attention :)
> LA_BLOWHARD: what do u like 2 do?
> QUEEN_MAB: :p
> QUEEN_MAB: :q
> QUEEN_MAB: :O
> QUEEN_MAB: :)
> LA_BLOWHARD: now u got my atnetion
> LA_BLOWHARD: attention :-/
> QUEEN_MAB: typing with 1 hand?
> LA_BLOWHARD: HAHAHAHAHA YES
> QUEEN_MAB: what will u do 2 me?

The response to that made Corbin want to scrub his eyes with soap.

"This isn't Guy. No way." He tossed the printout on the table and wiped his damp palms on his jeans. "My brother's a screw-up. Doesn't always have things squared away. But he is a decent man married to a good woman. They're expecting a baby. No way could he do this to her."

"During Ivan," Shay said, producing another printout, "he hooked up with a second-grade teacher from Wisconsin. During Hurricane Charley, he was with a Dallas architect."

"No," said Corbin, his gut hollowing. "He loves his wife."

"So did the guy in Pensacola. This family photo is from their church directory. It's not about love or sense or being squared away, Corbin. It's about need. That's what makes it possible for her to prey on these men."

Corbin leaned against the storm shutters, his backbone at odds with the scrolling trim, his shirt sticking to him in wet oblongs under both arms.

"Last week," said Shay, "when Katrina crossed Florida and started heading this way, she asked him for a photo. He sent this."

The picture she handed him was pixeled and blurry, having been upsized and cropped, but Corbin recognized it from his own digital camera. He'd snapped it the day they told him Bonnie was pregnant. Standing in the doorway of the shop, directly under the balcony where Shay stood now, Guy had tucked a round wicker basket under Bonnie's shirt, mugging with a hugely joyful expression. In the cropped print-out, all that was left of his wife was the tapering edge of her broad sun-hat and the prescient shadow of her basket-shaped belly on the door.

"That's where I drop out of the loop," said Shay. "I can't access phone calls or text messages. Protocol is to connect in public, exchange safe-words, and go somewhere conducive to fully experiencing the storm. Basic precautions and accommodations—toilet, food, water—opti-mally, you have good acoustics, sky view, some solid outside structure. He mentions a fire escape in one of the PMs, but he also talks about the possibility of a swimming pool, playground swings—"

"Geezes." Corbin recoiled. "I don't want to hear this."

"I'm sorry to be indelicate, but we need to figure out where he's going."

"Oh, he's not going anywhere," Corbin assured her. "He'll be right here with my boot up his ass."

"No, Corbin. Sykes would lose her."

"Which is to say, you'd lose your story."

"Yes," said Shay. "I won't pretend I don't care."

"If you want a major story, Shay, clever investigative reporting won't be necessary. Trust me, if you don't leave now, you'll be up to your neck in it. People will be dying."

"And if I wasn't standing here, your brother would be one of them. Corbin, if you derail this, someone else will very probably be killed, and that man's blood will be on your hands."

"My responsibility is to protect my family."

"Then I'll just have to tell Bonnie." Shay set her chin, keeping her voice low. "I'll forward every porntastic message and happily CC her divorce attorney."

"Bullcrap." Corbin looked toward the river, an immovable object. "You wouldn't do that."

Shay raised the window and called inside, "Hey, Bonnie? Could you please come out here one sec?"

"What the hell is wrong with you?" Corbin hissed, incredulous. "You'd be that cruel? Over a fucking cable pilot?"

"Cruel? It's worse to keep it from her. She has a right to know."

"And exactly how do you expect—"

"What's up?" Bonnie appeared at the French doors.

"Sorry to bother you," Shay said sweetly. "Could we please get a cold drink? I'm wilting like yesterday's daisies out here in this heat."

Bonnie turned to Corbin. "Seriously?"

"Please," he said. "If you wouldn't mind."

She huffed softly and disappeared into the house.

Shay slid the window shut and said, "I'll obscure his identity. Bonnie won't be publicly humiliated. He'll have to face the music eventually, but she wouldn't have to know until after the baby is born. Those are your options, Corbin. That or she finds out right now."

Bonnie returned with two tall glasses of lemonade. She smiled and squeezed Corbin's arm in a mother hen way that twisted his heart in a knot. He took a bottle of vodka from the baker's rack and laid a shot into his glass.

"Corbin has something to tell you," Shay piped up. Her eyes locked into his with an ice-cold charm school smile. "He's afraid you'll be upset."

Bonnie looked at him curiously. "What?"

"Belle soeur…"

Sweating, searching his brain for an off-ramp, then Corbin looked to Shay for help, hating it like hell. She slipped her arm around his waist, dependably quick on the uptake.

"Corbin invited me to the party tonight," she said. "I hope you don't mind."

"Of course not," Bonnie said crisply. "We don't turn anybody away."

"See, you big silly? Bonnie doesn't mind." Shay gave his ribs a tickle. "You'll pick me up at nine, right, baby?"

"Right." Corbin downed the hard lemonade in one drawn-out swallow. Cold pain ice-picked through the vodka, and he jammed his thumb against his eye socket.

"Bonnie," he said, "excuse us, please."

She stepped inside and closed the doors, leaving them to a thick silence in which Shay sat, hating how damp and duplicitous she felt, and Corbin stood, quietly resolving to beat his brother's ass.

Cars went by below, burdened with luggage, leaving town.

"There's a fire escape above the garage at the bike shop," said Corbin. "Basic precautions… heavy built loft, wire mesh windows. Generator. Facility's grungy but functional. Metal roofing for acoustics. That would be my guess."

"I'll tell Sykes to wait for us there," said Shay.

"And then what?"

"You've seen shows where they sting internet predators. When Guy goes, we follow, I get the money shot, and Sykes steps in before things get too nasty for prime time. If I get my birthday wish, Queen Mab will talk to me on camera while we wait out the storm. When the weather breaks tomorrow afternoon, my production unit rolls in from Baton Rouge, Sykes takes our girl to await extradition, and Guy—hopefully a bit the wiser—goes home to his lovely wife. Tuesday night, I'll meet you in the French Quarter and buy you a beer."

"When the weather breaks…" Corbin's clipped laugh was hard and humorless. "You haven't heard one word I've been saying."

"I'll come up with Plan B if necessary." Shay gathered her things to go, but she paused with her hand on the doorknob. "This isn't how I wanted to see you again, Corbin. Truth is, I've missed you."

Shay gave him time to answer before she left, but not enough to make it awkward when he didn't.

NEW ORLEANS

SUNDAY EVENING
AUGUST 28

From: Rhodes, Patrick

Sent: Sunday, August 28, 2005 8:59 PM

To: Altshuler, Brooks

Cc: Brown, Michael D

Subject: FW: IIMG

Mike,

Check out below - (Brooks, I thought the three of us might commiserate)

---------Original Message-----------

> From:...Lowder, Michael

> To:...Rhodes, Patrick; Heath, Michael; Altshuler,

Brooks; Burris, Ken;

> Cc:...Sharro, Stephen

> Sent:...Sun Aug 28 19:48:21 2005

> Subject: IIMG

Patrick,

Just received call from [—REDACTED—] water depth in New
Orleans may areas will be [—REDACTED—] said that he
wanted to let you know, that it was not to "get into our
knickers".

ML

From:...Altshuler, Brooks

Sent:...Sunday, August 28, 2005 8:28 PM

To:...Patrick.Rhodes@dhs.gov

Subject: Fw: IIMG

Importance: High

This is HSC pushing this. This is the job of the long term
recovery esf in the nrp and fema is the lead. Let them
play their reindeer games as long as they are not turning
around and tasking us with their stupid questions. None of
them have a clue about emergency management [or economic
impacts for that matter]

Sent from my BlackBerry Wireless Handheld

The first Thibodeaux Brothers Hurricane Bash was mostly Guy's doing. It was 1992. The boys had been on their own for four years. Corbin had quit high school after their father died, determined to keep his kid brother out of the foster-care system, so the minute Guy turned seventeen, Corbin joined the Navy, knowing it was his best hope for an education. He tried to force Guy to sign up as well, but Watts stepped in and said, "No. He ain't the type, bro. He'd end up in trouble, and that would break Bonnie's heart. You go. I'll keep an eye on him."

As Corbin cherished his last few days of civilian freedom, Hurricane Andrew raged into the city of New Orleans. Guy and Watts mixed a batch of Screaming Purple Jesus in the bathtub, gathered a cadre of rowdy friends, and the event went down in history. Corbin documented multiple funnel clouds, Guy and Bonnie popped each other's cherries, and Watts accidentally lit the sofa on fire when he coughed a spray of Everclear across a fondue burner.

At the height of the storm, the Thibodeaux brothers clung to each other out on the balcony, drunker than pump handles, red plastic fireman helmets duct taped to their heads, bellowing into the wind, shouting down the forces of nature, the God who'd taken their mother, the devil who was their daddy.

From that night forward, every big storm was an opportunity to get out the howling and host another party. These days, for Guy, it was an excuse to gather friends and neighbors for beer and loud music and bragging about all the big storms everybody had come through.

For Watts, it was a chance to shoot the bull with some of the steady customers, tattoo artists, and Harley enthusiasts who spent money at the bike shop. For Bonnie, it was a time to sit with her sisters in the kitchen, talking lively sister talk about matters too esoteric for anything less forgiving than candlelight. For Corbin, it was a way to get at least of few people up out of neighborhoods he knew would simply disappear should the levees give way.

The Katrina bash wasn't as well populated as some in the past. At the eleventh hour, officials had extracted their heads from their asses and ordered the mandatory evacuation of New Orleans, telling those who were unable to escape to bring three days worth of food and water to the Superdome.

The shelter of last resort.

Corbin's heart sank at the sound of that phrase. The words haunted him all afternoon, along with the twisted chat room exchange and everything else he wished he didn't know about Guy. It burned a hole in his liver to think what it would do to Bonnie if she ever found out.

Bonnie and Guy were best friends in first grade. She was his first and only high school girlfriend. She'd moved into this house when they were eighteen, and they married less than a year later. Over the years, Corbin had secretly wondered how that sort of monogamy was even possible.

Now he knew. It wasn't.

Night fell. Corbin met Shay at a downtown parking garage where she stashed her Escalade for safekeeping, and they drove back to Algiers without talking. She volunteered to help Bonnie and her sisters with the potluck spread. Corbin sat on the balcony, rolling a beer bottle back and forth between his hands, monitoring wind readings, watching the diehards arrive under the chaotic sky. Bonnie came out to watch the bewitched oak trees flail, and Guy stood behind her, arms around her blossoming belly, swaying her to the loud Zydeco music, talking low in her ear.

"Behave youself," Bonnie smiled and spanked his arm, and Guy tickled her neck with his whiskers.

Corbin went in and located a bottle of Jim Beam and sat on the couch.

Just before midnight, the lights started blinking and browning, then guttered out for good.

"Welcome to N'awlins, y'all!" Watts hoisted his beer. "*Laissez les bon temps roulez.*"

A whoop went up from the assembled lot. Leaning close to Corbin's shoulder, Shay said, "Did you expect the power to fail already? The weather isn't that bad yet."

"Sometimes they shut down the grids preemptively to minimize damage," said Corbin.

She pretended to nuzzle his ear, softly hissing, "Do not get drunk," then went back to playing the party girl, sipping Diet Coke, chatting people up, charming the tattoo ink out of Guy and Watts, who regaled her now with the Purple Jesus flaming sofa story.

"You gotta understand Everclear," Guy palavered. "That shit is some insanely flammable 190 proof alcohol."

"God created Everclear for two reasons," said Watts. "Get people stupid and start fires. Not a healthy combination."

"It has no taste, no smell," said Guy, "so you can mix it in anything, and Bonnie had grown these pineapples in some kinda psycho-botanical situation for the high school science fair, and whatever she did frankly made 'em taste like piss, but we don't want to hurt her feelings, so we're all gonna drink this Everclear pineapple piss concoction."

"I take a huge swig. Spew it forthwith. Fffffffooosh!" Watts reenacted the conflagration with sound effects that got bigger and more incendiary every time the saga was repeated.

Shay laughed her southern summer night laugh. Hot wind lifted her long ponytail. She hooked an ice cube from her glass with two fingers and held it against the back of her neck. Corbin rubbed his hand over his face, fighting the fatigue that weighted his eyelids and dragged his chin to his chest. The loud music and the length of the day webbed around him like the layers of a cocoon. He felt himself dozing.

Every once in a while someone came by and kissed him on top of the head or punched him on the shoulder.

"Hey, Doc."

Corbin didn't need to look up to see who it was. There were no strangers here. Just folks. The same shifting tidal eddy of people who'd been coming and going through stormy nights and crowded living rooms all his life.

He drifted into a shallow dream, and Shay was there in the green dress she wore the first time he saw her. From a distance, he heard her laughter again, not forced and fake, but easy and real, the way she was the last time he had her on her back. After Ivan. When he knew he loved her. Wanted to tell her. Screwed it up.

"Not dozing off, are you?" she whispered lightly, close enough that he felt her breath on his cheek.

"Resting my eyes," he said, breathing in the uncluttered pretty scent of her when she sat next to him. Cucumbers, crepe myrtle, and pretty, pretty woman. It made him wish he was still asleep and dreaming. She drummed her fingers on his kneecap.

"Corbin..."

The drumming turned to a lazy circle and moved up his thigh. He took her hand and laced his fingers with hers.

"I've missed you too, Shay."

"I'm Louisa, goose." She spanked his shoulder. "Thanks for making me feel special."

"Oh. Sorry." He sat up and clumsily withdrew his hand. "Louisa. I apologize."

"Long time no see, Dr. T-Bone," she said. "Except I saw you on TV this morning."

Corbin squinted at her in the non-light, trying to place her. Maybe the farmer's market girl Bonnie had tried to fix him up with. Or the book club girl Bonnie had tried to fix him up with. She definitely looked familiar. Blunt bobbed hair colored jet black. Pale heart-shaped face with full, fire engine red lips. Great body. She was wearing a pleasantly breezy summer dress that looked fresh off the clothesline and could have been in fashion in 1955 or '65 or '95 or now.

"So, um… how've you been?" he said.

"Good. How 'bout your own bad self?"

"Been better. This is a lousy week."

"Oh, sugar, do I know it. Lost half my dang work hours." She took the beer bottle and gave him her plastic cup. "Here. Have my Hurricane. Too much grenadine for me."

Corbin took a shallow pull on the silly twirled straw, cringed at the syrupy taste, and handed it back to her. "I'll pass."

"I haven't seen you since Uncle Tommy and Aunt Georgie's 50th anniversary picnic," said Louisa. "Gosh, that's… how many years ago now?"

"Geezes, six years, at least," said Corbin. Of course. Tommy and Georgie's Louisa. She'd changed her hair. Grown up. She was a college kid back then. She collected the cool condensation from the outside of her glass and laid her palm against her collarbone. The unfussy gesture reminded him of Shay. A lot about her reminded him of Shay.

"Y'all should have had more block parties," she said.

"Yup." Corbin felt a surge of loss, a sudden awareness of everyday things slipping into past tense. "That was a great time."

"Awesome food, good music, crazy hats, band up on the flatbed… you and me dancing."

"Not me," said Corbin. "I never dance."

"Well, you'd had a bit to drink," Louisa giggled, and he felt the tip of her index finger on his neck. "You tried to get fresh with me."

Corbin cringed at the thought of Tommy and Georgie seeing him drunk and hitting on their niece.

"Did your aunt and uncle get out okay?"

"Yes," said Louisa. "I told them as long as I was coming up to house-sit, they should leave Pincus and Pretty Cakes, but Aunt G just wanted to skadoodle, and Uncle Tommy was all, 'Last time I spent $1600 on rooms for the whole famdamily, and it didn't hardly tip over a flowerpot.'"

Corbin laughed at the dead-on impression of his neighbor. "He's never gonna let me live that one down, is he?"

"Nope. When you get it wrong, Slick, you get it seriously wrong." She giggled and crossed her smooth, bare legs so her shin bone rested against the back of Corbin's knee. "You think Katrina will be as awful as everyone's saying?"

"Yes, but apparently I don't know shit about it."

"Oh, *pshh*." Louisa tilted her head and laughed musical laughter. She laid her hand on his arm and left it there. "You're brilliant, and you know it. Aunt G takes everything you say as gospel. She wanted me to go with them to the timeshare in Florida, but I wouldn't miss this event for the world. Plus I work Monday."

"Trust me. That's not gonna be an issue."

"Personally, I don't want the weather to be predictable. What would life be without serendipity? Isn't it more fun to be surprised?"

"No."

"Is that a general aversion," she asked, "or hurricane specific?"

"Both."

"Maybe you just need to get your mind off it for a while."

She reached across him to steal his beer, and her breast brushed against his arm. Corbin felt an unwelcome stir low and tight in his midsection. Nothing to do with sense or being squared away.

"I thought I heard you were getting married a while back," he said, and Louisa's red lips froze in a slightly parted smile. There was a moment of something he couldn't read in her face, and he hastened, "I'm sorry. None of my business."

"It's complicated," she said. "Are you here with someone?"

"Yes. Yes, I am." Corbin nodded. "Lucky me."

"Oh, dear. I sense ambivalence."

"It's complicated." He felt himself sink a little deeper into the couch and couldn't tell if it was her perfume or the Jim Beam. "Maybe another time."

"I wouldn't hate that one bit." Louisa smiled and chucked him under the chin. "Stay high and dry, darlin.'"

Watts was dancing with her before she got three steps away. Corbin closed his eyes and tried to enjoy the lingering breeze of crepe myrtle.

"Corbin." Shay snapped her fingers in front of his face. "Wakey, wakey."

"Geezes." Corbin pushed the heels of his hands against his eyes. "Do you have to do that?"

"How much longer till the serious weather hits?"

"A while. Two, three hours."

"He'll be leaving soon. Look alert, would you?"

"Don't worry. We'll know when he tries to leave."

"Meaning what?"

"Meaning we'll know. Shay, I've had about ninety minutes sleep in the last two days. Just leave me alone. Half an hour. Please." He draped his arm across his eyes. "Kick me if it starts raining so I can log the time."

She sighed and headed down the narrow hall. By the light of a camp lantern, she stepped over pillows, blankets, and bodies. It was quieter than the living room and smelled like humans. People were settled on sleeping bags and futons, drinking wine, smoking grass, playing guitars, engaging in thinky philosophical discussions. Two people were going at it up against the wall in a dark corner of the laundry room. The hall was dark outside the kitchen, and Shay stepped into the shadows next to the door when she heard Guy's voice.

"Dog needs to get laid, Bon Bon. Praise God and pass the beauty queen."

"That's not a healthy relationship, Guy. It's a chronic one-night stand. When she kicked him to the curb, he got useless drunk for a month, slept with all my friends, and acted like a horse's ass."

"You can't lay that on her, Bonnie. Corbin had his finger on the eject button before her panties hit the floor, and it's his business, not ours."

"Whatever. I'm not putting up with that again. You love your brother, baby. I love him too. He's my beau frère—as much my big brother as Watts—but we got a family happening now. We need our own home. You gotta tell him to wake up and smell some get the hell out."

NEW ORLEANS

SUNDAY NIGHT
AUGUST 28

```
** WTUS84 KLIX 282242 ***
HLSLIX LAZ038-040-050-056>070-MSZ080>082-290100-
HURRICANE KATRINA LOCAL STATEMENT
NATIONAL WEATHER SERVICE NEW ORLEANS LA
545 PM CDT SUN AUG 28 2005

DIRECT STRIKE OF POTENTIALLY CATASTROPHIC AND LIFE
THREATENING HURRICANE LATE TONIGHT AND EARLY MONDAY...
SQUALLS SPREADING OVER SOUTHEAST LOUISIANA WITH CONDITIONS
DETERIORATING... KATRINA EXPECTED TO MAKE LANDFALL AS A
CATEGORY FOUR OR FIVE HURRICANE PACKING SUSTAINED 160
MPH WINDS. MANDATORY EVACUATION ORDERS ARE IN EFFECT
FOR MOST OF SOUTHEAST LOUISIANA PARISHES AND COASTAL
MISSISSIPPI COUNTIES. RESIDENTS SHOULD FOLLOW EVACUATION
RECOMMENDATIONS FROM LOCAL OFFICIALS AND LOCATIONS OF
SHELTER OF LAST RESORT.

$$
```

Shortly before one, Corbin stretched his legs and went to the dining room, where he cracked a beer from the cooler, worked his way down the potluck table, and settled into a straight chair with a paper plate full of dirty rice and deep fried turkey. Guy came and clapped his shoulder and parked backward on a chair next to him, half in the bag, all hail fellow well met.

"Hey, Doc," he grinned. "How's Miss Texas?"

"Fine," Corbin said without looking up from his plate.

"Get it while it's hot." Guy halved a dinner roll with his thumbs, layered it with a handful of turkey and wolfed it down. He finished off Corbin's beer and said, "Dude, hold down the fort. Before it gets too trashy, I'm gonna ride over and check the safety lights at the shop."

Corbin lurched from his chair, seized his little brother by the shirt and shoved him into a tight nook between the wall and their grandmother's bulky oak sideboard.

"I know where you're going, you greasy little shit, and you can forget it."

"Dude," Guy protested. "What is your problem?"

"I know what you did, you reprehensible little turd. During Charley. During Ivan. This stops now." Corbin throttled him hard against the woodwork. "Set one foot out that door, so help me Christ, I'll kick your ass."

"You couldn't kick my ass if I handed it to you in an Easter basket," Guy scoffed.

Corbin baffed him under the chin with the back of his fist, knocking Guy's skull sharply against the wall. Guy slapped him hard upside the head, and then they embraced, punching each other's ribs, as if they were still skinny, sweaty, sunburned boys.

"Guy," Bonnie shrilled from the doorway. "Corbin? What the hell?"

Her sisters and a few curious spectators gathered behind her.

"Bon Bon, I swear, I didn't do anything," Guy puffed like a guilty little crud. "Corbin just went apeshit on me."

"I got a houseful of your pit-stank friends and no AC. I am tired. I am hot. My two ankles are swelled up like goddang hog sausages." Bonnie's voice crumpled, almost crying. "Guy. You promised I could depend on you this time."

Guy punched Corbin's arm. "Show some freakin' restraint, dude. She's nine weeks from delivery. It's a very emotional time. Bon Bon, don't cry." He hustled over and got his arms around her. "Baby, it's okay. Corbin's worried is all. You know how he is."

"Corbin, you are outside your mind if you think I'm putting up with your drunk ass tonight," Bonnie glared. "Tomorrow's gonna be hard enough without you carping about what we should've done yesterday. Guy's a better man than you ever give him credit for, and you're no prince yourself, so you can take that almighty big brother act and shove it."

"Thank you, ma femme." Guy kissed the top of her head. "That means a lot to me."

"Damn straight it does." She flicked his hand from her shoulder.

"Want me to kick on the generator, Bon Bon? Run some AC for you?"

"Corbin made a schedule rationing the generator usage, and we're sticking to it," said Bonnie. "See, Corbin? We're following your generator rules. Happy?"

Arms folded, jaw taut, Corbin said, "Do what you need to do, Bonnie."

"Guy, if you need to check the lights at the shop, do it and get your flat white ass back here. Don't you even think about going to that poker game."

"Bon Bon, I'm almost even. Baby, don't make it be a fight."

"Do not test me." She drilled her index finger into his chest. "You come crawling home tomorrow, hung over like last time, you can kiss my ass on my way out the door. There's gonna be a huge mess up in here. I will not clean it up myself while you clear trees to pay back those jackals. That is not gonna happen again."

"It won't, ma femme." Guy pressed his palms to her belly, and the baby visibly pushed back. "I'll be back in two hours. I swear."

"Corbin?" Bonnie turned on him. "Shut it. And keep it shut. When that hurricane hits, y'all two better be sitting on that sofa like you're in a goddang boys' choir."

As she left the room, there was a spatter of applause. The spectators dissipated, leaving Shay standing in the doorway next to Watts, who tapped a spoon on the rim of his glass and said, "Thibodeaux, party of two? Your pussy-whipped is ready."

"How would you like to wake up with a fork in your eye?" Guy snarled.

"Do not test me!" Watts imitated his little sister in a nasal shrill. "Y'all two better be bent over that sofa like you's in a boy choir!"

"Watts," Corbin said wearily. "Give it a rest."

"I gotta go," said Guy.

"If you cross that bridge on your bike, you won't get home after the storm hits," Corbin said. "I won't lie to her to save your sorry ass."

"If you'd kept your mouth shut, I could have been there and back. She never would've known the difference."

"So that makes it okay? Christ, what is wrong with you? Brother, don't do this." Corbin was pleading now, not even trying to disguise it. "Guy, this woman loves you. She has your son inside her. She's as close as you'll ever get to salvation. Nothing you get out there is worth screwing that up."

"I know, all right? You think it doesn't eat my guts out every time I look at her?" Guy seized the overflowing trash bag, shoving in abandoned paper plates and plastic cups. "I didn't know the baby was gonna make everything so different. All I can do now is damage control."

"Dog, I already checked the shop," said Watts. "I got that covered."

Guy glared at him. "Watts, I thought you had someplace to be."

Corbin said, "Watts, you're not leaving Algiers, are you?"

"Nah," he said, "just gonna head over to the poker game."

"Okay, well, don't do anything I wouldn't do."

"Dude. You never do anything."

Guy cinched the trash bag and said, "Do I need y'all two's permission to take the garbage out before I sit on the couch like a choirboy?"

"You're doing the right thing," said Corbin.

"Screw you. Take your sunny little fuck buddy upstairs and stay out of my life."

As Guy stalked down the hall, Shay followed Corbin up the stairs to his bedroom. She kicked the door shut, seething.

"You just couldn't let it work out for me, could you, Corbin?"

"That's right, Shay, because everything is all about you."

"Oh, eat me, you self-righteous blowhole."

"Not a word to Bonnie," said Corbin. "There's no need for her to know now."

"What makes you think he won't do it again with the next storm, Corbin? What makes you so sure he won't still do it tonight?"

"I chained his Fat Boy with a combination lock. Just in case his better angels fall through." Corbin sat on the edge of his desk, listening to the wind, timing the lightning. "I won't apologize. I couldn't let him go."

"What the hell? Drive that final nail in the coffin." She paced the uneven floor, thumbs hooked on her hip pockets. "Sykes is stuck behind a roadblock in Gulfport, getting zero support from the cops here. Some weasel from the Discovery Channel hired my production unit out from under me. My cell phone signal is unusable crap. When I went to get my gun from the engraver, they'd closed early to evacuate, so thanks for that."

"Shay, it's all for the best. You can't confront her without Sykes." Corbin opened his laptop and keyed into readings from the remote anemometers on the roof of his office in the CBD. "There'll be another major storm in the Gulf this year. At least one. Probably more. You'll get another chance."

"I don't want another chance. I need this to work, Corbin. There has to be a way to make this work." Shay parked on a wooden desk chair, arms and legs crossed, foot bobbing like a sewing machine needle. "Reboot. Plan B. How long before the intense stuff hits?"

"We've got moderate storm conditions downtown right now," he said, tracing the readings on the screen with his finger. "That should continue for the next two hours, then that first feeder band comes down like a sledgehammer. Between feeder bands, we'll see severe storm conditions. About six hours from now, the eyewall hits, and all hell breaks loose."

"What about the eye? We have a window of opportunity there, right?"

Corbin shook his head. "It'll pass east of here. We'll get the worst of the eyewall without a break for several hours. I'm sorry things didn't go your way, but once that first feeder band hits, there's nothing we can do but hunker down and wait it out."

The bedroom windows were permanently fitted with heavy Bermuda shutters, pulled down for the storm. Shay stood looking between the slanted slats at the flittering leaves and wet street below.

"I need to go home before it gets any worse," she said. "Take me back to my car, will you please? You could get back here with time to spare."

"Shay, if the levees fail, you're looking at four or five feet of water at your place."

"I need my laptop." She pressed her temples. "The goddang cat is in my apartment."

"We have time to swing by and grab the laptop and the cat," said Corbin, "but for the next twelve hours, your car's better off in the ramp, and you're better off here."

"Doing what?"

"Exercising common sense."

Shay squared her shoulders. "I'm not your sunny little… what Guy said."

"I'll sleep on the floor."

"Sleep wherever you like. I'm not staying."

"Shay, please." Corbin came and stood beside her. "I apologize, all right? For whatever I said or did or didn't do—all-inclusive apology, okay? And I'm sorry I was an ass on the balcony this morning."

"Did I look surprised?"

"You looked pretty." Corbin moved a strand of brown hair behind her ear, letting his knuckle linger at a sensitive place he knew just behind her jaw. "I think about you a lot. I'd be embarrassed if you knew—Son of a bitch!"

Corbin yanked the curtain aside, peering between the rattling slats.

"That little bastard took my truck."

NEW ORLEANS

SUNDAY NIGHT AUGUST 28

THE WHITE HOUSE

Office of the Press Secretary

For Immediate Release

August 28, 2005

STATEMENT BY THE PRESIDENT ON HURRICANE KATRINA AND THE IRAQ CONSTITUTION

Prairie Chapel Ranch, Crawford, Texas

THE PRESIDENT: This morning I spoke with FEMA Undersecretary Mike Brown and emergency management teams not only at the federal level but at the state level about the - Hurricane Katrina. I've also spoken with Governor Blanco of Louisiana, Governor Barbour of Mississippi, Governor Bush of Florida, and Governor Riley of Alabama. I want to thank all the folks at the federal level and the state level and the local level who have taken this storm seriously…We cannot stress enough the danger this hurricane poses to Gulf Coast communities. I urge all citizens to put their own safety and the safety of their families first by moving to safe ground. Please listen carefully to instructions provided by state and local officials.

On another matter, today Iraqi political leaders completed the process for drafting a permanent constitution. Their example is an inspiration to all who share the universal values of freedom, democracy, and the rule of law... On behalf of the American people, I congratulate the people of Iraq on completing the next step in their transition from dictatorship to democracy.

And I want to remind the American people, as the democracy unfolds in Iraq, not only will it help make America more secure, but it will affect the broader Middle East. Democracies don't war with their neighbors; democracies don't become a safe haven for terrorists who want to destroy innocent life. We have hard work ahead of us, but we're on the – we're making good progress toward making sure this world of ours is more peaceful for generations to come. Thank you very much.

Watts stood on the steps inside Guy and Bonnie's back door, willing the flashlight to be steady in his hand. Despite his best effort, it trembled noticeably, casting the young woman on the stairway in a flickery French film. He tried to drag his eyes up from her body. Small at the waist, nicely dealt up top. She was a little taller than him, even in her beaded ballerina flats, and it was all in her legs. Her legs were long and tan. Her shoulders firm and smooth, softly blushed as nectarines. She leaned against the wall, looking him over.

"LA Blowhard," she said.

"You're Queen Mab?" Watts puffed a nervous laugh. "I thought I got stood up."

"Well, you didn't make it easy. Your photo doesn't do you justice, Watts."

"I uh… I've lost some weight."

"And some height," she said wryly. "And some hair."

"That's my brother-in-law." Watts shuffled his feet on the landing, avoiding her eyes. "My business partner down at the shop."

"Yes, I figured that out."

"The thing is," Watts said miserably, "I don't take a real good photo, and early on, I missed a couple events because of that, and I really didn't want to miss this one. The Big One, right? And let's be honest, a woman puts up a picture of herself twenty years and fifty pounds ago, nobody calls her on it. Last couple events, these gals looked less like their own photo than I looked like my bro, you know? I mean, forgive me for saying, but that photo you sent…"

She neither nodded nor shrugged, but made a gesture that combined the two.

"I never send a real picture," she said. "Safety precaution. Gives me a chance to scope things out. Make a quick getaway, if necessary." She smiled, her eyes like a doe's big, dreamy eyes. "Not all guys are nice like you, Watts."

"Me, I'm always sweating bullets that it might be a transvestite," Watts laughed awkwardly. "I couldn't handle that. But you—you're—you're—holy mother and Geezes H. Christopher. Now, I'm really nervous."

She laughed. Like a mandolin. Like a songbird. Watts was smitten with desire.

"If you're pissed," he said, "we'll go back to the party. No hard feelings. All good people up there. You'd have a good time. The storm's still gonna be a hell of a thing."

"Watts." She laid two fingers to his lips. "I didn't come here to party with those bozos. I came here to experience something important with you. I was happy when I figured out it wasn't Guy. Definitely relieved it wasn't his Mortimer brother. I prefer a man who's not overbearingly built. You're exactly the kind of man I hope for, Watts."

"Seriously?"

"Mm-hmm." She took his beer bottle and gave him her plastic cup. "Here. Have my Hurricane. A little too much grenadine for my taste buds."

He took a long pull on the bright-colored straw. It was sickly sweet, but he hoped drinking it would cover the taste of cigarette on his tongue when he kissed her. Hopefully, she wasn't the no-kissing-on-the-mouth type. Because Watts wanted to kiss her. On her mouth. Pretty much more than he wanted oxygen in his lungs, he wanted that.

"Is there a Mrs. Watts?" she asked, hooking her index finger through his belt loop.

"No. Absolutely not. I wouldn't lie about that. Other than the photo..." Watts felt bold enough to set his hand on her hip. "What I said about... everything else. That was for real."

"Reality is overrated," she smiled. "That's what the internet is all about, for goodness sake. It's a storefront for self-delusion."

He nodded, not knowing what the hell that meant, just looking at those red lips, wanting to taste the lipstick and grenadine.

"When you said you had family in Algiers—hell, I didn't know you meant Tommy and Georgie," he said.

"Small world, isn't it?"

"Yeah," said Watts. "It's like a good omen or—what's the word?"

"Serendipity," she whispered close to his cheek.

He took a shallow breath, and then a deep one as she explored his hip pockets. They stood like that for a while, the tension between their bodies as taut as a piano string. Footsteps scattered down the back stairs. Corbin and his girl burst onto the potting porch. They dragged a sheet of plywood onto the steps, and Corbin rolled his bike down to the courtyard.

"Let's go somewhere more private," Louisa whispered.

"We need to hurry and get over the expressway before the rain hits," said Watts. "I got a place all ready. Everything set up so you'll be comfortable. Food, wine, beer. Got you some of those Godiva chocolates. Over at the mall."

"Oh, Watts, that's so darling. But I'd feel safer next door."

"Sure. Sure. Anything you say," Watts said, his heart beating hard. "I want you to feel comfortable."

They crossed the courtyard to Tommy and Georgie's tall Victorian home. The wind was still in its infancy, caterwauling and colicky, but not steady on its feet yet and nowhere near the height of its destructive impulses. They climbed to the top of the fire escape outside a gabled third-floor alcove. She was wearing a modest summer dress, but as she climbed the fire escape, the wind kept casting it up, showing him glimpses of her panties.

Seemed to Watts like he lost some time. Like he drank more than he thought.

When the first rain hit, a fragrant wall of noise and motion, the cool water on his face brought him around, and he realized he'd been sitting against the wall for a long time. Louisa was at the edge of the fire escape, her legs dangling down, her face tipped up, hair drenched, skin vibrating. Every once in a while she opened her arms like she was taking in the thunder.

Watts struggled to his feet, and she smiled and came to him. She ducked her chin when he tried to kiss her, but when he reached up her skirt, got his hand in her panties, he found her silky and wet as the belly of a catfish, and she didn't resist that one bit.

Suddenly, it all came raging down.

Water. Noise. A rush of cool air when she jerked his pants open.

Watts leaned against the iron rail of the fire escape with his back to the storm. Reeling drunk and raring hard, he lost track of his own hands. She outfitted him with the promotional item, and the difference it made—that screwy little gadget. Watts was blind with sensation, deaf with wind, unsteady with wine, undone by the motion of her hand, her surprisingly strong grip on his throat when she said, "Relax. It's better if you don't breathe."

Release rolled over him and left him braying. Watts shut his eyes and came with the enormity of the storm, the weeping black sky, the living air.

It felt like falling.

NEW ORLEANS

MONDAY MORNING
AUGUST 29

From: Taylor, Cindy

Sent: Monday, August 29, 2005 7:52 AM

To: Brown, Michael D

Cc: Widomski, Michael

Subject: I know it's early, but...

My eyes must certainly be deceiving me. You look fabulous
- and I'm not talking the makeup!

From: Brown, Michael D

Sent: Monday, August 29, 2005 7:52 AM

To: Taylor, Cindy

Cc: Widomski, Michael

Subject: Re: I know it's early, but...

I got it at Nordstroms. Email McBride and make sure she
knows! Are you proud of me? Can I quit now? Can I go home?

From: Stephen-Sauls

Sent: Monday, August 29, 2005 6:11 AM

To: Brown, Michael D

Subject: Fw: Office Depot Pledge to Red Cross

We didn't wait to be asked to help.

Steve Sauls

----------Original Message ----------------

Subject: **Office Depot Pledge to Red Cross**

Steve Odland, new CEO of Office Depot, Florida's third largest company headquartered in Delray Beach, pledged $1 million to the Red Cross last night in anticipation of the disaster facing New Orleans from Hurricane Katrina. A leader in corporate governance reform, Odland will challenge his fellow members of the Business Roundtable to do the same.

Steve Sauls

VP, Corporate Relations

Rolling his old Harley Knucklehead out of the potting porch, Corbin felt the kick of the wind and smelled the onset of the first real rain band.

"Hurry," he told Shay. "We might not have as much time as I thought."

Surprisingly game or incredibly single-minded, she tucked her video camera in her leather messenger bag, looped it across her body like a pageant banner, cinched the stock half-helmet under her chin, and climbed on the Knucklehead behind him without hesitation or complaint.

They got lucky, riding out of Algiers under dry lightning. Circumventing the roadblocks and crossing the river on the express-way got a bit harrowing, but once they descended into the shady residential side streets of New Orleans proper, they were somewhat sheltered from the full force of the rising wind. As the first feeder band blew in, light-to-moderate rain fell periodically and the storm began to sound like an orchestra tuning. Shay kept her forehead tucked against Corbin's back, as he weaved as best he could between scattered branches, stray boxes, unidentified flying bits and pieces.

Nawlins Chopper sat a mile and a half outside the Central Business District in a mixed-bag neighborhood, surrounded by dilapidated houses, mom-and-pop stores, and a used auto parts yard. They approached the CBD, but the absence of the familiar skyline lights left Shay disoriented. Dark office buildings hulked under the clouds occasionally startled by lightning. Beyond the headlamp of the Knucklehead, the empty streets dropped away to nothingness, as if they were riding the narrow lip of a bottomless canyon.

Corbin cut the engine and headlight as they coasted down a shaded lane to the blacktop parking lot that wrapped around the bike shop and adjoining garage.

No truck.

Shay slid the garage door open, and pulled a pricey high-tech flashlight from her bag. Corbin rolled the Knucklehead inside, vectoring the possibilities: Guy dead in the truck somewhere between here and Algiers. Guy dead up in the loft and the truck disappearing into the night.

"I know what you're thinking." Shay squeezed his arm. "That's not part of the plan."

"Safety lights are on in the showroom," said Corbin. "Somebody started the generator."

He rummaged Guy's tool box for a chunky Mag-Lite and checked the fuel level on the generator, a cheap 3000 watt unit that kept the shop lights on until daybreak in an effort to ward off looters.

"Can you tell how long it's been running?" asked Shay.

"About four hours, if it started with a full tank."

In the showroom, strip lights on the floor illuminated a narrow path between two rows of restored bikes. Neon zigzags pulsed behind corner displays. Helmets and leathers hung on tall racks between a floor-to-ceiling selection of jagged items for which bikers had real or imagined need: gravity knives, multi-tools, brass knuckles, naked lady bottle openers, bag balm, sunscreen. The undisturbed items and ambient electric buzz of the glowing display cases were more ghostly than reassuring.

"He didn't put up plywood," Shay observed.

"They're impact windows. Pretty much unbreakable."

Shay opened a door near the boot and spur corner and tested the light switch at the bottom of the stairway to the loft, but the generator powered only the safety lights. Corbin laced his fingers through hers as they climbed the dark steps and beamed the flashlights across the clean-swept floor. In an area near the firewall, an inflated camping bed was spread with a clean chenille throw, surrounded by a flickering host of candles in glass jars.

On the floor nearby was a dented beer cooler and a pile of clean packing blankets. On an upturned crate, in a beer bottle next to a box of Godiva chocolates, was a single Black Velvet rose from Bonnie's hybrid garden. Corbin crossed the empty space in three long strides and hurled the bottle against the wall.

"So this is the place," said Shay. "We can assume—"

"We can't assume anything," said Corbin. "All we know is that she has her hooks in him. If he's still alive."

"The most likely scenario is that they met in public, as per protocol, and they're on their way here. Keep an eye on the driveway while I set up my cameras."

He tried Guy's cell, got nothing, swore softly. Shay positioned one digital camera in a corner at the top of the stairs where she could quickly click it to record when the truck lights appeared. She set a second on the window sill so she could shoot it handheld, leaving the third cam as a spare in her bag, which she stowed under the counter in the showroom so Guy wouldn't see it when he came in.

"Plan B is in swing," she said, posting herself next to Corbin at the wire-meshed window overlooking the driveway. "Turn off that flashlight."

Corbin clicked off the light, and shadows rose around them like a chancel choir. They stood for a long while, waiting, taking in the increasing shift and desperate whispers of the trees at the perimeter of the parking lot.

"Shay. Please."

Corbin touched her leg, and she realized her foot was going up and down like a piston.

"Sorry."

He set his elbows on the window ledge. "Scratch my back."

Fingers crooked, she briskly scoured over his shoulders, shoulder blades, ribcage, and kidneys. As she worked up the sides of his spine, Corbin rumbled like a mastiff and said "thank you," the way he always did at the end of the familiar ritual.

"That's the only reason you missed me," said Shay.

"No, but it's a good one." He leaned on the wall and looked out at the sky. "Our dad was a worthless piece of shit by the time Guy was ten.

I tried to teach him what's okay and not okay with women—a joke, I know. But I did try."

"You kept him fed and clothed and in school," said Shay. "What you did for him was extraordinary, Corbin. The choices he's making now don't diminish—"

There was a sharp whistle of swift wind above the high ceiling, then a suspended moment of what seemed like the trees holding their breath. Shay felt the caliber of the air pressure shift with the noise level; the ambient tuning orchestra sound was overrun by a galloping herd of yaks and belt sanders on the corrugated metal roof.

"No way," said Shay. "You told me two hours."

"I said *about* two hours. Ninety minutes ago." Corbin's cell vibrated, and he checked the ID. "It's Bonnie. What do I say?"

"Something vague. Ask her if she's okay."

He nodded and answered. "Bonnie, are you okay?"

"Nah, dude, it's me."

"*Guy*? Geezes. Brother. Thank God. Where the hell are you?"

"I'm at home," said Guy. "Where the hell are you?"

"I went looking for you, you stupid jerk."

"Doc, you need to get back here. It's raining like a—"

The call wrinkled and dropped.

"He's at home." Corbin raked his fingers through his hair, physically feeling relief in his veins. "He's home. He's okay."

Shay stood in the dark, gauging her mixed reaction: sympathetic relief, selfish disappointment, and a profound dislike for losing.

"So that's it," she said, looking at the rain thrashing the parking lot.

"I'm sorry, Shay."

"What now? Can we get back to Algiers?"

"No, that expressway bridge would be insane," said Corbin.

She opened her hands and made a *pffft* sound. "Nice. Guy's as snug as a bug at home, and we're stuck in the gitcherfreakon tree house."

"Between feeder bands, we'll hop on the bike and go to my office. We'd get wet on the way over, but the accommodations are more upscale."

Shay lifted the cooler lid. Beer, cold cuts, a bottle of cheap champagne and a quart of orange juice wallowed with a bag of rapidly melting ice.

"Welcome to my birthday party," she said dryly.

Corbin popped the cork on the champagne and mixed mimosas in plastic cups, and they sat on a packing blanket with their backs against the firewall. He set the Godiva chocolates on her lap and said, "Happy birthday, Shay."

"So sweet of you to remember."

He kissed her cheek, lingering for a moment, hoping she'd turn her mouth toward his, but she didn't.

"My father wanted to give me a Hummer for my birthday," said Shay. "Clever me, I told him, 'Daddy, I can't think of any scenario in which that would be an appropriate vehicle for me.'"

"I hate it when Republicans are right," Corbin harrumphed. "What did he give you? Private island? Yacht?"

"Nothing expensive," said Shay. "He gave me a Sig Sauer .38 with a handmade pink pearl grip. It matches the one he gave me when I turned thirteen. Back then, he taught me how to handle it, took me to the practice range every day. It brought us a lot closer, so this is a very sweet, meaningful gift."

"Till they pry it from your cold, dead hands."

She kicked his foot in the dark.

"It's his way of telling me to take the next step," said Shay. "And he's right. I need to launch my production company before my looks are gone."

"Your looks aren't going anywhere," said Corbin. "Every time I see you, James Brown takes over the left side of my brain."

"Oh! Two smooth points for the doctor." She smiled and held out her cup for another shot of champagne.

"You'll be a great producer," he said. "What are you waiting for? You with your big howdy resources. Screw the sunshine thing. And screw this cable pilot. It's not worth the chances you're taking."

"It's not just the pilot," said Shay. "Sykes is depending on me."

"Don't pretend it's about Sykes. It's about the giant panties. She outsmarted you and called you a fat-ass. Now you're mad, and you won't let it go."

"Corbin, this is not some sassy prankster. She kills people."

"Exactly," he said seriously. "Stop messing with her before you get hurt. Tell Sykes to step up and do his own job."

"Truthfully…" Shay cradled her lukewarm mimosa between her hands. "I wanted to prove that I could cover something grittier than a pancake breakfast. Somehow this racy little story about suburban sex-capades mushroomed into nine months of brain-consuming research, crime scene photos, dead bodies, genitalia, night after night of fetishist blather on the internet—gah. I'm so over it."

"A fundamental premise of risk assessment is that what you stand to gain has to be worth what you stand to lose. From what I've observed, this isn't."

"Millie keeps telling me the same thing," said Shay. "I can't let it go. The legacy of this crime for the wives of these men—it's emotionally shattering, financially ruinous, sexually humiliating. Queen Mab is clearly more interested in that than she is in the money. She could target guys with the greatest net worth, but she doesn't. She targets family men. In four cases, the wife was pregnant. That's not coincidence. She could fleece these guys without killing them, and she could kill them without screwing them, but she makes sure they're found with ejaculate in that kinky promotional condom. She's taken in close to four million dollars, but make no mistake, she's in this to brutalize those women. That's the aspect that's really under my skin. Who does that? Why? I need to know."

"I need to know why she went to Pensacola," said Corbin. "Down to the last few hours, I'd have bet paper money that Ivan was about to hit New Orleans."

"Luck?"

"I don't believe in luck." He refilled her cup and asked, "Who's Millie?"

"My father's secretary," Shay said, but she dropped her eyes to the left, the way she did when she was lying. "Anyway. Thanks for your concern. I can take care of myself."

She lifted the lid on the chocolate box. Nestled among the ornate confections was a HurricaneLovers promotional condom.

"Gosh, you Thibodeaux boys are classy." Shay clapped the lid down, tossed the box aside and got to her feet. "Time to do my KCs. A hundred pushups: morning, noon, night. No excuses. I'm cultivating Katie Couric arms. Ever notice the guns on that woman?"

"Can't say I have," said Corbin, but he noticed Shay's. Swan soft skin. Lean, animate muscle. Just enough baby fat to make them pinup girly.

She planked out for the pushups and said, "I also do yoga and kick-boxing. The TV body takes discipline. You can bet wherever Christa Mullroy is right now, she's either running on a treadmill or making herself throw up."

Corbin pulled off his boots and stretched out on the air mattress, watching her with his hands behind his head. After the pushups, Shay sat in the light of the waning candles, twined in a yoga pose that reminded him of a strange flower he'd seen once in a cypress glen. *Arundina graminifolia*, Bonnie had said when he described it to her. *Pagoda orchid.* A sudden gift, deep in the swamp.

He closed his eyes and drifted until something that felt like a jack-hammer wrenched him awake from an unpleasant dream of floating maps and drowning bicycles. Shay lay next to him, gripping his arm.

"Corbin, wake up. I heard a gunshot."

"Thunder," he said, stroking her shoulder. "Go back to sleep."

"Is this the eyewall?"

"Not yet." He took a swig of tepid champagne and handed the bottle to Shay. She took a swig and handed it back.

"Should we open a window?" she asked. "They say the building can explode because of weird air pressure."

"That's an old wives' tale."

"But I definitely feel that. I feel a weird pressure."

"C'mere, I'll help you with that."

"Hound dog." Shay punched his arm. "What time is it?"

"Time for you to get a watch."

She lifted his wrist and looked at his watch: 4:37 a.m.

"I can't wear a watch," she said. "Watches stop on me. I have a very strong magnetic field."

"Shay, that's another old wives' tale."

"No, that one's true. A human being has a certain energy."

"Yes, but trust me, you're not a magnet."

Outside, the wind pitched steadily higher, full of wailing babies, screaming wolves, howling fire drills. Shay startled again when something crashed down the sloping metal roof.

"That sounded large."

"This area's been dealing with a Formosan termite issue for the last ten years," said Corbin. "Infested oak trees won't stand this wind. Another Christ knows how many cubic yards of organic debris in the soup. Plus termite clouds."

"I hope you don't lose too many trees at your house. I can't imagine that neighborhood without those grand old ladies, all Spanish moss and elegant limbs."

"We'll lose some." He stretched and worked his arm around her. "We'll lose a lot of great old architecture. Parks. Sculptures."

"I hope the ferry jester survives," she said. "I always stop and say hi to him. He's kind of vulgar, but he says it all about how joyful and accepting and generous with a laugh this place is. I laugh at least forty percent more in New Orleans than anywhere else I've ever lived. And

I eat forty percent more. The food here—oh, Lord, the restaurants kill me. Old ice houses, grand hotels, barbeque joints. Any night of the week, you can go out and hear music and feel like people are glad to see you."

"The tourist industry will take an indescribable hit," said Corbin. "They'll really have to think outside the box to keep those businesses alive."

"Maybe this'll make people look beyond the bordellos and hot sauce image."

"Maybe. Obviously, we need Mardi Gras. It's a party town, and that's a relatively green industry. But there's also this mellow, early morning side. For every girl-gone-wild flashing her tits, there's two crotchety old men playing chess in the park. For every jester, there's a jazz artist. I go running just before dawn, and it's like that Louis Armstrong song. *Moss covered vines, tall sugar pines, that ol' lazy Mississippi rolling by.*"

Shay found his hand in the dark. "I like you when you wax poetic."

"There was a young man from Nantucket," he murmured in her ear.

She laughed, pressed an unhurried kiss to his mouth, and tucked into the crook of his arm, her head on his shoulder.

"This week seriously sucked," Corbin said. "I kept hoping I'd be wrong. Thinking the storm might do one of those last minute switchbacks. The last fifty hours or so, I knew, and it was... it's like when my mom died. She was only thirty-four. Came down with metastatic breast cancer, and that went the way that goes. I was fifteen. Guy was ten. Old enough to know what was happening when hospice showed up. That last night, our dad was off drunk on his ass somewhere. Guy and I sat on the floor in the hallway, waiting. Hour after hour, we're sitting there, and we were grateful—grateful, even at that age—for how beautiful and generous and crazy she was. And I remember feeling like guilty hell for thinking, geezes, it's inevitable, get it over with—feeling sick about this thing that's happening but actually wishing it would happen, because it was unbearable, sitting there with a sledgehammer six inches above my skull. Close to morning, we kept punching each other on the arm, trying to keep awake. We were so tired. Exhausted beyond belief. But we were afraid to go to sleep. We were terrified of what the world would be when we woke up. It didn't seem possible that the sun would be hot or brown sugar would taste right. We didn't know if the house would keep standing or there'd just be a giant sinkhole where our life used to be. If we'd hear music ever again. Or feel okay to laugh. We figured a few things might get better, but not before most things got a hell of a lot worse. All we knew for certain was that nothing would ever be the same. Because she'd be gone. And this whole week…" Corbin breathed a deep sigh that was lost in the wind. "This whole week, I've had exactly that same feeling."

Shay pressed her hand against his sternum and took the next several beats of his heart into her palm. Then she brought his hand to her lips and kissed each ungainly knuckle. She didn't insult him with attempts at optimism, just tugged his chin over and called him "baby" and kissed the downturned corners of his mouth.

In the darkness below, there was the intermittent music of breaking glass. In the darkness above, the roof bucked and shuddered. The air mattress sagged and made rubbery noises on the plank floor as they consumed each other's warm Brut kisses. Corbin rolled on top of her, nudging her legs apart with his knee. Shay opened to him like *Arundina graminifolia*, rocking against him in the fully-clothed, body-length embrace that trashy bad girls back in high school used to call "dry humping" until Shay, who was a classy bad girl, coined the less indecorous term "jean crushing." He growled her name or something else that didn't matter, dragging her shirt over her head, looting handfuls and mouthfuls. He breached the hardware on her bra, tossed it into the shadows, and went for the front of her jeans with one hand, wrangling his belt buckle with the other.

"Whoa. James Brown." Shay stopped his hands. "I need a visual on a condom."

"*Augh*," Corbin said hoarsely. "I don't have one. Unless you're okay with…"

He ticked a glance toward the Godiva box on the floor.

Shay seized him by the ears and said, "Get it. I need to pay a quick visit to the facilities."

"Me too."

"Me first."

"Hurry."

Shay broke away, nicked her flashlight from the packing blanket, skipped daintily down the shop stairs in her bare feet and yanked open the door to the showroom.

The flashlight clattered from her hand.

"Oh. Goodness."

Three teenage boys sat on the counter by the cash register, drinking beer in the staticky light of a small, battery operated TV. Their heads swiveled toward her, their slack, smooth faces illuminated by the grainy screen. Startled. Just kids.

"Holy shit," one of them said.

Shay stared at them. They stared at Shay. Awkwardly, she hugged her arms over the heated whisker burn on her breasts. They all blurted a nervous laugh—she and these startled boys.

"Um…you want a beer?" asked the youngest, or at least the smallest of them.

"No," said Shay. "No, thank you."

Her bag was behind the counter about seven feet away. She wanted to reach it so intensely, she could almost feel the leather strap in her fist.

"Shay." Corbin's voice was low and calm at her shoulder.

He stepped in front of her, took his shirt off and held it out to her. In his other hand, he had a crowbar. Shay pulled on the shirt, edged over to the counter and looped her bag across her body. The three young men had already helped themselves to boots, belts and leathers. The smallest guy was trying to extricate a multi-tool from its plastic packaging. The tallest had the curved handle of a serrated Urban Pal in his palm.

"Let's all be cool, okay?" said Corbin. "The bikes would get destroyed in the flood anyway. So y'all take what you need and head on out before the weather gets worse. Keys are hanging right there behind the counter. I'll keep my old Knucklehead back there. Everybody rides away happy. No problem."

"We don't want no problem," the smallest guy said.

"Good. Me neither." A trickle of sweat rolled down between Corbin's shoulder blades.

"So, what's up with the crowbar?" asked the tallest of the three. "Why you think we came for your bikes, anyways? You think we're looters cause we're black?"

"No, I think you're looters because you take shit that doesn't belong to you."

"Well, I ain't takin' any shit from you, motherfucker."

He advanced, and Corbin swung the crowbar. The Urban Pal clattered across the floor, but the young man caught the crowbar and brought his steel-toed motorcycle boot up between Corbin's legs, dropping him like a wrecking ball. The smaller two dove forward and tried to drag their friend back, but he managed to land several swift kicks to Corbin's face and midsection before Shay bellowed, "Freeze! Or I *will* shoot you."

Because you emphasize the *will*, the gun safety instructor had said.

"Get your punk asses down on that floor. Face down. Do not test me."

Because that had sounded so inarguable when Bonnie said it.

"It's cool, lady. Be cool." The two smaller fellows got to their knees, to the floor.

Shay moved closer to the garage door where Corbin was huddled in a fetal position, gasping for air, hands cupped over his groin. She tried to keep her hands in the deep shadows, but the tallest boy peered at her in the half-light, his curious expression widening to a grin.

"You ain't got no gun, bitch."

"Yes, I do," said Shay, fidgeting her hand inside her bag. "Right here."

"Then how come you ain't shot me?"

"I don't want anyone to get hurt."

"For real," he said. "Then you shoulda told your boy not to come at people who ain't doin' nothin' with a crowbar." He motioned the other boys to their feet. "Y'all, this bitch ain't got no gun. She got a gun, she blows my head off. All that shit talk is totally illogical."

"I didn't come here to mess with nobody," said the middle kid, and the youngest kid agreed, "I just wanted a bike, yo."

The biggest kid shrugged and sauntered toward Shay, sing-songing, "Whatcha gonna do, bitch? Whatcha gonna do?"

Shay drew her hand from the messenger bag and assumed Isosceles Stance.

Feet apart. Elbows locked.

Left hand cups the right.

Shoulders perpendicular to the target.

"Back off," she said. "*I. WILL. Shoot.*"

Eye the objective. Settling breath.

He laughed at the fluffy pink puppy in her hand. "What the f—"

Fire.

A tight stream of Mace Hot Pink pepper spray seared the young man full in the face. He screamed and recoiled, and just as Shay's kickboxing coach had promised—"As natural as a sneeze," he'd told her—muscle memory and adrenalin pumped outward from her core. Without even forming the intent, she boggie-hooked the kid under the jaw with the brass knuckles on her fist and landed a bony, barefoot roundhouse to his kidney. He went to his knees, choking, clutching at his streaming eyes. The other boys stood stunned, orphaned among the motorcycles.

Acrid pepper spray backdraft burning her nose and throat, Shay hooked her hand in the back of Corbin's belt and helped him drag himself through the door to the garage. She flung the heavy metal door shut and jammed a piece of 2x4 under the knob.

"I kicked his ass! I kicked his ass! Oh, my God, did you see that?" she jubileed, because it was horrible, but undeniably thrilling, until she knelt beside Corbin, who lay bleeding from his mouth and nose and a nasty gash above his eyebrow.

"Corbin? Oh, my God. Corbin, talk to me."

"Ah, Christ," he groaned. "Bloody fucking hell…"

On the other side of the door, the tall boy wailed that he'd been Maced, imploring his friends to get water, get milk, pour milk on his eyes. The brass knuckles clanged on the floor. Shay grabbed a roll of shop towels and frantically dabbed at Corbin's head.

"Okay. You're okay. Shake it off, baby, shake it off."

"You didn't have to do that!" The boy raged and hammered on the other side of the door, his voice choked with acid tears. "I was just messin' with you before. Now I'm gonna beat your skinny white bitch ass."

Teeth clenched against the agony, Corbin dragged himself up and limped to the door. "Dude. C'mon. Dial it down. Nobody wants this to happen."

"She broke my tooth! You're paying for this tooth, bitch!"

"Sure. Of course. I'm fine with that. Here you go." Shay rifled cash from her hip pocket, retained part of the wad, and shoved the rest under the door. "There's $200, plus the bikes and the other stuff. So, we're even. So… bye now. Y'all three be careful out there."

They heard quiet voices, quick scurries, unbreakable windows breaking. Raging wind combined with the sound of the showroom being trashed. Shay pressed her ear to the door, and Corbin slumped against the wall in misery, willing himself to breathe without vomiting. After a few minutes, engines bloomed, roared, and faded into the storm noise.

"Thank God," Shay breathed.

"Wait," said Corbin. "What's that smell?"

A curl of smoke trickled through the crack of light by his feet.

"No. They wouldn't." Shay wrenched the 2x4 away from the knob and opened the door. "Those little shitballs!"

The shelves and T-shirt carousels were engulfed in flame, despite the blowing rain from the open doors. Several bikes had been laid down, gas caps open and dribbling. Tanks on the standing bikes were wicked with bandanas. The wooden stairway to the loft was blackening rapidly. Even in the moment, the swiftness of the fire's progress astonished her.

Corbin slammed the door and coughed a gesture toward the far side of the garage, unable to go there himself. Shay ran over, yanked the fire extinguisher off the wall and ran back to him. He took it from her and yanked the pin.

"Open the door when I tell you."

Aiming the dented extinguisher, he squeezed the lever to test the trajectory. There was a brief, flabby stream of foam, followed by a hiss of dry air.

"God damn it, Guy!" He hurled the empty canister into the haze and limped to his bike, grimacing and swearing as he hoisted his leg over. "Get the door."

"My cameras," Shay coughed. "My shoes."

"*Door!*" He started the engine, coasting forward.

Shay managed the latch, but before she could anchor herself on the slippery floor, the wind caught the sheet metal door, jerking her out onto the cinder drive, casting her to the ground. She scrambled up and climbed onto the back of the Knucklehead, knees muddy and bleeding.

Corbin managed to keep the bike upright as far as the CBD. He fought it into an alley, and they found their way to a deep doorway behind a construction dumpster. They stood, faces tucked against each other's necks, with shrieking wind and scouring rain and flying garbage flogging them.

Corbin said something, but it was lost in the wind.

"What?" Shay shouted.

"We need to move," he shouted back. "We're in the eyewall."

NEW ORLEANS

MONDAY MORNING
AUGUST 29

From: Heath, Michael
Sent: Monday, August 29, 2005 10:20 AM
To: Brown, Michael D
Subject: FW: superdome

Marty. He is at the New Orleans EOC and is watching this as it unfolds. Mike Beeman is in Gulf port. However, we have not been able to establish communications with him.

Marty is going to try to send us photos shortly.

-------------Original Message--------------

From: Heath, Michael
Sent: Monday, August 29, 2005 10:12 AM
To: Rhode, Patrick; Altshuler, Brooks; Burris, Ken
Subject: RE: superdome

From Marty Bahamonde in the New Orleans EOC (next to the superdome)

-Severe flooding on the St. Bernard/Orleans parish line. Police report water level up to second floor of two story houses.

People are trapped in attics.

-Pumps starting to fail. The city has now confirmed four
pump3 are off line.

-Windows and parts of the east side of the Amaco building
blown out.

-New Orleans shopping center (next to superdome)
destroyed.

-Windows and parts of the East side of the Hyatt Hotel
have been blown out. Furniture is blowing out of the
hotel.

-Top floors of the Entergy building have been blown out
-Area around the Superdome is beginning to flood.

We should have pictures shortly.

Corbin was bleeding, trembling hard, and coughing. Shay held him against the brick wall and tried to cover him as best she could with her body, but his shoulders were several inches above hers.

"How far to your office?" she shouted.

"About a mile."

She tried to discern the line of the curb through stuttering blindness, pitch-blackness strobed with not-quite-continuous lightning.

"We have to cross the street," she told him. "Can you?"

He nodded.

"Go to that doorway. End of the block. Rest. Go to the next one. Yes?"

He nodded, and they stepped into the open maelstrom. The noise pitched up exponentially, shrilling higher, roaring wider. Debris rained from broken buildings. The wind made razor blades and scythes of paper and palm fronds. Rain sheared sideways, and every drop felt like it came out of a BB gun. There was an odd sensation of gravity having tilted. Walking felt like climbing a ladder, and under every rung was a wasp's nest. Standing still was not even within the bounds of physics. They kept their bodies bent low and tight together as wave-on-hasping-wave flayed their backs. They stumbled at the dark curb and ducked into another harboring doorway.

They moved to the next doorway. Rested. Made another move.

Doorway by doorway, they made their way up the street, around the corner, pushing into the wind for fifteen or twenty yards, ducking into the next little nook, pushing another thirty yards. Shay pounded on every plywood-covered door and window along the way. She drilled on every doorbell, shouted at each intercom, knowing there was no one to hear her and nothing to do but push toward the next doorway.

After a while, they began to find a rhythm to the resounding wind, and there was a brief period when they seemed to meet a little less debris. While Corbin leaned against the wall, Shay took her last camera from her bag, keeping it in the Ziploc, crouching low, trying to shoot and shield her face at the same time. A few doors down, Corbin got her into the corner, her head against his chest, trying to give her a moment of shelter from the shrilling wind.

"We're doing good," she called. "Halfway there."

They moved through another series of doorways. Then a long solid wall with no respite. Another street to cross. More doorways. Another street. Shay began to feel separated from her feet and legs.

"Ditch that camera bag," Corbin told her as they slumped into a doorway, faces pressed against the plywood.

"No. No way."

"Let me take it then."

"No. Let's just go." Shay gripped it tighter in the clawing wind, even though the strap cut into her shoulder and strangled her breath. She was down to her last, least favorite camera, but it felt like her only reason for being.

"Two blocks," Corbin shouted. "Two to go."

There were no more doorways, only boarded glass doors flush with brick walls and steel-shuttered windows. The front lobby of Corbin's building had been secured with heavy plywood. Corbin gestured toward a loading dock with a steep ramp down to the parking garage gate.

"Receiving entrance," he called over the fray, and Shay nodded.

Huddled against each other, they started down the oil-slicked ramp, but Shay lost her footing. Corbin tried to catch her and went down with her. They hit the slimy cement and slid down into a pool of dirty water that had collected with a mass of debris by the dumpsters. Corbin kept his head above water, but Shay went under briefly. Something soft curdled between her bare foot and the receiving door. A large rat, she realized, and when she came up screaming, she saw drowned rats bobbing in the water all around her. Thrashing to stand up, she shrieked and struggled. Corbin gripped her wrist and pulled her up, holding her tight to his body while he dug in his pocket for his keys, kicked away the garbage and offal and got the door open far enough for them to squeeze through one at a time. He wrestled the door shut and slumped against it.

"Jesus." Corbin's voice echoed in the stairwell. "That sucked."

Shay nodded, clutching her bag to her chest.

In the black but blessedly quiet stairwell of the parking garage, there was only the trickling echo of their breathing and the distant drum of a sump pump. Beyond the cinderblock walls, the muffled storm raged on, a muted thrumming cut by a thin, continuous scream. It was like being inside the beating heart of a man at a heavy metal concert. Knee-deep water shimmered under globed amber emergency lighting. A metal staircase rose like a broken pier on the opposite wall.

Shay felt smooth linoleum beneath her, and the sudden comfort of it made her stingingly aware of what the gritty sidewalks and cinder driveway had done to the soles of her bare feet. Core-deep trembling gripped her body. Her legs were shaking like she'd run a marathon.

"I need to sit," she said, sloshing toward the stairs.

Wading through the gloom, groping for the metal rail, Shay carefully slid her feet forward one at a time until her toes met the bottom of the first step. Corbin followed her up to a dry landing a few steps above the surface of the water. He was breathing unsteadily, shivering hard without his shirt. Dark-purple bruises had begun to blossom on his ribcage. He folded his arms on his knees and rested his head. Scooting close to him, Shay tried to warm his bare torso with her arms.

"My God. The levees must have failed almost immediately."

"No," said Corbin. "Pontchartrain is brackish. If this was coming from the levees, it would taste salty. This is just rainwater."

"With a twist of bubonic plague. My mouth was in rat water," she whimpered. "My hair smells like pigeon molt."

Shay excavated her cell phone from her bag and shined the light on Corbin's battered face. His breath was rasping and short, and blood dripped from his nose and the gash on his forehead. His eyes were flat and dark, his mouth dry and tight.

"Oh, Corbin," she said. "Baby, you don't look good."

"I'm fine." He squinted at the display light. "I can't believe your cell is still working."

"It was in a Ziploc bag."

They looked at each other and broke up in shallow, giddy laughter.

Corbin pushed an icky string of hair from her face, kissed her forehead, and said, "Let's go."

Shivering hard, he had to work to pull himself up by the railing. Shay pulled his arm across her shoulder, and they made their way up the stubby flight of stairs and opened the lobby door. The muffled heart split open, and the heavy metal poured in. It wasn't as bad as being outside, but it was a far cry from the sanctuary Shay was expecting.

Cross-hatched by a jet-sleek steel and hardwood staircase that zigzagged up the first fifteen stories, the open center column gave the building its towering light and high-tech appeal. It was the reason Corbin had loved the place as soon as the rental agent showed it to him, but even then, it had occurred to him that it would be an entirely different place with the soaring windows blown out, truncated electrical wires dangling and rainwater cascading down from a gaping hole 350 feet above, where skylights, solar panels, and a bus-size air conditioning unit had been torn off the roof. The faux marble floor was littered with broken glass, splintered plywood, and stray tree branches. Cardboard boxes, rafted paper, neon-colored Post-its, and clear plastic sheeting whipped in bewildered circles, up into the immense darkness of the building's high-rising hollow core. It was like the view from the bottom of a blender.

Shay's hope withered. Corbin's office was on the 27th floor.

He took her elbow. "We can make it."

"Are you high? It's impossible. We should at least wait until daylight."

"This is daylight. It's eight, maybe nine."

"Oh, God." She looked up into the howling blackness. "Let's go back to the parking garage."

"With water pouring in? Forget it. Shay, listen, it's open as far as fifteen, but the last twelve floors are inside a stairwell—a solid, safe core.

I practically live at my office. There's a shower, clean clothes, food, first aid kit. We can make it."

He slouched up the stairs, leaning heavily on the handrail. Shay shouldered her bag, taking one tender step at a time, not sure if she was feeling wet blood or water on the soles of her feet. Progress was slow, and Corbin was groaning by the time they approached the third floor. By the time they reached the fifth floor, the storm sounded like a subway stop. Another laborious flight up, it was like the underbelly of a plane crash. Shay could no longer feel the bottoms of her feet. Her wet jeans weighed and chafed like a coat of mail. The leather strap of her bag dragged painfully against her breast. Corbin staggered and slumped onto the steps. Shay squatted next to him and set her cool hand over the rapid pulse at the side of his neck. His skin was warm and dry, his eyes sunken and vacant.

"Corbin," she called out to him. "Corbin, other people live at their offices, too."

He nodded, clutching his midsection.

"That's where we're headed." She pointed down the hallway to a smoked glass wall lettered KENNET INSURANCE GROUP. "Sit tight. I'll be right back."

The hallway glowed with muted amber emergency lights. Shay spotted a water fountain set into a little recess. "Thank you," she whispered, hurrying toward it, but when she bent down to drink, a trickle came up, then an airy spit, then nothing. The elevator bay was merchandised with potted ficus trees and little iron occasional tables. Shay picked up one of the little tables and went to the glass door. Getting the best possible grip on the legs, she beat it against the thick glass, swearing and sweating, until the spindly legs paper-clipped in on each other, but only a small web of cracks slithered out from a center divot.

"Jesus, please," Shay panted. "Please, Jesus, *please*, break this fucking door."

She dragged over one of the Ficus trees and heaved it like a sledge-hammer. The door collapsed in a curtain of liability-friendly safety glass niblets instead of long scythes and splinters.

Shay clasped her hands in front of her forehead and breathed a humbly sincere, "Thank you. Sorry I said fuck. Amen."

The staid reception area inside Kennet Insurance was furnished with a large leather sofa and side chairs, an immense L-shaped desk, a woven Navajo wall hanging, and a group of framed Ansel Adams prints, but by cell light, Shay saw it the way a spider sees the inside of a drainpipe. She took the nearest Ansel Adams print and shoveled the glass niblets away from the entry, then headed back to the landing where Corbin lay shaking.

"Corbin? Baby, c'mon. Help me out here."

Shay slapped him awake and coaxed him upright, and together they stumbled back to the insurance office. Propping him against the reception desk, she worked out his belt buckle, dragged his wet jeans and boxers off him, yanked down the Navajo wall hanging and briskly rubbed his arms and legs, then kissed his cheek and helped him to the sofa.

"Hang tough," she said. "I'll find water and a first aid kit."

Peeling off her own wet jeans and panties, she draped them over the front desk before she set out scavenging, rifling cabinets and book-shelves by the filmy light of her cell phone. All the tall wooden doors to the executive offices were locked. There was a kitchenette in the break room, but the faucet puffed the same unwilling sigh as the water fountain in the hall. The vending machines and refrigerator had been emptied, unplugged and propped open in preparation for the power outage. Shay found melted remains in an ice cube tray, carefully drib-bled it into a "#1 Dad" coffee cup and allowed herself a small sip. If there was a first aid kit, she never found it, but she salvaged a half-full Diet Coke from a trash can, and when she looked in the coat closet, she discovered a squash racquet and gym bag.

"God, if you love me, let this belong to someone with bad knees."

She brought her treasure sack to the reception area, dumped it on the floor next to the sofa, and propped her cell phone on the coffee table. She shook out an LSU athletic department T-shirt and a wadded pin-striped dress shirt, sniffing under each sleeve, finding them only a little gamey. Sweat pants, more than a little gamey. Ace bandage. Deodorant. Altoids. Snickers bar. Her fingertips found a childproof cap.

"Yes. Pharmaceuticals, baby." She held the fine print close to her cell phone. "Survey says… Cialis. Oh, screw you, you limp—whoa. Hey, hey, hey…"

Another childproof cap. Larger.

"Lornexium? Take with food or milk. Substitute for Vicodin. Yes! Who's yer daddy?"

A fleeting movement at the door caught Shay's eye, and she scrambled back like a feral child before she realized it was her own reflection in the smoked glass across the hall. In a frame of shattered glass, she saw herself hunched over a stranger's belongings, sniffing through his dirty gym clothes. Corbin's sodden shirt clung to her body, spattered with filth, smeared with blood. Her hair hung down, dank and ropey, her pale skin cast bluish green in the eerie cell light. It was like seeing a corrupt version of herself in a zombie movie.

Corbin rattled a raspy cough and struggled to sit up. Shay crawled over to take his hand.

"Hey, baby." She dabbed clotted blood from his temple and held the coffee cup to his lips. "How are you feeling?"

"It's getting better. Geezes, I haven't taken a shot to the nuts like that since I was in junior high."

She shook the prescription bottle like a voodoo rattle. "How d'ya like me now?"

"I like you pretty good," he smiled unsteadily.

"That's it for water, but I found part of a Diet Coke." She pressed two Lornexium capsules into his palm. "What's wrong with these people that they don't have a water cooler? Where do they gather to gossip about each other's tawdry affairs?"

Corbin swallowed the painkillers and labored to sit himself up on the sofa.

"There's no water pressure?"

Shay shook her head. "What does that mean?"

"The pumping stations are failing."

Shay handed him the Snickers bar, shucked out of his filthy white shirt and pulled on the gamey LSU shirt.

"I wonder what time it is."

"Ten maybe," Corbin said.

"My God, it's so dark."

"That was some awesome eyewall action out there," he said. "Gorgeous. Could have been fun if I hadn't got my ass kicked beforehand."

"I say we crash here for a few hours. When the storm lets up later, you take a snootful of Vicodin Lite, and we make our way up to your office."

He nodded. "The National Guard should be on the ground by this—"

Shay's cell phone sang a little jingle. For a moment, they both felt a stab of hope that it meant she had a signal, but it turned out to be the low battery alert.

"It'll be dead in five minutes," she said. "Then we're in the dark. That cut over your eye needs attention."

"Water first." Corbin put the last bite of Snickers in her mouth.

"Whatever they had, they took it."

"The toilet in there—is it the kind with a tank on the back?"

"Yes, but... gah."

"It's clean," he said, pulling on the gamey sweats and dress shirt. "I'm already dehydrated. You probably are too. When was the last time you took a whiz?"

Shay didn't want to tell him she'd peed herself when she fell in the rat soup, so she bit her lip and said, "I guess looters can't be choosers."

In the ladies room, Corbin dipped the coffee cup in the toilet tank and offered it to Shay first. She had to force herself to take the initial sip, but the moment the cool water was in her mouth, she realized how badly she needed it and chugged three cupfuls. The walls were mounted with useless blow dryers instead of paper towels, but Shay found a little basket of feminine products under the sink. She dipped a tampon in the toilet tank to daub off the blood on Corbin's split lip and beleaguered face, then MacGyvered two panty shields to tape the gash above his eyebrow. They drank as much water as they could, filled the cup and soda bottle and groped their way to the sofa in the reception area just as Shay's cell phone powered down.

Corbin pulled her close in front of him and kissed the curve of her shoulder, and Shay closed her eyes, truly knowing for the first time in her life what weariness means, what shelter is. Beyond the haven of the insurance office, unbroken chaos raged in the open thoracic cavity above the lobby: shrieks of sheet metal, the drum of tumbling furniture, a corporate world coming apart at its riveted seams. It was hard for Shay to distinguish the shrill scream of the wind from the tympanic ringing in their ears as she drifted between roaring blackness and shifting dreams.

Without a concept of how many hours had passed, she became vaguely aware of being vaguely awake, and then acutely aware of Corbin's solid erection against the base of her spine. A wave of aching need surprised and humbled her. She shifted her hips and took him in.

The feeling was profound—fullness, pleasure, perfect dark—but it was the noise, Shay realized; the noise made it all-encompassing, suspending her in the multiple meanings of sound, incorporating their groans, his agony and her ecstasy, like the trickle of green around the blood red center of a Doppler image.

Corbin pressed his lips to her neck, mouthing words she couldn't hear but knew to be *I love you, I love you, I love you.* Shay brought his palm to her mouth. *Oh, my love, I love you.* A blue eye formed deep in her circulatory system and dispersed in a wrecking spiral, and he thundered into her with the final throes of Katrina's violent passage.

NEW ORLEANS

MONDAY EVENING
AUGUST 29

From: "FirstResponderTraining"

Date: 08/30/2005 12:25PM

Subject: DHS/SLGCP/ODP Cooperative Training Outreach Program

Dear Sir or Madam:

On behalf of the Department of Homeland Security (DHS), Office for State and Local Government Coordination and Preparedness1 (SLGCP), Office for Domestic Preparedness (ODP) Training Division, we would like to invite you to participate in a review and comment period for a new effort being instituted in Fiscal Year 2006 (FY 06) called the Cooperative Training Outreach Program (CO-OP).

The success we can achieve by working together will lay a solid, sustainable training foundation for a more prepared and secure homeland. Please review the attached document and provide feedback by September 20, 2005.

Thank you for your commitment to furthering our national preparedness, we look forward to your comments and suggestions.

Sincerely,

Barbara Biehn

Acting Director, Training Division

(See attached file: DHS CO-OP Letter.doc)

(See attached file: DHS CO-OP1.doc)

From:...Fugate, Craig

Sent: Tuesday, August 30, 2005 4:20 PM

To: FirstResponderTraining

Subject: Re: DHS/SLGCP/ODP Cooperative Training Outreach Program

just in case you missed it, we emergency managers are a little busy with something called a hurricane, I realize its not a terrorist incident, but we may not be able to respond to your request in a timely manner.

Craig Fugate, Director

Florida Division of Emergency Management

Shay opened her eyes, achy and alone, still wrapped in the woven Navajo wall hanging. The soles of her feet felt swarmed by fire ants. Her hunger went gut-deep. Muted daylight filtered in from somewhere down the hall, but the inner office hall was pitch dark. Seriously needing to pee, Shay groped a short distance down the corridor, but that sliver of daylight anchored her at the first turn; she couldn't separate herself from it. Knowing there was no way to navigate the ladies' room in utter blindness, Shay used the wastebasket under the front desk and made a mental note to anonymously send the receptionist a box of Godiva chocolates.

An odd smell emanated from her crusted jeans and stiff panties. Shay couldn't touch them to her legs, let alone her unprotected privates. The extra-large LSU tee fit her like a functional mini dress, so she left her clothes behind with a prayer of apology to Giorgio Armani, collected her bag from the coffee table, and made her way out to the twilit landing.

In the humid dusk, Corbin relieved himself over the railing into the misty wreckage below. Looking lanky and beaten, he cinched the gym bag sweats around his narrow waist and buttoned the pinstriped shirt over his bruised torso. Shay strained to see past the broken plywood and mud-spattered plastic sheeting that cloaked the lobby doors.

"Feels like we slept a long time," she said. "I wonder if I still have enough daylight to go out and get some footage."

"Forget it," said Corbin. "Even in broad daylight, there's open storm grates, downed power lines, every foul substance shit by man, beast, or machine. Let's go up to my office. At dawn, I'll get the solar-powered satellite unit situated up on the roof and get online. We'll find out what's going on and get you a ride out of the city."

Shay was forming her own agenda, and it didn't involve a ride out of the city, but it did involve a fully charged cell and camera batteries, so she avoided an argument by kissing Corbin's puffy lip.

"Is it crazy that I woke up feeling a little bit happy?"

"Don't start that," Corbin grimaced. "I'll say the wrong thing, and you'll worry it like a pit bull. Meanwhile, every step I take feels like another boot to the nuts."

"Aaaaand the good times roll on."

Feeling overexposed and irritable, Corbin climbed the stairs in steely silence. Shay cluttered the first few flights with chatter. The sound of her voice echoed through the towering ruins like a flock of jittery sparrows, grating on Corbin's last nerve as she went on about her Armani jeans and the smell of her hair.

"I wonder what Queen Mab is doing now," Shay said. "She hooked up with someone. I have zero doubt about that."

"She most likely hit the road two or three hours ago."

"She knew she wouldn't be able to fly out of any airport in the vicinity of New Orleans. Where would be the closest dependable flights?"

"Houston," said Corbin. "Jackson, maybe. You're assuming she doesn't live down here."

"You think that's not a safe assumption?"

"There's no such thing is a safe assumption. Especially when you automatically assume the best all the time."

"Or when you automatically assume the worst," said Shay. "I still have hope for the levees. I know this doesn't mean anything to you, but Mommi's church has been keeping a twenty-four-hour prayer vigil."

"That's very nice, but even if it's not part of your belief system, science is real. Levees are not maintained by spiritual placebo. I know you don't want to believe it, but climate change is a thing, and this is what happens when corporate rapists pollute with impunity. Not mentioning any names."

"My father is not a rapist," she said. "He invests a lot in compliance with EPA regulations, and he's funded solid research that proves global warming is a myth."

"If you listen to the fox, the chicken coop is an all-you-can-eat buffet."

"If I'd listened to the fox, we'd be driving out of here in a Hummer."

"Shay, Google Kerry Emanuel. He's a hurricane specialist at MIT, a conservative dude who's got no dog in the political hunt. Less than a month ago, he published a study linking climate change and mega-storms. Look it up. Or don't," he huffed. "Denial is pretty damn comfy for rich folks. I guess Mommi will pray for the rest of us."

"Don't you smack-talk my mother," Shay said sharply. "I kicked the ass of the fella who kicked your ass. Do the math."

Conversation was spare and awkward as they continued to the fifteenth floor and entered the eerie glower of the stairwell. The emergency lighting flickered and buzzed like cicadas. They fell into a bloodless silence weighted by the smell of wet cement.

Noticing a faint, smeary trail of blood on the steps, Corbin said, "I'm worried about your feet."

"Will you carry me, baby?" Shay batted her eyes, then laughed at his look of startled alarm. "Kidding. I'm kidding. Don't panic."

Corbin growled and clapped his hand to her backside and kept it there.

"Back atcha," he mumbled.

"Back atcha what?"

"Everything you woke up feeling. Back atcha. Don't talk it to death."

They trudged a few more stories in silence. The wall next to each doorway was marked with a large red number. For firemen, Shay supposed. As they rounded the landing marked 22, she sighed, "Dang, I'm so hungry."

"Think about something else."

"Dang, I'm so thirsty."

Nearing the uppermost landing, Shay skipped ahead and pressed her cheek to the big red number by the door.

"Oh, 27! My beautiful 27! You complete me."

The wooden door to Corbin's office was emblazoned with the EarthWeather Analytics logo, a striated globe that reminded Shay of Epcot Center. He rattled his keys from his pocket, but when he pushed it open, it wedged against some sort of debris. A telling breeze came from the other side. Corbin set his shoulder against the door and heaved it open, tipping a tall filing cabinet into the soggy drywall. Glass shards and splintered plywood carpeted the floor, along with calendar pages, Rolodex cards, manila folders, and parts of phones, fax, and copier. Maps, magazines, and other clutterabilia from the front desk were on the floor, stuck to the wet walls, or somewhere out in the world.

"Wait here while I fire up the generator," said Corbin.

He followed glowstripping down the hall to the equipment room where the operations gear and mainframe were housed. When he powered up the generator, fluorescent ceiling lights guttered to life. Out by the front door, Shay whooped.

"Clap on, baby! Where's the bottled water?"

"Under the pool table in the conference room."

"There's a pool table in your conference room?"

"Now you know how I negotiate my retainers."

Corbin scraped a path to his private office, relieved to find it dry and intact. He powered on a backup cell, tried Bonnie and then Guy. The inadequate signal was as useful as a soup can on a string. When he heard the rasp of his power drill from the conference room, he called, "Shay, whatever you're doing, please, don't."

The drill rasped again, and there was a loud thunk. By the time Corbin got to the door, she had one sheet of plywood down and was standing at the broken window, binoculars in hand, looking out at the falling dusk. A warm breeze from the broken window stirred her stringy hair.

"It's a beautiful evening, baby," she smiled, "and you are so full of crap."

Corbin took the binoculars from her and peered down at the dry street.

"Power of prayer," said Shay. "The levees held."

NEW ORLEANS

TUESDAY MORNING
AUGUST 30

From: Heath, Michael

To: Lowder, Michael

Sent: Mon Aug 29 11:51:18 2005

Subject: Re: Information

From Marty. He has been trying to reach Lokey. New
Orleans FD is reporting a 20 foot wide breech on the lake
ponchatrain side levy. The area is lakeshore Blvd and 17th
street.

From: Brown, Michael D

Sent: Monday, August 29,2005 12:09 PM

To: Lowder, Michael

Subject: Re: Information

I'm being told here water over not a breach.

From: Lowder, Michael

Sent: Monday, August 29, 200512.09 PM

To: Brown, Michael D

Subject: Re: Information

Ok. You probably have better info there. Just wanted to
pass you what we hear.

Corbin swabbed the bottom of Shay's foot with alcohol and took after the most obvious splinters with tweezers.

"The lack of water on the street doesn't mean the levees are intact," he said. "There could be hundreds of gallons per second pouring through. It would take several hours for us to see any sign of it in this part of town."

"It's been several hours," she said. "Turns out your Armageddon looks a lot like a flea market. I need to get down there before the Lady Foot Locker looter sells out of Nikes."

"It's not a joke, Shay. When that water starts rising, things will deteriorate rapidly. People will get nuts."

While he wrapped her feet with Neosporin, gauze and surgical tape, Shay carefully closed the gash on his forehead with two butterfly bandages and a kiss, thinking with relish about people getting nuts on camera, which people were more than willing to do even in the mildest circumstances. The possibilities gave her a physical shiver. She was essentially embedded in a war zone that every major news outlet would be scrambling to get into. Plan C was firmly in place: Focus on getting footage. Just shoot as much raw material as possible. Figure out what to do with it later.

After an ad hoc water bottle shower, she pulled on one of Corbin's clean white shirts and made coffee and sandwiches, delivering his to the equipment room. He squatted by the mainframe, tinkering with a wireless anemometer and other equipment that would need to go up on the roof as soon as it was light enough to venture up there without undue risk of accidentally stepping off into pitch-black oblivion. Shay plugged in her cell and camera chargers, pulled out the sofa bed in Corbin's office, and curled up with the radio. Conflicting reports threaded weakly through the static, bumping up against oblivious computer-programmed music from oblivious remote translators, the band that played on.

Corbin eventually came in and found her dozing. He set an apple in her hand and gently bit her earlobe, whispering that he'd found a condom in his desk drawer. In his experience, Shay was a ready lover who seldom required a lot of hijinks or hand cramps to get the job done, and he was particularly grateful for that now. The ache in his ribs was excruciating, but having her was still less painful than not having her. It was the only way to slow down his brain, the only way to feel something other than dread and sorrow.

After, she ate the apple while Corbin changed the dressing on her feet. He stroked her instep with antiseptic and kissed it before he wrapped it with fresh gauze and pulled clean socks over the surgical tape.

"Thanks," she said. "These poor little doggies are in for a long day."

In Corbin's walk-in closet, she commandeered a pair of cargo shorts and paired a white tank shirt with a white dress shirt tied at the midriff. She did her best to rock it but longed for the bra he'd cast into the darkness back at the loft. In the bathroom, she splashed bottled water on her face and scrubbed her teeth with a washcloth. As she gathered her hair into a ponytail, she realized her hands were shaking.

Shay looked at herself in the mirror and said, "Go. Just go."

"Sunrise in about forty minutes," Corbin called from the closet, pulling on jeans and a fresh shirt. "Should be light enough up there to safely situate the satellite unit."

"I'll help you carry the gear up. Then I gotta bounce, lover."

"Shay, wait till I get this thing up and running. I want to see what's out there, too, but there's an intelligent way to go about it."

She leaned on the door and said, "Why would you assume I can't be intelligent about it?"

"Stay till we get online. If the levees are holding, fine. Do what you need to do. If there's a breach, the National Guard will have enough to do without rescuing people who could have stayed safe to begin with."

"Corbin, I appreciate that you care, and if the water starts to rise—"

"I'm asking you for one hour. Do you have to be so pig-headed?"

"Don't yell at me," Shay said evenly. "I can take care of myself, and breach or no breach, whatever happens out there today, I am by God getting it on camera. I can still salvage a great opportunity here."

"Right. Thousands of people dying. Terrific photo op."

"For five years," Shay flared, "I have worked my ass off and paid my dues, and every sunshiny little segment was rehearsal for a moment when what I do actually matters. Because history requires a witness, Corbin. An unsentimental, technically proficient eye that happens to be in the right place at the right moment. I won't cower here while that moment passes me by. It's my privilege and responsibility to be that witness, and if that seems immoral or whoring or foolish to you, then there's nowhere for us to go from here."

"Fine. I give up, Shay," he said broadly. "You're a human magnet, and the awesome power of Jesus held up the levees, so go ahead. Risk your life for these unshakable principles you stand for when it suits your agenda."

"Go to hell."

Shay went to the conference room, took two water bottles from the bar, and jerked her cell phone from the charger. She sealed her camera and memory cards in Ziplocs and tucked everything into her damp but serviceable leather bag.

"Why, why, why don't we ever part well?" asked Shay.

Corbin stood by the pool table with his palm pressed against his throbbing eyebrow. A breeze from the broken window rattled the old-school maps mounted on the wall. Apparently unable to leave anything alone, Shay had pulled down the geologic map of the Eastern hemisphere when she first came in. Corbin fixed his gaze on Northern Africa so he wouldn't have to watch the familiar pattern play out in her face: the need to hear him say something turning to raw hurt, then wounded pride, then a composed pageant mask as her heart closed like a fist.

"Whatever." She shouldered her bag and looped the strap across her body. "I owe you a beer."

"Wait." Corbin yanked a pool cue from a rack on the wall, placed it in her hands, and closed her hands tight between his own. "When the water starts rising, you don't take a step without testing the ground in front of you. Understand? Not one step, Shay. You don't take foolish chances. You don't get into it with people or try to be a tough guy. And you get back here before dark. Promise me you'll be in that stairwell at sunset."

She shook her head. "I think I'm better off on my own."

"That's what it always comes down to, Shay. But it won't work this time."

She took the pool cue and left without meeting his eye.

Cursing himself with every blackened epithet he could think of, Corbin returned to the equipment room to muscle the router. *Priorities*, he instructed himself as he headed down the hall to the roof access ladder.

Get the internet connected and find out about the levees.

Contact the NHC and activate the backup telemetry units.

Get hammered and pass out.

Not necessarily in that order.

NEW ORLEANS

TUESDAY MORNING
AUGUST 30

From: Worthy, Sharon

Sent: Monday, August 29,20057:22 PM

To: Brown, Michael D

Subject: Tuesday morning media schedule

All times are central and the location is the Holiday Inn
Select Executive Conference Room, Baton Rouge.

5:20: CBS Early Show - Robin Wood,

5:30: Good Morning America - Ari Meltzer,

5:40: NBC Today Show - David Sullivan

5:50 : CNN American Morning - Alex Powers

6:00: MSNBC - Bruce Carter

6:15: Fox & Friends - Kim Agle

S hay used her pool cue to pry loose a sheet of plywood on a broken window in the lobby and emerged through the hole on Perdido Street just before sunrise. The Central Business District was already bustling like a school carnival.

The place had the look of something shaken out of a toy box. An upside-down dumpster in a shop window. A store mannequin in a tree. A pink flamingo jammed through the screen on an ATM machine. A desk with a reading lamp still firmly affixed sat up on one end at a bus stop. Inside one of the open drawers, Shay saw a cell phone, two pens, and an undamaged packet of Otis Spunkmeyer chocolate chip cookies, which she scavenged into her bag without a second thought. Clothing, paper, coffee cups, office chairs, and a potpourri of incongruous items randomly scattered the sidewalk. Blaring from a car stereo behind the spidered windshield of a Chevy Nova, the Blackeyed Peas thrummed "Don't Phunk With My Heart," the watermark song Shay would never be able to separate from that summer.

People in slow-moving cars honked and waved, negotiating the obstacle course of broken branches and furniture on the street. Strangers on the sidewalk struck up shaken conversations, telling each other their storm stories, asking after information, searching for friends and family. Everyone was asking everyone else if they had a cell signal, if the National Guard was coming soon, if they'd heard anything about the levees.

Someone told Shay the radio was saying there'd been no breach, that the water over the levee was just storm surge, but somebody else reported a text from a friend on Lakeshore Boulevard saying, "GET OUT!" Shay laid in a direct course for the shoe salesman, trusting nothing but the dry ground beneath her feet.

Looters wheeled by with shopping carts and picnic coolers, setting up shop, calling out cheerful greetings, sales-pitching like sideshow barkers. Shay hooked up a pair of Nike Air Zooms. She took a moment to sit on a bench and put them on and half a moment more to breathe a prayer of thanks for the extraordinary gift and privilege of shoes.

Down the block, she scored a legendary Louis Vuitton mono-gram Luco tote for forty bucks. She ditched her leather messenger bag, which was still damp and stank like a roadkill mofo, but because extreme circumstances call for extreme measures, she unhooked the shoulder strap from the old bag and snapped it onto the LV Luco tote. She traded a convenience store looter one of her water bottles for a Diet Coke and paid him a dollar for a tin of Altoids, then procured a nice racerback bra from a girl who'd looted a local Sports Authority.

"Necessities, check," Shay smiled to herself.

She'd shifted so far from her frame of reference over the preceding thirty-six hours, it took her a moment to recognize the sound of her cell phone. She rummaged for it and looked at the screen.

MOMMI HOME

With one bar of signal.

"Mommi?" Shay heard her mother's voice for a moment. Then nothing. She extended the pointless little antenna and pointed it one direction and another. "Mommi, can you hear me?"

"Shay!" she cried. "Baby girl. Thank you, Lord Jesus, thank you."

"Mommi, everything's fine. Calm down."

"All night, I was praying, hitting the redial. God's hand is on you, Shay."

"Mommi, please, don't cry. I'm fine. Is Daddy there?"

"He's getting a helicopter to come get you. Millie's trying to call you."

"Mommi, there's no need for that. It's okay. Please, don't cry."

"Fox News—Lake Ponch—by tonight—water coming—all—"

"Wait, what? Mommi, turn to CNN and tell me what they're saying."

"—hole in the roof at the Superdome and black men are raping and kill—"

Shay's cell triple-beeped as the call was lost. She cussed it, shook it, held it upside down, blew on it, all the usual voodoo, which she knew in her heart only served to pass the time until the thing decided on its own to reconnect to the matrix of the living. She started jogging toward the parking garage, but two blocks up the street, she spotted the *NOLA Now* satellite van weaving carefully through the debris field. Shay ran up to the passenger side, waving her Louis Vuitton tote.

"Renny! Renny, can I get a crew?"

As the tinted window eased down, she saw Christa and Jonas craning forward in the back seat.

"Shay, what are you doing here?" said Renny. "You smell like a frat party. There's a giant hickey on your boob. And what are you *wearing*?"

"Give me a ride to my car. I'll be back in twenty minutes in makeup and wardrobe. Twenty minutes, I swear."

"Look, I applaud the effort, okay? But this is not the time or place. Stop screwing around and find a ride out of the city."

"Send one camera guy with me, Renny. Please. Or one camera. I'll shoot it myself."

"Go. Find. A ride," said Renny. "We don't have time for the spunky kid with the fire in her belly storyline today, and frankly, Shay, you're too old for it."

Christa leaned forward from the back seat and said, "Shay, when we get back to regular programming, you'll have some great human interest pieces to sink your teeth into. Somewhere in there, we'll find an Emmy for you, I promise."

"That's right," said Renny. "This city is gonna need some sunshine. Okay, angel? We're gonna need a cheerleader, Shay, and that's you."

"No. That is not me," said Shay. "I quit."

"Shay, you're being ridiculous. And you have a contract."

"My attorney will be in touch to resolve that."

"Seriously?" He opened his arms to the scene around them. "You're choosing this moment to pull some diva trip on me?"

"No. I'm choosing this moment to do what I should have done five years ago. Me and my big howdy resources."

"Listen to me, you stuck up little twat—"

"*Renny.*" Christa set her elegant hand on his shoulder. "Shay, please, don't do this now. Go somewhere safe. When this is all over, you and I will have lunch and work it out."

"Bite me, Christa." Shay shouldered her bag. "And FYI, hon, forget about Corbin Thibodeaux. He's gay."

She headed up the street, humming *don't phunk with my heart.* She didn't need this job. She didn't need this man. She was better off alone. Buttoning up Corbin's shirt to cover the hickey on her chest, she jogged down the block toward a woman selling iPods and digital cameras.

Reboot. Plan C. Plans D, E, and F, if necessary.

The camcorders were straight off the shelves. The batteries would have to be charged in her car. The parking ramp was a little over a mile away. Her feet hurt like blazes, but she was certain she could still jog that distance in ten minutes or so.

"How much for the digi-cam here?" she asked the woman on the corner.

"Three-fifty."

"I'll give you seventy-five bucks," said Shay. This wasn't her first trip to the Casbah.

"Two-fifty. That's half price."

"Well, I'm assuming I won't be offered the extended service warranty."

They eyed each other without blinking. Bargain Samurais.

"Ninety bucks," said Shay. "And I need extra batteries and memory cards."

"Maybe we could work a trade," the woman said, eyeing the Louis Vuitton Frankentote.

"I'm not parting with the bag, but let's try this." Shay pulled out her wallet. "Here's my Victoria's Secret credit card. I'll write a note with my signature, authorizing you to charge $150 worth of merchandise. Plus the ninety bucks cash."

"Forget it. How do I know the card's any good?"

"Same way I know you won't go in there and buy $700 worth of stuff," said Shay. "Honor among thieves. What do you say?"

"Two-seventy-five," said the woman, "and I'll throw in a couple of MREs."

"What's that?" asked Shay, perusing the haphazard merchandise display.

"Meals Ready to Eat. Generic survival rations. It's like you're labeled HUMAN, and it's labeled FOOD."

"Okay. I'll take two of those. Do you have any socks?"

"Just men's."

"Final offer," said Shay. "Two hundred on the Victoria's Secret card plus seventy-five in cash for the camcorder, two memory cards, the MREs, and three pairs of socks."

"Two-fifty on the card."

"Done."

They shook hands. Shay wrote the note, tucked her purchases in her tote, and started jogging down the street in the direction of the parking ramp, keeping an eye out for someplace she could duck in and put on her new bra. In a little while, her feet were splishing on wet pavement, then splashing in two or three inches of water. She moved up onto the littered sidewalk, above the streaming gutters and gargling storm drains, traversing the aftermath in long, lean strides. A battered blue van sprouting with satellite dishes, antennae, and coaxial cables pulled alongside the curb and paced her as she kept jogging.

"Hey, you need a ride?" called the driver.

"Yeah," she said. "Can you take me to the parking garage on Seventh?"

"Sure, hop in."

Shay stopped running, but waited a thinking distance back from the door as it slid open. Scoping out the interior, she saw three scrubby guys and two girls packed into what looked like a cobbled together version of Corbin's equipment room, almost as high tech, but dented and bastardized and carpeted with fast food trash.

"Storm chasers," said Shay. There was a rowdy affirmation from the motley crew.

"Tornado pirates," said one of the girls, and sure enough, she was wearing a pirate's hat, and her teeth were a treasure collection of silver hooks and bands.

"Awesome." Shay took out the camera with the full charge. "Where are you from?"

"Purdue," the girl said, and the guy in the driver's seat gave off some sort of yell, which presumably had something to do with being a Boilermaker.

"Are you online?" Shay asked, framing her opening shot of the van. "What are you hearing about the levees?"

"Head of FEMA says there's no breach. CNN says they're looking right at it," said Boilermaker. "If it's the hotel parking ramp you're going to, forget it. The MIT people we were supposed to meet up with said it's flooded at the bottom. They couldn't drive out."

Shay cussed and powered up her cell. She had six text messages from Corbin. First the backup cell number. Then five more that all said the same thing:

BREACH CONFIRMED.

Guiltily, she texted him back:

OK.

"I'll give you five thousand dollars to take me to Metairie," Shay told the storm chasers. "Wait for me for fifteen minutes, then drop me off at the Superdome."

The girls exchanged glances.

"Hang on." Pirate girl laid a transparency of the Formosan termite infestation map over a map of the city streets. "No can do. That'll be a bunch of broke-ass trees around there. We'd end up wasting our gas."

The other girl elbowed her. "Yeah, but five grand?"

"That's a thousand dollars each," said Shay.

"With which we cannot buy gas," the pirate girl enunciated. "Post-apocalypse, lady. Cash doesn't mean crap. From here on out, fuel is fricking unicorn tears."

"I need to charge my other camera battery," said Shay. "Can you help me out there?"

"I can charge it for you," said a boy sitting on a folding chair in the back of the van. "I mean, you know, ride around with us for a while and charge it. In here. No problem."

He frankly looked too young to be in college. Painfully thin. Peppered with acne. Pushing classic wire-rimmed glasses up on the bridge of his hawkish nose. Shay felt a glimpse of what Corbin must have been like at that age.

"Okay. Thanks," said Shay, starting toward the sliding door.

"Hold it!" said the pirate girl. "Show us your tits."

"What?"

"Yeah, show us your tits!" It quickly became the consensus.

"You're kidding me," said Shay.

"Come on," the girl chided. "You have to. We're in New Orleans!"

The way she pronounced New Orleans—three syllables, accent on the *leans*, instead of the gentle *N'awlins* Shay was accustomed to—this told Shay they were Yankee children. They were far from home, rolling on a road trip to everywhere, infatuated with esoteric things like the weather and the internet and their own spectacularly nerdy piracy. Standing on the sidewalk, a little too late to be twenty-something, Shay envied them.

She rolled her eyes and untied Corbin's white shirt at her waist.

The boy in the wire-rimmed glasses immediately started wheezing.

"You don't have to," he blurted between inhaler hits.

Shay hoisted her T-shirt and a group howl went up.

"Welcome to N'awlins, y'all," she said. "*Laissez les bon temps roulez.*"

NEW ORLEANS

TUESDAY AFTERNOON
AUGUST 30

From: Rule, Natalie

Sent: Tuesday, August 30, 2005 10:40 PM

To: EST-ESF15

Subject: FYI - News Report Coming out of New Orleans

Please forward only to the Talking Points - Detailed list....thanks..

Just FYI:

FROM WWL-TV, CBS New Orleans website

****ALL RESIDENTS ON THE EAST BANK OF ORLEANS AND JEFFERSON REMAINING IN THE METRO AREA ARE BEING TOLD TO EVACUATE AS EFFORTS TO SANDBAG THE LEVEE BREAK HAVE ENDED. THE PUMPS IN THAT AREA ARE EXPECTED TO FAIL SOON AND 9 FEET OF WATER IS EXPECTED IN THE ENTIRE EAST BANK. WITHIN THE NEXT 12-15 HOURS****

Jeff Parish President. Residents will probably be allowed back in town in a week, with identification only, but only to get essentials and clothing. You will then be asked to leave and not come back for one month.

From: Lowder, Michael

To: Edward.Buikemaadhs; Patrick.Rhode

CC: Michael.D.Brown

Sent: Tue Aug 30 00:26:42 2005

Subject: Moving teams

Just got off the phone with Lokey. One of the hospitals in
NO is starting to flood and it is going critical. They are
evacuating patients to the Superdome. We are flying some
of our NDMS strike teams in to provide medical support at
the SD, and will be providing additional support to the
hospital. We will also be moving additional DMATs from the
MOB centers into Baton Rouge and NO.

More to follow later this morning.

ML

Purple afternoon shadows crept like kudzu up the delicate pin-striped wallpaper in the living room where Shay lay sleeping on her red leather sofa, smooth and pale as a swamp orchid, the god-dang cat nestled in a softly vibrating ball behind her knees. She stirred slightly but didn't awaken as water seeped under the door, through the mail slot, cracking a corner pane in the stained glass window, lapping higher, floating her up above the well-appointed furniture and the preaching television and the ticking clock. Her arms opened on the oily surface, creating gasoline rainbows and angel wings. Her blouse clung to her, as if the fabric had been dripped on her like wax. Her hair became a mermaid's cobwebbing mane. Her skin took on a bluish cast, her face as close to the ceiling now as it would be to a coffin lid, and then she was clawing, panicked, screaming and hissing with the drowning cat, clutching at Corbin as he fought for the inch of airspace between his groping mouth and the underside of the attic. Shay's arms were around his neck, choking him, dragging him down into the dark. The thrashing cat clawed at his face, and a thin burning line through the throbbing over his eyebrow stung him awake.

Corbin sat up swearing and sweating, not knowing where he was, then he remembered where he was and swore at that. He hadn't intended to sleep more than an hour, but slanted shafts of sunlight through the office window told him it was mid-afternoon. Whiskey and faux Vicodin burdened the back of his neck like a bag of wet concrete. He lumbered to his feet and followed the graveled hum of the generator to the equipment room. Almost a quarter of his fuel was gone.

Down the short hall in the kitchen, he went to the tepid refrigerator, cracked a warm bottle of Dr. Pepper, and sat at the counter, holding his head, heart still hammering. He considered turning on the air conditioner for a bit, but decided every available minute of energy needed to be spent keeping the dehumidifier and mainframe going. He checked his cell and found a fragmented message from Bonnie.

"Hey, beau frère, check in if—worry—Guy's signal is better—if you—"

Shay hadn't called or texted him back. It was possible that she'd tried and it didn't come through, but not probable. This was the way it habitually played out between them. Corbin vacillated between cursing her for being a Charybdis of volatile wrong-headedness and cursing himself for being the kick-dog who allowed her to T-bone him again and again.

Back in the equipment room, he turned on the monitor array and checked the RTU while the system was booting up. Winds were still gusting and had apparently shifted the satellite dish. Corbin searched for a Wi-Fi connection to piggyback. Nothing. No surprise there either. Rubbing his hands over his face, he accepted that he would have to climb the ladder to the roof hatch again. Stout drugs and a few hours of sleep had done him some good. He was able to trek the three floors to the access door without too much difficulty and squat with only a modicum of agony to check the surge suppressor and solar power supply.

Standing at the edge of the roof, Corbin raised the binoculars and surveyed the shipwrecked city. The shambled office buildings of the CBD extended to the horizon and disappeared into the dark as the rising water met the last remnants of sunset. Vanishing gas stations, stores, and neighborhoods, truncated streetlights and flag poles, palm trees stripped bald by the wind and up to their necks in water. A few scattered vehicles provided a rough standard whereby he could estimate the water depth. A little over two feet, he figured. Deeper in the side streets. People waded past, floating plastic storage bins and Styrofoam coolers piled with boxes and babies and jumbled belongings. Still no Guard in sight. A few canoes here and there. One good size bass boat, carrying a news crew.

"The good ship Opportunity," Corbin said bitterly. "History's witness, my ass."

At the corner of the roof, Corbin had installed a webcam that fed a continuing view of the sky above New Orleans to his company website. School children could click on it, watch the clouds roll by, and compare what they saw to diagrams on the side of the page to see what kind of clouds they were. Stratus, cirrostratus, cumulonimbus. Using both hands to bend the metal bracket that housed the webcam, Corbin refocused its unsentimental eye down toward the flooded street.

In the absence of city lights that usually competed with and easily overwhelmed them, the first evening stars emerged bright and insistent overhead. Corbin sat for a long time with his back to the access door, watching as they intensified and were absorbed into the brilliant clutter of planets and suns and satellites that reeled over an abject blackness that slowly enveloped the buildings below.

Shay Hoovestahl was not a reasonable person, he told himself. Common sense couldn't sway her any more than a red plastic fireman's hat could ward off lightning. And she couldn't just walk out the door— no, she had to make sure she got that last thing in there so she could leave him twisting in the wind. Corbin kicked a pile of shingled debris by the circuit panel and stopped pretending he didn't have to go out and find her.

Back in the equipment room, he shoved a flashlight and a handful of Sharpies in the hip pocket of his jeans, yanked another pool cue from the rack, and began the agonizing descent to the lobby. Even fortified with the generic Vicodin, the impact of every step shot up from his groin and pinballed back and forth across his ribcage. The amber emergency lighting in the stairwell had long since given up the ghost, so every once in a while, he stumbled, grinding his teeth, cursing Shay anew. Pushing through the door to the jet-sleek open stairway, he called down into the dark.

"Shay?"

There was no response except his own echo over the ambient trickle and hush of water far below. Corbin continued down, shining a limp beam of light into the abyss.

"Shay?"

At the point where the steps disappeared into the black pool, he tested the depth with his pool cue and stepped into it. A visceral awareness of the floodwater's chemical composition crawled over his skin as he slid one foot and then the other forward to the edge of each step, testing with the pool cue, dropping another step, then one more. When he found the floor, the oily soup lapped at the top of his knee-caps. Wading through the toxic sludge to a broken window from which someone had wrenched the plywood, he went out onto the sidewalk, calling her name, knowing it was pointless. It was a prayer, he realized to his discomfort.

Corbin took a thick Sharpie from his pocket and printed on a cov-ered window:

SHAY H: CALL ASAP! CT

Below that, he scrawled his backup cell number. Wading up the block, he beamed the flashlight down the alley.

"Shay?"

The service entrance at the bottom of the ramp was almost com-pletely submerged now. A snare of trash, rats, and pigeon wings floated inches below the light fixture above the door. Corbin scrawled the mes-sage on a dumpster that had been blown to the other side of the alley, then waded to the other end of the block and scrawled it on the hood of a waterlogged Chevy Nova. Work a perimeter, he decided. Expand block by block. If she was trying to find the building in the disorienting dark, she's hopefully hear his voice or see one of the scrawled messages. Though he was trying to conserve his battery, Corbin allowed himself to try her number a few times. He felt it in his diaphragm when the call finally went through, but it automatically tripped to her voicemail: "Hi, this is Shay. Tell me sumpthin' good."

"Shay, this is my backup cell. I texted you earlier. Hopefully, you get one or all of these messages. Look, I'm sorry I upset you. I don't know what else to say. We can talk about it if you come back. Whatever you want. I just need to know you're okay. Please. Call me or come back, and—and just—please. Please be okay. Call me. Immediately. Don't be stupid."

Corbin had nothing else, but he held the connection close to his chin until Shay's voicemail timed out, then he sent Guy a text.

SHAY SHOW UP?

The most sensible thing for her to do would have been to find a way back to Algiers, but apparently, that made too much sense for the Hoovestahl hierarchy of ego-driven needs.

NO, Guy texted back. LOTS PEOPLE HERE. SITUATION APESHIT.

Corbin came to a broken-out store window and stepped up into a display of office furniture, needing to get out of the water for a minute, knowing this whole excursion was idiotic and accomplishing nothing. He scrolled through the uploaded phone book, trying to think of any acquaintance they might have in common, finally striking on Shay's boss, the producer who'd booked him on the morning show. The phone rang three or four times before it rattled to life and a muffled voice croaked, "What the... who is this?"

"Renny, it's Corbin Thibodeaux."

"Corbin?" Renny coughed a phlegmy first morning cough. "What time is it?"

"Early. Late. About three. I apologize. I'm trying to reach Shay Hoovestahl."

"Shay? What for?"

Corbin hesitated. Shay had always been adamant about keeping their relationship on the down-low. In harsh moments, he'd said it was how she kept her distance when she was slumming, but in this moment, he realized he'd gone along with it for his own reasons.

"Her father contracted my services," he said. "It's very important that I reach her. Have you seen her?"

"Not since yesterday," said Renny, clearing a little as he came awake. "She was obviously out partying all night. Goes off on me with a bunch of bratty crap, and I was like, whatever, sister. You are so fired."

Corbin set his head in his hand. "Any idea where she might have gone?"

"Superdome, probably. Look for the greatest concentration of national media vehicles. My guess is you'll find her trying to beg, borrow, or blowjob whatever face time she can get."

"If you see her, please, tell her it's extremely important that she call me."

"Will do. So, Corbin." Renny cleared an owl's nest from his throat. "When this whole thing is over... maybe we could have a beer sometime?"

"Sure," Corbin said absently, climbing down from the office store window, plotting the best route to the Superdome.

"Great. I'll give you a call," said Renny with surprising warmth. "Hey, here's an idea. Come with us today. This could be a great angle. Native New Orleans environmentalist-slash-meteorologist. Could be an interesting opportunity for you. I'd love to get you in on it. We're shooting all over the city. Feeding stuff to all the majors."

"All over the city?" said Corbin. "How are you doing that?"

"We've got one of those monster trucks that sits way up with the big tires and hydraulics, and we're porting a couple small pontoons for anything too deep for the truck. Interested?"

"Yes. Very interested. Where can I meet up with you?"

"We're shooting at the Superdome at first light."

"I'm on my way over there now."

"Excellent," said Renny, wide awake now. "I'm looking forward to getting to know you better, Corbin."

14

NEW ORLEANS

TUESDAY AFTERNOON
AUGUST 30

From: James, Tillie
To: Brown, Michael D
Sent: Tue Aug 30 22:43:17 2005
Subject: U ok?

.

From: Brown, Michael D
To: James, Tillie
Sent: Tue Aug 30 22:52:18 2005
Subject: Re: U ok?

I'm not answering that question, but do have a question.
Do you know of anyone who dog-sits? Bethany has backed
out and Tamara is looking. If you know of any responsible
kids, let me know. They can have the house to themselves
Th-Su.

From: James, Tillie

To: Brown, Michael D

Sent: Wed Aug 31 05:49:23 2005

Subject: Re: U ok?

No I don't know anyone. Want me to see if my son is in town and can do it? David Trisself was looking for someone recently too. Maybe he knows someone.

Don't answer my question then. Still working on project today from home. It's crazy I hear in the office.

From: Brown, Michael D

To: James, Tillie

Sent: Tue Aug 30 22:52:18 2005

Subject: Re: U ok?

Sure, if he likes dogs. Check with David, too.

I should have done my announcement a week early.

❝I know folks think I'm outside my mind, but I won't ever leave the house for a hurricane. I can't leave my babies." The old woman in Shay's viewfinder thoughtfully stroked the little French bulldog in her lap. "If the Lord wants me home, he calls me home, and I'll be glad to see him. I never got afraid. Not when I was a child and not last night. Was it last night?"

"Yesterday morning, Ms. Martineau," said Shay.

"Oh, yes. Yes, the darkness makes it like black night." The old woman nodded with her whole body. "Like a great wild animal swallowed up the sun."

Seated in a wooden rocker on a little balcony outside the second floor of her ramshackle Ninth Ward shotgun house, Ms. Martineau was framed in the viewfinder with a trace of wrought-iron railing behind her and the massive river of slow-moving trash and branches traveling past in the shady street below. The water was only ten or twelve inches deep, but in the shade of the broken oaks, it appeared as dense and unknowable as the muddy Mississippi. Shay was afraid to breathe, the shot was so perfect, the old woman so unbearably beautiful.

"You were saying… you weren't afraid," Shay prompted gently.

"Oh, no. I don't get afraid. I always know that my mama is praying for me."

"Me too." Shay smiled and blinked back the sting that came up behind her eyes.

"If you see my granddaughter," said the old woman, "you tell her I'm all right. This house is a good house. Never takes water above that third step right down there."

"How long have you lived here?" asked Shay.

"Oh, longer than I been alive. I baked my bread and had my babies in this house. My nephew—he's passed now—he put in the new water heater…oh, three years ago. Was it three years? Maybe it was seven. I wasn't driving anymore. I know that. We enjoy sitting out here when the mosquitoes aren't too bad. My great-grandchildren have a sandbox down there."

She pointed a knobby finger toward the surface of the water that had crawled from the curb to the sidewalk in the forty minutes or so that Shay had been sitting here.

"I'll stop talking now," said Ms. Martineau. "I get dry and these new teeth, they rub."

"Thank you so much for visiting with me, ma'am. Do you have water set aside in the house, Ms. Martineau? It's hot. You have to drink lots of water."

"Yes, my nephew put in the new water heater last year."

"Here, drink this." Shay handed the old lady a water bottle she'd been hoarding all day, along with the last MRE. "I want you to stay up here and eat this tonight. Don't go downstairs to your kitchen."

"Well, you're too sweet," said Ms. Martineau. "Did you bake this yourself?"

Shay packed her camera in her tote bag, then took off the white shirt from Corbin's closet and tied one sleeve to a scrolled frou-frou at the corner of the balcony rail.

"I'm putting this here so they'll know someone needs help, all right, Ms. Martineau? Don't you take this down now. Someone will come along in a boat and see it. The National Guard or the police." Shay tried not to think about the possibility that the white flag might be under water by morning. "If someone comes for you with a boat, you go with them. They'll take you somewhere safe. Your granddaughter will know to look for you there."

"Oh, no, honey. I can't leave my babies."

"Ms. Martineau, you have to go." Shay's eyes dropped to the left. "I'll come back and take care of the dogs."

"Oh, would you, dear? Take them for a walk and feed them? And Sweet Bay—he needs his daily glucosamine."

"Sure. Of course," Shay lied, caught in one of those horrible Chinese finger puzzles where anything you say is wrong. "You stay upstairs until the boat comes. Promise?"

"All right, dear. So long as I know my babies are in good hands. If you see my granddaughter, you tell her I'm all right."

The two exchanged a warm embrace, and as Shay made her way down through an angled stairway tiled with family photos to the front parlor that was everyone's grandmother's parlor in some respect, she made the conscious decision to take this sort of story with her when she left the sunshine gig. The intensely beautiful faces and voices of folks who were no one in that they were everyone. The hardcore news was only a fraction of the story without Ms. Martineau's face, soft as onion paper, alive with history. Shay made another slow, deliberate trip up and down the stairs, with the camera on this time, knowing this history in faces, in button shoes, in old-timey clothes and funeral portraits would be lost to the water within a matter of hours. The voices would last only as long as Ms. Martineau's memory, and that was fading with the light.

Shay had filled a third memory card on the camera, and before she left Ms. Martineau's parlor, she took it out and added it to the Ziploc bag in her bra. It wasn't particularly comfortable portaging the memory cards this way, but she'd gotten some amazing footage and would have sacrificed a finger rather than lose it. The stuff with the Purdue storm chasers was nothing short of priceless, poignant in contrast to the stately old houses steeped in black tea and storm ruin. She shot hours of fathers making their way through the streets with their children on their shoulders, mommies floating babies along in plastic storage bin boats, firefighters struggling to put down flames that flared up out of the greasy water like dragon's breath.

Stepping off the porch steps into the shin-deep water, Shay heard Ms. Martineau's dog barking out back.

"I'll be right down, babies," Ms. Martineau called from the balcony. "I know it's past your supper time."

"Ms. Martineau, I'll feed them," Shay shouted up. "You stay up there."

"Oh, thank you, Sugar. The food's right inside the screen door out back."

Shay found herself wading deeper as she went around the side of the house. Ms. Martineau's back yard sloped down a good two feet from the front. At the end of the walk, cement steps disappeared into the water, and only an inch or two of the dog kennel showed above the filthy surface. The three larger dogs were already dead, suspended still and matted in the clouded water. The smallest of the dogs frantically paddled toward Shay, jamming its narrow, bloodied snout between the cage wires, grasping at the slip of air there.

Shay approached slowly and felt the edge of the sidewalk with her foot. In order to free the little dog, she'd have to descend the cement steps into the deeper water, then reach down and feel around for the latch. Testing the ground with her pool cue, she took the two steps down and felt the earth go mushy under her feet, grass and weeds tangling at her ankles. She made an attempt to lift the kennel to give the little dog a bit more room to breathe, but the weight of it and the instability of the ground made that impossible. She'd accepted the feeling of wet filth inch by inch, to the point where it was now above her knees, but her hands and body were still relatively clean. The thought of bending her face to that water, leaning her chest into it, ducking her head under—

Shay couldn't do it.

When she tried to move her feet, she felt mud sucking at her shoes, and she experienced a stab of panic about losing them, but she managed to stumble back up the cement steps to the sidewalk. She should go, she decided. Walk away quickly. Walk away. Just walk.

The yapping of the little dog rose and fell.

"Is that Sweet Bay?" Ms. Martineau called from an upstairs window. "Did he tangle himself again? I'll come down."

"No, ma'am, I'll get him."

Shay leaned over the water and tried to pry the kennel door open with her pool cue, tried to pry the kennel roof up, tried to pry the kennel corner apart.

"Hang on, Sweet Bay," Ms. Martineau called. "I'm coming down."

"No!" Shay shouted up. "You stay put, Ms. Martineau! I have the dog food now. I have it right here. You stay right there where you are."

The little dog paddled to her, yelping piteously, bleating really, like a lamb, its bright eyes never leaving her face.

"I'm sorry," Shay whispered. "I'm sorry."

She eased the pool cue between the cage wires, touched it to the back of the little dog's neck, found a purchase at the line of its leather collar and pushed down. There was no noise and only a little resistance in the twenty seconds of eternity before Sweet Bay went as still as the others. Shay didn't realize she was biting her lip until she tasted blood in her mouth.

"Everybody settled in down there?" Ms. Martineau called.

Shay cleared her throat and said, "Yes, ma'am. I'll be going now, Ms. Martineau."

"Thank you, angel. God bless you, sugar!"

Shay took out her camera, shot a minute or so of the kennel, then walked away quickly, contemplating something her father once said about his time in Vietnam: "You don't know what you'll do until you do it." He'd said the same thing years later when Shay questioned him about some disturbing talk surrounding a political PAC he'd funded. Whatever he did, she believed beyond any doubt, he had a good reason, the best intention, and until this moment, she would have said that a righteous intention made the doing of a terrible thing less appalling. It was a mercy to the dog and necessary to Ms. Martineau's survival, but Shay felt the cost of it. A knot of murderous sorrow tightened in her empty stomach.

"Shit!"

She impulsively hurled the pool cue like a javelin out over the water, realizing as it left her hand what a stupid, stupid thing she'd done.

"SHIT! Shit. Shit."

She waded the shady street for what seemed like a long time, keeping her eyes open for another good walking stick. She saw some men in a bass boat about a block away and hurried to catch up to them, dredging her legs through the stiff current, trying to splash as little as possible, but they disappeared around the corner of someone's garage before she could get to the intersection. This was an unfamiliar part of town for Shay, though she thought she remembered being somewhere near here to do a story about a lady who was turning a hundred years old. A jazz singer back in the day. Daughter of a freed slave who wrote poetry. Shay was certain she remembered shooting B-roll on a tall gingerbread-trimmed porch just like Ms. Martineau's, but that was a standard set piece in any number of New Orleans neighborhoods.

Was the water getting higher or the street sloping lower? Shay couldn't tell, but she was soon knee deep, then a little over her knees. She started feeling seriously afraid when it reached her mid-thighs, but on the corner up ahead, she noticed, there was a car with half the hubcap still visible above the black surface. So even if it got a little deeper at first…

Focused on the far corner, Shay didn't see the branches drifting in front of her. When she stumbled, her first thought was for her camera, her second for the legendary tote. She fought to regain her balance, but went down on one knee, holding the Louis Vuitton bag over her head. With the water at her waist now, the oily chemical stench of it was eye-watering. Shay held her breath, purposefully engaged every muscle in her exhausted core, and struggled to her feet.

Heart beating hard now, she walked a little further and realized the car was up on a flatbed trailer. Turning back, she tried to get her bearings, tried to remember if she'd already gone past this particular house with the fallen tree across its collapsed front porch or a hundred other houses with fallen trees and collapsed porches. Shadows were getting longer. She decided to make her way back to Corbin's office. It was the logical base camp. She could preview her footage on his big conference room monitor. After a shower and a nap, she'd download some editing software and work through the night. Drinking beer. She'd make him laugh, make him run the AC for a little while, make him get over himself, and if he played his cards right...

But maybe the hundred-year-old lady was more toward Metairie. This felt too far east of the CBD. And bottom line, it didn't matter, because the putrid water was hip deep now, sloshing at the crotch of the baggy cargo shorts. Shay had no choice but to go whichever direction seemed like it was uphill.

She kept wading, crossing paths with someone every once in a while. If it was a young black man, she guiltily cast her eyes away from his, hating herself for being a person who does that, but keeping her keys clenched in her right fist, the jagged Mustang tooth jutting forward like a bayonet between her middle and ring fingers. If it was a woman or an older man or a group of people, she tried to get directions. As long as the light held, she asked if she could film them for a few minutes, and they were eager to share their stories. Her spare battery was almost gone now. The sun sank into the shattered trees, and she sloshed onward, meeting with fewer and fewer people, changing direction when the street seemed to be dropping away from under her feet. She gripped the leather shoulder strap with her fist against her chest, trying to manually hold her heartbeat steady as the shadows on the water fell longer and more impenetrable.

The porch steps and garden walls disappeared, along with any hope of getting back to the CBD. It was miles away, Shay was certain, but she didn't know in which direction.

"God's hand is on me," she said with grim faith, mounting fear, and throat-deep thirst.

There was nothing inviting about the house with the mustard-yellow sofa on the porch. The steps and roofline sagged in need of repair. The paint was a mildewed avocado green. Iron grates barred the windows and door. There may have been some intent to have them look decorative at some point in the distant past, but the clear purpose of the security bars gave the house a sad, besieged feel. It seemed to sit a bit higher than other houses on the street, however, with three porch steps still visible, while the rest of the neighbors already had the devil at their front doors.

Shay slogged toward the steps, weighed down by the soggy shorts, fighting fatigue. She reached the slanted railing and dragged up the wooden steps, out of the unremitting movement of the flood. Easing her camera bag off her aching shoulder, she looked out across the rolling river of debris and decided it would make an impressive shot.

The street moved like a coal train, carrying jagged planks, rafts of drywall, the occasional mattress, coffee table, or couch cushion. Rainbows of gas and oil swirled in vast, graceful slicks on top of the murky water; just below the clouded surface, immense shadows shifted and swam. Something that looked like a dog lolled over and sank into the dark. Something that looked like a kitchen chair rose to the top and floated away. Great tangles of branches and debris tumbled into each other and snagged on street signs. Close to the porch, a succession of small items sailed by like a carnival game—a basketball, a Styrofoam clamshell, a plastic palm frond, a platform shoe with a high cork heel—bumping into the submerged steps, spinning, bobbing, sailing on. Something thumped against the bottom banister with a wet, wooden sound, and a heavy mass of debris stalled there, hung up on the submerged steps.

A baseball cap. A backpack. A pair of jeans. A shoe.

It took Shay a moment to sort out the understanding that it was the body of a woman. She recoiled, twisted, staggered back on the porch boards. Her breath went out of her chest in what felt like a raw scream, but came out small and guttural.

"Oh, God… oh, God… oh, Jesus…"

Shay walked quickly to the farthest part of the porch, trying not to see anything, not to smell anything, not to taste tar and dark rot. She pounded on the door through the grate, scuffing her wrist on the rusted iron.

"Hello? Hello! Is anyone there?"

No sound or movement inside. She tried to throttle the bars loose from the windows, but they were bolted fast.

"Dang it. This is not good. This is not cool."

She should get moving again, she decided. It didn't matter where. Just get away from here. She saw herself climbing the steps to Corbin's office, welcoming the sear of venom in her thigh muscles at the seventeenth floor, but even if she'd had the slightest inkling of the direction she should move in, she was terrified to step back into the flowing street. Shay sat gingerly on the arm of the fusty sofa, trying to be as unafraid as old Ms. Martineau. In the few minutes since she'd arrived, the water had risen from the bottom of the third step to the kickboard of the fourth.

She dug into her bag, drew her cell from the Ziploc, and powered it on, thrilled to see two bars of signal. She tried 911, just for drill. She got a recording. No emergency services. She tried Corbin, but it went straight to voicemail, and she realized this was his defunct cell number, not his live emergency phone. She was about to leave a message, thinking he might check the voicemail, but the phone suddenly vibrated in her hand.

DADDY OFC

Shay clicked to it. "Millie?"

"Shay! Thank God. Bob, I have her. Take this. I'll call Char."

Shay heard her father's big steps, his big voice. "Shay, are you all right?"

"Daddy! Daddy, hi. Hello." Shay clutched the cell to her cheek. "Oh, God, you don't know how good it is to hear your voice right now."

"I got your mama on the other phone. She's beside herself."

"Tell her I love her so much, and please don't stop praying for me. I'm scared, Daddy. It's getting bad. I'm alone, and I can't get back to my base, and there's not much daylight—but don't scare Mommi. Tell her everything's fine. Daddy, say it."

"Char, she says she's fine. She loves you. Char, honey, don't cry. Just let me talk to her. I'll call you back. Shay? Your mama loves you. And you know I love my Blueberry." Shay's father cleared his throat, tempering with an unsteady laugh. "You took a year or two off your old man's life today. I got a few new gray hairs."

"I'm sorry, Daddy. Everything's going wrong."

"We're gonna get you out of there. I got a chopper on standby. Where are you?"

"I don't know."

"God damn it, Shay—"

"Daddy, I don't know! I'm not familiar with this area. It's a bad neighborhood. I couldn't go back because… Daddy, somebody's coming."

"Shay. Tell me what you see. Stay low," he said, and his voice felt oaky and calm. Shay held the cell tight to her temple.

"Heavy set. Tall. Black. Older, maybe. I can't tell…" She strained to make sense of the odd angle of his arm. "He has a gun."

"What kind of gun?"

"Shotgun," she whispered. "Short barrel."

"Good girl. That's two in the magazine, one in the chamber. Can you get—"

"Shit! Shit! Daddy, he's coming this way."

"Shay," he said sharply. "Shut your mouth. You soldier up and shut that mouth and stay calm, you hear me?"

"Mm-hmm." She nodded, holding her hand tight over her mouth.

"Get low and cover the light on that phone. Is it covered?"

"Yes, sir," she whispered. "Daddy, don't leave me."

"I'm here, baby girl. I'm with you, Shay. Can you reach your pepper spray?"

"No, sir." She crouched beside the sofa, barely breathing.

"Knuckles?"

"Daddy, I lost them."

"Car keys."

"Yes."

"Okay. You know—fist with shark's teeth. Keep that fist tight—up—walk by. He's not gonna see you, but if—the gullet, then straight for that eye—"

"Daddy?" She looked at the fading bars on the cell. "Oh, God, Daddy, don't lose me."

"Shay? Shay!"

She'd never heard her father's voice like that. Choked. Terrified. She couldn't imagine any expression she'd ever seen on his face that might go with the sound.

"*Daddy.*" The cell was an empty seashell at her ear.

"Who's over there?" The man in the water swung his arm up, training his weapon toward the porch. "Police! Up on your knees! Hands where I can see them!"

A police officer. The uniform was soaked and too filthy to recognize, but as he came out of the shadows into the streaming street, he was the most enormously comforting sight Shay could have imagined. She almost laughed at her own ridiculous cowardice as she scrambled down the steps into the thigh-deep water, sloshing toward him, coughing through the contaminated taste in her nostrils.

"Officer! Thank God. Officer, I need help."

"Don't come any closer." He raised the shotgun and held it with both hands at the level of Shay's forehead. "Stop right where you are."

"No, no, it's okay." Shay held her hands up. "I don't belong here. I'm lost. I'm not—"

"Drop the Taser!"

"It's just my phone."

"Drop it! Drop it, or I will shoot!"

Seeing only the short barrel at the level of her eye, Shay gritted her teeth and let the cell phone plunk into the dragging current.

"Okay. See? I'm—I'm a good person. Please, lower your weapon."

"I got nothing," he said, still pointing the gun at her head. "I can't do nothing for you."

"Okay, but—"

"Hands! Keep your hands where I can see them!"

Shay held her palms up wide, trying to maintain her stance in the swift water, trying to keep her voice calm and placating.

"Officer. Please. I can't imagine what this day has been like for you. I know you're in a terrible situation here, but please, please, lower your weapon. It's okay."

He folded his arms in after a moment, but kept the gun in both hands at his chest.

"There's nothing I can do for you," he said. "Get on back up there where you were. Wait there till daylight. Then get to the Convention Center. Buses are taking people out."

"No, I need to get to the CBD before dark," said Shay. "Can you take me there? Or I'll just go with you—wherever you're going—it doesn't matter. Let me go with you."

"Convention Center," he enunciated. "That's all I can do for you. Now get over there."

"No, Officer, a woman is over there. In the water. There's a woman."

"Is she dead?"

Shay nodded.

"Get her secured," he told her. "Leave some kind of marking."

"What?" Shay shook her head. "How on earth would I do that?"

"Get her on top of a car or on a porch or tie her to a fence or a tree."

"Officer… my God. No. You have to take care of that. You have to help me."

Shay meant to reach for his arm, but before she'd taken a full step forward, the barrel of the shotgun was in her face again.

"Back off!" he bellowed. "Do not step toward me again or I will shoot. Turn around and get back up there like I told you. Do it!"

Shay turned away, fighting the current that wanted her to go sideways, fighting the fear that wanted her to cry like a child, fighting the anger that wanted her to lunge for his gun and kill him with it. Sloshing back toward the porch, she paused in what must have been the middle of the street, looking at the bobbing shape of the body, splayed now across the full width of the stairway as the rising water lifted it to the next step.

"I said get up there!" the officer barked, and from twenty feet across the water, Shay felt the cool gun barrel sighted on the back of her skull.

She strode forward, but in the fractured moment when she tried to step up over the woman's body, she lost her footing and stumbled backward, the fetid current closing in up to her neck. Flailing against an unknowable snarl of God knows what—spider legs, cypress roots, rats, shrunken heads, voodoo hair—she fought for her feet, gasping, gagging, slapping at the twigs and piano wires and unidentified, terrifying shit that tangled in her ponytail and clothes. Trapped between the woman's backpack and a tree branch, she went down again, grinding her knees against a submerged row of pointed pavers that lined the sidewalk to the porch. A rubbery blue hand slipped across Shay's arm, and she reflexively kicked and scrambled, clambered up onto the porch steps, spitting and swearing, coughing out dry, shrill cries, half-horror, half-terror, all disbelief, no air.

"Now stay there," the officer called across the current. "Do as you're told."

"Officer!" Shay rasped after him.

She wanted to beg him not to leave her, to threaten him with her father's iron hammer of influence, to tell him to go fuck himself, but her throat was closed and retching. He sloshed away into the shadows. She paced the porch boards for a moment, twisting her shirt in her hands in an attempt to wring out some of the filth, then returned to her perch on the arm of the sofa, clutching her arms in front of her, breathing in small, baffled chirps like a hatchling. Hearing the sound echoing on the water, Shay slapped herself hard across the face.

"Suck it up."

The sting was true and present, and it helped. She slapped herself again.

"Suck it up, you fat, pathetic twat."

The stench was unbearable now, permeating her hair and clothes, burning deep into her sinuses, behind her eyes, under her tongue, between her legs. The white tank and khaki cargo pants were the same shade of greenish-sludge gray now and stank of flood and sweat. Shay tried not to swallow and to find a clean part of her hand with which to cover her face. She tried to cough up and spit out the taste, but she had no spit left. Her tongue was thick with thirst and the urge to vomit. She instructed herself to inhale and exhale, to be calm, to form a plan, to know that her mother was praying.

Dragging the quilt from the sofa, she wiped her neck and arms and legs and her torso inside her shirt. When she first arrived on the porch, the old quilt had seemed dank and dirty. Now it was a gift, the hem of a benediction stole. When she'd done as much for herself as she could, Shay went to the edge of the porch, intending to do the right thing. The What Would Jesus Do thing. What the police officer said. Tether the woman. Leave a mark. The sofa seemed like a right place, but Shay could not even form a vision of the physical task of getting the bloated body on it. She fingered the bungee around her waist, the leather strap on the Luco tote. The first thing, she felt, was to cast the quilt over the body of the woman, to cover her.

Shay knelt at the edge of the porch floor, intending to do that, but then…

"Oh. Oh, goodness."

Inside the meshed outer pocket of the backpack, protruding above the water, there was a plastic bottle of Sprite, two granola bars, a packet of baby wipes and a cell phone, all neatly sealed in a large Ziploc bag. The urge to take it struck Shay like an open hand on her back, shoving her physically forward, against her own shame and decency, but when she leaned forward, the smell of the water and the body pushed her back. She recoiled into a tight ball against the newel post and sat still for what seemed like a long time, her eyes riveted to the Velcro stays on the bobbing backpack.

Twilight lingered above the water. A luminous wetland stretched between the besieged house and turbid shadows across the street. The misted air glowed with the last of the late afternoon sun. Golden hour, as they say. Shay took her camera from her bag and sat on the porch floor with her back against the sofa, allowing the passing current to create the shot. The slow moving train. The swirling rainbows. The random spray cans, hats, and plastic toys. A large mass cruised through the middle of the frame. A picnic table all involved with tree branches and yellow caution tape. It created enough of a wake to dislodge the woman's body, roll her sideways. Shay zoomed in on an earring. A white daisy with a yellow center and little butterflies that dangled down. The ear teemed with silverfish. She followed the soft line of the slender neck to the precious contents of the pack.

The camera took her close enough to see what she hadn't seen before. Just behind the lip of the Ziploc. A jar of pureed peaches. Gerber baby cheeks on the label beamed up in the brief instant before another lap of passing wake dragged the pack aside. At first, Shay thought the woman had another rucksack on the front of her. It took the physical turning of the next moment for her to accept that it was a snuggle sling. The type one sees in the mall with a mother's protective arms around it and an infant's chubby legs kicking below.

Shay made a small, involuntary sound, trying to steady the camera in her unsteady hands. The golden hour light gave up the perfect form of the baby's porcelain foot just below the surface. Unbearably sweet, inconceivably wrong. Shay breathed through her teeth, pulling back to frame it with the cherub face on the baby food jar, holding there until another passing wake rolled the woman forward again, thunking her head between the posts of the wooden railing, lifting her to the next step, shifting the Sprite and wipes and cell bag into view.

"How do you like to go up in a swing," Shay whispered. "...up in the air so blue..."

She set the camera carefully aside and crawled to the edge of the porch.

"Oh, I do think it the pleasantest…thing…ever a child…can do."

She breathed for a moment, lowered herself to the second step down.

"Up in the air and…and over the wall," she whimpered, pressing her wrists against her thighs, clenching and unclenching her hands. "…till I can see so wide…"

She was even with the sodden backpack now. It was an arm's length away.

"River…and trees…and…and cattle…and all…all over the countryside."

Clutching the quilt in front of her, all in one motion, like an asana, Shay cast the fabric over the Madonna and child, scooped her arms under them and heaved as hard as she could, dislodging them from the wooden railing, hefting them off the step, shoving them out into the stream of debris until the current caught hold and took them into the crowded tide.

Shay crawled back to the foot of the sofa and clicked the camera off, carefully bagged it, and pulled the Luco tote between her knees. She took out the dead cell phone she'd scavenged from the bus stop desk, removed the back, carefully cleaned the screen, keypad, battery chamber, and connections with a bit of foam from the tattered sofa cushion. She reassembled the cell, blew on it, shook it, begged it, beat it against the floor, and finally pitched it out into the slipstream behind a passing rack of croquet mallets. Only the top porch step remained above the floodwater now, and the tide moved more swiftly, carrying ever larger artifacts. A dresser. A wingback chair. A spinet piano.

Night fell.

Dark shadows and dark water melted into each other. Sporadic cries and mystery noises caused her heart to knot up. Shay posted her tote bag up on the back of the decaying sofa and huddled on the less rotting cushion, hands folded in her lap, eyes focused on the first of the evening stars. She looked up from the abject blackness to the brilliant clutter above. Inhale. Exhale. God's hand is on you, Shay. Thou art strength to the needful, a refuge from the storm. Thou art strength to the needful, a refuge from the storm. She closed her eyes, allowing herself to drift.

Shay smiled when she felt the gray tomcat licking her hand.

She opened her eyes, sitting in an inch of warm, stinking water. A brigade of oily rats had taken refuge on the arms and back of the sofa.

"Shit! Shit!" She scrambled to her feet on the sofa, trying to seize hold of her slamming heart. "Okay. Okay. Calm down, goddamnit! You soldier up. You get a grip."

The darkness around her was a living, liquid thing. The water was knee deep on the porch floor, which made it neck deep in the street. Standing on the arm of the sofa, Shay clutched her camera bag in one arm and linked the other around the porch post. Two solid things. She would not let go of these. Time went by.

"If it gets above my ankles," Shay told herself, "I will… something. What will I do? Form a plan. Set a deadline. If it gets above my ankles, I will… do… that."

When the water was just below her knees, she shouldered the tote and hoisted herself up on the porch rail. If it had been a little wider, she thought, she might have been able to stand on it until first light, but as the water continued to rise, the perch felt impossibly unstable. Shay reached up one hand and took hold of the rain gutter above her. She let the camera bag slide down from her shoulder, caught the strap in her fist, did two slow practice pendulums, then slung it up onto the porch roof. A small cry came out of her when she let go of the leather strap, and she held her breath, praying to hear a thump instead of a splash. The bag thumped onto the roof overhead and slid a little on the shingles, but stayed put.

Shay whooped out loud at that victory. Sliding her feet sideways along the railing, steadying herself with one hand on the ceiling, she made her way to the trellis at the front end of the porch. The roof stuck out beyond the posts a good eighteen inches, but she was certain that if the lattice was strong enough to support her weight until she got her elbows up onto the shingles, she'd be able to get a foothold on a gnarled oak tree growing close to the house and push herself up. If the lattice was strong enough.

But it wasn't.

When the narrow slats gave way beneath her feet, Shay grasped at the rain gutter. It came away from the roofline with a rusty shriek. There was a fragmented moment when she had one hand on the tree trunk and one foot on the rail, and in the crack between that moment and falling, she saw clearly that she should have tried to climb the tree instead. She saw the branches spread out above her against thin gray dawn and reeling stars. For that moment, the world was beautiful, and then the black water closed over her head.

15

NEW ORLEANS

WEDNESDAY MORNING
AUGUST 31

From: Bahamonde, Marty

Sent: Wednesday, August 31, 2005 12:20 PM

To: Brown, Michael D

Subject: New Orleans

Sir, I know that you know the situation is past critical . Here some things you might not know.

Hotels are kicking people out, thousands gathering in the streets with no food or water. Hundreds still being rescued from homes.

The dying patients at the DMAT tent being medivac. Estimates are many will die within hours. Evacuation in process. Plans developing for dome evacuation but hotel situation adding to problem. We are out of food and running out of water at the dome, plans in works to address the critical need.

FEMA staff is OK and holding own. DMAT staff working in deplorable conditions. The sooner we can get the medical patients out, the sooner we can get them out. Phone connectivity impossible

From: Brown, Michael D

Sent: Wednesday, August 31, 2005 12:24 PM

To: Bahamonde, Marty

Subject: Re: New Orleans

Thanks for update. Anything specific I need to do or tweak?

Corbin made his way through a thin gray dawn to the Superdome, one arm held tight across his aching ribs. A two-hour search of the facility left him sweaty and sad, the postapocalyptic stench clinging to his dank white shirt. Despite the media hype about violence and chaos, all he saw was weariness and worry, people sitting on the floor, mostly silent, many praying, all sharing what less-than-little they had, sustaining on nothing but stale air, treating every Twinkie and Dr. Pepper like loaves and fishes. Much to his cynical surprise, there was an element of Woodstock in it. He asked around for directions to the freezer where they were keeping the dead, located a guy there who was somewhat in charge, and asked if they'd seen a woman who fit Shay's description.

"She was here yesterday," the guy reported.

He remembered her because Shay had asked if any of the stiffs were sporting the unusual promotional item and hadn't been shy about describing it.

"Interesting girlfriend you got there," he smirked.

"Did any of them have it?" asked Corbin. "The, uh… the unusual item?"

The guy recoiled. "How would I know, ya sick screw?"

Outside under the humid sunrise, people milled and mugged for the cameras, cluster-shuffling like inmates in a prison yard until they realized they had to do something more interesting to stay in the frame. The monster truck pulled up on the corner of Lasalle and Girod with Christa perched up in cab like an English dame on safari.

"Let's get some B-roll." Renny dispatched cameramen and approached Corbin with obvious dismay. "Good morning, Dr. Thibodeaux. What happened to your face?"

"Corbin?" Christa called from the open window. "Good God, are you all right?"

"I got into a thing with a looter," Corbin said. "It's not as bad as it looks."

"Come on up." Christa patted the back seat of the truck and opened her makeup kit. "I'll see what I can do."

"No, don't," said Renny, stepping closer, peering at Corbin through a square eyepiece. "That actually works. Very 'that's gotta hurt,' you know? Battered but not beaten. And it's—wow. Incredibly masculine. I think I'm loving this."

Renny's cell jingled in the pocket of his fresh shirt, and he held up his hand while he conversed urgently with someone at a remote studio he'd arranged outside the city.

"We're here now," he said. "There's national media all over the place. I hear it's like hell on earth inside. Gang rapes happening right out in the open. They're totally raping babies and children. Forty bodies in the freezer."

"What? No, no, no. That's bull," Corbin tried to tell him. "Everybody's basically being cool. And there's only four bodies in the freezer."

"You were in the freezer?" Christa was instantly attentive. "Doing what?"

"Looking for a friend," said Corbin. "I saw four bodies."

"Make that forty-four bodies," Renny said to his cell. "Forty-four bodies confirmed."

"No, not—" Corbin started, but Renny gave him a thumbs up and clapped him appreciatively on the shoulder before heading toward the editing truck. With his pool cue in one hand, Corbin struggled into the back seat of the monster truck beside Christa.

"Might be interesting to start in Metairie at the apartment you used in your hurricane prep material on Saturday." He tried to make it sound like a casual suggestion. "There's four to five feet of water in it. You could get a pretty striking before and after."

"Love it," Christa agreed and radioed to the other truck.

The water on Shay's street was only a few feet deep, so the monster truck easily rolled up in front of her condo, but sitting several cobblestone steps down from the sidewalk, her garden level apartment wallowed in five feet of flood, muck, and palm fronds.

They unloaded the pontoons, and Jonas and Corbin each got into one with a cameraman while Christa did an exterior bit from the bed of the truck to set it up. Jonas and his cameraman pulled the larger pontoon close to the broken windows and shot from outside, but Corbin and the cameraman in the smaller craft approached the patio entrance to Shay's bedroom and determined they could fit through the sliding doors. Corbin used his pool cue to break the glass. They crouched forward, squeezing under the top of the doorway.

"Shay?" Corbin coughed at the flood stench in his throat. "Shay, are you in here?"

His voice echoed strangely between the high ceilings and calm wall-to-wall water. The tall bedposts and heavy pole lamps grew up from the swamp like cypress trees. The cameraman pointed to a nest of decorative pillows that bloated and bobbed near the headboard. When Corbin prodded them with the pool cue, a snake slid out of the shadows and rippled away, abandoning a crew of mice that frantically clawed at the pleats and ruffles. The walk-in closet door stood ajar, and a clogged mass of shoes and boots circled slowly, as if they were feeding on the random clutch purses, belts, and bras in the murky water.

Shay's peach-colored easy chair lumbered like a cartoon hippo beneath the surface, and discernible on a table next to it was the wavering shape of her white laptop. If Shay had come back here before the flood, Corbin knew, she'd have taken her computer with her.

They nudged through the wide French doors and moved down the hallway, pushing themselves along with their hands on the walls and door jambs, ducking their heads for ceiling fans and hanging light fixtures. Corbin reached up and rapped with his pool cue on the hatch leading to the attic.

"Shay? Are you up there?"

There was only the scurrying of rats and squirrels in answer.

They drifted into the living room, where the wide yellow eyes of a large Blue Dog painting peered at them from a wall above a jumble of submerged furniture. After Shay outbid him at an auction to benefit the Humane Society, Corbin had offered to follow her home and help her hang it, and she made him move it at least fourteen times before he parked it there and pulled her down on the red leather sofa.

The cameraman focused on a grid of watercolor and ink originals.

"Holy crap. This art collection is worth a fortune. Rodrigue, Sandhue, McCrady... what a tragedy."

Some smaller paintings and kinetic sculptures were up on top of a bookshelf, but the larger pieces including the Blue Dog were all several inches or more into the water, the canvases sweating and rippling, frames expanding and separating at the seams in the thick, wet heat. Shay's antique Oxford Shakespeare, cumbersome old Webster's dictionary, and a signed copy of *Leaves of Grass* sat open on beveled bookstands on an étagère, onion-paper pages warped and curled, covers swelled and flaking like the layers of a croissant.

Barstools and wooden chairs traveled gracefully around the open kitchen and dining area. As Corbin slid the pontoon over the sunken cooking island, guiding the craft by grasping hanging pots and pans, the cameraman zeroed in on the top of the refrigerator where some kind of animal—perhaps the goddang cat, Corbin speculated—had apparently survived for at least a little while, gnawing on a box of Special K bars.

He caught the freezer handle to stop the slow glide of the boat, and as he scrawled the backup cell message on a white cupboard door, he saw the cat's matted form just under the surface of the water, caught between the stovetop and mounted microwave.

Back in the truck, they lumbered through town, cruising slowly up Canal Street, shooting B roll of a bloated corpse, broken windows, tumbled brick walls. Corbin's cell chimed. A text message from Shay.

SPRDOME

Corbin rubbed his hand over his face. There was no way to know when the message had been sent, what she was responding to. But at least he knew what her priorities were.

They set up a shot with Christa on the cracked lip of a demolished fountain questioning Corbin about various aspects of the storm itself. Wind speeds, rainfall, the data he'd been able to gather during the hours he spent at his office. They drove up an overpass from which they could see one particularly bad section of the failed levee, and she interviewed him about the history of the structure and asked how the salt water was going to affect area ecology.

Pontooning through submerged neighborhoods, past brimming porches and drowned playgrounds, Christa asked him what exactly was in the water below them, what the impact would be in the opinion of an environmentalist, but as they floated past the rooflines of the sagging shotgun houses, she skillfully finessed him into talking about his childhood in New Orleans and what the city meant to him.

"Go down the street here and turn left," Corbin said.

As they drifted through the old cemetery, headstones and angel wings scraped the bottom of the boat. Corbin found himself peering into the water despite his own dread, watching for old lace and white bones.

"Why are we here?" asked Christa.

Corbin nodded toward the sundered cement walls of a collapsing mausoleum. The roof was gone, the wrought-iron gate twisted off into the arms of a broken oak tree.

"My grandparents' ashes," he said. "My mom and dad…"

He felt his throat closing and tried to clear it, tried to blink back the sudden burning in his eyes and sinuses. He said something clumsy about the flood stench getting to him, and Christa put her hand on his arm. The crew was immaculately silent. The craving was palpable.

After that, Corbin kept his answers brief, factual, and to the scientific point.

They made the best of the lighting at dusk, and as darkness gathered, the monster truck rolled back into the CBD, stereo blaring a Bob Dylan song Christa had proclaimed their official anthem. Corbin found it helped cut the stench in his nose if he sang along at the top of his lungs.

"Take a deep breath, feel like you're chokin'…" Here they all played an air guitar riff before bellowing, "Everything is broken!"

Six blocks or so from Corbin's office, the driver stopped and climbed down to assess the water level down the street, leaving Jonas asleep in the front seat and Christa and Corbin talking quietly in the back.

"This was by far the most intelligent conversation I've had about all this with anyone in the media," Corbin told her. "I appreciate it, Christa."

"I appreciate your appreciation," she smiled. "I was that compulsive little homework doer who always threw off the class curve. Not an endearing trait to most people."

"I hear ya."

"Jesus, what we saw today." She took a deep, exhausted draw from a little silver flask. "The nursing home. That cemetery… everything. God almighty."

"Are you okay?" he asked.

"No, I'm not okay. Are you okay? How the hell is anybody okay?" Christa peered through the dark window down the dark street. "I wish he'd hurry. If I don't cold pack my eyes, I'll look like Courtney Love on camera tomorrow."

"Christa?" The PA's voice crackled in a walkie-talkie on the seat. "My Guard source says they're clearing the bodies out of that old folks home at first light. Renny said to ask if you want to cover that or have Jonas go."

"I'll cover it," Christa said, but when she set the walkie-talkie down, she caught a hitched breath and turned to Corbin. "Jesus. Can someone remind me why I have to do that?"

"Because history requires a witness," Corbin told her. "An unsentimental, technically proficient eye in exactly the right place at the right moment. It's your privilege and responsibility to get it right."

Christa took another hit from the flask and set her head on his shoulder.

"Thank you, Corbin. It means a lot to me that you think of my work that way."

"Don't give me any credit for that," he said sheepishly.

"Rather than climb all those stairs again," said Christa, "you should come with us to the hotel in Baton Rouge."

"I doubt there's a room," Corbin said.

"There's my room, Norbert. Do I have to spell it out?"

She'd been drinking Disaronno from the little silver flask. Corbin tasted burnt sugar and apricot on her tongue when she kissed him. He deepened the kiss with his hand on her hip, possible outcomes and algorithms vectoring across his mind. Christa moved his hand inside her blouse, and he explored a bit, then touched his forehead to hers and said, "Good night, Christa."

Christa sighed. "Maybe some other time."

Corbin opened the door, but as he climbed down onto the running board, Renny's voice crackled from the walkie-talkie. "Christa, come back to the trailer right now. I need you to see something. Tell Thibodeaux he'll want to see this."

The mobile editing suite was up on a flatbed behind the monster truck. Corbin crowded in with Christa and Renny and two other producers in the close corner behind the PA's chair.

"Okay, first there's this," said Renny.

He rolled footage of heavily trafficked water, expanding the image to full-screen as the camera zoomed in on a sodden backpack and golden hour light gave up the porcelain foot of a dead baby.

"Oh, my God," Christa whispered.

"That is a powerful image," said Renny. "That's an Emmy right there."

"*How do you like to go up in a swing,*" whispered the tinny laptop speakers.

The back of Corbin's scalp went ice cold. Mud-spattered arms—lean with a hint of pinup girl—reached into the frame and pushed the corpse into the turning floodwater with a swallowy slosh, followed by a small, terrified bleating.

"Where did we get this?" asked Christa.

"One of the network crews found it on a roof in the Ninth Ward," said Renny.

"I don't understand," said Christa. "Why did they bring it to us?"

"Press credentials in the bag."

Renny fast forwarded through a jumble of unintelligible images. When he pushed play, the lens peered out of the Luco tote like a half-closed eye. Moonlit shingles were discernible through crinkled plastic. Under the ambient drone of the passing flood, there was the crack of breaking lattice, a glimpse of a frantic white hand, the metal shriek of the storm gutter coming away. There was a long moment of ambient water noise. A rat scuttled across the shot.

"Wait for it," said Renny. "Wait for it...here."

There was a blur of frenzied clawing at the edge of the crumbling shingles. A swampy Gollum form heaved itself from the tangled arms of the oak tree and scrambled to the highest part of the hipped roof, retching and wheezing.

The camera jerked to a series of rough cut daylight images. Floodwater lapping at the soffit. A foosball table floating by. A bloated dog, the body of a man, a disembodied arm. A flotilla of porn DVDs and sex toys on an amorphous pond lily of bubble wrap. The neighboring house shifting on its foundation, tipping, folding like a card table. And then, sunburned and filthy, lips cracked and bleeding, Shay turned the camera on herself.

"Whoever finds this," she said, hoarse with thirst and resignation, "my name is Shay Olympia Hoovestahl..."

Corbin made a sound like he'd been kicked in the solar plexus.

Christa leaned in. "Turn it up. Turn it up."

"You'll receive a generous cash reward if you return this to Millie Teasdale at Hoovestahl TransGlobal." Shay spelled Hoovestahl and gave her date of birth, social security number, and Millie's email address.

"Her body was on the roof?" Christa said. "They found her body?"

"No body," said Renny, "but clearly, she died on the job, so anything on that camera—"

"This does not mean she's dead," said Corbin, needing to say it out loud. "This means she lost the bag. That's the only fact in evidence."

"Right," said Christa. "No assumptions. Technically, she's still alive and under contract, which makes this work product. Until there's a body—bagged and tagged—we have the right to cut, air, and license this footage any way we see fit."

"Whoa, whoa, we need to consider her family," said one of the other producers. "Hoovestahl TransGlobal is a major system-wide advertiser. The vehicle dealership alone has a seven-figure quarterly ad budget."

"If Hoovestahl attorneys make noise," Renny said, "we hand over the bag with condolences and help them understand we're making the most dramatic use of the footage because that's what our Shay would have wanted. We owe it to her to do this footage justice. She's our angel, right?"

"Right, right," was the consensus as the video played on without pause.

"So, for now," said Renny, "the approach is we've lost one of our own, so on and so forth. Until we get positive ID on a body, there's an interfaith prayer vigil. Let's get some national follow-through. I want transition graphics—'fearing the worst' to 'confirming the worst'— maybe a thirty-minute special report."

"I could use the footage to reconstruct her final hours," said Christa.

"Yes. Loving that," said Renny. "Let's put together a sizzle reel of Shay's cutest bits, charity events, the rah rah Special Olympics stuff."

"Not that last Sunshine Girl segment. That shelter in place thing is kind of an irony suck now."

"Millie, when I was a little girl," said Shay, "I pegged you as the doer of impossible deeds. I'm so grateful. You know about my projects, the endowments, and all that. Also, Mills, I want you to have my little house in Hawaii. I was planning to give it to you when you retire. The property taxes are insane, so set up a perpetuating fund to cover that, okay?"

"Let's loop Anderson Cooper in on this," said Renny. "She was a major AC fan."

"Also reactions from the reigning Miss Texas and Miss USA," said Christa.

"Someone needs to hit every body retrieval site until we find her. Someone who can make a positive ID."

"I'll go," Corbin said.

He peered into the monitor, trying to discern the time of day, the extent of her exposure, anything that might give a clue to her exact location. The sun appeared to be straight overhead. Estimating by a telephone pole that remained fairly upright, the water depth was approximately thirteen feet. That meant she was alive less than eight hours ago.

Shay pushed the heel of her hand across her cheek and hacked a dry cough.

"McKecknie, precious baby sis, be sweet and help Mommi. Take care of Namma. Mommi and Daddy, thank you for being the most wonderful people in the world. Mommi, I'm so sorry to put you through this. Daddy…"

She smiled and pushed her hand against her heart.

"You're right here, Daddy. And Mommi, I feel you praying for me. God's hand is on me. I'm not scared. I'll see you again with Jesus. I will see you there, Mommi. You know that. *Joy cometh in the morning,* okay? You hold onto that, and just… just hold onto me, and know that I'm holding onto you, and I love you, I love you, I love you, Mommi.

I'm so sorry. And um… my battery's about gone, so… I just love you all so much."

"Oh, my God," Renny whispered. "Tears. Are you seeing this? I'm in tears."

"Millie, one more thing." Shay tried to swallow, but she had no spit. "If they can salvage the Blue Dog painting from my condo, send it to Dr. Corbin Thibodeaux at EarthWeather Analytics. Tell him I said…"

When Shay's voice faltered, Corbin felt his heart collapse.

"Tell him I hate it when Democrats are right."

16

NEW ORLEANS

WEDNESDAY EVENING
AUGUST 31

From: Piotr Dmkier

Sent: Wednesday, August 31,2005 4:16 PM

To: [-------------------------]

Subject: Hurricane Help - Forensic Anthropology

Importance: High

Dear Sirs,

I am a Polish forensic anthropologist visiting the
U.S. on an internship at Smithsonian in Washington,
D.C. My colleagues here in the States and I are
forensic scientists specializing in human recovery and
identification. We worked for International Commission on
Missing Persons in the former Yugoslavia recovering and
identifying thousands who were killed during the wars in
the Balkans.

We read of the terrible tragedy that has struck the
gulf area and we would like to volunteer our services
in assisting in recovery of those lost due to Hurricane
Katrina and perhaps coordinate a Missing Persons call
center for families searching for loved ones.

We look forward to hearing from you soon and perhaps
coming down to help with the recovery and identification.

Lying next to her messenger bag on the roach-infested shingles under the searing afternoon sun, Shay reached the decision that, if she survived this, she would go back to the Sunshine gig. She'd beg Christa for her old job. She'd cover pancake breakfasts and fashion shows.

She'd be good, she kept promising God, she'd be a good girl and find a decent man to marry and do everything she was supposed to do, because this was ridiculous, this sucked, this was butt-sucking ludicrous, and she was an idiot for thinking she could make any difference in the unstoppable rising tide of human suffering and bullshit. She was born to privilege, and that wasn't her fault, and if she survived this, she was going to appreciate and enjoy all the comforts and perks that were her first-class-swilling birthright, and fuck this—and she apologized to God for saying fuck again—but screw this, screw the rats and roaches and the bludgeoning sun, and screw loving somebody who wasn't a suitable or even functional partner. Screw Corbin and his bleeding heart and his global-warming hysterics. If half the people on Earth died, it wouldn't be the half on her side of the tracks, so screw white guilt and rich girl guilt and pretty girl guilt. Screw political correctness and WWJD lip service.

Screw this, Shay would have wept if she hadn't been so desperately dehydrated, *oh God, oh Jesus, I'm so screwed, I'm so screwed.*

The next thing in her murky consciousness was the wet floor of a bass boat. A National Guardsman held a plastic water bottle to her lips, and it was like drinking cold diamonds. Then there was blackness again.

"How's our customer in first class?"

A nurse lifted the tent flap and knelt beside her cot near the swamp cooler in the officer's mess tent. He took her vitals and pushed a syringe into the port on her IV.

"This is a megadose of penicillin for the rat bites. Since you spent time in the water, we'll give you a round of tetracycline to take home. Don't want those feet to get infected."

"Thank you," said Shay. "Were you able to relay a message to my father?"

"Yes, ma'am, Ms. Hoovestahl. The general spoke with him directly."

"Oh, thank God. Thank you so much." She sat up and pushed her dirty hair away from her face. "Y'all were very sweet to make a special place for me. I feel much better."

"Basically, you're in good shape. Let's keep the fluids going tonight while you get some sleep. I'll give you a vitamin B shot and some potassium." He bit the cap off another syringe and pushed it into the IV. "I don't know how, but your dad got a helicopter for you. You'll be home in time for breakfast tomorrow."

There was no tacit "must be nice" in the way he said it, but Shay had been watching the trail of dire misery since they triaged her, the critical shortages, all the too-little-too-late the Guard and the Red Cross were coping with.

"Tell them I'm grateful," she said. "I'll make sure Daddy knows y'all were wonderful, but don't waste the helicopter. Use it for medevac."

"You're sure?" he said. "Believe me, we won't turn it down."

"Of course. But if it's not too much trouble, could I get a ride back to the CBD?"

"No, ma'am. They're clearing the city."

"What about Algiers?"

He nodded. "We've got people headed over first thing in the morning, but they'll be clearing Algiers, too. The whole metro area."

The sun was coming up when they dropped Shay off on the curb in front of Bonnie's Bloom & Grow. The house was packed and full of activity. Upstairs, music, and people spilled out onto the balcony, making coffee, cooking breakfast on the grill. Down on the sidewalk, Bonnie was spray-painting a message on the plywood that covered the shop windows:

GOING TO HOUSTON THRS AM

"Shay? Thank God. Corbin has been going out of his mind." Bonnie's first impulse was to hug her, but she recoiled from the smell of Shay's crusty hair.

"Do you still have water pressure?" asked Shay.

"Yes, but they're saying it might be contaminated. And there's no gas, so it's cold."

"I don't care. I just need soap and water. Please."

"C'mon out back." Bonnie called over her shoulder to the balcony, "Guy? Call Corbin. Tell him we have Shay."

Out on the potting porch, Shay stripped out of the tee-shirt and boxers volunteered by one of the Guard women and sat on an upturned bucket, hanging her fetid hair in front of her as Bonnie hosed her down with the garden sprayer and worked shampoo into her scalp.

"Oh, God," Shay said, "I just want to peel my skin off."

"With this sunburn, you'll get your wish," said Bonnie.

"My hair is never going to smell right again."

"You'll be fine. This is my sister Zenobia's homemade lemon soap."

Bonnie produced a large bar of plain white soap and two hand towels. While she scrubbed Shay's neck and back and arms, Shay scrubbed her privates and legs. They rinsed and repeated, wearing the white soap down to a crescent moon. Bonnie brought out a bowl of grapefruits and cut them in half. As Bonnie scrubbed her down, Shay's body stopped shaking, and that was a relief. The sudsy water and citrus seeds washed into the long drain channel that ran the length of the cement floor and dripped down into the courtyard.

"I don't know what stinks out here," said Bonnie. "It's not just you. I'm afraid maybe somebody's dog died." She rinsed Shay's hair again and sniffed delicately. "Maybe tomato juice. Like if you get sprayed by a skunk."

Bonnie went to the kitchen and came back with the tomato juice.

"No one came back to open the church parking lot," she said as she poured it over Shay's head. "Guy cut the fence and siphoned gas from the cars into the church's praise team bus. Last word we got was that people are being taken to the Astrodome, and FEMA is there, and I guess they're putting people in shelters."

"You and Guy can stay with my folks," said Shay.

"That wouldn't be awkward?"

"Why? Because you hate me?" Shay looked up through her tangled, Bloody Mary hair. "You just scrubbed my naked ass with a grapefruit, Bonnie. Staying in my parents' guest wing is no longer the gold standard for awkward."

"Guest *wing*?"

"Just go with it."

Bonnie hosed down Shay's hair and twisted it into a soggy knob at the back of her head.

"Stand," she said, and Shay stood.

Bonnie had harvested a good number of roses before the storm so she could keep a bucket of water and rose petals out in the sun. She ladled the warm rose water over Shay's head and shoulders, breasts and backside. Shay closed her eyes and let herself be baptized. Fresh, fragrant petals clung to her skin and scattered on the floor at her feet. This tender conclusion to the drawn-out process of her unstenching felt like ablution instead of decontamination. Shay gratefully dried herself with a beach towel from the clothesline, and Bonnie went to the laundry room and returned with faded crop jeans, a muslin peasant blouse and gardening clogs.

"Proof that I wasn't always shaped like Mrs. Potatohead," she said. "Feels like a thousand years ago."

"Sunday morning feels like a thousand years ago." Shay pulled on the jeans and blouse.

"Everybody decent?" Guy rapped on the door before coming out onto the porch.

"We're good," said Bonnie. "How many people are going on the bus?"

"About two dozen," said Guy. "We're almost out of food since all these additional people showed up. I put Zenobia in charge of rationing. Finding gas is gonna be the tough part. But you don't worry, baby. I'll get us there."

"Did you get through to Corbin?" Shay asked.

"No. We'll keep trying once we're on the road."

"We can't leave without him and Watts," said Bonnie.

"Baby, that freeway's gonna be an unholy mess," Guy said. "We need to get rolling now so we can make the whole way in daylight. Those two assholes can take care of themselves. You're the priority, here on out. You and the baby." He rubbed the small of her back. "Geezes, what is that smell? It's worse than yesterday."

"Did you check for Watts at Jimmy G's?" Bonnie fretted, her eyes exhausted and brimming. "What about Little Bill's? Was he at the poker game?"

"What..." Guy pushed his hands in his hip pockets. "What poker game?"

"Guy. I know you were there, and we got a ten-hour drive to discuss it. Right now, I want to know about Watts."

"He had a date," said Guy. "A girl he met on the internet. Do not tell him I told you. It's none of your business. But I got a text message from him yesterday, so..." Guy ducked his head and grinned. "Apparently, it was going good."

Bonnie rolled her eyes and said something Shay couldn't hear over the sound of her own pulse just below her eardrums. She pushed through the screen door, out into the morning mist and the unspeakable smell of the courtyard. She bunched the front of the borrowed blouse in her fist and pressed it under her nose as she approached a cloud of flies on the other side of the hydroponics wreckage.

Horrified understanding unfolded like a roadmap.

The computer. The credit card. The photograph.

Watts.

Shay took in the horribly wrong angle of his leg, the presence of the promotional item, what was left of his face.

It was Watts. It had always been Watts.

17

NEW ORLEANS

THURSDAY MORNING
SEPTEMBER 1

From: Fugate, Craig

To: William Carwile; Michael D Brown . \P*P

Cc: Deirdre Finn; Mr. Scott Morris

Sent: 9/1/05 5:42 AM

Subject: Good Morning

I'm out of water and ice from my stocks. I've directed
Mike DeLorenzo to start purchasing and shipping product
into the coastal Mississippi Counties. Not sure I have an
EMAC mission, but our folks on the ground have concerns if
they run out. Not sure how much and when, but will try to
keep you updated on progress.

If this works, will continue until told to stop. So far
we have only been shipping water and ice. No food or baby
products.

craig

Craig Fugate, Director

Florida Division of Emergency Management

From: William Carwile

Sent: Thursday, September 01. 2005 10:26 AM

To: Fugate, Craig; Brown, Michael D

Cc: Deirdre Finn; Mr. Scott Morris; Latham, Robert;
Lowder, Michael

Subject: RE: Good Morning

Craig:

You are doing the right thing. Thanks. Know Robert would
concur. Will police up paperwork later - you have my
guarantee.

Food is also critical. Need MRE and/or heater meals if you
have any. Water, ice, food in eastern counties should be
your priority. Recommend Allen coordinate with Red Cross
(TAG, MS) for integration into their distribution system.
Also, know FL is providing law enforcement. Need all you
can send. Public safety major concern (looting, etc.).

Have used Dixie Co. body bags (250) got more?

Thanks, old friend.

Bill

Corbin spent the night visiting the body repositories with the PA and slogged back to his office before first light on Thursday morning, heavyhearted, his brain replaying everything that wasn't being done and shouldn't have been done and couldn't be undone. Shay was only part of the overwhelming picture, but the immediacy of his need to know what happened to her felt like an open incision. Entering the building through a break in the plywood, Corbin paused at the bottom of the stairs, sorting out what he was hearing in hallway above him. Someone snoring. Gruff laughter. Corbin stood in the knee-deep swamp, unaccustomed to the two distinct feelings that cut through the heaviness in his chest: fear and indecision.

"Hey, man, how's it goin'?" asked a voice from above his head.

"Not well," said Corbin, stepping out of the water onto the stairs. "What's..." He wasn't sure how to finish it. What's happening? What's up? What's the dealio?

"C'mon up outta there. We're just hangin.'"

Scrolling methodically through the various options that fell on the spectrum between fight and flight, Corbin climbed the steps to the first landing. From there he could see that a small but functioning community had taken shape in the second-floor hallway in the twenty-eight hours since he'd gone out looking for Shay. He recognized the wall hanging and sofa from Kennet Insurance among the furnishings that also included side chairs, coffee tables, and rugs from other offices on the first few floors. Camp lanterns and candles created a lighted common area close to the top of the stairs, where three young black men sat in canvas chairs around a portable barbecue pit. Corbin smelled coffee, bacon, and eggs cooking and hunger struck him like a boot to the gut. He was uncomfortable confronting the reality that his reaction to the age and race of these men was just that visceral.

"Morning," he said, cautiously approaching the top of the stairs. From there, he could see their warehouse area stacked with boxes, bags and mounted merchandise.

"Man, you stink like a motherfucker," one of them said. "Need some dry shoes, dog?"

"I don't have any cash," Corbin lied.

"Don't worry about it. What size you need?"

"Thirteen."

The guy whistled through his teeth and said, "You got some big ass feet for a white man, my brother." And they all laughed as he hoisted out of the sling chair. "You run?"

"Yeah," said Corbin, who would probably have been running already had there been anywhere to run to.

"I got you covered."

He went to the warehouse area, perused a stack of shoe boxes, selected one with a Reebok logo. He went to another neatly piled aisle and came up with a package of athletic socks.

"You be runnin' like a fool in these here. Insta Pump Furies," he said, handing them to Corbin. "Gotta take care of the dogs, dog. Sit on down and get rid of them stank shoes. This is some toxic mother-fuckin' shit you been walkin' in. Man, you don't wanna know."

"Thank you," said Corbin.

"You look low down, dog. Lose somebody?"

Corbin nodded. Around the campfire, there was a low, mumbled condolence.

"I don't suppose you could spare some coffee," said Corbin.

The man tending the grill opened a Hallmark giftbox and withdrew a mug scripted with the words "This is the day the Lord has made!" under a pastel rainbow.

"With or without Baileys?"

"With, please," said Corbin.

He pulled off his stank shoes and seaweed socks and let his feet dry while they drank their coffee and ate eggs and bacon, talking sad, head-shaking talk about what they'd seen in their journeys so far and what they might see in these streets over the coming days, weeks, months. The coming years. Hoarse from hacking and coughing on the stench of the flood, their raspy voices echoed in the lobby like a dour company of trolls talking in the bottom of a well.

"Yesterday, some dude down here from New York offered me a job collecting architectural features. Door knobs, hinges, stained glass windows, everything like that. Said he'll sell that shit at flea markets up north and make a hundred grand before Christmas. Said he could make two hundred if he had some good help."

"Town's getting' raped while we sit here."

"Not one thing you can do about it."

"I got to get mine is all I know. I took my wife and baby up to my sister in Texarkana before the storm. Me and my brother-in-law came back with his Hummer, laid out a route—pawn shops, sporting goods, WalMart. Already got stuff on Ebay. Holiday season, we'll make good money at gun shows all over Texas. Hey, I ain't saying it's right, but somebody was gonna do it."

"Might as well be a man who's taking care of family instead of doing drugs and runnin' with gangs and shit."

"Insurance'll cover it. It's not like you're robbing from people."

Corbin finished his coffee and pulled on the clean socks and shoes.

"Thanks for your hospitality," he said. "Good luck to you."

Handshakes were offered from around the circle.

"Hope things work out for you, dog."

In the dark stairwell, Corbin's phone chimed with an incoming call: UNKNOWN NUMBER.

"Shay?"

"I know where she is," said the voice on the other end. "Have you got cash?"

Corbin clicked off. Since he started leaving his number on plywood windows, dumpsters, and bus stops around town, he'd heard from a dozen fake Shays, several people claiming to have her body and several others offering to locate her for a price. Sea monsters and night crawlers were out now, as ubiquitous and single-minded and attracted to ruin as roaches.

As Corbin entered the fifteenth-floor stairwell, his cell chimed again.

"Shay?"

"It's Christa. The National Guard has her."

"Oh, Jesus." Corbin leaned on the wall, breathing for the first time in ten hours. "Is she okay?"

"She's fine. Dehydrated, but still the irrepressible Sunshine Girl." Christa took a dry, sifting drag on her cigarette. "Renny asked her to do a segment, and she said she's saving herself for Anderson Cooper."

"Thanks for letting me know."

"The Guard is clearing the city. Algiers. French Quarter. Everything. If you're trying to connect with people, Houston's the place. I'm staying here. Jonas is covering I-10 and the Astrodome. If you want to catch a ride, you can roll out with the crew at noon."

"Thanks. I appreciate it."

"Look, I know you and Shay have a history," said Christa. "I may have come off a bit cold last night. All's well that ends well, right?"

"Right," he said. "Christa, I should conserve my cell battery."

"You said it yourself, Corbin. An unsentimental, technically proficient eye."

"Good luck to you, Christa."

Back in his office, Corbin collected a few small but expensive bits of equipment, jump drives with his client files, a change of clothes and his passport in a leather backpack. Up on the roof, he secured all the connections and the solar collector in hopes of keeping the webcam operating after the generator died. His cell chimed in his pocket. The caller ID said BONNIE CELL, but when he answered, he heard Guy breathing hard, choking on sorrow.

"Doc... Watts is dead."

It was like stepping on a broken bottle: a bright flash of agony, followed by sickening realization. Corbin saw exactly what had happened, saw with searing clarity what he should have seen from the beginning, everything Shay had no way of knowing as she formed her airtight impeachment of Guy.

Twenty hours earlier, floating over the fractured angels and open graves, Corbin had passed the point of consolation. There was no emotional vocabulary to encompass it. Loss of that caliber became a concept. Subject to semantics. Prone to round numbers. Seen from a thirty-thousand-foot view, it was mapped like a geological survey after a tsunami. But now, the death of his friend knifed through the vast, dreamlike drowning of New Orleans. It was precise and cruel to the bone, and it was a relief, weirdly, like a hole drilled in the skull to relieve pressure. For the first time since he saw it all coming in the turbid oracle of the satellite feed, Corbin clamped his hand over his mouth and cried.

18

HOUSTON

FRIDAY MORNING
SEPTEMBER 2

From: Worthy, Sharon

Sent: Friday, September 2, 2005 10:17 AM

To: Brown, Michael D

Subject: Your shirt

Please roll up the sleeves of your shirt…all shirts. Even
the President rolled his sleeves up to just below the
elbow. In this crises and on TV you just need to look more
hard-working…ROLL UP THE SLEEVES!

"Austin-Seybold. Winnie Austin-Seybold, please report to the pharmacy."

Before she was fully conscious, Shay was on her feet, unkempt and sweaty in Bonnie's old garden togs, her heart upturned and pounding like she'd been awakened with jumper cables.

"Houston welcomes you. Please remember that the Reliant Center is a nonsmoking facility. Sidwell, Arthur Sidwell, please return to the intake center for a lost item…"

It was early. The lights were still low, most of the cots still occupied with sleeping evacuees, but a few people were stirring, speaking quietly, carrying their plastic toiletry bags to and from the shower lines. A generic voice on the PA system recited and repeated a hypnotic stream of names and announcements.

"Hoovestahl, Shay Hoovestahl, please meet your party at staging area C… Austin-Seybold. Winnie Austin-Seybold, please report to the pharmacy… Sidwell, Arthur Sidwell, please return to the intake center for a lost item… Houston welcomes you. Please remember that the Reliant Center is a nonsmoking facility… La Pierre, Kenya La Pierre, please meet your party at the intake center…"

Since she arrived at the Reliant Center, Shay had been watching people find each other, shrieking in harmony, crashing together, holding on for dear life. But those were families and lovers, people who knew for whom they were waiting and why. Approaching Staging Area C, she wanted to run, but she wasn't sure in which direction. She'd watched Guy's face when he was on the phone with Corbin the day before. She'd stood very still, thinking Corbin would ask to speak to her, but that didn't happen. Guy hung up and said, "He said to tell you he'd be in Houston Friday morning."

"Dubois, Octavia Dubois, please return to the clinic for an important message…"

Corbin didn't call out or move toward her. Just watched her walk the long alley between rows of rumpled cots. When Shay finally stood in front of him, breathing the same air again, they studied each other's dry eyes, looking for someone lost.

"You owe me a beer," said Corbin.

Shay wanted to laugh, but her body couldn't quite remember how laughter worked. Like a cough, she thought, but she was afraid if she coughed, something black and unspeakable would come out of her throat. She stepped into his arms without answering.

Looking past her shoulder, Corbin watched the weary tide of people shifting and flowing through the arena. The cavernous space was muted with shell-shock. He was keenly aware of all that he still had: promise and premise that made going forward possible, a home and work to return to. Few people in the room were so fortunate. Grief and gratitude warred in him. Hope and bereavement. Corbin bit down on his back teeth, taking deep, ragged breaths, holding Shay hard, saying thank God over and over as he kissed her forehead, face, and salty neck. She smelled earthy and sweaty and tired, but on her skin, there was a faint scent of roses.

"Let's get out of here," she said. "Daddy sent me a car."

Out on the sweltering street, people waited in long lines to be processed into the shelter. Beet red volunteers from local churches, temples, and mosques wore bright yellow "Operation Compassion" T-shirts and pushed beverage carts down the sidewalk, doling out water bottles, juice boxes, handfuls of ice.

"My parents' home is in the Woodlands, about an hour north," said Shay. "Or there's our beach house in Galveston, about an hour south."

"We'll be on multiple shit lists if we go south," said Corbin, "starting with your dad and Bonnie."

Shay nodded. "South it is."

Down the block, behind a long line of buses was Shay's new car, a little red Mercedes-Benz Roadster. Water bottles and sunglasses had been thoughtfully deposited in the center armrest. She inserted her smart key, and the driver's seat and steering wheel eased into conformance with her personal specs already on the hard drive.

"Geezes. It's like a spy car," said Corbin.

"It'll get me from point A to point B," Shay said, equal parts smug and guilty, spoiled rotten and dearly loved. She dropped the retractable hardtop and thumbed her father's cell.

"Hey, Daddy. I'm in the Roadster. Thank you so much. I love it. No, no, I'm fine to drive. Really, Daddy, I can drive myself. Daddy, I know how to drive. Listen—I need some private time. I'm going down to the beach house for a few days. Tell Mommi I'll check on Namma and be home soon. Not that soon. Next week. Hey, did she take Bonnie to the obstetrician?" Shay gave Corbin a thumbs up for the healthy baby report. "No, don't come down, please. That defeats the purpose of private time. I just need a few days by myself. I will, I promise. B'bye. Wait! Daddy?" She sighed and said to the empty cell phone, "I love you."

"Mind if I turn on the TV?" Corbin asked.

"Knock yourself out," she said. "But we're keeping the top down."

The TV was preset to CNN. President Bush was speaking from the tarmac of a cracked and sodden airport somewhere in Alabama. Corbin cranked the volume and leaned closer.

"…faith-based groups and the community-based groups through-out this part of the world—and the country for that matter—are responding. If you wanna—wanna help… give cash money to the Red Cross and the Salvation Army. That's where the first help will come. There's going to be plenty of opportunities to help later on, but right now the immediate concern is to save lives and get food and medicine to people so we can stabilize the situation. Uh… again, I want to thank you all for—and Brownie, you're doing a heck of a job!"

"*Fuh!*" Corbin pushed his thumb knuckle against the bridge of his nose and muttered something Shay didn't try to hear.

"The FEMA Director is working twenty-four—they're working twenty-four hours a day. Again, my attitude is, if it's not going exactly right, we're going to make it go exactly right. If there's problems, we're going to address the problems."

"If there's problems?" Corbin barked a sharp laugh. "Ya think?"

"And… and that—and that's what I've come down to assure people…. of. And again, I want to thank everybody. Uh… uh… and I'm not looking forward to this trip. I got a feel for it when I flew over before. It—for those who have not—it can't do—ah, trying to conceive what we're talking about. It's as if the entire Gulf Coast were obliterated by a… uh… the worst kinda weapon you can imagine. And now we're gonna go try to comfort people in that part of the world. Thank you."

"That part of the world," Corbin echoed. "It's not Rwanda, asshole, it's Louisiana."

"Corbin. Please." Shay flipped the TV into the dashboard and punched up the satellite radio. "We'll be drowning in coverage for the next three months. Let's take a minute, okay?"

Corbin squeezed the back of his neck, watching the city go by. "This might be a mistake, Shay. I'm not very good company right now."

"Nothing feels right today," she said. "Let's just do what's necessary."

"What about tomorrow?"

"When the adrenaline wears off, we'll be too tired to give a crap."

They stopped at Target for a brief wardrobe of serviceable clothes and underwear. Corbin picked up his standard cargo shorts and white shirts. Shay took ten easy summer dresses off the rack without trying them. Leaving their dirty clothes on the fitting-room floors, they offered themselves with Shay's credit card at the counter and went out to the car with tags fluttering from the backs of their necks.

"Laptops," said Shay, swinging into the Best Buy parking lot. "No shopping. Just get two of the most expensive one while I pick up the peripherals."

Corbin did as he was told, glad that Shay shared his basic definition of necessity: food, shelter, computer. Ten minutes later, they were back on the road, their purchases in the trunk of the Roadster. As she ramped back onto the freeway, she said, "Let's plan to camp out at the beach until Nagin reopens the CBD. That puts a nice, logical egg-timer on it."

"That'll be two or three weeks. At least. It could be a month."

171

She flashed a sideways smile. "We'll be okay if we spend most of our time in bed."

It was hot, but they drove with the top down as they surfed the traffic out of the city. Shay needed to feel the speed and the sun, and Corbin was grateful to make the trip without talking. She slowed some when the air started to feel salty, and he sensed her shifting gears. A sea change.

"This is where I always get that almost-there feeling," she said.

They cruised onto the palm-lined boulevard and passed the same brightly painted Victorian houses and crummy Nixon-era apartments she'd passed when she was a little girl. She turned onto Seawall Boulevard and headed out along the shore, past the surf shops and fishing piers and the souvie stores that sold cheap Mexican necklaces and coconut heads and painted hermit crabs.

They stopped at a convenience store on San Luis Pass Road and wandered the cramped aisles, not knowing what to pick up or why. Shay gathered Diet Coke, Tylenol, and condoms. Corbin took apples, butter, bread, eggs, and a bottle of Jim Beam. He took a Houston Chronicle off the rack. She scanned a rack of paperbacks, selecting an Elmore Leonard novel.

"Revelatory," Shay said, looking over their respective purchases. "C'mon. Let's go be beach bums."

They passed the state park, and the road dropped closer to the coastline. Shay pulled into a picturesque little neighborhood and stopped in front of an Edwardian bungalow.

"I need to check on my grandmother," she said. "Sit tight. I'll call you if she wants to meet you."

Shay bounded up the porch steps and disappeared inside the screen door for a few minutes, then came back to report, "The nurse says Namma's a little out of it today."

She knew that last stretch from her earliest childhood memories, the quiet mile or so between her grandmother's bungalow and the beach house. The seaside picnic shelters, weathered condos, and cloistered mansions all jumbled together. The lifting gulls and tufted sand grass, always changing but never different. A sleepy peace always came over her as soon as her beloved house on stilts came into view.

Corbin whistled softly as she turned down the palm-lined drive. "One of us is unclear about the meaning of beach bum."

Shay pulled into the wide garage between the jet skis and fishing boat. From there, wooden stairs and short boardwalk extended down over the shifting dunes to the front porch, where thorny bougainvillea climbed out of enormous pots beside the arched windows of the Spanish multi-level. Shay bypassed the front door, and Corbin followed her into a breezeway that wrapped around the house and stepped down to a flagstone patio out back. The airy lanai was tinted with the sound of wind chimes and the scent of Char Hoovestahl's potted herb garden. Beyond the lanai, a wide cedar deck looked out over the Gulf of Mexico.

Corbin piled their bags on the wrought-iron and marble patio table and went to the boardwalk that extended along the dunes. He took the wooden steps dropping down to the bleached brown sand, walked a few paces, then broke to a loping run. Shay took their purchases inside and went around the kitchen, breakfast nook, and great room, turning on ceiling fans and opening blinds to let in the daylight. She cracked open a Diet Coke and went to the pantry to inventory the nonperishable supplies.

She heard Corbin come in and turned to ask if he was hungry, but he pulled her ponytail back and put his mouth to her neck, groping her, wrangling her dress up. A few plain words were spoken. Shay appreciated the blunt exchange the way she appreciated that first water bottle in the rescue boat and the white bar soap on the potting porch. What was needed. Nothing squanderous like foreplay, no profligate talking. He tore her panties and got her hips onto the kitchen counter, supporting her open thighs as if he were pushing a wheelbarrow. The utilitarian nature of the act reminded Shay of an MRE. She was labeled HUMAN, it was labeled RELIEF. Corbin clutched her to his chest when he came, and when he could breathe again, he thanked her and offered to do something for her, but it seemed like a chore.

"Let's just find some food," Shay said, and they wordlessly did that.

More than anything right now, she wanted to get in the bathtub, scrub her skin, wring out her muscles, reduce herself to powder-white bone. She was achingly grateful for the nearness of that moment when she would lie down on clean, white linens in a clean, quiet room, reach out her clean, dry hand, and turnoff the light.

She made the bathwater lukewarm because of her sunburn and sank into the oversized tub in the master suite, looking out the bay window at the Gulf of Mexico.

Long before baby McKecknie came along, Shay used to play in this big tub in the evenings while her mother sat at the vanity mirror, teasing her hair huge and touching up her lips. Before she changed from her crisp white beachcombers to a summer-colored cocktail dress, she'd come to the side of the tub and work shampoo through Shay's hair and wash under her arms and dry her off. When Char left for the evening, there was always a faint whiff of Johnson's baby powder slightly to one side of her expensive perfume.

Corbin rapped lightly on the open door.

"Yup," Shay said without opening her eyes.

He took a long, hot shower, then knelt beside the tub, scrubbing the bridge of her nose, the nape of her neck, her jawline, all aspects of each ear. He spread her fingers and worked each knuckle, blotted her lacerated shins and skinned knees. He worked a washcloth between her toes, cupped fresh water between her legs, then helped her out of the tub and dried her with a white towel. They lay far apart on the king size bed, staring up at the ceiling fan, fading in and out of sweaty, disjointed sleep. A gull cried outside, and Shay jolted upright, heart racing.

"Oh, God. I can't get—I have to…"

Corbin laid his hand on her leg and murmured, "You're fine."

Shay curled up against his body and pulled his arm across her middle.

"I keep dreaming about that goddang cat," she said. "I don't even know the cat's name. I never signed up to take care of a cat. I thought it would be cruel to leave it out in the storm. Now, I can't stop seeing how it must have…" Shay shook her head. "Maybe it found a way out."

"No," said Corbin. "It's dead."

Oddly, Shay found his cold response kinder than the rosy lie she'd been trying to tell herself. It freed her from the sunshine story about the miraculous cat; that was not the story they were part of now.

Corbin was troubled that his brain felt so blunted, unwilling to process the exponential consequences of all the small details that kept rewinding in his mind. The cat on the refrigerator and mice scuttling onto the ruffled pillows vectored to elderly people abandoned by caregivers, to uncounted denizens of the Ninth Ward scrambling into their attics only to find they were entombed there as water rose over the rooftops. The shortage of body bags and ice, the endless march of rats over every unflooded cobblestone in the French Quarter. His throat ached with equations, cubic tons of debris, depths, and measures of measureless things.

"Where do you supposed Queen Mab is now?" Shay wondered.

"Houston. Or Dallas. She could have gone east to Atlanta."

"Maybe she'll book a flight using Watts' credit card. That would be perfect. We'd know exactly—"

Corbin rolled away from her and sat up with his feet on the floor.

"I need a drink," he said stiffly.

Shay pulled on a blue silk kimono from her mother's closet, made a cup of chamomile tea for herself, and poured a highball glass of bourbon for Corbin. The soles of her feet were exquisitely tender on the flagstones. She lit citronella candles to keep the mosquitoes down, and they sat talking quietly through the night, comparing notes, telling each other their storm stories. The only thing Corbin left out was the moment with Christa. Shay told him everything except the last thing she did with the pool cue. Each of them sensed a deliberate omission, but they both knew it was something they didn't want to know and let it go.

"You would have been proud of Guy," said Shay. "He was the undisputed captain of our lifeboat. He was on a network news segment about renegade buses coming out of New Orleans. One look at the tattoos and Jesus hair, and the cameras were all over him. Meanwhile, I sat on the ground snarfing a hot dog. How's that for irony?"

"How long did it take you to get there?"

"About eleven hours, but when we got to the Astrodome in a stolen bus, they wouldn't let us in. Authorized vehicles only. We just sat there for a while, not knowing what to do, and then the most amazing thing happened." Shay cradled her teacup between her hands. "People came out of the neighborhoods, dragging grills and little red wagons and garden carts loaded with water, food, blankets. We were hungry, and they fed us. No questions. No politics. Nothing but 'Love thy neighbor' human kindness. I hope stories like that make it through the noise."

Corbin smiled and said, "That sounds suspiciously sunshine-like."

"I guess it does."

"It was good of your folks to come down for Bonnie and Guy," said Corbin.

"Daddy was already at the Reliant Center, washing dishes in the cafeteria. Mommi and her church ladies were doing pedicures for women at the Astrodome. Pedicures and Bible study. That's Char Hoovestahl."

Eventually, Shay went back to bed, hoping Corbin would follow, but he stayed outside. From the dark bedroom, she watched him for a long time, pacing, studying the tide as the haze came up and dawn hinted. He gazed at the muted television over the bar on the lanai. Watery light shifted and flickered on his skin, reflected images of the ruined city. Corbin rocked on the edge of the chaise, pushing the heels of his hands against his eyes, his shoulders heaving unevenly.

In the hazy white hour before sunrise, he finally came inside. Shay remained perfectly still and pretended she'd been sleeping when he pulled the sheet off her and dragged her hips to the edge of the mattress. Corbin moved a chair over so he could devote the necessary patience without putting pressure on his bruised ribcage. He nosed her legs apart, pulled her to his open mouth and wouldn't let her give up until a dense orgasm broke over her.

They worked at some of their old methodology, but he was so weary now, all he really wanted was to lay on top of her and get it over with. When he was almost there, he felt Shay's strong hand on the back of his head. She held him mouth to mouth, and Corbin felt flooded with breath, a drowning man surfacing, taking life back into his lungs. He wanted to tell her then what she meant to him, but he didn't know how, so he thought he should tell her that, but in the end, all he could say was her name and "don't move."

Shay slept after that, dead to the world, dead to dreaming. Corbin lay next to her, remote control in hand, bloodshot eyes riveted to the 24/7 news cycle.

19

GALVESTON

SATURDAY MORNING
SEPTEMBER 3

** WTNT44 KNHC 032038 ***

TCDAT4

TROPICAL STORM MARIA DISCUSSION NUMBER 10

NWS TPC/NATIONAL HURRICANE CENTER MIAMI FL

5 PM EDT SAT SEP 03 2005

THERE HAS BEEN AN INCREASE IN ORGANIZATION DURING THE DAY.
THE CENTER IS WELL EMBEDDED WITHIN THE DEEP CONVECTION AND
THERE IS A WELL-DEFINED CONVECTIVE CURVED BAND WRAPPING
AROUND THE CENTER. THE OUTFLOW HAS BECOME ESTABLISHED
AND LATEST MICROWAVE DATA SHOWS THAT MARIA IS DEVELOPING
AN INNER CORE. OBJECTIVE T-NUMBERS HAVE BEEN AVERAGING
AROUND 4.2 ON THE DVORAK SCALE. INITIAL INTENSITY HAS BEEN
INCREASED TO 60 KNOTS. AN ENVIRONMENT OF LOW SHEAR AND A
WARM OCEAN IS AHEAD OF MARIA...

 FORECASTER AVILA

$$

Sometime around noon, Shay stirred and kissed Corbin's elbow. "Hey there."

"Hey," he said in a way that sounded like "be quiet" more than "good morning."

NBC's Brian Williams, on location in New Orleans, tasked an increasingly badger-on-the-freeway Michael Brown about why the helicopters and Black Hawks flying over the city couldn't lower water and MREs to people trapped and suffering on the roofs of abandoned buildings.

"The federal government just learned about those people today," said Brown. "I've gotta tell ya, we are gonna move Heaven and Earth to get food and water to those people."

"Whatthefuckever," Corbin growled.

"I've watched all day long," Brown complained, "the stories of people who are causing trouble, who are, you know, screaming and yelling about things and just being thugs. And then I hear about this group today, and I told my team, I don't care what it takes. You get stuff to them and you get it to them now."

"But you know," Williams said wearily, "you had twenty thousand, thirty thousand absolutely miserable people in the Astrodome with no basic human needs."

"*Super*dome." Shay tossed a pillow at the screen. "The Astrodome is in Houston, and they have all the comforts of home, including my mother."

"Cut him some slack," Corbin said. "They've got a tough job over there."

"Oh, now you're defending the media vultures?" she said with some amusement.

"No, but Williams is one of the good ones."

Shay rolled out of bed, thirsty and stiff, went to the bathroom, washed her hands, and brushed her teeth, puffy-eyed and aching, but consciously grateful for the stinging clean water in the tap. She opened the drapes and cracked the patio door to let in the daylight air and monotonous white noise of one breaking wave following another. Then she climbed back in bed and kissed Corbin's bruised ribs and warm belly, lowering on him like a fogbank, encouraging his morning wood. He breathed something appreciative. Williams moved on to task Brown about the Convention Center evacuation.

"Give us some hope," he said. "When?"

"That's actually moving along pretty darn well," said Brown.

Corbin crowed in disbelief. "Geezes, this guy. Bush rolls FEMA into Homeland Security, sucks that funding into his war chest, and plugs in this yes man who doesn't know the difference. Now they're like, National Guard? Oh, sorry, they're busy in Iraq."

"The Guard is doing an amazing job," said Shay.

"What's left of them, yes."

"Their lives have been upended," Brown said dolefully. "They have nothing. They have no place to go."

"This guy doesn't know shit about disaster management," said Corbin, "and Bush doesn't give a crap about anything except dick swinging and oil money."

"You want to blame Bush for every fire ant hill and cancerous mole in America," Shay murmured against his hip bone. "This could have been prevented by Clinton."

"Or Reagan or Bush 41."

"Or your personal Jesus, Jimmy Carter."

"We're going to take care of them," said Brown. "That's me talking. That's the president talking. That's the entire country talking."

"Too much talking," said Shay.

Corbin muted the TV, and she lay on top of him like a lazy hunting dog. He moved his hands over her, relearning the muscles that defined her back.

There was a sudden jangle from the cowbell that dangled on the front door. Shay heard her father's voice booming from the foyer.

"Where's my blueberry?"

Shay swore, scrambled out of bed, threw on the kimono, and spritzed herself liberally with perfume from the vanity. She sprinted for the hallway, slamming the bedroom door behind her, calling, "Daddy! Gosh. What a surprise."

Bob Hoovestahl stood in the kitchen, customary ten gallon hat on his head, canvas grocery totes looped over his wrists.

"You brought food. You're so sweet." Shay took the bags and set them on the counter, took his hat and hung it on the little antelope antler rack next to the pantry door. "Well. Wow. You, um… here you are."

"Don't get your Irish up. I won't stay long. Had to lay eyes on my little girl." He swept her into a bear hug and pressed kisses to the crown of her head, murmuring, "Here's my blueberry. Everything's okay now. I got my cupcake."

Shay's arms didn't quite reach around his middle, but she hugged as much of him as she could, breathing in the familiar smell of dry-cleaned suit and new car interior, surprised to realize how much she needed this feeling and feeling a little stupid about trying so hard to act like she didn't.

"It's good to see you, Daddy," she said around a sudden lump in her throat.

"Let me look at you." He held her at arm's length and nodded. "You look like you got a story to tell."

"Yeah," Shay laughed thinly.

"Christ almighty, Shay. I about tore down the walls. That about killed me."

"I know. I'm so sorry."

He blinked and cleared his throat. "I'm proud of you, Shay. You stayed strong."

"Oh, Daddy, I didn't. If you hadn't been with me—and not just on the phone—"

"When we heard from the Guard command that they had you—"

"How's Mommi? Is she okay?"

"She's worried about you being down here all by yourself." He tapered off, looking past her shoulder. "Well. I see she didn't need to fret."

"Good morning, Mr. Hoovestahl."

Corbin was barefoot, and his hair was wet, but he looked somewhat respectable in a fresh white shirt with the sleeves rolled up just below his elbows.

"Daddy," said Shay in proper Junior League form, "may I present Dr. Corbin Thibodeaux of EarthWeather Analytics in New Orleans."

"I know who he is," her father said curtly.

"Corbin," she persevered, "my father, Mr. Robert Hoovestahl of Hoovestahl TransGlobal and Gulf Coast Luxury Transport in Houston. Daddy, Corbin. Corbin, Daddy. My father. Bob."

"Pleased to meet you, sir." Corbin extended his hand, but Shay's father left him hanging.

"Just happened to stop by, Dr. Thibodeaux?"

"I invited Corbin to hang out with me for a few weeks," said Shay. "Till things get squared away back home."

"Hang out," her father echoed.

"Yes."

"Well," he said darkly. "You're a grown woman, Shay. I guess you don't have to explain yourself to me."

"I don't intend to, Daddy. I'm just giving you the information."

Hoovestahl folded his arms over his ample midsection. Awkward silence smoldered. Shay excused herself to slip into something more appropriate.

"Have a seat, Dr. Thibodeaux," said Hoovestahl.

Corbin shuffled to the kitchen table and sat opposite the obvious captain's chair. Before Hoovestahl sat, he opened a narrow door at the top of the ornate sideboard and brought out a bottle of Glenfiddich and two shot glasses.

"A little early," he said, "but I think it might serve the greater good."

"Won't argue with you there, sir."

Shay's father poured the shots, nudged Corbin's glass across the table and wafted his own under his nose.

"I'm familiar with your work, Dr. Thibodeaux. I'd hire you myself if you weren't intent on being a thorn in my side, vilifying me in the media and what not."

"I'll take that as a compliment. Thank you, sir."

Corbin threw back the shot of Glenfiddich, and it slapped him upside the head like a bare-naked lady.

"Holy hell," he rasped. "That is good."

"Thirty year old single malt. Three hundred dollars a bottle," said Hoovestahl, reaching across the table to fill Corbin's glass again. "Considered a sipping whiskey in polite company."

"I hear ya." Corbin nodded, blinking back the raw ecstasy in his tear ducts.

Shay returned to the kitchen, hair combed into a smooth ponytail, demeanor as bright and modest as her yellow summer dress.

"Daddy, how's Bonnie? Is she well?"

"Well enough, considering what she's been through," he said. "Guy's already set to work rebuilding my 1970 Suzuki Honcho."

There was another heavy silence as Shay ground coffee beans and started a kettle of water for the French press. Corbin and Hoovestahl sipped their whiskey.

"Corbin's done a lot of fascinating things with his work," said Shay. "He used to be on a team that flew airplanes directly into hurricanes."

"Why would a person do a jackass thing like that?" said her father.

Corbin smiled. "I was in the Navy, so I pretty much did like I was told."

"It was very brave, important work," Shay gushed. "They gathered data that revolutionized storm track forecasting."

Corbin shifted uncomfortably. He was used to being oversold by Bonnie, but he would have preferred that Shay not feel the need for it.

"Navy man, huh?" said Hoovestahl.

"Yup." Corbin nodded.

"Former Marine, myself. But I'm a fan of the Navy. When there's a job to be done, you fellas always give us a ride. OORAH!" he added heartily.

Corbin smiled tightly and politely sipped his whiskey, as if he hadn't heard that line a thousand times since *A Few Good Men*.

"Tell me, Dr. Thibodeaux, what's your take on this Tropical Depression Maria? Boys on one of my Atlantic rigs are getting nervous."

"Last I was able to check, she was moving pretty good about midway between Cape Verde and the Lesser Antilles," said Corbin, relaxing a little. This was his comfort zone: whiskey in hand, talking about the weather. "It's a significant storm, but nothing out of the ordinary for this time of year. I think people are skittish because of Katrina. Hurricanes don't usually get this much network face time."

"So, in your expert opinion, we're looking at another hurricane?"

"Possibly. She's got some warm water and an interesting set of pressure variables to work with. As soon as Shay and I set up our office space, I'd be glad to look into it and help you out any way I can."

"And what would that cost me?" asked Hoovestahl.

"How about one more kick in the head? We'll call it even." Corbin grinned affably and slid his empty shot glass across the table.

Shay cleared her throat daintily, trying to communicate to him that he was being tested, but he just smiled at her like a happy, beef-headed puppy.

Hoovestahl filled the glass, slid it back.

"Why don't we settle a C-note on it?" he said. "When, where, and category. I'll bet you a hundred dollars this ol' country boy calls it as close or closer than you with your PhD."

Corbin tented his fingers over his glass and said, "I'll pass."

"Afraid to stick your neck out?"

"No, sir, but I don't make judgments without proper data. And I don't game on things that kill people."

"Daddy, Corbin is very serious about his work," said Shay. "Just like you."

"So I see," said her father. "Serious about anything else, Dr. Thibodeaux?"

"I'm not sure I get your meaning."

"My meaning's pretty clear, I think."

"No, sir, actually, it's not."

"I'm well aware how you've been sniffing around my daughter off and on for four years. Now you're shacked up with her here at my beach home. A man your age. Never married. What am I supposed to think?"

"I wouldn't presume to tell you," said Corbin. "Think whatever you like."

"I think you've been mighty casual with my daughter's time, and now you're mooching off her money."

"Shut up, Daddy," Shay said abruptly. "That whole act is so tired."

Unsettled by the flat cast of her voice, Corbin felt a surprising shot of empathy for her old man. Hoovestahl's neck flushed scarlet above his shirt collar.

"Corbin," said Shay, "weren't you going for a run up the beach?"

Corbin pushed back from the table, figuring it was the better part of valor.

"Pleasure meeting you, Mr. Hoovestahl. I sincerely appreciate your kindness to my family. And you should know, sir, I have a lot of respect for your daughter. She's an extraordinary woman."

Hoovestahl wafted his whiskey under his nose. "Enjoy your day, Dr. Thibodeaux."

As Corbin went out across the patio and down the boardwalk, he heard Shay's father excoriating her in good ol' boy basso profundo.

"Well, this is a hell of an eyeful for the neighborhood, isn't it, Miss Don't Give a Goddamn? Cheapening yourself with that boozy liberal swamp hound. Don't even try to bring that socialist son of a bitch up home. I will not be affronted and deceived in a house I bought and paid for."

Corbin walked to the water and followed the shoreline. The Hoovestahl house and a few other swanky dwellings shared a neatly manicured private beach, but in the public area further on, people were allowed to drive trucks and sport vehicles through the tide pools. There was trash tangled in the seaweed and stray beer cans by the low dunes. Corbin pulled a plastic grocery bag from under a dead seagull, collected as much manmade debris as he could stuff into it, and deposited it in a garbage barrel chained to a piling under a beachside bar.

He clambered up the riprap seawall that armored the shore-line with broken concrete and construction debris, crossed the long boardwalk that connected the front porch to the two-lane road, and bought a beer at the long mahogany bar. Out back, at the end of the long fishing pier, there was an old-timey coin-operated binocular unit. Periodically, children ran up, parents and nannies scolding after them, to climb on the heavy metal base, plug in their quarters, and swing the bulky viewer toward the Gulf. Dolphins were spotted, boats followed, topless sunbathers spied upon.

Corbin sat on a bench and rolled his beer bottle between his hands, thinking about the year Watts got his driver's license, loaded all his sisters and the Thibodeaux boys into his Dodge Duster on the last day of school, and they all camped out under a railroad trestle by some bayou. They'd jumped, one by one, into a deep spot between the pilings.

The drop seemed like an immense height, an enormous act of courage, but it was probably only ten or twelve feet in reality. Watts missed the deep spot and gashed the heck out of his leg on a submerged cypress knee.

It was one of those things that scared the shit out of everybody at the time, but they laughed about it in retrospect, when it had passed into legend with the Everclear and the burning sofa. Corbin flinched as the memory was invaded by the sickening thought of Watts rotting in the courtyard. He had to physically shake his head to keep the two bloody images separate.

Hooking his phone from his pocket, he hit Guy's cell.

"Corbin." Bonnie answered after one ring. "Where are you?"

"I'm in Galveston with Shay," he said. "How ya holding up, belle soeur?"

"I'm okay," said Bonnie. "Thank God for Char Hoovestahl. I was completely beat down when we got here. Couldn't stop crying. This total stranger takes me in, treats me like one of her own, takes me to the best obstetrician in Houston, sits up talking with me till all hours. She's so gracious and kind and has this amazing faith in the goodness of the world. Bob is this big jolly salt-of-the-earth type. He took Guy right under his wing. Got him working on a bike, which is the best therapy. I hope Shay knows how lucky she is. And I don't mean the swimming pool."

"Shay has her family issues, same as anybody," said Corbin, dropping a quarter in the binocular unit, swinging the viewer toward the beach house half a mile down the shore. Bob Hoovestahl sat in an Adirondack chair on the deck. Shay paced nearby. The conversation looked strongly animated. Lots of gesticulations on both sides.

"Can I talk to Guy?"

"He's out in the garage," said Bonnie. "He's pissed off at me because he cried last night, and I guess I was supposed to pretend like I didn't hear. He feels responsible for Watts. Says if he'd looked out for Watts like you looked out for him, Watts would still be alive."

"That's bullcrap. It's not his fault, it's..." Corbin set his jaw, eyes fixed on the line where the Gulf met the sky. "Just tell him that's bull."

"He needs to hear it from his big brother," said Bonnie. "You two should come up for a visit. Char would like to meet you."

"I don't see that happening, and I wish y'all would leave me out of the conversation up there."

"Corbin, they already knew. Char told me Shay's father had a background check done on you three years ago."

As Corbin absorbed that, the binoculars timed out, and the viewer blinked off.

"I told them you're a good man," said Bonnie. "And you are. You lose your way every once in a while and say idiot things, but only because you believe so hard in what you believe. You're good in your soul, and you'll keep it together now, won't you, Corbin? I can't lose another big brother."

Her voice choked with tears, and the sound provoked a lump in Corbin's throat.

"Belle soeur," he mumbled lamely. "C'mon. Don't cry."

"It's all you now, beau frère. You're all the uncles Baby T gets. He won't have Watts to look up to the way I did growing up. My big brother who could do no wrong, always fixed everything that needed fixing, made us talk straight and take the high road. After you left for the Navy, Watts made Guy grow up and be a man for me. Helped him start a business that gave him something to be. Now that's burned to the ground. Watts is dead. New Orleans is gone." She caught a deep hiccup of breath. "Corbin, I don't know how we get home from here."

"Christ, Bonnie, I'm so sorry. I'm sorry, belle soeur."

Hearing her weep, Corbin reached for anything comforting—platitudes, resolve, silver lining. He had nothing for her, and he couldn't bring himself to tell her that Watts' blood was on his hands. He tried to stay quietly on the line with her, but knowing he was no good with this sort of thing, Bonnie mercifully let him go.

Corbin was left alone, caught off guard by a spike of bitter anger.

Saint Watts, who could do no wrong—that stupid bastard leaked the seamy realities of his private business into that kinked-up chat room exchange. The words were stuck in Corbin's brain like an infected sliver. Corbin had whispered some twisted things in Shay's ear over the years, but no decent man would spell that shit out on the internet.

Watts had screwed strange women and used Guy's photo to deceive strange women into screwing him. He'd brought disaster on himself. Brought it on Bonnie and her sisters. Dragged Corbin into it by setting Guy up as the straw dog. And as much as Corbin hated himself for thinking all this, he hated Watts for having the kind of secrets that should never outlive a man. It made the loss of Watts feel like being hit with the claw side of a hammer instead of the head.

Corbin leaned on the binocular unit and looked across the water at the beach house, letting the Gulf breeze move through him. When Hoovestahl's behemoth black Cadillac SUV rolled out of the carport, Corbin headed back to the house at a moderate lope, sending up tufts of wet sand, scattering seagulls.

Shay was out on the balcony with a brushed brass telescope on a heavy tripod.

"Hey," she called as he came up the boardwalk. "You came back."

"I left my looter shoes under your bed."

"I see you found Billy Oyster's." Shay peered into the telescope at the bar down the beach. "Back when Billy's daddy first owned the place, they put that big old binocular thing out on the pier. Billy and I were about eight years old. So, he's looking at me over here, and I'm looking at him over there. Each of us is thinking the other kid's life is way better. We met up halfway down the beach, and we've been best buds ever since."

She waved and blew kisses, peered into the telescope and laughed out loud.

"He moons me," she explained. "That's the tradition."

Corbin went inside and up the steps, through a large, open area with a billiard table and barrel chairs to the pink-and-tangerine bedroom shared by Shay and her little sister, McKecknie.

"Everything okay with your dad?" he asked.

"Sure. That's my second-favorite dysfunctional relationship."

Shay goosed his backside on her way to the lowboy dresser, where she poked through drawers of spare summer things and came up with a pair of white linen Capri pants and a sky-blue bikini top beaded with tiny seashells.

"Hungry?" she said. "Mommi sent broiled chicken with mango salsa, beer bread, black bean salad, and key lime pie."

"Thank God for Char Hoovestahl," Corbin said sincerely.

"She's an excellent cook and a very sweet lady."

"I guess you take after your dad."

Shay stopped short. "Is that an insult to me or to him?"

"Neither," said Corbin. "Shay, c'mon, I was teasing."

"Don't you start cracking on my father."

"Don't you start cracking on me. I did everything I could to make nice with the guy."

"Except swallow one ounce of your voluminous ego instead of eighty bucks worth of Scotch."

Shay pulled on the Capris and exchanged her bra for the bikini top. Corbin leaned on the lowboy, watching her.

"If you could get past your myopic politics," she said, "you'd see that my father is a principled, intelligent, goodhearted man. The greatest man I've ever known. The only man I've ever been able to count on."

"He's also an obnoxious blowhard."

"Said the pot calling the kettle black." She turned her back to him, holding the bikini strings between her shoulder blades. "Tie this for me, please?"

Corbin tied it. Then he untied it, pulled her back against him and whispered something twisted about the Barbie bed. As the words left his mouth, he felt a dark tentacle connecting him to Queen Mab and the chat room, another unwelcome spike of bitterness toward Watts.

Shay brought his hand to her mouth and sucked his middle finger. That was the end of cogent thought for a while, and Corbin was grateful.

Later, as they lay in a confusion of fussy pink sheets and ruffled pillows, Shay said, "That storm Daddy mentioned. Off the record, is it going anywhere?"

"Not to make landfall, but like I said, the water's warm. That makes for a lot of activity." Corbin studied an incongruous shape among the vintage Barbies in a tall corner cabinet. "Moxx of Balhoon?"

"With antigravity chair. Scored that at a head shop in Amsterdam."

"You're a Dr. Who collector?"

"I'm into a lot of nerdy things." Shay teased her foot against the back of his leg. "My favorite piece is the British police box time travel machine. TARDIS: Time And Relative Dimension In Space. I love the idea of something bigger on the inside than it is on the outside. I kept my smokes in it during my Ani DiFranco phase."

"So you weren't all that nerdy."

"Heck no," said Shay. "I was one of the cool kids. Homecoming queen. Captain of the cheerleaders. I merely aspired to be a nerd."

Salt breeze from the balcony brought in the sunset mosquitoes, and Corbin blew gently to shoo one away from her shoulder.

"Bonnie's having a bad time," he said. "It'll get worse. Eventually, she'll know what really happened, and it'll ruin every good thing she believes about her brother."

"You see what I mean now," said Shay. "About the legacy."

"We have to find her."

"We?"

Corbin nodded. "This is way too close to home."

II

OPHELIA

20

GALVESTON

FRIDAY MORNING
SEPTEMBER 9

```
** WTNT44 KNHC 090858 ***

TCDAT4

TROPICAL STORM MARIA DISCUSSION NUMBER 32

NWS TPC/NATIONAL HURRICANE CENTER MIAMI FL

5 AM EDT FRI SEP 09 2005


MARIA CONTINUES TO BE QUITE RESILIENT AS LATEST SATELLITE

IMAGERY SHOWS THE CYCLONE IS MAINTAINING DEEP CONVECTION

AROUND AN EYE-LIKE FEATURE. HOWEVER...SATELLITE INTENSITY

ESTIMATES CONTINUE TO DECREASE AND ARE NOW UNANIMOUSLY

T3.5...OR 55 KT...THE SATELLITE SIGNATURE STILL IMPLIES A

PRIMARILY WARM CORE STRUCTURE.

$$
```

The simplified assumptions of the Limited Area Barotropic forecast model compromised accuracy more than Corbin was comfortable with, but it was about the best he could do on his laptop. Between the LBAR and what he was getting from the NHC forecasts, it seemed like Maria was going to remain at sea, more decorative than destructive.

Meanwhile, Tropical Storm Nate opened a sleepy eye near the Bermuda Triangle, developing enough of a woody to be called a Cat 1 hurricane for a few hours. Now Tropical Storm Ophelia was giving Corbin the biggest headache and Shay the most hope.

"She'll go one of two ways," he said. "Up the Atlantic coast or across Florida into the Gulf of Mexico."

Corbin's colleagues were evenly split on which it would be, and Corbin wasn't ready to make a call, given the limited technology available to him at his makeshift office. The storm had briefly upgraded to Hurricane Ophelia the previous day, but Corbin was preoccupied with Rhett Butlering Shay on the staircase, then sleeping like roadkill on the living room floor for four hours, so he missed it.

Now Ophelia was parked off the Outer Banks with her legs crossed, pouting about being downgraded to tropical storm status again, and Corbin was backpedaling, trying to make it right with his clients, who were already on edge.

Nerves were raw out on the oil rigs and along all coasts with one storm after another roiling out of the warm water and the aftermath images of Hurricane Katrina dominating every network, newspaper, and twenty-four-hour news cycle. Every outlet had its own theme song for the travesty: a slick compilation of music and images that set up the premise with all the subtlety of the Brady Bunch theme song, typically some spyrotechnic graphic mixed with soggy images—humanitarian aid on overwhelm, Bush and Brown on underwhelm—smartly punctuated with an authoritative music stinger.

Talking heads blustered about one thing and another. Investigation. Accountability. More endless replaying of the now familiar footage from outside the Superdome. More endless replaying of helicopter rescues and scattered houses and water-logged neighborhoods.

Shay, who was a bit jaded by nature, purposefully ignored the coverage after day seven, with the exception of the ten o'clock news, which had been part of her bedtime ritual since early childhood. Corbin remained glued to it for a while longer, but on day twelve, as he watched a reporter in the littered street outside Johnny White's basically pronouncing New Orleans brain dead, Corbin was suddenly unable to locate his outrage. He wanted to feel as gutshot by it as he had the first week, but even he was beginning to numb. He wanted to turn away. Mix another margarita. Enjoy this woman who was ready and willing at any given moment. It made him feel like guilty hell.

In the first ten days after the storm, approximately a quarter of a million evacuees poured into the city of Houston. Hotels and goodhearted homes filled up quickly. Almost two weeks later, the Astrodome and Reliant Center were still overflowing, and the kind citizens of Houston were feeding everyone to the tune of $6 million per week without a dime from the federal government.

"I'm pretty dang proud of my town," said Shay. "This is some serious money-where-the-mouth-is 'love thy neighbor' action."

When FEMA announced the distribution of $2000 debit cards to evacuees, many of the 10,000 homeless people who were on the streets of Houston on any given day hustled to get in line. A chauffeured parade of celebrities visited the facilities, which made for both fundraising and paparazzi ops out the wazoo, and those who knew how to make hay out of such things were doing a brisk business, along with purveyors of generators, duct tape, hurricane shutters, and pet insurance.

"It's the land of opportunity," Corbin observed. "She could be right there under our noses, taking advantage of the strain on Houston's infrastructure."

"A major missing piece all along," said Shay. "What does she do between hurricanes?"

"Probably the same thing everybody else does," he said. "Works a job, pays rent, buys groceries."

"There are plenty of regular jobs where her skill set could be applied. Computers, notably."

"This level of forecasting proficiency is a very marketable skill. And it doesn't happen without a focused formal education."

"Then there's the people skills. And a lot of travel. She uses those cards all over the world. So airline, maybe. Or oil industry. Some conglomerate like Halliburton."

"Or Hoovestahl TransGlobal," Corbin said.

"Oh, God, I hope not. To have something like this linked to Daddy's name…"

"We need to build a multi-dimensional cross-reference: potential employers, dates, places, information access, cash flow."

"Not just cash flow," said Shay. "Spending patterns that indicate preparation, celebration, conservation. Retail profiling, if you will."

"Yes. Brilliant. I didn't think of that," Corbin said, and Shay was embarrassed by how good that made her feel.

She kept four windows open on her laptop, constantly monitoring Watts' debit card and three credit cards that had been set up and activated in his name by the time Corbin and Shay had their office space online. Each window was set to refresh every thirty seconds, and Shay kept it in sight, on the dresser in the bedroom where they slept spooned together at night, on the vanity in the bathroom while she shaved her legs, on the coffee table in the great room while they made love and listened to the rain, on the kitchen counter while she read the *Houston Chronicle* op eds to Corbin as he cooked dinner, on the patio table where they spent most of their days, soaking in sunlight, bantering over coffee in the morning and margaritas at night. Shay had one eye on it all the time, except when they were jogging on the beach and visiting Namma, who entertained them in varying states of fog and clarity and was delighted to meet Shay's young man for the first time every day.

Twelve days after Katrina, not a single transaction had posted on Watts' accounts, but Shay and Corbin had settled into an odd mélange of domestic bliss, lively debate, and what Shay called "Kama Sutranicity" backdropped by the room to room omnipresence of the Weather Channel. They hardly recognized themselves anymore. She was a pussycat, eager to please; he was an optimist with a condom in his pocket.

As they lay together in the hammock on the lanai, Corbin worked an orange peel in a long, curled helix, and Shay told him, "The beach agrees with you. I've never seen you so happy and relaxed."

"You too. And you're even more beautiful. Geezes. Your body is so alive."

"As opposed to… inflatable?"

Corbin teased her lip with an orange section and put it in her mouth. "I mean physiologically, you seem—"

"Baby, she tapped a card!" Shay rocked out of the hammock and scrambled to her computer. "Debit card. North Carolina, Newport News. She paid at the pump."

"She's calling Ophelia for the east coast," Corbin said, looking over her shoulder. "I was starting to think this one was a non-starter."

Shay speed-dialed her cell phone. "Detective Sykes, please. Shay Hoovestahl. It's an emergency. C'mon, c'mon… Berto! She tapped his debit card. Watts—Eldridge Watts—seven minutes ago at a gas station. I'm sending the store number and location. My weather guy says she's going for Ophelia. Right. Go, go, go. Call me back." She clicked off and got up to pace. "He's getting them to dispatch someone."

"Seven minutes," said Corbin. "She's long gone."

"Yes, but hopefully, the gas station has security video of her and whatever she's driving. Oh, God of Glory, please, let there be video, and please, please, please, don't let some morbidly obese trucker be eating a Moon Pie in the foreground." Shay slapped the table. "I knew if I sat on that debit card, she'd go for gas." Shay flipped off her unseen adversary with both barrels. "See how ya like payin' at my pump, bi-otch!"

Corbin smiled and offered her a high five. "You did good, babe."

"I bet anything we'll see a hotel charge on that phony baloney MasterCard. The questions is, what took her so long? Did she want us to assume she was in Houston? Was she in Houston?"

"She could be based here," he said. "It would be a logical hub."

"It would." Shay bit her bottom lip. "I don't like it, but maybe we'd better have Millie check into the consulting meteorologists Daddy has on the payroll."

"I'm a little vague on Millie's job description."

"That's for the best," Shay said cryptically. "Let's stay on Ophelia. We need to know exactly where she's going to make landfall. Can you run that forecast thing again? That Limited Barometric Expialidocious?"

"Rather than the LBAR, I'll run SHIFOR and see if anybody salutes."

"What's that?"

"Statistical Hurricane Intensity Forecasting System. It's a fairly simple climatology and persistence model," he said, tapping parameters into his laptop. "Geezes, I wish I was in my office. Anything you can run on a PC is really not as accurate as I'd like it to be."

"Why not?"

"Well, the LBAR, for example, uses a simplified version of the equations of fluid dynamics. It makes assumptions in order to reduce the necessary computer time and power. Upside is, you can run it on a fast PC or Sun/HP-type workstation, but those simplifying assumptions impact accuracy. And making assumptions…" Corbin shook his head. "Assumptions make me nervous. I tend to get burned."

"Okay," said Shay. "For the sake of flow, I'm going to nod, but I need you to flip that to me in an email so I can see the words. Are you saying only certain kinds of computers would give her the level of information she's getting? Because that might narrow the search parameters for Sykes. A lot."

"Yup." Corbin nodded. "The better models require access to a supercomputer. These systems aren't available to just anybody."

"Keep talking."

Shay propped her feet in his lap, taking notes on her laptop.

"GFS, for example," he said. "Global Forecasting System, the National Weather Service's global forecasting model. And the GFDL, Geophysical Fluid Dynamics Laboratory, a high-res hurricane forecast model. That one requires a supercomputer and data from a global model, but it would give her exactly the kind of information she's looking for. Then there's NOGAPS, the Naval Operational Global Atmospheric Prediction System, and UKMET, the United Kingdom Meteorological Office global model. Those are just a few."

"Your life is all about the anagrams, isn't it?"

"Mostly FUBAR lately."

"Okay. Email all that to me, please? ASAP. SWAK. FYI. Add a brief note about exactly who does have access to those supercomputer models. I'll forward to Sykes and start lurking the forums. See who's looking for a date for Ophelia."

She got up and squeezed him briefly before she went to pacing again, working her phone voodoo. "Call me back, call me back, call me back."

21

GALVESTON

SATURDAY EVENING
SEPTEMBER 10

```
ZCZC MIATCDAT1 ALL

TTAA00 KNHC DDHHMM CCA

TROPICAL STORM OPHELIA DISCUSSION NUMBER 16...CORRECTED

NWS TPC/NATIONAL HURRICANE CENTER MIAMI FL

5 AM EDT SAT SEP 10 2005


...CORRECTED 72 HOUR INTENSITY...85 KT...IN TABLE...

 RECON REPORTS THROUGH 06Z LOCATED THE CENTER WITHIN A

LONE BURST OF DEEP CONVECTION THAT HAS BEEN ROTATING

SOMEWHAT WITHIN A LARGER MID-LEVEL CIRCULATION... THE

WEAKENING IS ONLY SLIGHT AND RESTRENGTHENING IS FORECAST.

... NORTHEASTWARD MOTION IS DECEPTIVE SINCE IT IS EXPECTED

TO PERSIST FOR ONLY ABOUT 12 MORE HOURS... OR LESS. A

STRONG AND DEEP RIDGE IS FORECAST BY ALL OF THE DYNAMICAL

MODELS TO BUILD IN ITS PLACE.

 FORECASTER KNABB

 $$
```

Sykes called back, but only to tell her there was nothing to tell. The useless security video was clouded with dirt and rain, the camera shuddering with gusting winds from Ophelia's ragged sleeve.

With the sun low on the smudgy horizon, Corbin and Shay headed up the shore to Billy Oyster's, wading along the edge of the water, carrying their shoes in their hands.

"It's so lovely this year," she said. "Usually it gets chilly after Labor Day."

"It's noticeably warm," Corbin nodded. "I need to double check my readings."

"Why?"

"Short version: warm water transfers more moisture and energy to the atmosphere."

"I'll bite," said Shay. "Give me the long version."

"Here's the Gulf Coast." Corbin squatted to draw the broad cauldron with his finger in the sand. "Straits of Florida at three o'clock. Here's Sykes in Tampa at two. New Orleans, straight up at twelve. Here we are on Galveston Island at eleven o'clock. Here's Tampico, Veracruz, Tabasco. Down here at six is Cancun at the tip of Quintana Roo. Over here at five, you got Cuba and the Yucatan Channel. The Loop Current—eddies of warm water coming out of the Caribbean, travel through the Yucatan Straits, into the Gulf. This year, that Loop Current is deeper and warmer than I've ever seen it. It's like a factory, churning out one storm after another. The Gulf of Mexico is like a shallow little kiddie pool compared to the Atlantic Ocean. You stick a little kiddie pool out under the blazing sun all day, and the water heats up in a hurry. You take a look at it that night when the air cools down, and what do you see?"

"Evaporation. Vapor rising," said Shay. "And what goes up..."

"Right. The hurricane is basically a community of thunderstorms being fed by moisture and energy coming up off that warm water. There's a lot of other factors in the atmospheric environment as a whole, but as it gets bigger, it's getting its spin from the rotation of Earth, and those storms are passing over the warm water one after another, taking up moisture, unloading that precipitation, taking up more moisture, generating more storm clouds. So when a tropical depression moves over water this warm, it's like pouring high octane fuel into a fire."

He stood and brushed his hands off on the seat of his pants as they walked on.

"You haven't changed your mind about Ophelia, have you?" said Shay. "Do you think she'll cross into the Gulf like Katrina did?"

"No, but there's usually a comforting consensus of the smartest people," said Corbin, "and that's not happening. I hate to admit it, but I felt a little more confident about calling it when I saw our girlfriend going for the east coast."

"Wait, wait," Shay said with some amusement. "Are you saying she's better than you?"

"Going over her activities during the storms in your files, comparing it to my own records—technically, yeah, her track record is better than mine, and I like to think my track record is pretty good." Corbin pushed his hands in his hip pockets. "Maybe she's Navy."

"Why would you say that?"

"Seems like her methodology is pretty similar to mine. There's a way you learn meteorology in the military that's not like private sector. The objectives are different, which steers the process. That would also explain how she's in a position to access data from the more advanced computer models."

"Sykes needs to hear all this," Shay said as they approached the pilings under the packed icehouse. "And he needs to hear it from you. I'm sorry, but my eyes glazed over somewhere in the Yucatan Straits."

"Now that we know she's in North Carolina, I can tweak my projections, maybe narrow the corridor of opportunity for him."

Music throbbed from the open windows of the bar overhead, and Chinese lanterns turned in the breeze under the bright halogen lights all down the length of the fishing pier. Shay saw Billy smoking a joint with some bikers on the side of the road by the end of the boardwalk.

"Hey, Billy Bud," she called as she and Corbin climbed the rip-rap seawall.

"Shay Bomb!" Billy croaked without exhaling, then bounded over and expelled a cloud of fragrant smoke before he bear-hugged her. "Took you long enough to get over here. I was starting to wonder."

He held her somewhat longer and a lot closer to his crotch than necessary, it seemed to Corbin. Stevie Ray Vaughan's "Pride and Joy" pulsed out through the swinging doors, and as Billy danced Shay down the boardwalk to the front porch, Corbin could see the deep muscle memory that existed between them, the long history of him carrying her to the tideline when the sand was too hot for her feet, rubbing her back as she threw up at a kegger in the state park, lugging a succession of suitcases to and from every car she'd ever owned, and taking his reward for all that as deeply and as often as she'd allow.

"Who the hell are you?" Billy asked Corbin over the top of Shay's head.

"Billy, this is Corbin," said Shay. "My friend from New Orleans."

"Whoa. Dude." Billy offered the sort of sympathetic handshake you'd offer to someone who's had a death in the family. "Boilermakers?"

"Not me." Shay stepped into her sandals. "Counting calories."

"How 'bout you, bro?" he asked Corbin.

"Sure. Thanks."

As they headed into the noise and music, Billy grabbed a passing barmaid and kissed her lavishly on the mouth. "Heather, honey, this is Shay."

Shay offered her hand. "Nice to meet you, Heather."

"Yeah. Super nice." Heather deftly lofted a tray of drinks and bar food on her shoulder. "'Scuse me. I gotta do this."

"Goodness," Shay said as Heather walked away. "Is she old enough to work here?"

"Just barely," said Billy, "but she's got an impressive résumé."

"Yeah, I see that."

"Hey, Hoots," he said. "New house rule: Iciest bitch has to mop up."

"Touché," she conceded. "Is my Ramones music still on the box?"

"Till death do us part." He parked a plastic cup of quarters in front of her.

Shay went to the jukebox. Billy knocked out two shots from a bottle of Jim Beam.

"So, you're with the Shay Bomb."

"Yup," said Corbin.

"Met her dad yet?"

"Oh, yeah."

"Somebody needs to tell that dude he's Foghorn Leghorn."

Corbin shrugged. "He's all right."

"Shay's not as tough as she pretends to be. If you mess her up," said Billy, drafting two beers from the tap, "after her dad rips your head off and grinds out the stump, I will find you. And gut you. Like a fuckin' tuna."

"If you say so," said Corbin.

Billy dropped his shot glass into his mug and threw back the whole assembly, chugging the overrunning beer, foam and amber dribbling down the front of his shirt. He tipped the shot glass into his mouth, the centerpiece of an aspiring heavy metal grin. Corbin drank his without showmanship. Simple shot with a beer back. He'd be going home with Shay and didn't need to make any statement beyond that. The Ramones pounded into the crowded room, and Shay returned to the bar, singing along unselfconsciously despite her appalling singing voice.

"Teepee men in tender century. Dee dee and my hat on a mercury."

"Stop desecrating the place," Billy groaned. "You don't know the words, and you suck."

"This was my downfall in the Miss USA pageant," she told Corbin. "No talent. I can't sing, can't twirl baton, and with these Mermans," she pointed to her chest, "you're allowed to dance only at your wedding or on a table."

"Okay, Hoots, it's time." Billy hitched himself up on the bar and swung his legs over, singing like a lounge lizard. "Happy birthday to you, happy birthday to you..."

"My birthday was two weeks ago," said Shay. "Statute of limitations."

"Ladies and gents, Miss Hooterstall is thirty-one," he called out to the bar. A cheer went up, and the assembly joined the chorus. "*Happy Birthday, dear Hooterstalllll, Happy Birthday to youuuuuuuu!*"

Another cheer rose, followed by chanting: "Lock'er up! Lock'er up!"

Shay shrieked as Billy caught her by the waist and hoisted her over his shoulder in a fireman's carry, slapping her backside, counting with the crowd, "1, 2, 3, 4..."

Corbin stood at the bar, astonished and intensely uncomfortable.

"Don't sweat it." Heather nudged his shoulder. "He's just playing. She has to stay in the liquor lockup until she earns thirty bucks for a children's charity."

"Liquor lockup?"

"It's to keep spring breakers from stealing the good stuff." Heather indicated a gated length of tall wrought-iron fencing that partitioned off a corner of the bar by the back door. The makeshift ten-by-ten cell was stacked with cases of good-name beer, Bacardi, various vodkas, and a supply of extra glasses to address daily breakage.

"How's she supposed to earn the thirty bucks?" Corbin asked warily.

"Nothing bad. Show some skin, dance, belly shots, whatever."

"...29, 30, 31 and one to grow on!"

Setting Shay back on her feet, Billy kissed her long and hard on the mouth, then clanked the heavy iron gate closed, hooked a padlock in place, and strutted back to the bar. Corbin handed him thirty dollars and said, "Let her out."

"I just remembered," said Billy. "We raised it to fifty."

"And this goes to what charity?"

"Children's charity," said Billy. "You know. Kids and shit."

Corbin laid another twenty on the bar, and Billy slapped the key painfully into his palm. As Corbin freed Shay from her cage, Billy victory-lapped the pool tables, waving the fifty dollars in the air, collecting high fives from his fellow dirt bags and baguettes.

Shay perched like a budgie on a barstool next to Corbin, flushed and disheveled. "Thank you for rescuing me."

"Did you want to be rescued?" Corbin asked dryly. "I couldn't tell."

"Don't be like that." Shay punched his arm. "You don't see me getting jealous about you and Bonnie."

Corbin huffed a short, sharp laugh. "Bonnie was a tenth-grade science geek when I left for Japan. When I came home six years later, she was married to my brother. Never—not ever—would I ride up her leg the way that guy was on you just now. Geezes. She'd put my lights out."

"It's hilarious that she thinks you'll ever live with another woman," said Shay. "You already have the perfect wife. All the comforts of home with none of the annoying sobriety or faithfulness."

Corbin downed the rest of his boilermaker. "I'll leave you to hang out with your friend."

"Baby, don't go." Shay got her arms around him, but he was immovable as a barnacled piling under the pier. "C'mon. Embattlement is part of our chemistry. I make it hard, and you hold it against me."

"It's not funny, Shay."

"Beertender," she called. "We need a Sam Adams. It's an emergency."

"Right away," Billy grinned. "I promise not to piss in it hardly at all."

Shay caught his hand and said, "Hey. I'd be sad if I felt like I couldn't come in here with a friend, Billy Bud. I'd miss you. Know what I'm saying?"

He set up the Sam Adams and a Heineken Light for Shay. She collected the bottles by the necks and said, "Your girl is lovely, Billy. And the fifty bucks is our bar tab."

Out on the pier, a bachelorette party was winding down. A few old men were fishing. A sunburned couple peered into the binocular unit. Assorted people watched the sunset over the incoming tide.

"I love it when the clouds go all Spanish olive grove like that," said Shay.

"Cirrocumulus. Those are good ones."

"Ah. Nice."

"I did live with a woman," Corbin said abruptly. "For two years. In Japan."

"Was she—"

"She was a geologist." His inflection closed the subject like a steam trunk. "The point is—that embattled chemistry thing, Shay—on a long-term daily basis, that works about as well as a pet crocodile."

Shay studied his face for a trace of wistfulness or better-to-have-loved-and-lost, but there was only a hard-tasked recall, which she found enormously sad.

They walked to the end of the pier and watched the sun disappear.

"So, what was your talent?" Corbin asked.

Shay laughed, but there was a cringe in it. "Swinging."

"Excuse me?"

"I had a big swing unit built and this billowy peach dress and white petticoats made to look like the girl on the swing in the Fragonard painting. I did some little quasi-trapeze tricks and recited a Robert Louis Stevenson poem. *How do you like to go up in a swing? Up in… up in the air so*—oh… goodness…"

Shay had to turn away from the water. Suddenly the salt air held a sickening undercurrent of decay and gasoline rainbows.

"Are you okay?" Corbin touched the small of her back.

"I need to stay by the rail for a minute." Shay poured her beer into the water and held the cold bottle against her neck. "Stress doesn't usually get to my stomach like this."

"Stress about the Mab thing? Or is it me?"

"It's her. Every time I think the end is in sight, she takes me further down the rabbit hole. It was already at critical mass. Now you're dragged into it."

"If you hadn't come to me, no one would have ever known what really happened to Watts."

"Maybe that would have been for the best."

"I'm not a believer in 'what you don't know can't hurt you.'"

"How does this end, Corbin? The gas station video was useless. She hasn't gone for the Master Card or the AmEx. My stomach is a mess, and I can't let this consume another year of my life."

"There's nothing you need to do about it tonight."

Corbin set her arms around his middle and massaged her neck. The moon drifted over the water. Music drifted from the open door.

Shay said, "Dance with me," and did her best to sway him, but he planted his feet and said, "I don't dance."

"Everybody dances. You can't go through life and never ever dance."

"Yes, I can. Ask Guy. It doesn't matter if I'm three sheets to the wind, I never—" A chill came off the water, touching the back of his neck like a spider. "I don't dance. She said I was drunk and we danced. That never happened."

"Who said?"

"Louisa. Tommy and Georgie's niece." He swallowed, realization and anguish rising in his chest. "She's Queen Mab. She killed Watts."

"What? How long have you known this girl?"

"I don't know her. It wasn't—*shit*. How fucking gullible could—I watched him dance with her, Shay. I sat there thinking how lucky—oh, Christ, I would have—I'd have gone with her myself if you hadn't been there."

"Start at the beginning," said Shay. "Tell me what happened."

"She sat down. We talked. Watts said he was going to the poker game." Corbin raked his hair back from his forehead, replaying the conversation in agonized real time as the whole thing worked forward from the back of his brain. "She acted like she knew me. She knew Tommy, knew the neighborhood. She knew the names of their friggin' cats."

"She must have been in their house after they evacuated. Think what you could find out in an hour or two. Photo albums, home videos, email. Look what we knew about some guy from his gym bag. She passed herself off to neighbors, did what she came to do, and sheltered in place until the storm passed."

Shay pushed her fists together in front of her, trying to figure out what to do with all this.

"Corbin, we need to get in touch with Tommy and Georgie. That house is a crime scene. It has to be processed before they go back in and contaminate the evidence."

"The whole city is a crime scene," said Corbin. "There's no processing it. You and I both know Watts is lying there right now getting eaten by rats. It'll take months to sort things out, and I guarantee, this will not be a top priority. Isn't that the point? She was counting on it playing out exactly like it did."

"Could you identify her if you saw her again? What did she look like?"

"She was…what I wanted to see."

"Corbin, you have to be more specific."

"She looked a bit like you. A little taller, maybe. Dark hair. Athletic, white, early thirties. Voluptuous up front. Great legs. Her perfume was nice."

"Maybe there's something Sykes can do about the crime scene," said Shay. "We'll keep him in the loop and watch the cards. She used the one in North Carolina yesterday, so she's probably assuming that in all this confusion, no one knows he's dead."

"No," said Corbin. "My gut feeling is she doesn't like assumptions any more than I do."

22

THE WOODLANDS

SUNDAY AFTERNOON
SEPTEMBER 11

```
** WTNT41 KNHC 112100 ***

TCDAT1

HURRICANE OPHELIA DISCUSSION NUMBER 22...CORRECTED

NWS TPC/NATIONAL HURRICANE CENTER MIAMI FL

5 PM EDT SUN SEP 11 2005

...CORRECTED GFS TO GFDL...

CURRENT INTENSITY IS ADJUSTED DOWNWARD TO 65 KT. BECAUSE

OF THE INFLUENCE OF UPWELLED COOLER WATERS AND DRIER AIR

TO THE WEST... SOME RE-INTENSIFICATION MAY OCCUR BY 48-72

HOURS DUE TO THE ENERGIZING EFFECT OF THE GULF STREAM AND

A MODIFICATION OF THE AIR MASS.... INTENSITY PREDICTIONS

CAN EASILY HAVE ERRORS OF 1 SAFFIR-SIMPSON CATEGORY IN 2-3

DAYS. ...

FORECASTER PASCH

$$
```

The long driveway at the Hoovestahl home was lined with little American flags on sticks. Old Glory flew at half mast in the center of the ChemLawn-green yard, in honor of 9/11. All the way from Galveston, Shay had recited a litany of instructions about what Corbin was allowed to do, not do, say and not say in front of her parents.

"Small talk," she said. "Nothing political, religious, environmental, social, industrial. Talk about the weather. Do not engage. Whatever Daddy says, just do not engage."

"I don't need you to coach me, Shay. My mother housebroke me just fine."

He pulled to the end of the long driveway and parked the Roadster in front of an enormous open garage where the Hoovestahl vehicle pool stretched out like a parking lot, every car, truck, and SUV sporting a "We Support Bush and Our Troops" yellow-ribbon magnet.

"Be mellow," said Shay. "Please, baby."

"I'll be mellow. I'll be Perry friggin' Como."

Following her up the wide porch steps, through a massive front door, Corbin entered the foyer, which essentially functioned as a shrine to Shay Olympia Hoovestahl. The walls were a mosaic of academic awards and Miss-one-thing-or-another banners. Framed studio portraits showed an evolving Shay in her little patent leather tap shoes, her cheerleading uniform, her voluminous prom queen dress. Shadow boxes contained baby booties, ballet shoes, pageant crowns, graduation tassels, corsages the size of a human head, homecoming mums like parade floats. The rising expanse above the grand staircase was dominated by an enormous oil painting of her swinging in her frothy Fragonard gown.

"And suddenly, it all makes sense," said Corbin.

Shay flipped him a pageant wave. "Bite me."

"Baby girl!" Shay's mother came fluttering down the stairs. "And your handsome young man. Welcome to our home."

Char Hoovestahl was Nancy Reagan slim with a Lady Bird swoop of champagne-blonde hair. She'd had a facelift, but she'd gotten her money's worth. She was a slighter, tighter, reluctantly aging version of her daughter. Char wore bright-red lipstick on Shay's soft smile, thin brows penciled over Shay's big eyes, beefy diamond studs on the perfect earlobes where Shay generally posted nothing fancier than small opals or solo pearls.

"Mommi," said Shay, "this is Dr. Corbin Thibodeaux of the Louisiana Thibodeaux family. Corbin, my mother: Charlotte McKecknie Hoovestahl of the Dallas McKecknies."

"Honored to meet you, Mrs. Hoovestahl. Now I see how Shay got to be such a knockout." Corbin extended his hand, and Char grasped it between both of hers.

"Oh, now, you charmer, you!" Char kissed his cheek and rubbed the lipstick mark with her thumb. "Why, he's just a big ol' charmer, isn't he, Shay?"

"Regular Perry Como," said Shay.

"Corbin, honey, please call me Char. You're home folks now. Bonnie's been telling us how brilliant you are, how you were Shay's knight in shining armor during that awful mess."

"Actually, it was the other way around," he said.

"Come say hello to Bob." Char linked her arm through Corbin's, calling out over the squawk of a screen door that led to a side porch. "Robert, honey? Corbin's here!"

Robert Hoovestahl came around the corner of the house, hefting a silver wash tub full of ice and beer. He set it on the porch steps and galumphed up to lasso Shay in his arms.

"Hey there, Blueberry. How's my pretty princess?"

"Very well, thank you, Daddy. How are you?"

"We'll be all right." Without letting her go, he extended his hand toward Corbin. "Good to see you again, Dr. Thibodeaux."

"Likewise." Corbin accepted his hand, and the mutually firm grasp made him think of the ancient original spirit of the handshake; one man trying to dislodge the weapon from another man's sleeve.

"I've been instructed to mind my Ps and Qs," said Hoovestahl.

"Likewise," said Corbin.

"How 'bout something to wet the whistle?" Bob handed Corbin a dripping bottle of Shiner Bock from the tub. "Finest dark lager in the world, brewed right here in Texas."

"Thank you, sir."

"Mud in your eye." He clinked his bottle on Corbin's.

"Bob, don't forget coasters," said Char. "Shay, come help me in the kitchen."

Shay touched Corbin's elbow and followed her mother through the screen door. Bob and Corbin sat beside a coffee table made from a wagon wheel. The porch fell silent except for the strained squeak of the wicker rockers. They drank their beer. A woodpecker nattered on a pecan tree in the yard.

"Hot enough for ya?" Corbin ventured.

"Yup."

"Quite a little high-pressure system moving through."

"Oh?"

"Yup. Warms things right up."

Corbin heard boots on the steps behind him, felt a firm clap on his shoulder.

"Hey, Doc. How ya doin'?"

He turned to find a face he didn't know. Corbin hadn't seen his brother clean shaven since Guy was sixteen. Freshly shorn Presbyterian choir haircut. Polo shirt and khakis. Nothing about this man was familiar except Guy's whiskey-graveled voice and tattoo sleeve.

"Cleaned up pretty good, huh?" Guy proudly stroked his naked chin. There was a cleft in it. Corbin had completely forgotten. "I'm working in the motor pool up at the country club. Me and Bonnie wanted to contribute something to our upkeep."

"Here's a man I can respect." Hoovestahl clapped Guy on the back and offered him a Shiner. "Family man. Hard worker. Wouldn't be caught dead mooching off a woman."

"Mr. Hoovestahl, is that—" Corbin stopped himself and modulated his tone. "Is that a Maserati I saw in the garage when I pulled in?"

"1973 Ghibli Spyder SS," said Hoovestahl.

Corbin fished another beer from the tub. "Care to introduce me to her?"

Hoovestahl regarded him hard and said, "Smart move, Navy."

"And… they're off to the garage," said Char, observing from the kitchen window.

"Where's Bonnie?" Shay asked.

"She went for a walk in my prayer garden. She's darling. I'm so glad to be an instrument of Christ's love in her life." Char set about arranging dinner rolls in baskets. "She says Corbin is a good man. Has his own money. A good business. You'd be Mrs. Dr. Somebody. And he's good-looking, in his way."

"Mommi. Please."

"I know the two of you are intimate. I hope you've had the good sense to hold something back."

"Well, I haven't cooked for him."

"Don't get tart with me, missy." Char took Shay's face between her hands. "Baby girl, you've always got that wall up. Any man who's willing and able to climb over it—you better pay attention."

"Mommi—"

"Oh, here's Bonnie! Sit down, sweetie," said Char, waving Bonnie in the door. "I'll get you some ginger ale. Shay, Fostella did all the foundation dishes before church. You should do something for Corbin's dinner. Summer crudités—avocado burst, cherry tomato roses, cucumber tendrils. Use the spiral slicer."

"Mommi, I'm no good at that. I'll make a salad. I'm sure Corbin will want to marry me the moment he sees it."

She went to the produce cooler and brought salad makings back to the vegetable sink in the prep island while Char went to the dining room to prepare the table. A horn blast out on the driveway announced the arrival of McKecknie's bright-yellow Hummer. She roared to a halt and hopped down from the running board with club-kid nonchalance, hair unevenly razor cut, streaked auburn and magenta, baggy jeans low slung to show a dangly navel ring. As McKecknie pushed through the screen door, Shay embraced her and whooped, "Oh Mickey, you're so fine! You're so fine you blow my mind!" But the exuberant hug quickly transitioned to a latched hand on the back of McKecknie's neck.

"You smell like Amsterdam," said Shay. "You've got five minutes to take a shower and put on a dress before Daddy gets a whiff of you, and if I catch you smoking weed again, I will snap you like a twig."

"The Annihilator is in the house."

McKecknie disappeared up the kitchen stairs, leaving an awkward silence.

"Your parents are lovely people," said Bonnie.

"Yes. I'm incredibly blessed."

It came out a little brusque, but Shay didn't know how to fix it, so she focused on snipping the tips off pea pods, and Bonnie excused herself to help Char with the table.

McKecknie returned with wet hair and a short jersey dress from Shay's closet. She peered out the window and said, "That's the orgasmonaut you've been telling me about?"

"The very one."

"Lanky fellow, isn't he?"

"He's in good shape," said Shay. "Runs eight miles every morning."

"Go go Gadget details."

Shay glanced over her shoulder and whispered in her sister's ear.

"Oh, my," McKecknie giggled into her hand. "I'm telling JoJo to do that."

Out on the porch, Guy distributed another round from the silver tub. Corbin's third beer, by Shay's count. Her father's second. Corbin always hit a little jovial spell right before Beer 4, and Shay prayed this would be the window into which dinner dropped.

"Daddy says he's an alcoholic," said Mick.

"No. Just an overachiever."

"His nose is like a hatchet."

"I love his nose. I love his hideous feet and his snoring and his good, good soul." Shay got a little misty. "I love this man. I have no fluffy fantasies about how it might work out, because it won't, but Lord help me, I love him, and I intend to enjoy the hell out of him right up to the minute he breaks my heart."

"You are a total pod person right now," McKecknie frowned.

Shay set her arm on her sister's shoulder. "Tell me about you and JoJo."

"We decided to close the deal," McKecknie said. "You made me promise not to do it in high school, so we didn't, but we've been together three years. I feel ready. I just don't want to be a suburban cliché and get nailed in my dorm room."

"The vibrant pink hibiscus of womanhood is a treasure to be respected and celebrated, not nailed."

"Says the girl who gave it up to Billy Oyster under the boardwalk."

"He was very sweet and gentle," said Shay, rinsing a red bell pepper. "Remember the Zip Rule."

"No zippers till you get a visual on the condom."

"That's my girl."

Char and Bonnie brought linen napkins from the dining room, and Char showed them all how to fold the napkins into swans.

"It's the details that make dinner a special event," she said. "Especially when there's a special someone at the table. We want to show some home skills."

"Mommi, please don't make more of this than it is," said Shay.

"Well, tell us what it is, honey. Then I'll know what not to make of it."

"We're enjoying each other's company for a few weeks. That's all," said Shay.

"Does Corbin know that?" Bonnie asked, fluffing napkin wings.

"In your twenties, you don't hear that biological clock ticking, but girls in their thirties?" Char placed a tomato on the cutting board for each example. "Bitty Fairbrother's daughter: age 32, about to marry a 64-year-old man. Bootsy King's girl: age 35, reduced to -nternet dating. Your sorority sister, Huntington Ford-Holmes: age 39, third year on the IVF. Even the prayer circle has despaired."

"Mother. Stop." Shay shoveled the salad veggies into a ceramic bowl and gave them a perfunctory toss. "I offered a friend a place to stay during a difficult time—the worst natural disaster in the history of the United States. And I don't mean my thirties."

Char and Bonnie exchanged a loaded glance, and Shay experienced a swift little shrimp fork of jealousy. Certainly hadn't taken long for Bonnie to become the daughter Char never had.

"I need some jeans from my closet," she said. "Mick, come up and help me."

"Oh, Shay, honey," said Char. "I gave all that to the refugees."

"Mommi! Those were my specifically tailored Armani fat jeans. And I am a refugee."

"Refugee with a Neiman's card," Char huffed. "You're breaking my heart."

"They're 'evacuees'," said McKecknie. "Stop saying 'refugee,' you bimbos."

"Watch your mouth, missy," said Char, setting the last napkin swan on the tray. "Put these on the table. Make sure they're all facing east." She leaned out the screen door and called down the porch, "Boys, come in and wash up. It's dinner."

As they milled toward the table, Char micromanaged each napkin swan, seating everyone according to an instinctive boy-girl-boy-girl chart in her head.

"We're an odd number, unfortunately. Oh, wait!" she delighted. "We have Baby T on this side of the table with Guy and Bonnie. Everything's perfect!"

"Thank you for going to all this trouble," Corbin said.

"We're just so happy to have you," said Char. "Corbin, I had Fostella prepare one of her famous dessert carts. And Shay wanted to create something special for you herself."

Char proffered a fancy crystal crudités plate, and Shay was disturbed to see that Corbin seemed genuinely pleased by it. Seated between the Hoovestahl sisters, he brought her slender hand briefly to his lips and said, "Thank you, babe. It looks great."

Across the table, Char beamed. "Bob, will you say grace?"

Corbin was stunned to see Guy tuck his head down, eyes screwed shut, as they all held hands around the table, and Shay's father led the prayer.

"Heavenly Father, we thank you for bringing us together today. Sunday. The Lord's Day. September 11th. A day of remembrance. Lord, hold our fallen heroes up before us as beacons of freedom's light as we go out in your name to bring liberty and justice to the world."

He wasn't tipsy, but that second Shiner always brought out the patriot in him, and this made Shay nervous. She squeezed Corbin's hand, and he shrugged and smiled. Praise God and pass Beer 4.

"Lord, I thank you for the magnificent woman at the end of the table. My beautiful wife. Foundation of this family. We thank you for our beautiful children. For this beautiful child on the way. For the bounty and blessings poured out on this household. We thank you, Father, for the Christian leadership of our president and those who guide our nation in the way of Jesus Christ, despite fools and detractors who—"

"Amen," Char said softly, but without one centimeter of slack.

Corbin glanced up to see Robert Hoovestahl's eyes locked with his wife's. It was like watching two sumo wrestlers square off before embracing.

"Amen," Hoovestahl said, and a mumbled "amen" echoed around the table.

"Dig in, y'all!" Char smiled brightly and allowed just a moment of muted clatter and clink of silverware and china, so as not to seem anxious when she got the small talk train on the tracks. "Corbin, Bonnie tells me the Thibodeaux family has a long, proud history in Louisiana."

"Well, it's long." Corbin tried to smile. It was hard to think of anything benign or chatty to say about the Thibodeaux family. "Guy and Bonnie's son will be the seventh generation born in New Orleans."

"Actually, Doc…" Guy shifted nervously, and glanced at Bonnie. "The obstetrician recommended we stay here until the baby's at least eight weeks old."

"Our Baby T's gonna be a Texan!" Char delighted.

Corbin chuffed a sharp, disbelieving laugh.

"Bro," said Guy, "we gotta do what's best for Bonnie and the baby. Bob and Char were kind enough to extend the invitation."

"It's our privilege," Char said warmly. "Bonnie and I have been *shop till ya drop*, getting the nursery ready. Little Boy Blue is the theme. I don't know when I've been so excited. I'm practicing for being a doting namma someday."

Shay strained a smile and moved her water glass from ten o'clock to two o'clock, the Hoovestahl sisters' code for "change the subject."

McKecknie elbowed Corbin. "Hey, Gandalf, did you see my Hummer?"

"Hard to miss," he said.

"I fixed her up with a 2005 H2," said Bob. "Sunflower yellow. Upgraded five-link air suspension. Touring edition. MP3 docking, Surround Sound. The whole package."

"Sweet," said Guy.

"JoJo and I are driving to Marfa next weekend to shoot a music video for his band, Hats of Smallness."

"You'll be spending next weekend at Namma's," said Char. "I promised her you'd make it fun."

"Namma's house smells like witchcraft," McKecknie grumbled. "Her idea of fun is driving her Buick through a crowded marketplace."

"McKecknie," Char chided quietly.

"Corbin," said Bob, "you drive a full-size pickup for your line of work?"

"Mostly I ride my bike," said Corbin. "Guy rebuilt me a 1947 Harley Knucklehead."

"Nottingham Firemist green." Guy's voice clouded with nostalgia. "That sucker could climb trees."

Corbin saw Bonnie smile when Guy said that. It was a Watts line.

'at sucker c'd climb trees

Suddenly unwilling to add another item to their growing museum of gone things, Corbin said, "I'll find it. I'll get it back when they reopen the CBD in another week or so."

"We'll see some progress now that there's law and order instead of people acting like jungle apes," said Bob. "Once Halliburton gets in there, things'll shape up in a hurry. Those fellas know what they're doing."

Shay felt Corbin's knee turn to stone.

"Corbin, I'd like to put some decent wheels under you," said Bob. "Gesture of good will. I'll fix you up with a 2006 Dodge Ram Mega Cab 2500 Laramie 4x4, and I'll give it to you at half cost, son, because I love my little girl."

Shay said, "Daddy, you're so sweet, but—"

"That has the Cummins Turbo Diesel," said Guy.

"It's a hell of a vehicle," Bob declared. "Luxury interior, six-foot-three-inch cargo box, 12,400 pounds of towing power. You'll get some serious business done with that bad boy."

"I prefer something more mileage conscious," Corbin said.

"Son, when you're in the crosshairs of a Cat 5, your main concern better be gettin' the hell out of the strike zone, am I right?"

"Actually, I'm more concerned about irresponsible oil consumption provoking wars and causing climate change." Corbin physically felt Bonnie's laser-sharp gaze on the side of his skull. "I appreciate the offer, sir, but that's more vehicle than I need. I've been told good stewardship of one's resources is a Christian family value."

Shay put her hand firmly on Corbin's knee and whispered, "Perry. Como."

"I figured we'd get to the liberal chest-thumping before the dessert cart rolled out," said her father. "It so happens, Dr. Thibodeaux, that while great humanitarians like yourself were protesting the war from a barstool, I personally donated 200 sets of body armor for soldiers who didn't have any. I funded over a million dollars' worth of USO performances and scholarships for war widows and outfitted four handicap accessible vans at my own personal expense for men who got their legs blown off." Bob Hoovestahl raised his coffee mug to his lips, glaring over the rim. "What have you done for anybody lately?"

"Well, for starters, I don't ask men to sacrifice their legs so my little girl can drive a Hummer to the mall."

"Dude," Guy said uncomfortably. "That's uncalled for."

"You and your ilk," Hoovestahl said disdainfully. "If you were in charge, we'd all be vegetarian atheists, burning flags and riding bicycles."

"Yes, sir," said Corbin. "Better we should be praying at football games and torturing illegally held prisoners."

"Go ahead and boohoo about that raghead on his box in Abu Ghraib. I'll spare my tears for the American heroes who died at his hands on 9/11."

"Corbin," said Shay. "Do not engage."

"Iraq had nothing to do with 9/11, Mr. Hoovestahl, and you know that better than anyone at this table. This war was orchestrated in boardrooms and sold to the American people with lies and fearmongering. You and your cronies basically used a dog bite to justify your drunk driving accident on the other side of town."

"I don't have to justify jack to you, you swamp-running socialist piece of shit."

"Oh, you proved that when you bought and paid for an American president."

"George W. Bush was elected by the people, for the people!"

"In a pig's ass! The 2000 election was a bloodless coup, and 2004 was the result of swiftboating and target-marketed mass hysteria."

"Right there!" Hoovestahl shook his finger in Corbin's direction. "Right there's the difference between Republicans and Democrats. We lose an election; we take our lumps and do what we gotta do to win the midterm. You lose an election; you spend the next four years cryin' like pansies. In a time of war, a patriot stands behind his Commander-in-Chief, but men like you—oh, you're happy to enjoy the fruits of freedom, but you hold yourself morally superior to those who serve their country and get the job done. Just like you're happy to sit in judgment of my family values, but you don't feel any compunction about sleepin' under my roof, do ya?"

"I served my country, so don't lay that crap on me," said Corbin. "And frankly, sir, your daughter doesn't let me get much sleep."

"Corbin!" Bonnie hissed. "What is wrong with you?"

"THAT WAS OVER THE LINE, YOUNG MAN!" bellowed Robert Hoovestahl.

"Daddy, please, sit down," Shay implored.

"THAT WAS OVER THE LINE!"

"Over the line?" Corbin scraped his chair back and threw his napkin on the table. "Blindly goose-stepping behind a catastrophically inept leader because doing the right thing would gore your private ox—that's over the line. Using your money to install an administration that pampers the haves while the have nots drown, and then swaggering around congratulating yourself about how charitable you are. Curious George saying, 'No one anticipated the levees would fail. Heck of a job, Brownie!' Handing Halliburton eight billion dollars to raze the remains of my hometown, when I and my ilk couldn't get seventy million to save it. That, sir, is over the goddamn line."

"Shut up! Both of you!" Shay put one palm toward Corbin, the other toward her father. "Corbin, sit down. You're behaving like an ass. Daddy, enough with the jingoism. You've been baiting Corbin since we got here." She made a regal gesture and resumed her seat. "Reboot!

That did not happen. We're being nice and innocuous, making banal chit chat about meaningless crap while we all enjoy this lovely fucking brisket."

"Shay," Char whispered. "That language from a lady."

Corbin and Bob sat down without breaking eye contact. After a brief silence, they picked up their forks and sullenly stabbed at the food on their plates.

"Mommi was right about the napkins," said McKecknie. "This is an awesome event."

"Shut up, McKecknie," Shay snarled in unison with her father.

"Dr. Thibodeaux," Char said carefully, "I feel it's important to say that Mr. Hoovestahl and I are sincere in our charitable efforts. I think the real difference is that liberals care about humanity, and conservatives care about people. Seems like it shouldn't be so hard to build a bridge between the two."

"Yes, ma'am," Corbin said, duly abashed.

She placed two warm biscuits on a bread plate with a dollop of strawberry jam and passed it to him.

"The pedicures, for example." Char folded her hands, speaking with quiet dignity. "I know it seems silly in the face of such an overwhelming tragedy, but I think about how our Lord Jesus Christ, on the very night He was betrayed to be crucified, gathered his friends to celebrate the Passover. For them, this was the end of a long road and the beginning of a terrible journey. They'd walked many miles that day— hot, thirsty, weary beyond belief. Anyone could see they needed food and shelter. But Jesus saw their need to be comforted. So, the Lord of Love... He washed their feet." Her voice trembled with emotion. "The Son of God humbled himself on His knees and tended to their filthy, aching feet. And then He broke bread."

"Gah," said McKecknie, "I hope he washed his hands."

Shay strangled an involuntary snort of laughter.

"Excuse me, please." Char covered her face and crumpled into tears as she walked quickly away from the table.

"Oh, Mommi, no." Shay hurried after her. "Mommi, we're sorry."

"GODDAMNIT, MCKECKNIE!" Robert Hoovestahl slammed the flat of his hand on the table, and all the flatware jumped. "I've taken all the crap I'm gonna take today," he roared, "and don't think I'm not talkin' to you, too, Miss High'n'Mighty!"

He jabbed his index finger into Shay's shoulder, and she protested, "Daddy, ow!"

"The two of you are beautiful, intelligent women, and that ain't how you fell off the supply wagon. Everything you are, your mama made you. There's not a goddamn soul on the planet more deserving of your love, respect, and gratitude, and so help me Christ, McKecknie, if I don't see a sincere display of all three when you get up those goddamn stairs, you're going out on your ass like the cat who ain't comin' back. I am under no obligation to subsidize the education, transportation, and pot-smokin' bullshit of a by-God legal adult who treats me and my wife with disdain and audacity." He rounded the table and put his face nose-to-nose with his intimidated daughter. "Something this poor little rich girl better cotton to in a quick hurry: I'm the one who's rich. All you are is goddamn lucky. Understand?"

McKecknie glared past his shoulder at the front door, her mouth set in a hard line.

"Do you understand?" he enunciated.

"Yes."

"Yes what?"

"Yes, sir," glared McKecknie. "Yes, great patriarchal figurehead. Yes, my destiny is in the palm of your hand. I am nothing without your largess. You could crush me on a whim."

Hoovestahl gave her a curt nod. "Glad we're finally on the same page."

23

GALVESTON

MONDAY EVENING,
SEPTEMBER 12
2005

```
** WTNT41 KNHC 130248 ***

TCDAT1

TROPICAL STORM OPHELIA DISCUSSION NUMBER 27

NWS TPC/NATIONAL HURRICANE CENTER MIAMI FL

11 PM EDT MON SEP 12 2005


THE STRUCTURE OF OPHELIA HAS CHANGED LITTLE OVER THE PAST

SEVERAL HOURS...ALTHOUGH THE CONVECTIVE TOPS ARE A LITTLE

COOLER THAN THEY WERE EARLIER. THE MOTION REMAINS SLOW AND

ERRATIC... GIVEN THE SIZE OF THE WIND FIELD...WINDS AT OR

NEAR HURRICANE STRENGTH COULD BE A PROLONGED EXPERIENCE IN

MANY LOCATIONS.

FORECASTER FRANKLIN

$$
```

It was a quiet week at the beach house.

24

GALVESTON

THURSDAY MORNING
SEPTEMBER 15

```
** WTNT41 KNHC 150257 ***

TCDAT1

HURRICANE OPHELIA DISCUSSION NUMBER 36

NWS TPC/NATIONAL HURRICANE CENTER MIAMI FL

11 PM EDT WED SEP 14 2005


OPHELIA MAY HAVE REACHED ITS PEAK INTENSITY. WATER VAPOR

IMAGERY SHOWS THAT A SURGE OF NORTHWESTERLIES IN THE MID-

TO UPPER-TROPOSPHERE IS RAPIDLY UNDERCUTTING THE OUTFLOW

IN THE NORTHWEST QUADRANT. WHILE THIS MAY BE TEMPORARILY

ENHANCING CONVECTION IN THE WESTERN EYEWALL...I HAVE TO

THINK THAT THIS FLOW WILL BE A DISRUPTIVE INFLUENCE ON

THE CIRCULATION IN ANOTHER 6-12 HOURS. ... GIVEN THE

CONSISTENT SHIFT IN ALL THE GUIDANCE...I HAVE ADJUSTED

THE TRACK TO THE LEFT... BUT FURTHER ADJUSTMENTS IN THAT

DIRECTION DOWN THE ROAD MAY BE REQUIRED.

FORECASTER FRANKLIN
```

On the television over the bar on the lanai, Keith Olbermann was ripping the administration a new one. "Lord knows, no one is suggesting that we should ever prioritize levee improvement for a below-sea-level city, ahead of $454 million worth of trophy bridges for the politicians of Alaska…"

Leaning back in an Adirondack chair, laptop on her knees, Shay watched the Hurricane Lovers forums, hoping to see something that seemed like anything.

321BOOM: me = outy

321BOOM: sorry kidz

321BOOM: this one's not packing much of a package…

321BOOM: IYKWIM

Another week was passing by with plenty of speculation and rumors but no definitive commitment from city officials about the reopening of New Orleans. Corbin and Shay moved between the kitchen and makeshift office spaces in guarded, eggshell conversation. The Kama Sutranicity continued, but the original brio had taken on a tinge of all-you-can-eat-buffet that mandated multiple daily incursions and left them both exhausted and irritable. Shay massaged her temple, their numbered days bumping into her dull headache and monumental failure as an investigative journalist.

Corbin ran forecast models in rotation, hoping to see anything he could offer her in addition to three hundred dollars worth of flowers he'd sent to Char and, as much as it galled him, the bottle of Glenfiddich he'd had delivered to Bob Hoovestahl at his office. But Ophelia kept playing with him, tempting him to see what he wanted to see, then dropping her skirt, flouncing off in a different direction.

For the fourth day in a row, he was fielding emails from clients, who were disgruntled about his flabby performance, and fielding phone calls from Bonnie, who kept thinking of things that had pissed her off over the years but she'd been too nice to tell him. These offenses were legion and ranged back to when she and Guy were seven, and Corbin, who was twelve, made them be Ewoks whenever they played

Star Wars and never once let Guy be Han Solo, and who was the real Han Solo now, asshole, so stick that in your light saber and smoke it.

"...devastated by infrastructure collapse in New Orleans," Olbermann continued his righteous tirade, "even though the government had heard all the 'chatter' from the scientists and city planners and hurricane centers and some group whose purposes the government couldn't quite discern: a group called the U.S. Army Corps of Engineers..."

"Corbin?" Shay said. "Must we?"

He clicked to a Fox report about Bush's request for 10.5 billion dollars in aid to the ravaged Gulf Coast and his promise to lead an investigation into the slow response. Then he clicked to something about hundreds of firemen from Atlanta who'd been waiting at an airport for days, hoping to be deployed to search and rescue teams, but sitting instead through hours of classes on the history of FEMA and the legal ramifications of sexual harassment. When a few of them were finally sent to the affected area, it was only to accompany the president and other dignitaries for a series of soggy photo ops. Corbin clicked away from that to a story about a spate of New Orleans police officers killing themselves, to a segment about the long stringer of political and entertainment luminaries still visiting the Astrodome and Reliant Center. Chris Rock, Bill Cosby. Macy Gray was one of the few who actually got in there and worked alongside the volunteers.

"They're here. They've gotten out of that disaster," she said in her distinctive gravel. "But it's like, now what?"

An unfortunate remark by Barbara Bush was getting a lot of play. "So many of the people here, you know, were underprivileged anyway," she said, bubbling the sound bite with a grandmotherly chuckle, "this is working out very well for them."

"I knew she'd get horsewhipped for that," said Shay. "And why don't they hire a stylist? They trot her around in the worst possible clothes for her body type."

"A stylist." Corbin huffed. "Yeah, that would fix it."

"Corbin, my mother says that same sort of para-clueless thing with purely benign intentions. This is a very sweet elderly lady, making a gesture of goodwill, and she slipped and put her foot in her mouth."

"If you say so."

He clicked to CNN, and they both sat forward when they saw Christa Mullroy, disheveled but beautiful, wearing jeans and a T-shirt now instead of her designer safari getup, on location at the Convention Center where the last of the least were still being bused out.

"…but the encouraging news is that, so far, about five hundred children have been reunited with their parents in Houston."

"Thanks, Christa," said Anderson Cooper. "Christa Mullroy, one of many dedicated New Orleans journalists determined to stay and tell the story unfolding here."

"It's been very hard. Very hard," she said.

Shay rolled her eyes. "Stop saying everything twice, Fork Tongue."

"What keeps me going," said Christa, "is that history requires a witness, Anderson. An unsentimental, technically proficient eye in the right place at the right moment. It's my privilege and responsibility—"

Corbin muted the TV, feeling the silence like an oncoming bus.

"Shay. Please. Let me put that in context."

"Don't bother," she said tightly. "I know you. I know her. I can connect the dots. Frankly, I'd feel less betrayed if you'd slept with her."

"Shay—"

"*Did* you sleep with her?"

"No! Hell, no. Of course not."

"Goodness. Protest much?"

"Okay, technically, Shay, I did nothing wrong here."

"Yeah, technically, you never do."

"How do I fix this?" Corbin said. "Tell me what to do or say or jump off of to fix it, and I will."

"I don't know," Shay said honestly. "This is a tough one."

She went back to her laptop, scrolling to the last of the ongoing chat room exchange.

TARAFIRMA: next best thing if ur in the area
TARAFIRMA: we put on some led zep
TARAFIRMA: LOUD
TARAFIRMA: and f#ck our brains out
321BOOM: maybe next time, firm one
TARAFIRMA: by by boom boom

Corbin went in to start dinner, the clatter of pots and pans back-dropped by the drone of the Weather Channel, which was now as deeply ingrained in the soundscape of the house as the constant lapping of the waves.

Shay closed the forum message window, closed her eyes.

When she woke up, her laptop had been set aside, and a selection of mint leaves and rose petals had been carefully scattered over her dress. Close to her hand was a note scratched out in Corbin's small, squarish penmanship on a piece of graph paper: "Please forgive my para-clueless behavior. I have purely benign intentions. C."

Having made his best attempt to feed the pet crocodile, Corbin was talking on the phone with his feet up on the deck rail.

"Julia, hi. Corbin Thibodeaux calling about your email. I'll be back in my office in New Orleans any day now, so... But the basic infra-structure in the CBD—please, hear me out. The infrastructure we need to carry on business as usual will be there, so if y'all can sit tight for one more week... What about five days? Give me three days, Julia. I'm willing to adjust my fee to reflect—of course. I understand. I can rec-ommend a colleague in Miami. I hope we can do business again in the future. Sure. Have a good one."

He clicked off the phone and cursed softly, then thumbed in another number.

"Charles. Corbin Thibodeaux. I lost another one. ProPetroCal. I'm emailing you her contact info now. You're welcome. No, it's all good. No complaints. I'm living with my girl on the beach in Galveston."

He laughed, and for some reason, the sound of it bothered Shay.

"Oh, absolutely. I'm on board with a Chamber of Commerce effort to keep small tech businesses based in New Orleans. Heading home as soon as Nagin reopens Algiers. Soon, I hope. I'm rapidly working through the list of things I can do here to lose money and piss off my girl. Anyway. No worries. I expect to see the favor returned. Miami takes the hit next time. Have a good one."

Corbin stood at the deck rail, looking out at the Gulf. When he felt Shay's arms around his waist, he took her in and kissed her.

"We don't have much time left," said Shay. "Let's not fight."

"Please," he said, strengthening his hold on her, "don't use that Christa thing as an excuse to cut me loose."

"I'm not, but you need to know… I bought an apartment in New York."

He stepped back, trying to read her expression. "You're not coming home?"

"Houston will always be home for me, Corbin. New Orleans was a train stop. A vibrant, lovely train stop, but nonetheless—and now the New Orleans I loved…" She didn't finish the thought, but Corbin noted the past tense.

"Can I still see you?"

"If you make the effort," she said. "I thought you'd be relieved to be off the hook."

"Well, you think a lot of things that are bullcrap."

Shay's cell phone buzzed in her pocket. The ID said SYKES.

"I can't talk to him right now." Shay looked out at the waves, and each one unsettled her equilibrium a little further. "When is this over? How does it end? I swear, this thing is giving me a bleeding ulcer. She won. She has officially kicked my fat ass, and I'm sorry for everyone involved, including Sykes and you and Bonnie, but I can't do this anymore."

"You don't owe this to me or anyone else, Shay. You've done more than your share." Corbin put her cell phone in her hand. "It's over when you say it's over."

Shay took the phone. "Hey, Berto."

"Any action on the credit cards?" Sykes asked.

"Nada. And she never even tried to tap his life insurance."

"Okay," he sighed. "We'll get 'er next time."

"Berto, there's no next time for me. I'm sorry. I'm done."

"Shay, don't quit on me. Not until I get the FBI involved. We're closing in. We're gonna nail this bitch."

"Nailing this bitch is not my responsibility," Shay flashed angrily.

"I'd like to snap my fingers and make this happen, Shay, but the FBI doesn't take kindly to the way you procure your information, and none of these vics, including your pal Watts, are in my jurisdiction. Please, hang in here with me. Finish the job you started."

"The job *I* started?" Shay echoed with an abruptly cut laugh. "When you contacted me, I was working on a sordid little story about fetish sex and chump change fraud on a credit card. Nine pointless months later, I have no job, no home, and almost got myself killed. I'm trying to start over somewhere south of zero, and I can't do it with this thing destroying the lining of my stomach. I'm sorry, Alberto. I hope you get her. And when you get her, I'll do a great story about it. Because from now on, that's what I do. I tell the story that's in front of me. I don't manufacture a chain of events designed to pull the story out of someone's ass."

There was a tight silence on the line. Shay sat down and reopened her laptop.

"Berto, I'm sending you access codes to my online storage. It has all my research files. Hard copies are under water. Nothing I can do about that, but… hang on." Shay covered the phone with her hand. "Corbin?"

"Tell him I'll continue to help any way I can."

"Berto, I'm forwarding email from my hurricane guy. Feel free to call him. He's one of the top people in the field, and Watts was a close friend of his."

They ended with forced courtesy, and Shay hung up, feeling kicked down, tired, and defeated. Corbin came and put his arms around her. "Are you okay?"

"You know me," she said brightly. "Plan Z will be in swing any minute."

He rubbed her back and stroked her hair, and Shay stiffly endured that until he returned to his computer, his pile of file folders, the sort of work top people feel the need to wave in other people's faces. Shay felt another wave of dark offal somewhere deep in her stomach. She opened the long list of email she'd been ignoring.

"Dear Ms. Hoovestahl: Thank you for your generous donation to the New Orleans Humane Society in memory of Goddang Cat. Your gift will save the lives of…"

"Dear Ms. Hoovestahl: Thank you for your generous donation to support the families of New Orleans police officers…"

"Dear Ms. Hoovestahl: Thank you for your generous donation to the New Orleans Museum of Art…"

"Dear Ms. Hoovestahl: The New Orleans Library Association appreciates your generous donation…"

Wondering if anything she ever did would take the edge off everything she'd failed to do, Shay deleted the long list and went on to idle through the headline news feeds. One item in particular elicited a sharp half-laugh.

"What's funny?" Corbin said absently.

"Halliburton's contract for Katrina cleanup," said Shay. "They got twelve million on August 29. They'll probably get a total of about eighty million."

"Geezes. Appalling."

"But you said they were getting eight billion."

"What?" He glanced up at her.

"You were hollering at my father, and you said, and I quote, 'Halliburton got eight billion dollars to raze the remains of my hometown, when I and my ilk couldn't get 70 million to save it?' Eight billion versus eighty million? That's a pretty broad margin."

"Shay, even at eighty million—and leaving aside the fact that the vice president of the United States stands to reap significant personal gain—the American people are still paying more for the destruction of countless lives and historical treasures than they would have paid to protect them."

"Whatever. I didn't realize your standards for fact were so flexible."

"My standards. For fact. Are not flexible."

"Not when it comes to other people," she said, "but apparently you don't hold yourself accountable for whatever wild misstatements support your position."

"Fine. Noted. I'll keep that in mind next time I'm defending my family jewels from your father's barrage of right-wing bullshit." Corbin went back to work, but he couldn't stop himself from adding, "Just to clarify, that doesn't reflect what's being siphoned to Halliburton's subsidiaries—including Hoovestahl TransGlobal."

"Fine. And just to clarify, Corbin, I am a woman, not a girl. And I'm not *your* girl, because you don't own me. And you don't *live* here, you're my guest. So don't be telling people, 'Ah'm livin' with mah gurl,' which is really code for 'I'm bangin' one of the broads I hooked up with at the hurricane. Not the real journalist, of course. No, I got the unemployed one who has unprotected sex and drinks out of the toilet. Yep, that's mah gurl!'"

Corbin walked down the boardwalk to the sand and kept going until the sickly warm Gulf waters closed over his head.

The way she'd escalated, picked up speed, circled around the rhetoric—it was a cyclonic event, feeding off the heat, humidity, and its own momentum. Observing it, Corbin instinctively understood, the way he understood the dynamics of an accelerating storm, and he had an uncomfortable gut feeling about the direction she was taking.

25

TAMPA

FRIDAY AFTERNOON
SEPTEMBER 16

```
** WTPZ45 KNHC 162035 ***

TCDEP5

HURRICANE JOVA DISCUSSION NUMBER 20

NWS TPC/NATIONAL HURRICANE CENTER MIAMI FL

2 PM PDT FRI SEP 16 2005


SATELLITE IMAGERY THIS AFTERNOON SHOWS THAT JOVA REMAINS

A COMPACT STORM... THE INITIAL MOTION IS 260/11. THERE IS

LITTLE CHANGE IN THE FORECAST TRACK OR FORECAST PHILOSOPHY

FROM THE PREVIOUS ADVISORY.


FORECASTER BEVEN


$$
```

Alberto Sykes pushed his lawnmower in long, straight passes across his front yard, ducking his head to rub the shoulder of his T-shirt across his face every once in a while. It was past what a person would call the heat of the day, but it was still too damn hot. Probably too hot to be out mowing, but he wanted to do it. He found it therapeutic after a frustrating day. He liked the readily measurable progress being made, the finishing of the job—the fact that it was a job he could finish. There was an end, and he could get to it, and when he did, his yard looked better than his neighbor's and smelled like his childhood and made him feel like a good husband.

His wife, Jeanette, had started working an additional swing shift in the ER after their youngest daughter went off to school in Gainesville. They needed the money. She deserved something nice, and Jeanette loved a nice yard, so it was worth the effort, but damn, was it hot.

"Hot enough for ya?" people always said, and the answer for Sykes was invariably "yes." He was heavyset, and heat is hard on heavyset men. Sykes was sweating like a horse. He was self-conscious about it when the pretty young woman skimmed into his driveway on her bike.

"Is this the place with the Nissan Sentra?" she asked.

"Sure is," he said. "Are you Sandy?"

"Hi," she smiled, and she was sweaty, too, having been riding her bike in the heat. She seemed embarrassed, which actually made him feel less so.

"I'm Alberto," he said, wiping his hand on his shorts before offering it to her. "That was my wife you spoke to on the phone."

"Hi," she said again, and wiped her hand on her skirt before she took his. "Phew. Sure is hot."

"Would you like something cold to drink?"

"Um, no offense," she said, "I brought something. I don't wanna be rude, and you seem nice enough and everything, but how easy would it be for some guy to put an ad in the paper and… you know, like, do that date-rape drug. I took a self-defense class. They said girls should never drink anything from a stranger."

"Right, right. Of course," said Sykes. "Smart girl. In my line of work I see a lot of young women who, um… well, suffice to say I wish more girls would be like you."

"No offense," she repeated, zipping open a little cooler pack on the back of her bike. She took out two water bottles and offered one to Sykes.

"Thanks," he said, holding the cool plastic against his neck. "So that Sentra? It's six years old, but it's been well-maintained. My daughter had it through college."

"You wife told me she went overseas to the Peace Corps."

"Yup. We're real proud of her," he said. "She loved this little car, I'll tell you that. Took excellent care of it."

"Do you mind backing it out so we don't have to go in the garage?"

"No problem," he said, and he had to smile. She was running the show exactly like he'd want his daughters to do.

Sykes moved the Sentra out on the driveway, and they walked around it, examined the tires, opened the hood. She seemed to know her way around the engine and had already checked the book value. She took her time, though. The sun beat down. Sykes' shirt was soaked through.

"My dad thought the price was a little high for the mileage." She slid her fanny pack around to the front and took out her cell phone. "How flexible is that?"

"Oh," he shrugged, "there's some wiggle room. We could come down another two hundred, I guess."

"Excuse me one sec," she said, flipping open the phone. "Hi, I'm here looking at the car. No, she's not here, but he seems cool. Dad, it's so great. I'm dying. Kind of like silvery bluish. Yeah, I asked, and he said two hundred." She looked up at Sykes, her big eyes begging. "He wants to know if you'll do three hundred off the asking price."

He smiled again. "I can live with that."

"Dad, he said yes! Well, yeah, I'm going to drive it, but it seems to be in really good shape. Daddy, thank you! You're the best. Love you, too."

Sykes felt a pang of nostalgia for his faraway girl. He also felt the heat. The driveway was like a frying pan. Sykes cracked the water bottle she'd handed him, chugged it in one swath, and tossed the empty in the recycling bin.

"Okay, let's take it for a drive," she said, fairly dancing with anticipation. "He says if it runs okay, he'll meet us at the bank with the money."

"Pretty eager about having more than two wheels?" Sykes grinned.

"Oh, my gosh, yes. The AC doesn't work so great on the bicycle," she said, and he laughed, easing into the passenger seat, closing the garage door with the remote.

"Buckle up," she said.

He flashed her a copilot salute, buckled his seatbelt, and cranked the AC as he pointed out some of the instrumentation upgrades. She adjusted the driver's seat and mirrors and played with the windshield washer and high beams and other incidentals before starting the engine and driving carefully out of the manicured subdivision.

"Why don't you get on the highway up here after the light?" Sykes suggested, still feeling the heat despite the AC. "You'll be amazed how much get up and go this little bugger has."

"Yeah, I was thinking it drives pretty well for four cylinders," said Sandy.

"Okay, you, um… you wanna hang a left here."

"Right here?" she said, glancing over at him.

Sykes meant to point to the next intersection, but his hand didn't rise to the level of the windshield. The word "left" didn't come up as far as it was supposed to either. It kind of came out… *luhf*. He looked out the window toward the corner where he'd wanted her to make the turn, but his eyes felt only half connected to the rest of him. He watched the intersection roll by as she continued straight on the feeder.

And then there came an odd, sluggish lapsing, as if he was watching the two halves of his brain separate.

"Feeling a little woozy, Detective Sykes?"

"Huh-uh... huh-uh... *nuh!*"

She cruised up the onramp and traveled past an exit or two as Sykes labored inside himself. Seeing it all like a movie: how she gave Watts' credit card to some itinerant on his way to North Carolina and told him exactly where and when to use it, how she'd go back to his house now and open the door with the keys dangling from the ignition and search his computer and know everything. She would untie the knot he'd been worrying at since his friend died in Hurricane Charley.

The girl drove on with that bright, excited smile. She turned on the radio, tuning around until she found a station playing soft rock music. The cheesy stuff from the 80s. Sykes hated that. Hair bands. Power ballads. The way Jefferson Airplane became Jefferson Starship. That wasn't right.

She changed lanes, took an exit, went under the overpass. When she made the U-turn, Sykes slid to the side. His seatbelt kept him from slumping down or forward, but his face mashed against the window. Taking the onramp heading back toward his home, she reached over to hoist him upright again. A small stringer of saliva momentarily connected his mouth to the glass. He looked at his oily face print on the window and tried to put that together with some way to open the door.

There was a John Wayne movie on TV late one night when Jeanette was at the hospital working graveyard shift and Sykes was alone in bed missing her. *Flying Leathernecks* it was called. Was it called *Flying Leathernecks*? The Duke is paralyzed from the waist down, but determined to move his toe, and he says over and over, "I'm gonna move that toe." And he does move that toe. The damn thing does move.

She took his exit and eased the Sentra down into the slower traffic on the feeder as Sykes thought more thickened thoughts about the cell phone in his pocket, the service revolver in the glove compartment.

The Duke. Jefferson Airplane in their "White Rabbit" days. Somebody to love. Jeanette in her sky-blue scrubs and orthopedic shoes.

I'm gonna move that toe, said the Duke. I'm gonna move that toe.

He wondered muddily what this slip of a girl was planning to do with his bulky body. For Jeanette's sake, Alberto hoped for something away from the house, but of course, the girl pulled into the garage and lowered the door and left the Sentra running.

26

GALVESTON

SUNDAY EVENING
SEPTEMBER 18

City modifies return schedule

Plan for Uptown, Quarter could be pushed back

Gordon Russell, Staff writer NOLA Times-Picayune

New Orleans officials pulled back a bit Friday from the ambitious timeline for resettling unflooded portions of New Orleans that was announced a day earlier by Mayor Ray Nagin. The first two phases of the plan will go on as scheduled, Col. Terry Ebbert, New Orleans' director of homeland security, said at an afternoon news conference. Business owners in the French Quarter, Central Business District, Algiers and parts of Uptown will be allowed to return beginning today at 8 a.m. And Algiers residents can return to their homes beginning Monday morning… In a PowerPoint presentation for reporters, Ebbert displayed a grid showing the status of various services in the areas in question, with levels ranging from green, for fully operational, to amber, for partly operational, to red, for mostly non-functioning

The press release about the reopening of Algiers came not a moment too soon for Corbin. The honeymoon with Shay had pretty much unraveled that morning. She'd locked herself in the bathroom for over an hour. Preoccupied with a troublesome storm he was watching, Corbin didn't realize until late afternoon that she hadn't spoken to him all day.

Tropical Depression 18 had organized and blossomed to Tropical Storm Rita on her way over Turks and Caicos. She wasn't a hurricane yet, but as she scoured across the Bahamas toward the warm Loop Current, intensification was favored. The Florida Keys were being evacuated.

With one eye on the Weather Channel, Corbin put together a good paella for dinner, but Shay said she wasn't hungry. She dragged an Adirondack chair and ottoman down the steps to the sand, and was sitting out there now with a book propped on her chest, apparently wishing he didn't exist.

Margaritas, Corbin decided. Not bastardized yuppie blender Slurpees: proper cocktails with exact amounts of tequila, triple sec and fresh-squeezed lime juice, shaken with ice, strained into two tall glasses that he chilled, dipped in lime, and rimmed with coarse salt. He set them on the wide arm of the wooden chair, sat on the ottoman, and took Shay's hand.

"Come home with me," he said without preamble.

Shay closed her book and took off her sunglasses. "What do you mean?"

"I mean, screw New York. There's plenty of New Yorkers. New Orleans needs you."

"Oh." She withdrew her hand and opened her book again. "Corbin, I have no job in New Orleans. There's four feet of water in my apartment."

"Start your production company. Get an office in the CBD. Find an apartment in the French Quarter." He nudged her knee and added, "I'll be your bed and breakfast while you're looking."

"It's not as simple as 'Woohoo, y'all! Nagin says c'mon home.' Given the enormous ongoing problems—infrastructure, power, drinking water, the smell of the place, for God's sake—I'd be in worse professional limbo than I am now and a lot less comfortable."

"You'd be a lot more comfortable than most people."

"Corbin, we agreed this would be a logical place to—"

"Do not say *reboot*," he cut in. "There is no reboot. You can't just get in your TARDIS time machine and decree that something didn't happen. That's a copout."

"Oh, this from the Elvis of copouts."

"Look, the last few days haven't been great, but it'll be different when we're home, living our lives. I'm asking you to make some concessions so we can give it a try."

"Corbin, just go home. Please. I don't want us to part company arguing."

"I don't want us to part company at all!"

"Okay, then let's hear about the concessions you're willing to make. Are you willing to move to New York? Or even Houston? Are you suggesting some kind of meaningful commitment? No. All you're saying is that I should ignore what's best for myself so I can be booty-call convenient for you."

"I'm saying that I—that you—you are important to me." The botched declaration sounded limp and sweaty of palm, even to himself. Corbin took her feet in his lap, moving his thumbs over the fine bones of her ankle. "Babe, you know I can't leave New Orleans."

"Well, I'm sorry. I can't go back there."

"Bullcrap. Give me one valid reason that doesn't boil down to your frilly pink sense of entitlement."

The salt breeze was brittle and clammy, the way it always was at the end of summer. Shay took a tight breath of it and said, "I'm pregnant."

Corbin pushed his sunglasses over his forehead, blinking at the sudden brightness, the piercing daylight on her white skin.

"Holy hell," he said woodenly. "Are you sure?"

"I did the test this morning. Just to reassure myself I wasn't."

"Holy hell," he said again, forcing his brain through the equation. Katrina was August 29, today the 18th of September. "Twenty-one days."

"Right."

"So, it's… it's early. If you..." Corbin's chest constricted, worlds warring in his heart and head. Finally, he mumbled, "I don't know what to say."

"Well, everything you're feeling—*back atcha*."

"Oh, screw that. You lay this on me like a meat cleaver—expecting what? If I say you shouldn't go through with it, I'm a bastard. If I say I love you, I get kicked in the teeth." He raked his hair back from his forehead. "Jesus Christ, can we pile one more millstone on top of this mind-fucking disaster?"

Corbin immediately wanted to break his own jaw.

Shay pushed the back of her hand against her mouth and started crying. She tried to contain it, but it was like trying to hold sand in her fists. She crumpled forward and sobbed, and it was jarring, not only because she was so cracked open and flood-sieged, but because Corbin realized that in all that had transpired, he'd never once seen her cry.

As the jag wound down to hitched but quiet breathing, he stroked and rocked her, scrounging for something other than these idiot words that kept whiplashing on him.

"I'm sorry. I'm sorry," he said. "I'm a moron, I'm a dick."

"It was an honest response," Shay said. "I felt the same way this morning."

"How do you feel now?"

"Bigger on the inside than I am on the outside."

Corbin kissed her temple and burning cheek and lamely said, "It'll be okay."

"No, it won't. I can't do this alone. We can't do it together. My parents will be devastated, privately and publicly—spray tan harpies clucking behind Mommi's back about how the mighty have fallen, every gas bag in Daddy's cigar bar scuttlebutting about his whore daughter in bed with the enemy."

"Your father," Corbin winced. "He's gonna rip my head off and grind out the stump."

"Maybe he doesn't have to know," said Shay. "One of my sorority sisters is an attorney in Boston. She and her husband have been trying for several years to conceive. This baby would be a miraculous blessing to them."

Corbin studied her face, trying to read her expression through the wreckage.

"Guess I should have known you already had a plan in swing."

"It's not a plan," said Shay. "It's an option."

"Really? Because it sounds a hell of a lot like a plan. It sounds like you thought it through and tried to send me home without telling me."

"I thought you would react badly, and you did. Spare me the indignation."

"Give me a little credit," he said. "I will step up and do the honorable thing. I'm willing to make the best of a bad situation."

"A child's life should not be a *bad situation*. It certainly shouldn't be a *mind-screwing disaster* before he's half the size of a sugar cube."

"That's semantics," said Corbin. "Let's just deal with reality."

"Okay, here's the reality: I'm a driven bitch, and you're a drunken asshole. We'd be horrific parents. A baby should be loved and celebrated and welcomed into a functional family like Baby T. Clearly, Corbin, that is not happening with you and me." Shay straightened her spine. "I'm not making any decisions today, but rest assured, I don't need anything from you. I'm fine on my own."

"You always are," Corbin said bitterly. A wave of relief made him feel like guilty hell. Then a wave of heartache took his breath away. "What happens now?"

"Now you go home. Go home tomorrow and get your life back."

He huffed a dark half-laugh, going bleak, shutting down.

"I'll never see you again, will I?"

"I'm sorry, Corbin. I can't do this anymore. I can't." Shay kissed his hard-set jaw and grand nose. "I'll always love our pet crocodile. But it bit me, baby. It'll kill me if I don't let it go."

III

RITA

27

ALGIERS

MONDAY MORNING
SEPTEMBER 19

```
** WTJP21 RJTD 180600 ***

WARNING 180600.

JAPAN METEOROLOGICAL AGENCY.=
```

```
** WTPQ30 RJTD 180600 ***

RSMC TROPICAL CYCLONE PROGNOSTIC REASONING

REASONING NO.12 FOR TS 0516 VICENTE (0516)

1.GENERAL COMMENTS

...REASONING OF PROGNOSIS THIS TIME IS SIMILAR TO PREVIOUS
ONE.

2.SYNOPTIC SITUATION

...NOTHING PARTICULAR TO EXPLAIN.

3.MOTION FORECAST

...TS WILL MOVE AT THE SAME SPEED FOR THE NEXT 24 HOURS.

4.INTENSITY FORECAST

...TS WILL WEAKEN BECAUSE LANDFALL IS EXPECTED WITHIN 6
HOURS.

5.REMARKS

...THIS IS FINAL PROGNOSTIC REASONING ON TS 0516 VICENTE
(0516).=
```

Guy and Corbin set out before dawn and kept to I-10 as far as the border and a fair distance into Louisiana. The battered freeway ran parallel to the coast, inland enough to still be intact for the most part, but there was plenty of wreckage. Billboards and road signs flattened face down, poles snapped and severed, trees stripped and splintered, buildings thrashed to ruin. Corbin stared out the window at the bullied swampscape. Guy repeatedly called Bonnie to ask her how she was feeling and tell her how much he loved her and let her know their exact location per the snazzy GPS display on the dashboard. Every time he got off the phone with her, he looked at Corbin, shook his head, and sighed, "Geezes, dog. Geezes."

Gas was as precious as griffin's blood, and Corbin was nagged by the knowledge that they were burning through it at a ridiculous rate in the candy apple red behemoth Guy had driven hot off the lot at Hoovestahl Luxury Transport. The truck's vast club cab and command deck were tricked out like a Vegas showgirl, and of course, with great delight, Hoovestahl had slapped a bright yellow ribbon magnet—"We support Bush and the troops!"—high and shiny on the ass end.

The back of the truck was loaded with relief supplies donated by Char's church—boxes of clean T-shirts in all sizes, cases of antibacterial wipes, pallets of bottled water—and they dragged a large trailer stacked to the ceiling with Recovery Buckets. Char's church ladies had spent three sixteen-hour days assembling the five gallon pails with essential elements needed for basic survival and remediation of sodden, moldering homes.

The Cleanliness is Next to Godliness Bucket included bleach, dish soap, Ajax powder, scrub brushes, and steel wool, rubber gloves, Lysol and the like. The I Am Jesus' Little Lamb Bucket contained formula, diapers, and other baby care items. The Family That Prays Together Stays Together Bucket contained powdered milk and children's vitamins, along with crayons, coloring books, and other quiet toys and activities designed to preserve the sanity of a mother miles from the nearest working television. Each bucket included prayer request postcards, angel pins, and a pocket-sized New Testament with the words of Jesus in red.

Shay's mother, who had spearheaded and financed the effort in addition to coming up with the clever and inspirational bucket themes, added her own special touch, a little mani/pedi kit. Char, Bonnie, and Fostella sat up late into the night, using Sharpies to inscribe several hundred pairs of canvas work gloves with the reminder "He's got the whole world in his hands!" and instructed Guy and Corbin to give out all this merch however they saw fit as they traveled back to New Orleans.

From Lafayette on, they had plenty of opportunities. With all the media and fundraising focus on New Orleans, the tiny parish towns that had been turned inside out were struggling up out of the mud all but unnoticed by FEMA and the rest of the world. The Red Cross was here and there. Local churches and charities offered whatever broken shelter they had. Houston to New Orleans was normally a five or six hour drive, but the trip ended up taking all day, partly because of the road damage and detours, but mostly because the Thibodeaux brothers' mama didn't raise them to drive on by without lending a hand to the elderly couple struggling to drag a row boat out of their living room, or the young woman carting water bottles and toddlers up the muddy road in a little red wagon, or the boy and his father wrestling with the remains of an old oak tree that leaned dangerously over their roof, a tire swing strangling its shattered trunk.

Bone weary and out of sorts, they reached Algiers Monday evening as the humid dusk descended. The air inside the house was hot and swampy. There was no power, no gas for the stove or water heater. While Guy fueled up the generator and swept a legion of roaches out of the kitchen, Corbin rigged a solar-powered Wi-Fi unit on the roof so he could get his laptop and RTUs online. Tropical Storm Rita was crawling over Cuba like a lap dancer. No complete eyewall, but wind speeds were sustaining close to seventy, and Katrina-fatigued media outlets had begun to take notice. Desperate for something fresh to talk about between the belabored images and scratched up stories, they began speculating on various worst-case scenarios.

Corbin stood under a cold shower, thinking about how it was making love to Shay before he left her that morning. No hope of redemption, no need for a protective barrier between them. Only what people grab onto as they flee a burning building. Sleepless and clammy, wishing he could feel a breeze or feel release or be unconscious and feel nothing, he took his laptop to the kitchen, poured himself a tall glass of bourbon, and sat on a wooden chair, craving her companionship with a physical ache that extended from his tailbone to the front of his throat. The longer he sat, the more he loathed himself with a specific sort of loathing he'd traditionally reserved for his father. Unexpected yearning engulfed and confounded him. Corbin held the bourbon between his hands. Drank it as a tall shot. Thumbed his cell. Shay's number went immediately to voicemail.

"Hi, this is Shay. I'm not happening right now. If this is an emergency, call 911."

"Shay, it's me again. Please, call me. Tropical Storm Rita's going to upgrade to a Cat 2 hurricane by morning. I know you don't want to see me right now, but you need to evacuate with your grandmother. I think I should come back and help you get preparations squared away. Also, this other issue merits further discussion, and…I just—I need you to call me. Please."

Corbin poured another bourbon and waited, thinking he should call her back and say something about wind speeds and path projection. Or tell her that he loved her. Or remind her that a child conceived in a hurricane—some people believed that meant something, even though Corbin himself had been conceived in a hurricane, according to family lore, and evidence would suggest that it had endowed him with nothing remarkable except the ability to damage people the way his father did.

He set his watch to alert him if she didn't call in forty-five minutes and studied the storm on his laptop until the alert pipped in the quiet kitchen. He speed-dialed her again, but when he heard the cheery beep, something turned a page in his head, and he said, "If you don't want to talk to me, fine, but don't sit there listening to your own bullshit. You're scared. And you're spoiled. And you're selfish. But I reacted badly? You set me up to react badly. You wanted me to react badly. I call bullshit on all that—horrific parents—speak for yourself, Miss Universe. I'm not the one who was incapable of keeping a fucking cat alive."

Corbin poured another tall shot, feeling better briefly, then wanting to call back to apologize, but not wanting to be the pathetic asshole who calls back apologizing. He set his watch for forty minutes.

Guy shook his shoulder sometime around noon. "Dude. Wake up."

The bourbon bottle was empty. Corbin's neck was cricked stiff. His pulse throbbed like a dying star at the base of his skull. He looked at his phone to see if Shay had called, and she hadn't, but Corbin saw that he'd called her eleven times. He cringed to think what she was hearing on her voicemail right now.

"I'm going to get Watts' ashes," Guy said. "You coming?"

Corbin shook his pounding head, feeling like a miserable shit-heel. He stumbled to the bathroom and leaned against the door until he heard his little brother leaving alone, then he stood under the cold shower again, his fists clenched hard against the tile wall, a tight knot of loss clenched hard against the inside of his chest. He stood naked by the kitchen table, staring at his laptop. Hurricane Rita was howling at the mouth of the Gulf of Mexico, a Cat 2 with sustained 100-mile-per-hour winds. Media was hitting the story hard. A mandatory evacuation would be called for Galveston. Corbin sat down to see to his clients, reminding himself that Shay neither needed nor expected anything from him.

When Guy returned with an unadorned plastic box containing Watts' remains, Corbin was out in the courtyard, scrubbing the back wall of Tommy and Georgie's house where Shay had spray-painted a large white arrow, and Guy had lettered beside it: R.I.P. ELDRIDGE C. WATTS 10/12/71—8/29/05 A GOOD MAN. PLEASE BE

RESPECTFUL. Leaving the ashes on the potting porch steps, Guy rolled up his sleeves and stood beside his brother, scrubbing in silence. Sweat rolled down their faces and soaked their shirts.

"I need a beer," Corbin said after a time. "You want one?"

"Yeah," said Guy, without looking at him.

Leaning on the spiraled metal stairs at the bottom of Tommy and Georgie's fire escape, they silently tipped the beers and wiped their mouths with the backs of their hands. Corbin studied his little brother, looking for anything recognizable about the way he was talking, the cut of his hair, the clean-shaven assurance in his face. Guy was as lost to him as Watts, the courtyard, the neighborhood, the city itself. The street in front of Bonnie's Bloom & Grow was a jungle of downed trees and branches. The French Quarter looked like the set of a gothic horror flick.

Past Guy's shoulder, only a faint white ghost remained of the legend scrawled for Watts on the red brick wall. That wasn't part of the story they would tell Baby T about his lost uncle, Eldridge Watts, a good man taken by the storm, deserving of respect. The family this child should have been born into no longer existed. The New Orleans this child would grow up in was a place Corbin couldn't even envision, much less call home, and that gutted him, because he knew he'd never use that word anywhere else.

Guy shook his head heavily and said, "Geezes, dude."

"What," Corbin barked. "If you've got something to say, say it."

"You're a fucking hypocrite," Guy burst out. "All your crap about 'This woman loves you, brother. She's as close to salvation as you'll ever get.' After everything you always told me, you took this woman and wrecked her. She's wrecked. Mick told Bonnie, and Bonnie has seriously had it with you, man."

"Bonnie needs to rezone her bitching to her own business." Corbin resumed scrubbing at the spray-painted epitaph, close-mouthed and angry.

"It's not just Bonnie," said Guy, blinking back sun, sweat, and enormous resolve. "I don't want you living here anymore, Corbin. You don't get to be a pussy hound and a drunk and have a family life with my wife and kid in your spare time. I saw enough of this crap with Dad. Bonnie and me are both getting life insurance money from Watts. We want to buy the house."

"My house," said Corbin. "The house I was born in. Quit school so you'd have a home. Paid taxes by consigning my ass to the military. The house in which your wife has lived and conducted business rent-free for thirteen years. And now you think you're gonna throw me out?"

"When this house was yours, dude, it sucked. You left without checking the rearview mirror. Bonnie moved in—eighteen-year-old girl—fixed the plumbing and drywall, painted, did the kitchen, built the shop. Everything that's *home* about this place, everything that made you want to come back—that was all Bonnie. This is already her house, Corbin. She deserves to have it on paper."

When Corbin didn't answer, Guy cast his scrub brush into the Jesus bucket and said, "Screw you. Keep the place. Because you know what? This ain't my home. Bonnie is. And that piece o' shit..." Guy pointed across the ruined courtyard to the empty, shuttered house. "That's all you got."

Guy wiped his hands on his pants and took a last look around.

Seven hours later, he called to let Corbin know he'd made it home.

28

GALVESTON

THURSDAY MORNING
SEPTEMBER 21

```
** WTUS84 KHGX 220336 ***

HLSHGX

GMZ330-335-350-355-370-375-

TXZ200-213-214-226-227-235>238-221000-

HURRICANE LOCAL STATEMENT

NATIONAL WEATHER SERVICE HOUSTON/GALVESTON TX

1100 PM CDT WED SEP 21 2005


...RITA IS A DANGEROUS CATEGORY 5 HURRICANE WITH WINDS

NEAR 175 MPH...

...CURRENT STORM INFORMATION...

LATITUDE 24.5 NORTH... LONGITUDE 86.8 WEST... 585 MILES

SOUTHEAST OF GALVESTON TEXAS MOVING WEST AT 9 MPH. MAXIMUM

SUSTAINED WINDS WERE ESTIMATED AT 175 MPH WITH HIGHER

GUSTS.

...EVACUATION INFORMATION...

TRAFFIC HAS BEEN HEAVY WITH VOLUNTARY EVACUATIONS...

TRAFFIC MANAGEMENT PLAN IMPLEMENTED AT 6 PM... DO NOT LET

TRAFFIC DELAYS HALT YOUR EFFORTS TO EVACUATE.

GALVESTON COUNTY GOVERNMENT FACILITIES WILL BE CLOSED

TODAY. JAMAICA BEACH OFFICE OF EMERGENCY MANAGEMENT HAS

BEEN CLOSED. NO MEDICAL CARE WILL BE AVAILABLE AT UTMB

HOSPITAL FROM THIS POINT FORWARD.

$$
```

Namma's house did smell a bit witchy. Shay lay awake on the brocade sofa in the parlor long before dawn, waves of morning sickness rocking her empty stomach, the answering machine blinking with a fresh spate of messages from her mother.

Namma's live-in caregiver had left with the first wave of traffic on Wednesday, which turned out to be the smart choice. Careful plans had been laid out, evacuation zones defined, departure times designated, but media hype took effect like a sneeze of Everclear over an open flame. Round-the-clock coverage of Hurricane Rita took on more spin than the storm itself, relying heavily on regurgitated images of the Katrina aftermath to maximize every marketable minute of can't-turn-away TV. The storm headed for Houston was proclaimed to be even bigger, but the developing news coverage rapidly became more about the panicked mass exodus.

Two million city dwellers and suburbanites—most of whom were not in mandatory evacuation zones—blew off the official shelter-in-place recommendation and poured out of the sprawling city. The Houston metroplex was now gridlocked in a chokehold almost two hundred miles wide. Small-towners on the coast had been ordered to leave their homes, but were unable to move once they got on the roads. Gas was gone. Cell towers jammed. Businesses closed their doors and posted signs: "No toilets for evacuees." Watching the hysteria play out on TV in Namma's dark parlor, Shay wanted to seize Corbin by the collar and say, "See? See what happens when you incite effing panic?"

Galveston was all but deserted now, with every store and gas station closed and all police and emergency services suspended until after the storm. The weather forecast was calling for relentless sun, smothering humidity, a heat index near 110. Shay and her mother had been trying for two days to arrange a medical transport, but people like Namma were in a gray area: not critical enough for an ambulance, just a bit iffy for a private car. At first Shay and Char readily conceded that more critical cases should take precedence; now Shay was getting nervous, and Char had reverted to the persona Mick called "Momzilla."

Shay went to the gabled guest room and lay down next to McKecknie, who was under the embroidered coverlet, giggling with JoJo.

"Mick, get off the phone. We need to get moving."

"The Annihilator speaks," McKecknie told JoJo. "Later, dude."

"How much gas is in the Hummer?" Shay asked.

"Quarter tank," said McKecknie. "I had to wait in line at the gas station like a Czechoslovakian, and they only let me get ten bucks worth."

"Dang it. Mommi's having a cow. You should have gone home when they closed the campus, Mick. I told you not to come down here."

"How could I not come down, Shay Shay? You're always there for me, and it scares the crap out of me when you cry. It's like seeing the Statue of Liberty get her period. I hope he gets hit by a bus, that scurvy, hatchet-faced pissninja. I hope he dies nine days a week till there's not a hairy nevus left to bury."

"Mick, that's not helpful," said Shay, fighting tears that welled up behind her cheekbones. The first crying jag of the day was the worst, she'd learned, and today, there was no time for it. Downstairs in their nightgowns, they stared in disbelief at the alarming images on the countertop TV as Namma turtled out of her bedroom with her walker in front of her.

"Good morning, Shay, honey. Did you make my toast points?"

"In a sec, Namma."

"Goodness, you have filled out." Namma extended a translucent hand to plump Shay's breast like a pillow. "You be careful. Busty girls turn trashy with the difference of an inch. You'll get in trouble like your mother."

"Okay, Namma." Shay kissed Namma's onion paper cheek and started the tea kettle while McKecknie settled their grandmother in her favorite chair.

"This reeks." McKecknie frowned, doing the math in her head. "Average speed on I-45 is twelve to fifteen, so 89 miles to home at the breakneck top velocity of fifteen miles per hour—that's like six hours."

"With stop-and-start gas mileage," said Shay. "That Hummer is a major problem. We can't be stranded on the road with Namma in this heat."

"Did you call Daddy?"

"He's on a flight back from Dubai. It'll probably get diverted to Newark."

"What about the limo service?"

"Millie tried. With contraflow starting, southbound lanes have been reversed. They can't get here." Shay pressed her fingertips to her temples. "Okay. Plan B. We siphon the gas from the Hummer to fill up the Roadster. It'll get four times the mileage and be a lot easier to maneuver through traffic."

"Yeah, but all three of us? Squished in that tiny car?"

"No." Shay took McKecknie's hand. "Just you and Namma."

McKecknie's eyes went wide. "No. Effing. Way."

"The nurse said to give her a little something to help her sleep. We'll do that right before you leave. Keep the top up so you can run the AC. With contraflow kicking in, you'll make better time. You'll be home in three or four hours."

"But what about you? You can't stay here."

"I'll go with Billy to San Antonio. Mick, help me out here. I just don't have it in me to deal with Mommi right now."

Shay deftly siphoned the gas from the Hummer, topping up the Roadster with a little left over. She put a fresh Depends on Namma and assembled a small cooler with water bottles, sandwiches, two bags of ice cubes, and a little flask for Namma's afternoon nip of gin. On the curb, with Namma pleasantly high and installed in the passenger seat, McKecknie grasped Shay's hand, serious as the edge of a volcano.

"Shay Shay, can I tell you something off topic?"

"Mick, are you and JoJo…" Shay pulled her into a hug. "Oh, Mickey, I hope it's lovely for you. When? What's the plan?"

"Totally not cliché," said McKecknie. "We're doing it in the hurricane. Did you know people do that? There's this whole website about it."

An icy finger traced the length of Shay's spine. "How do you know about that?"

"There was a flyer on the Hummer a few days ago."

"At school? At the dorm?"

"Where else would I be?"

"Mickey, the flyer—did all the cars have them or just yours?"

"All, I guess. Some, at least. I don't know. Why?"

Shay took her sister's face between her hands, processing the best course of action based on what she knew, what she shouldn't assume, what she couldn't afford to panic over.

"McKecknie. Listen to me. You go home and stay there until you hear from me. You do not go back to campus, and you do not get on the internet. No blog, no Facebook, no email, and you do not get on that website again. Ever. Do you understand me?"

"No. What's wrong?"

"I'll explain later. Just promise me."

Mick rolled her eyes and nodded. Shay gave her a tight squeeze.

"How's your phone battery?"

"It sucks. And my car charger is in JoJo's truck," McKecknie said. "I'll get another one on the way."

"No! You don't stop for anything. Take mine. The charger's in the console." Shay handed over her cell and took McKecknie's. "Check in every hour. Text messages take less bandwidth, so they go through sometimes when calls won't. If Corbin calls, let it go to voicemail. Call me on the landline the second you get home."

"Stop spazzing. We'll be fine," said McKecknie.

"I know," said Shay. "Mick, I'm sure you won't need it, but there's a gun in the glove compartment. You know how to handle it properly."

McKecknie held up Shay's cell. "Lurch is blowing up your phone."

"Ignore it," Shay said, but McKecknie showed her the incoming text.

MA FEMME. PLEASE CALL. I LOVE YOU.

"Aw." McKecknie crinkled her nose. "Now I feel kinda sorry for him."

"Don't."

"Shay Shay, you don't always have to be the Annihilator."

"In this case, I do, Mick. And you need to go."

Watching the Roadster disappear, Shay weighed McKecknie's cell phone in her hand, needing to hear Corbin's voice close to her cheek, his calm extrapolation of this flyer thing, his sober assessment of Hurricane Rita. But that's not the voice that was in her head now. Listening to him that first night was like following him down a hole. She'd seen Corbin drink—seen him drunk—many times over the years, but never like that. Stooping to sloppy affection, hollowing to antagonism, darkening to anger, devolving into someone she didn't know. Using Namma's rickety rotary-dial landline, she called Sykes' cell. The call went immediately to a generic voicemail.

"Berto, it's Shay. Please call me ASAP. I don't know what this means, but a few days ago, there was a flyer for the Hurricane Lovers website on my sister's car outside her dorm at Rice. At the very least, this was supposed to send me a message, and worst case—I can't even think about it. Call me. Text if you can't get through. I'm still in Galveston."

Shay pulled down the hurricane shutters and dragged in Namma's outdoor things, rolling bougainvillea pots into the entry, lugging garden gnomes to the breakfast nook. She packed her camera bag and a small overnight satchel. She'd come into town with next to nothing and intended to leave with as little baggage as possible.

She met not a soul as she left Namma's abandoned neighborhood and cruised the Hummer down San Luis Pass Road to the turnoff at the bar. When she saw a number of vehicles parked on the shoulder above the riprap seawall, she thought Billy might be having a hurricane party, but pulling in across the road, she noticed how dilapidated they all were and realized they were insurance bait. The tide was already rising. On the thin strip of sand still visible between the water's edge and the bottom of the seawall, Billy had tied several janky old motorboats to the pilings.

"Shay Bomb?" He bounded up from the beach and met her on the boardwalk. "I thought you'd be long gone with your grandma."

"Mick took her in the Roadster. Can I get a ride out with you?"

"Sure. Of course," he said, taking her bags from her. "I'm not going till tomorrow, though. Probably split around five."

"Billy, are you serious? That's ridiculously late to be leaving."

"I know, but I gotta finish this project. The evacuation craziness will let up by then. We'll make better time than we could make today."

"Will Heather mind having me along?"

"She took off yesterday with her family," he said. "Took thirty hours to get to Dallas. Ten miles an hour up that I-45 corridor. Stuck between construction barriers. No exits. Hundred five degrees. Her mom passed out and pissed herself. It was totally batshit."

"Billy, Mick has my phone. If you see a call from her, grab it right away, and call me on her number. I brought the Hummer so we could siphon the rest of the gas into your truck."

Billy opened the front door, and Shay looked around the disorderly bar.

"What's all this?"

"Stuff from my place," he said. "For the insurance pictures."

He parked her bags on a table next to an old computer, a broken TV and his boom box from high school.

"I'm in for a big, fat payday" he grinned, stacking empty cartons in the liquor lockup. "I went to every liquor store on the island last night and got empty boxes out of their recycling. Help me set these up. Keep the expensive brands in front."

"No way." She showed him the hand. "I am not involved."

Shay walked down the pier to the old binocular unit. She had a quarter in her pocket but didn't put it in the slot. Forty hours from now, her beloved home on stilts would likely be gone. Let the storm have it, Shay thought. It should have been the place she retreated to after a sorry love affair, not the place where she had one. She couldn't sleep there anymore. Without Corbin spooned behind her, the mattress in the master bedroom felt like an empty parking lot. Her little Barbie bed upstairs was a dirty joke. The austere guest room smacked of "get thee to a nunnery." Shay decided she'd rather spend another night on the lumpy Edwardian fainting couch in Namma's dusty parlor.

McKecknie's cell vibrated in her hip pocket. A text message from Sykes:

FBI GOT HER! WILL CALL AFTER RITA. R U OK?

"Thank God," Shay breathed. "God, thank you."

Standing in the sun, able to feel its warmth for the first time in weeks, she sent Sykes a message of affectionate congratulations.

BERTO! YOU EFFING ROCK! IM OK. LEAVING GVSTN TMORO AFT.

She thought about calling Corbin, but she didn't know what to say. One less millstone for him to worry about?

Better to just go forward.

Shay's plan fell quickly into place. Tomorrow, she'd swing by the house, get her laptop, and go to San Antonio with Billy, maybe even take some comfort from him there. Next week, she'd go to New York, embrace the traffic and the hard Rs. She'd move on and reserve for Corbin the same hard-tasked recall with which he revisited his old lover in Japan. Corbin had shown his true colors. So be it. If her father turned his back on her, so be that, too. Shay had always planned to spend her life working for a living.

Billy came out and said, "Take my picture with today's paper. I want good money for this pier. There's not a rotten board on it."

"Maybe it'll hold up," said Shay, feeling a breeze of her old optimism.

Billy shuffled one foot. "What happened with the dude from New Orleans?"

"He's back where he belongs."

"Are you okay?"

"I will be. Eventually."

Shay turned her back on the beach house and walked arm-in-arm with Billy to the door.

"This mahogany bar is worth big bucks," he said as they went in. "Handcrafted by my father, a bastard, but a fine carpenter. And I want money for these valuable antiques."

He gestured to the walls, which were barnacled with bits and pieces that had washed up on the beach below the bar over the last twenty years. Patrons would pick things up and bring them in, and Billy would unceremoniously screw, nail, or chicken wire whatever it was to the wall. A plastic baby doll, a shapely mannequin everyone called Myrtle, a steering wheel, lots of driftwood, thousands of shells, crab nets, shrimp nets, fishnet stockings, a sullied bridal veil, a selection of bras, boat oars, and even a rowboat, broken in half.

Stacking soda pallets under a porthole window at the back of the liquor lockup, he said, "Put those bottles in the Svedka boxes, would you? Everclear's illegal in Texas."

"Billy, I won't be party to you defrauding your insurance company."

"You say that now," he said. "Wait till you see the view from my new place."

"It'll probably look something like this." Shay closed the wrought-iron gate and latched the padlock. "How do you like it?"

"Fine." He jingled the keys from his pocket. "Better if you were in here."

Taking a silver box from the windowsill, he tamped grass from a plastic baggie into his favorite pipe, struck a kitchen match, and held the flame above the bowl.

"C'mere," he said. "I got sumpthin' for ya."

He drew a deep toke on the pipe, reached through the bars to cup Shay's chin, and brought her mouth to his. She accepted a warm ball of smoke and let him dart the tip of his tongue across her lips while she delayed the exhale.

"C'mon, goody two shoes, suck it in," Billy said.

"Can't." Shay puffed a smoke ring over his shoulder. "I'm pregnant."

"Oh, my God!" Billy swooped his arms around her, crowing, laughing. "Are you kidding me? Shay, that's awesome. Baby Bomb? Freaking off the hook."

The metal bars bruised into Shay's collarbone, but with his unbridled joy, an initial glimmer of happiness unhuddled in her. She almost didn't recognize it.

"Thank you, Billy Bud," she said, hugging him hard. "I haven't been able to process it beyond the mind-numbing fear. Corbin was the opposite of thrilled. I can't even think about telling Mommi and Daddy."

"Don't tell them," Billy said, suddenly serious. "Marry me. Marry me right now this weekend in San Antonio. We'll tell them in a couple months. They'll never know the difference." He kissed her through the bars. "Forget that douchebag. It's always been you and me, Shay Bomb."

"What about Heather?"

"Shay, she's dumb, but she's not stupid." Billy closed his hands around hers. "This place is going in the drink tomorrow night. I'm gonna buy a house in Sugarland. I'll go to college, like you always said. I'll get a degree in marine biology and be a teacher, and we'll come to the beach on weekends with our kids. It'll be awesome."

"That sounds like a wonderful life, Billy. You deserve to share it with the right person."

"You are my right person," he said in earnest. "I've been waiting twenty-two years for you to figure that out."

"Billy…"

"Don't say anything right now. Just think about it. No matter what you decide, Shay, I'm here for you with this baby thing. Anything you need."

"How would you feel about a godfather gig?"

"Godfather. Yeah…" Billy stroked his chin and did a raspy Brando. "I swear on the souls of my grandchildren that I will not break the peace we have made here today."

Shay laughed and said, "You are so hired."

"May your first child be a masculine child," said Brando.

"I'm staying at Namma's, so I'll meet you here. Five o'clock sharp."

Before she could walk away, he pulled her back and kissed her, and she let him. Shay was ashamed of herself for taking advantage, but Billy had a capacity for great tenderness, and she needed a moment of that right now.

As she walked away, she said, "See you tomorrow, Billy Bud."

"We're getting married," he called from the gate of his private zoo. "I'm gonna woo you. Woo my ass off all the way to San Antonio. You won't remember that chump's name."

NEW ORLEANS

THURSDAY NIGHT
SEPTEMBER 22

```
** WTUS84 KHGX 220336 ***

HLSHGX

GMZ330-335-350-355-370-375-

TXZ200-213-214-226-227-235>238-221000-

HURRICANE TRACKING DATA

NATIONAL WEATHER SERVICE HOUSTON/GALVESTON TX

1013 PM CDT WED SEP 22 2005


HURRICANE RITA

ADV LAT...LON... TIME... WIND PR STAT

15  24.30 -84.60 09/21/09Z 105 956 HURRICANE-3

16  24.30 -85.90 09/21/15Z 120 944 HURRICANE-4

17  24.40 -86.80 09/21/21Z 145 914 HURRICANE-5

17A 24.50 -86.80 09/22/00Z 145 898 HURRICANE-5

18  24.60 -87.20 09/22/03Z 150 897 HURRICANE-5

18A 24.80 -87.60 09/22/06Z 150 898 HURRICANE-5

19  24.90 -88.00 09/22/09Z 150 897 HURRICANE-5

19A 25.20 -88.30 09/22/12Z 145 907 HURRICANE-5

20  25.40 -88.70 09/22/15Z 145 907 HURRICANE-5

20A 25.50 -89.20 09/22/18Z 130 915 HURRICANE-4

21  25.80 -89.50 09/22/21Z 125 913 HURRICANE-4
```

Corbin stood over the pool table in his conference room, vectoring probabilities on a large sheet of graph paper. A computer model would have been superior, but he didn't know if the technology to present that would be available when he needed it. He'd positioned the main computer so he could monitor the movement of Hurricane Rita as he worked. She'd gone to Cat 5 over the warm Gulf water and seemed intent on Galveston until now. But as he worked at mapping the probability web on the graph paper, Corbin thought he saw something from the corner of his eye. Nothing he could quantify. The slightest shrug of her shoulder. A subtle but distinctly bitchy side glance to the east.

It was enough to prompt an update to his clients, adjusting his landfall and path projections. Galveston and Beaumont would go for a pretty good ride, but Houston wouldn't take the hit after all.

He worked through the night with one eye on the Houston evacuation debacle on CNN. By Friday morning, the traffic gridlock had broken up and much of the adrenaline had drained from the media hype, but dozens of people were dead, including a two-year-old girl who was run over by a truck in a median strip where her family had stopped, a number of people who were essentially broasted in their stalled vehicles, a busload of elderly folks who burned to death when an oxygen tank exploded, and uncounted other elderly and infirm who would fail and fall in the coming weeks as a result of heat stroke and the strain of travel. It was worse than yelling fire in a crowded theater; it was as if the theater doors were barricaded, the windows smothered in Homeland hysterical plastic and duct tape.

Corbin kept trying Shay's cell, not knowing if the calls were strangled by the jammed towers or she still wasn't willing to talk. Shortly before sunrise, he sent her a text.

NEED TO KNOW YOURE OK.

A moment later his cell vibrated, and he seized it when he saw her name appear.

"Shay, are you all right? Are you out of Galveston?"

"I hope you slam your cloven man hammer in a car door."

"McKecknie, put Shay on the phone."

"Shay stuffed me in the Roadster with Namma yesterday. She's still in Galveston, rebounding with that low-rent Twisted Sister reject. Mommi's freaking out, and it's your fault, you dickwidget."

"Shay's not answering at the beach house. How can I reach her?"

"Grow some emotional balls."

"Mick. I'm making an effort here. Can the hipster crap and help me out."

"Text my cell. Or call Namma's."

Corbin set the numbers on his speed dial as she gave them to him and went for the landline with no caller ID. When Shay answered, he said, "Please, don't hang up."

She didn't say anything, but she didn't hang up.

"Shay, you need to get out of Galveston. Hurricane Rita's downgraded to a Cat 4, but this is a massive storm." He gave her the rundown on sustained wind speeds and central pressure, encouraged when she listened and even asked a few pertinent questions about the storm track and timeline. "I'm projecting a shift to the east, but if I'm off, there won't be much left of the island. You can't stay there."

"I'm not," she said. "I'm going to San Antonio this afternoon."

"With the bartender?"

"With my friend."

"Does he know that?"

"I'm not obligated to explain myself to you just because you're finally drunk enough to say you love me."

"No," Corbin said evenly, "but I do love you. And I've been drunk only that one time since I got home."

Right before he said it, he heard Watts in the back of his head—*Thibodeaux, party of one, your pussy-whipped is ready*—but Corbin said it anyway, wanting to offer her that, and he didn't hate it that for the first time in a month, an involuntary memory of Watts provoked a smile instead of sadness.

"Shay, we need to talk about—"

"No. Please, don't call me again," Shay said.

But there was a soft catch in her breathing, a slight shift just before the disconnect.

Corbin sat on the edge of the pool table, rolling the cue ball between his hands, sorting through his options. Certainly, the least intelligent choice was anything that involved rushing into the strike zone of a Cat 4 hurricane.

"South it is," he said grimly.

30

GALVESTON

FRIDAY MORNING
SEPTEMBER 23

```
** WTNT33 KNHC 230542 ***

TCPAT3

BULLETIN

HURRICANE RITA INTERMEDIATE ADVISORY NUMBER 22A

NWS TPC/NATIONAL HURRICANE CENTER MIAMI FL

11 AM CDT FRI SEP 23 2005


 ...EXTREMELY DANGEROUS CATEGORY FOUR HURRICANE RITA

MOVING WEST-NORTHWESTWARD TOWARD THE SOUTHWESTERN

LOUISIANA AND UPPER TEXAS COASTS WITH LITTLE CHANGE IN

STRENGTH... PREPARATIONS TO PROTECT LIFE AND PROPERTY

SHOULD BE RUSHED TO COMPLETION.


FORECASTER BEVEN

$$
```

The sky was blue as a bell, and the hurricane only beginning to tease, as far as Billy Oyster could feel. He pushed his hands deep in the pockets of his cargo shorts, jingling some loose change on one side and feeling for his lucky charm on the other.

"TARDIS," she'd said when she gave it to him, back in the day. "It's a time machine."

It took all of his going-on-seventeen-year-old manliness to not say something about "RETARDIS" or "FARTIS."

"Basically, it can take a person anywhere they want to go in time or space," she told him, latching it onto his car keys. "It looks like a police box, like they have in England, but it can actually change to like blend in, you know? Like camouflage. So wherever it ends up, it just kind of is. And the interior is way bigger than the exterior, so it's like a whole 'nother thing in there."

This was something Billy came to understand about Shay over the years. How she could change to blend in, how she did that without hesitation or remorse. Everybody thought she was the big shit up at her pricey private school, but she was painfully nerdy in real life. Reading all the time. Watching the news on PBS. The Dr. Who obsession—that was just wrong for a girl in the business of flaming tasty hotness. That shit was for geeks and freaks. But Billy didn't say a word about it that day. He had high hopes, and he was not going to blow it.

Fifteen years later, with the same resolve, he reached in his pocket and located the TARDIS keychain with his fingertips, just to reassure himself it was still there, securely linked to his bar keys and the diamond ring he'd gotten for her. He'd get her a better one after they were married. He'd get better everything. A better life. He'd be a better person. He'd be a father, and maybe even get some respect from her dad. Maybe go into the business with him.

Billy walked toward the beach house with the same high hopes he'd had back in the day, the same vague quasi-hard-on that stirred whenever he thought about being with her. She was out on the deck, but her back was to him.

"Shay!" he called, but she didn't hear him over the sounding waves. The sun was still broad and bright as a platter, but the telltale harbingers of the superstorm had already arrived: an obstinate wind, a grayness to the choppy water, a clawing quality in the surf.

Shay was wearing a silky robe with wide sleeves like a dragon's wings. The sky-blue fabric moved like a parasail on the Gulf breeze. Her hair was in a knot with chopsticks stuck through it. She walked to the edge of the steps, opening her arms wide, and the robe unfurled behind her on a gust of incoming wind. Billy couldn't tell if she was wearing a bikini or if she was in her bra and panties, but the sight of her body—her legs longer and leaner than he remembered and those incredibly firm, full tits—it knocked the cartilage right out of his knees.

"Shay Bomb," he called, getting closer, ambling across the sand.

"Well, hey there," she waved. Something about her voice caught him by surprise, and closing in on the last few yards of sand between them, he shaded his eyes with his hand and realized it wasn't her.

"Oh, sorry," he said. "I thought…"

It wasn't a bikini. It was a lacy bra and panties, and the woman who was not Shay stood there in them, unselfconscious, the robe fluttering open every time the air stirred.

"Is Shay around?" he managed to ask.

"She had a quick errand."

Billy puzzled a moment, trying to find someplace to settle his gaze. She came down to the second step. He could see her dark nipples through the fabric of the bra, which was right at eye level to him now.

"I'm kind of confused here," he said. "She told me she was staying at her Namma's. We were supposed to go to San Antonio today. Did she say anything about that?"

"Oh! You're the San Antonio guy. Right. Right. She did say that. The thing is, I got stuck over here with that wonky traffic issue, so we had a little slumber party over here last night. She said I could ride over there with y'all two crazy kids today."

"Sure. That's cool, I guess." Billy's heart and quasi-hard-on collapsed into the usual shit. She'd called in a friend for backup. Real nice. "So…how do you know Shay?"

"Sorority sistah," she said.

"Huh. Okay, cool, so…"

"Did you need something from the house here?"

"No. It's not important."

"I don't believe you." She smiled and pointed her finger at him. "You look like a man on a mission."

"It's stupid. She has this toy collection. Dr. Who paraphernalia. She'd be bummed if it got trashed, so I was gonna throw a few things in a box is all. Just as like a surprise or whatever. Anyway, it doesn't matter."

"Oh, I see how it is," she smiled. "Now, are you the guy from the place or the one doing the thing?"

"Oh. Sorry. Billy Ostermann. That's my bar up the beach. Billy Oyster's."

"So pleased to meet you, Billy." She offered her hand.

He wiped his palm on his Bermuda shorts and came to the bottom step. It was like shaking hands with a tiger lily. Softly curved, exquisitely light, delicately fragrant.

"You're so sweet to rescue us poor little damsels in distress," she said, holding on a little longer than a person has to.

"No problem." Billy swallowed, trying to force his eyes up to her face. "I better get back. I left the bar open, and I got a thing I'm working on, so… anyhoo. Better get back."

"What time will you pick us up?" she asked.

"Oh, I thought we were meeting up at the bar at five."

"Oh, yes, that's right. She said the bar. At five."

"I know she's buggin' over how late that is. If you want to shoot for four…"

"Five is good," she said. "Five works."

"Hey, if Shay wants help with this patio furniture—well, never mind. I'll give her a call. See ya later."

"See ya, Billy."

She waved a parade girl wave. He grinned and turned to head back to the bar.

The sky was still blue as a bell, but the first dark breath of wind teased up his spine as he took his cell phone from his pocket. There was a split of lightning cut with thunder. Billy felt a wasp on the back of his neck. He clapped his hand against it, dropping to his knees in the sand.

His throat is thick and hot.

He feels his heartbeat in it.

"Spritz," Shay commands.

Shay is on her stomach, bleached hair flipped up in a banana clip, the back of her bikini top untied, because she'll turn seventeen over Labor Day Weekend and will be allowed to wear a strapless dress when some rich guy takes her to a dance at her whoopty-shit prep school, so Shay doesn't want tan lines.

"Spritz, please?"

Billy spritzes her with a pink pump bottle of water and lemon juice, not because he always does what Shay commands, but because he loves the taste of her lemonade sweat. He leans forward to taste it.

He falls forward, hot sand on his face.

He sees her feet at the level of his eye, she bends down to touch his neck, takes his hand, which is heavy and sags like a wet towel. She lets it drop.

In his pocket, Billy feels the jagged edge of the keychain from her dumb TV show she always watches and pitches a fit if the VCR screws up, which Billy doesn't mind. He loves her jagged edges and fitfulness as much as he loves the taste of the warm cunt honey between her legs, even when she's on her period and his fingers come away painted with blood.

He sees blood on his fingers now and wishes he could taste it.

He's going to pop her cherry today. They're going all the way.

"Lovers for real and forever," she said.

Billy has a love gift for her in the pocket of his cut-offs, tangled up with the RETARDIS, an actual 14-karat-gold necklace that cost almost forty dollars at Tejas Pawn-All, your one-stop source for guitars, guns, and gold off the southbound feeder on I-45. Real gold, not fake, and not because Shay is rich and knows the difference, but because his love for her is real. He intends to honor that as a man, marry her after they graduate, work a real job to support her, and never smoke pot or disappoint her or be a stupid screw-up kid anymore, and Billy knows he can do all this, because Shay makes him feel manly in a way that eclipses everything bad he's been told about himself all his lowdown life.

She breathes beneath him in the sand. The light catches the love gift, rising and falling on her chest. Her top is untied. She moves it aside. Billy feels the sharp edges of the time machine in his pocket. Shay loves him, for real and forever, and knowing that now, he experiences an ecstasy so specific it seems the sun has stepped forward from the sky.

His throat aches with happiness.

He waits for her to say when.

And when she says when, he enters in.

31

GALVESTON

FRIDAY MORNING
SEPTEMBER 23

```
ZCZC MIASPFAT3 ALL

TTAA00 KNHC DDHHMM

HURRICANE RITA PROBABILITIES NUMBER 24

NWS TPC/NATIONAL HURRICANE CENTER MIAMI FL

10 AM CDT FRI SEP 23 2005

 PROBABILITIES FOR GUIDANCE IN HURRICANE PROTECTION

PLANNING BY GOVERNMENT AND DISASTER OFFICIALS... AT 10 AM

CDT...1500Z...THE CENTER OF RITA WAS LOCATED NEAR LATITUDE

27.4 NORTH... LONGITUDE 91.9 WEST… CHANCES OF CENTER OF

THE HURRICANE PASSING WITHIN 65 NAUTICAL MILES OF LISTED

LOCATIONS THROUGH 7AM CDT MON SEP 26 2005  GALVESTON TX...

37 X X X 37  PENSACOLA FL... X X X 3 3 CORPUSCHRISTI TX 1

X X 2 3  NEW ORLEANS LA... 6 3 1 2 12  GULF 28N 93W... 74

X X X 74

$$$
```

It was approximately 381 miles from Corbin's door to Shay's. Counting on an average 51 miles per gallon from Guy's Fat Boy, Corbin estimated he'd need approximately 7.45 gallons of gas. He'd filled the Fat Boy the day before, so there was five gallons. He siphoned two gallons more from the generator and carried it in the saddle bags. He topped off the tank when he passed Bayou des Ourses and made it all the way to the Bluewater Highway bridge before the fuel gauge hit E. He negotiated the contraflow roadblocks and passed signs for the state park before the bike coughed and sighed, rolling to the shoulder about six miles from Shay's place, half a mile less to the bar.

Leaving the Fat Boy tucked under a concrete picnic shelter, Corbin took off at a carefully paced lope, budgeting his sweat and energy, working the evolving math in his head: one mile at approximately seven miles per hour alternating with fifteen minute sprints at approximately 10.4, divide the total distance for an average of X miles at Y miles per hour, all of which was irrelevant, because he didn't know if they were still on the island at all, but he needed the order of the numbers to keep him from thinking about what he'd be left with if he was too late.

Corbin felt a surge of hope when he saw the yellow Hummer parked across the road from Billy Oyster's and heard loud music thumping from inside the bar. Breathing hard and drenched in sweat, he stopped to drink from the red spigot and douse his head with cool water. He didn't want to think about how he'd smell to her, but he felt sure of what he wanted to say as he approached the front door.

Choppy water rose and fell below the boardwalk, lapping at the graffiti on the pilings, casting occasional spray as high as the rail. The barroom was empty and redolent with lingering pot smoke. The liquor lockup stood open, the padlock dangling by its claw on the rusted hasp. Shay's camera bag sat on a table nearby. Corbin unplugged the jukebox and called her name. Only the rising surf answered. He checked the facilities and the office behind the bar, then went out to the long fishing pier.

The haze was moving in, precursor to the storm clouds, and it magnified the sun's brightness as he walked to the old binocular unit, feeling for a quarter in his pocket. He came up with one and plugged it in, swinging the bulky viewer across the Gulf to the beach house, training in on the balcony above the lanai. Shay's telescope had been taken inside, and hurricane shutters covered the sliding glass doors.

Corbin shifted the viewer to the lanai. The shutters were in place, but the marble table and Adirondack chairs were still outside. The dirt-bag bartender stood below the steps. Blue silk flicked the corner of the image like a dragonfly. Shay's kimono billowed open, revealing her lacy bra and panties and smooth white belly. The binocular unit whirred and went dark.

He let it swing back toward the sea and stood for a long, hard-breathing bit, calculating how many minutes it would take him to run the six tenths of a mile to Shay's place, trying to discern if he loved her more than he hated her at this moment. He strode down the pier to the barroom, helped himself to another Sam Adams and a handful of the juke box quarters, strode back down the pier, plugged in a quarter and dragged his eyes back to the patio steps.

Shay waved a little princess wave. Billy turned to walk away. The sleeve of the blue kimono rose up as graceful as a kite. There was a sound like a black dot on the air. A pencil point in the huge ambient scribble of wind and water. The bartender clapped his hand to the back of his neck. His knees folded. Arterial spray—three distinct plumes of descending magnitude—pulsed from the front of his throat. His chin went to his chest, and he slumped boneless to the sand.

Corbin stumbled back with a guttural "*fuh!*" and the quarters scattered on the planking.

"What the fuck…"

His hands were shaking when he gripped the viewer again. Shay's back was to him now. She stood over the dirtbag's body, prodded it gently with her bare foot. A pool of blood blossomed like a red hibiscus on the ground beneath his head. She stood for a moment with her hands on her hips, then, holding the hem of her robe carefully away from the stain in the sand, bent to primly check his pulse, first with two fingers below his jaw, then with thumb and forefinger lifting his inert wrist. She let it drop and stood for another moment, arms akimbo. She went to the patio, removing her robe on her way up the steps.

When Corbin saw her body uncovered, he realized the woman was not Shay. His relief in that was quickly supplanted by understanding along with dark fear for where the real Shay might be now. If she was still alive. The viewer whirred and went dark again. By the time Corbin managed to scavenge his quarters and find the beach house, the woman was attempting to drag the beefy bartender, first by an arm, then by a leg, to the deck. She managed a few feet, straining and stumbling in the sand, rested a moment, dragged him another two feet.

Corbin fumbled his phone from his pocket and called 911. A recording reported that the island had been evacuated, and there would be no emergency services until 6 AM Tuesday.

Sykes then.

Corbin scrolled through the contacts to the DA's office, feeling a small victory when the call went through.

"You've reached the voicemail for Alberto Sykes. Detective Sykes passed away September 16, 2005. If you're calling about a case, please call back on the main number and you'll be connected to the appropriate personnel. If you'd like to leave a message of condolence for Mrs. Sykes, please do so at the tone."

Heart pounding in his throat, Corbin fed another quarter into the viewer and found the woman who wasn't Shay log-rolling the bartender's body under the deck. It was a laborious process, heaving him in quarter turns, onto his left side, onto his back, onto his right side, onto his front, onto his left side, onto his back.

Corbin speed dialed Namma's landline. No answer. He tried McKecknie's cell. No go. He tried again, but quickly cut it off. If the call went through and Shay was trying to hide, the ringer might give her away.

Corbin trained the viewer on the crawl space below the deck, peering for any glimpse of Shay's pale skin in the black hole, the garden outside the kitchen, each shuttered window, the front veranda and drive. He scoped the narrowing stretch of beach between the house and bar. By the tidal pools, the water had risen enough that it might make her take the road.

The viewer went dark. Corbin swore and searched for another quarter.

On the last quarter, the bartender was no longer visible. The woman at the beach house kicked clean sand over the red stain and tromped up the steps. She took a white towel from the cabinet on the lanai and patted at her chest, the back of her neck, under her arms, and donned the kimono, the weight of the gun swinging heavily in the deep pocket. She draped herself on an Adirondack chair, fanning herself with something flat, pressing a Diet Coke to her forehead.

Corbin eased the binocular toward the driveway, to the road, and along the coast. In all that he could survey, there was not a car passing, not a flag flying, not a dog or bird or bicycle. One small movement snagged the edge of the image.

It was Shay. Walking toward the house on San Luis Pass Road.

32

GALVESTON

FRIDAY MORNING
SEPTEMBER 23

```
ZCZC MIATCPAT3 ALL

TTAA00 KNHC DDHHMM

BULLETIN

HURRICANE RITA ADVISORY NUMBER 24

NWS TPC/NATIONAL HURRICANE CENTER MIAMI FL

10 AM CDT FRI SEP 23 2005


...RITA A LITTLE WEAKER...STILL A VERY DANGEROUS

HURRICANE...

AT 10 AM CDT...1500Z...THE CENTER OF HURRICANE RITA WAS

LOCATED NEAR LATITUDE 27.4 NORTH...LONGITUDE 91.9 WEST

OR ABOUT 220 MILES SOUTHEAST OF GALVESTON TEXAS AND...

MOVEMENT TOWARD...NORTHWEST NEAR 10 MPH. MAXIMUM SUSTAINED

WINDS...135 MPH. MINIMUM CENTRAL PRESSURE... 929 MB.

$$
```

A little after noon, Shay headed for the beach house to pick up her laptop. Despite the clarity of the blue sky, there was something terribly forlorn about the salt breeze off the Gulf. The palm trees whipped and shivered. Shay felt the heat of the day as thick as mercury in her veins. Looking out over the wheat-colored sand and sequined waves, not knowing what it would look like this time tomorrow, she decided to walk out to the water instead of climbing the stairs to the wraparound porch.

She should change the sheets instead of leaving them for the cleaning lady, she decided. She should have done it when Corbin left, but she didn't want to breathe that last breath of him or think about how it was making love before he left, thrashing against the inevitable, sinking with him like a shipwreck. Shay paused on the steps below the kitchen window and looked back over her shoulder. For a moment, she thought she heard someone say her name.

Also the refrigerator should be emptied and propped open. That was the thought at the front of her mind the moment the blunt force knocked the wind out of her.

Not understanding.

Deep inhale, all heat, no oxygen.

Sky reeling sideways, beach grass in her face, iron grip over her mouth.

Shay and her assailant hit the ground hard. She knew what to do in theory, but her body didn't automatically spring to it this time. Instead, a small, scrambling animal inside her took over. She clawed on squirrel instinct at anything she could reach—a face, a fence post, a rock, a wrist—as she felt herself dragged into the darkness under the deck, the way crocodiles spin their prey into a deep hidey hole under the calm surface of a bayou. Blinking sand from her eyes, Shay struggled to make sense of the slashes of sunlight above her, the familiar weight crushing her body against the seaweed under the deck.

Overhead, on the patio table, the phone was ringing.

Corbin buried his face against her breast, struggling to silence his labored breathing, shirt soaked with sweat, hand clamped tight over Shay's mouth.

Footsteps crossed the cedar floor. Shay's blue kimono floated above the sunlit cracks, tenting a pair of long, lean legs.

"Yes, this is Shay. Hello there. You got my picture?" She giggled brightly, fanning herself with a flat leather folio of credit cards from Char's kitchen desk. "Oh, you're too sweet. Looking at you right now. You obviously take good care of yourself. How tall are you? Oh, goodness. That bodes well."

The kimono billowed in the breeze. She took a .38 from the pocket and laid it on the table next to Shay's open laptop.

"Your profile on the BDSM subforum hints at a taste for the, um… extraordinary. Oh, I agree. Why invest this kind of effort for some vanilla experience, right?"

Corbin tipped Shay's head slightly to the side. Billy lay in the sand an arm's length away. A roach trundled down his shirt collar, and he seemed a little puffy, but other than that, he just looked startled, his eyes only a little more vacant than when he was stoned. It took Shay a full beat to understand the rusty spill down the front of his shirt, the exit wound that looked like a cigarette burn on the front of his throat. Corbin felt her whole body react. He clamped down hard on her mouth, confining her screaming to her eyes and the inside of her chest. Tipping her face away from Billy's vacant stare, he pressed his lips to her forehead, silently stroking her temple, hoping she would feel it as *shhhh*.

"Of course, I don't go into an extreme play session without a safeword. Perfect! Love it. 'Halliburton' it is." The long legs stretched out in front of the Adirondack chair. She lit a cigarette, her voice low and languid. "Here's the plan. There's a bar on San Luis Pass Road. Billy Oyster's. Door's open. The owner's a friend. Be there at four. Get everything ready for me. I'll be along, oh, five-ish. I'll pretend I'm there to get a ride to the mainland with my friend. 'Billy, where are you? Billy, help me!' Only Billy won't be there. Just you and me. When you take me, I'll put up a fight, and I fight hard. I fight dirty. So don't go easy on me. The more I struggle, the more I want. If you don't hear that safe word, zip tie my hands, duct tape my mouth…"

Shay focused on breathing shallow, remaining still. Hard trembling had overtaken her, and the only thing that made it bearable was the weight of Corbin's body on top of her. She felt an overwhelming need to pee, to scream, to get away from Billy's startled stare and the smell of cedar and beach rot under the deck.

"You have my permission to do anything you want to any part of my body. This is such a rare opportunity. I want to be reminded of it every time I see my body in the mirror for the rest of my life."

She tucked the phone into her shoulder, removed the dozen or so cards from their plastic slots, and resumed fanning herself with the empty folio.

"I don't want it rough. I want it brutal. Beat me, burn me, humiliate me. Take me to the extreme, and when it looks like I can't take any more…"

As she described the indescribable, sweat and tears rolled back on Shay's temple. Corbin could feel her heartbeat like a television on the other side of a motel wall.

"I've been a very bad girl, Daddy. I deserve to be punished." There was liquid laughter and some words they couldn't quite hear. "See ya later, alligator."

The lipstick-rimmed cigarette flicked to the sand with a soft-finished hiss twenty inches from Shay's face. The kimono sailed to the table. A graceful hand picked up the gun and dropped it in the pocket. The kimono sailed to the patio door. The door slid open, slid closed.

Corbin brushed at his sandy handprint on her cheek. "Are you all right?"

"*Billy*," she whispered, choked and small. "*It's Billy.*"

"Shay, we can't let the tidal surge take his body. It's evidence."

She nodded. Corbin undid his belt buckle, crawling low and quiet. As he rolled Billy to a pressure treated post, Billy's keys jingled from his pocket. Shay reached over and closed her hand around the TARDIS. Corbin cinched Billy's thigh to the post and crawled back to her.

She pointed to the cigarette butt. "Fingerprints and DNA."

He felt in his pocket and came up with the folded graph paper. Tearing off a square, he fashioned a little envelope and collected the cigarette by the ash end.

"We need to get out of here," he said. "Suggestion?"

"I used to sneak out under the boardwalk." Shay nodded toward the steps that led out to the beach. "Crawl under, all the way to the sand dunes. Don't come up till you get to the fence. You can get most of the way without being seen from the deck."

"Okay. You go first. If she opens the door, I'll give a whistle, and you run like hell, and you don't look back." He listened for a moment, then whispered, "Go."

Shay scuttled like a hermit crab across the tight corner between the deck and the steps and scrambled the length of the boardwalk on her hands and knees when she could, on her belly and elbows the rest of the time. She reached the fence, raw and bleeding from periwinkle and clam shells, stumbled to her feet, and hit the deserted road at a sprint, straining for any sound behind her, groping for her phone. She called 911 and got the recording. She tried Sykes and got the all circuits busy message.

"Shay?" Corbin caught up and briefly squeezed her hand. "What's our objective?"

"Namma's," Shay panted, pointing to the turnoff. "Landline. Call Sykes."

"He's dead."

She stumbled and cried out like she'd been stung by an arrow, pushing her hand to her side, unable to grasp enough air to ask questions. They turned on a residential street that cut across the narrow island to Galveston Bay.

The sky was coming alive with tumbling clouds now. The ground swarmed with blowing leaves and sand devils. On the screened porch behind Namma's house, Shay untangled her keys from Billy's and let herself and Corbin into the kitchen. She stepped into the pantry, closed the door and started screaming. Raw, uninterrupted grieving gave way to unmistakable rage, then revulsion, more grief, then rage again, throaty, serrated with hate.

"You fucking bitch! You fucking bitch! You're dead! You're dead, you bitch!"

Corbin heard cans and boxes hurled against the wall. After a moment, Shay came out, leaned over the sink and cupped cool water over her face and neck. A crackly but functional connection was still in place on Namma's rotary phone, though the process of dialing her father's office number seemed to take forever.

"Millie, I'm hacked," Shay said, trying to push the panic out of her throat. "Cut me off. Lock everything down. Don't believe it's me unless I'm standing in front of you. No, I'm fine. Everything's fine. Everything's under control. Wait—Millie, a call came to the beach house about twenty minutes ago. I need a name and number." She waited, flushed and grim, hands shaking, then wrote on a little chalkboard above the telephone stand. "Got it. Thank you."

Shay hung up, dialed again, and said, "Halliburton." Jaw clenched, she tersely nutshelled it for him. "That was not me, and we do not have a date. Get some therapy, jackoff."

Corbin soaked a dishtowel in cold water and pressed it to the back of her neck as she sorted immediate questions and obvious answers.

"Billy... why would... what happened?"

"They were talking. He started to walk away. She... she just plugged him."

"You saw this?"

"From the pier," Corbin nodded. "There was nothing I could do."

"What about Alberto? I got a text from him yesterday saying—"

"No, Shay. He's been dead for a week."

She hugged her arms across her body. "It was her. I told her I was here."

"Whatever evidence he had on his computer is gone."

"Along with my online storage. I gave him the keys to everything I had on her. Now she's on my computer. She knows everything about me."

Corbin took Billy's keys from her hand. The TARDIS had bitten deep red marks in her palm. "Does your grandmother have a car?"

"Not for years. Mick's Hummer is at the bar, but it's almost out of gas."

"We need to get off this island and contact the police in Houston."

"And say what, Corbin? That someone was murdered outside their jurisdiction, and if they come here after the storm, they'll find absolutely nothing? Gee, officer, I no longer have my illegal evidence about the unidentified person who's not there, but you're welcome to check for pieces of my old boyfriend under my father's tiki bar."

"We have the DNA on the cigarette."

"So they can convict her of smoking?"

"Shay, let's just get over the bridge before the storm hits," said Corbin. "If there's no gas in the Hummer, we'll hotwire one of the junkers. We'll call—I don't know. Somebody. FBI, *Sixty Minutes*. Hell, call your personal Jesus, Anderson Cooper. What else can we do?"

"Kill her."

He rubbed her hands between his. "Babe. Take a deep breath."

"That's how it ends, Corbin. I kill her or she kills me. I was an idiot to think she'd let me walk away."

Corbin would have been hard pressed to find a word for her expression. There were tears below the surface, but she wasn't crying. She was Shay, tough and particular, like she was when it all started. But now instead of wearing that toughness like a skiff of television makeup, she wore it the way a person wears their capillaries, a fine web of resolve just beneath her skin. It sent a frisson of cold through his gut.

"What's happening with Rita?" she asked.

"She shifted east. Lost some speed. Landfall looks to be Cat 2 between Beaumont and Lake Charles. New Orleans and Galveston are both outside the eyewall. Houston will basically see a severe thunderstorm."

"So she's planning to ride this out at the beach house," said Shay.

"Possibly. It was built to withstand some intense weather."

"What about the bar?"

"It's already survived a number of storms worse than this. Pilings appear well-maintained and sound. I wouldn't bet on the fishing pier or the boardwalk, though, and when that boardwalk goes, you're stuck twenty feet offshore until the tidal surge goes down. Or you swim through ten-foot swells with a bunch of debris toward a riprap wall."

"Then I have to kill her at the house."

"Shay, stop it. For Christ sake. You don't just decide to kill somebody."

"You don't know what you'll do until you do it."

"I know I'm not a cold-blooded murderer, and neither are you."

"She knows who we are, knows where our families live. She sent a message to show me she could get to McKecknie. Corbin, she knows I'm pregnant."

She went to the pantry, climbed up on a red step stool and brought out a metal strong box. She twisted Namma's birthday into the combination lock, but it didn't work. Char must have changed it, Shay realized. Of course. Namma was no longer right enough in the head to be packing heat. Shay tried her mother's birthday. Then she twisted in her own birthday, and the tumblers clicked.

Namma's snubby little Bursa Thunder .380 hadn't been loaded or properly cleaned in years. Shay wasn't completely confident that it could be cocked and fired without jamming, but the moment she had it in her hand, for the first time in twenty-eight days—possibly for the first time in thirty-one years—she felt like she was the one in control.

It felt good.

33

GALVESTON

FRIDAY NIGHT
SEPTEMBER 23

```
** WTNT33 KNHC 240100 ***

TCPAT3

BULLETIN

HURRICANE RITA INTERMEDIATE ADVISORY NUMBER 25B

NWS TPC/NATIONAL HURRICANE CENTER MIAMI FL

8 PM CDT FRI SEP 23 2005

...CONDITIONS DETERIORATING IN SOUTHWESTERN LOUISIANA
AND SOUTHEASTERN TEXAS AS DANGEROUS HURRICANE RITA
APPROACHES... REPEATING THE 8 PM CDT POSITION...28.7 N...
93.0 W. MOVEMENT TOWARD NORTHWEST NEAR 11 MPH. MAXIMUM
SUSTAINED WINDS...120 MPH. MINIMUM CENTRAL PRESSURE... 931
MB.

$$
```

Comforted by the cool weight of the little Thunder in her hip pocket, Shay stood alone on the end of the fishing pier at Billy Oyster's. The crowded sky loomed low over the Gulf. Salt spray and stinging rain singed her cheeks. The surf rose and fell in powerful voice. Between the breakers, the Gregorian chant of the generator droned. The golden hour was bruised dark with scudding purple clouds.

Scanning the shore with the binocular unit, Shay couldn't see an electric light anywhere on the island except for the barely discernible glow behind the shuttered windows at the beach house and the long blaze of pier lights over her head. Namma's orange kimono fairly glowed under the bright halogen bulbs, flagging and snapping in the wind.

Shay kept the binocular unit trained on the side windows in the pink-and-tangerine bedroom until the hurricane shutters did their smooth electronic rise. She could just make out the shiny line of her telescope and the form of the woman bending to the eyepiece. Shay cupped her hand in a pageant wave, then extended her middle finger. The hurricane shutters made their smooth electronic descent. She fought the wind on her way back to the bar and wrestled the door open and closed. The phone was already ringing over the cash register.

Shay picked it up and said, "I have your butt."

There was a brief, baffled laugh on the other end of the line. "What?"

"I already know the brand of your cigarettes. By this time tomorrow, I'll know where you bought your lipstick. In seventy-two hours, I'll have your military record. And if you work for TransGlobal, I'll have you."

"Oh, you are an optimist, aren't you?"

"I have every reason to be."

"Shay. Let's not have this end badly."

"See you soon."

Shay hung up and poured herself a ginger ale. She left the pier lights on but kept the barroom dark as she rigged the camera in the fish net on the wall and checked the playback to make sure it was positioned for the widest possible shot. She put Namma's orange robe on Myrtle the mannequin and posed her in a sleepy slump in a booth by a window near the liquor lockup. She raised the window shade to the level of Myrtle's ear, then, scuttling low as a hermit crab, lit candles on the tables near the dance floor.

She retreated to the base of the bar, tucked in a small, tight ball, wet hair clinging to her neck, finger aching on the trigger of the little Thunder. After what seemed like a very long time, the muscles in her legs began to tremble and sear. Shay forced herself to stay quiet, to breathe around her rushing heartbeat.

"She's coming. Stay still."

Outside, spray lashed at the pilings and wind howled through the planked teeth of the boardwalk. Lightning leaped and volleyed between the tall shadows of the empty boxes stacked outside the liquor lockup. The rolling thunder was like a relentless freight train now.

Shay stayed perfectly still, focused on her grip, the gun in her hand.

The front door creaked open, and the wind took it and banged it against the wall, allowing a broad roar of storm noise and damp salt air that snuffed the guttering candles. Backlit by the halogen glow from the pier, a graceful shadow sidled curiously toward Myrtle, arms out straight, both hands on the .38. Three shots cracked in quick succession. Myrtle keeled at an angle. Her arm fell out of Namma's sleeve and clattered on the floor. Plaster shards from her shattered cheek littered the table.

"*Shi—*"

The truncated glottal lodged in Mab's throat. The .38 clattered on the floor. Corbin's grip on the front of her gullet was strong enough to lift her feet off the floor. He held her against his body, one arm tight across her slender neck, the other pinning her arms at her sides as she rasped and kicked, digging her heels into his shins. Shay flipped on the house lights, kicked the gun away from Corbin's feet and pressed the barrel of the Bursa Thunder against Mab's temple.

"Three. Two. One…"

Mab stopped struggling. Her lips were blue, her mouth searching for air like a landed goldfish. She clawed at the back of Corbin's hand, her toes straining for the floor like a ballerina on point as he walked her briskly to the liquor lockup and shoved her forward into the tumble of empty boxes. She took a moment on her hands and knees, clutching at her throat, swallowing and sucking at the air, coughing saliva and swear words.

Corbin closed the gate and hooked the padlock in place. Shay met him at the far end of the bar, and put her arms around him.

"Okay," she said unsteadily. "Your idea was better."

"We're feeling the outer edge of the first feeder band. Too windy to drive over the bridge, but there's a good safe core option at the house."

"There's a generator, too," said Shay.

She produced a Ziploc bag from under the bar and held it open as Corbin picked up the gun by its warm barrel and dropped it in. She sealed the bag, tucked it in a side pocket on her camera bag, and tucked Namma's gun next to it. While he shook out another plastic bag, she unfolded the makeshift graph-paper envelope on the bar, carefully transferring the cigarette butt without touching the lipstick-marked filter.

"How long before it gets intense?"

"About two hours," said Corbin. "Let's expedite this and get across that boardwalk."

"Agreed." Shay fetched her camera from the fish net on the wall.

In the liquor lockup, their guest stepped up on the soda pallets and peered out the little round porthole, spanning her hand across the diameter, taking measure of the wire mesh glass. Corbin pulled a table and two wooden chairs over to the lockup and set them about three feet from the iron bars.

"Can I get you anything?" he asked.

She turned to him with an unreadable smile. "Diet Coke and Bacardi, please."

Corbin went behind the bar and returned with a Diet Coke, a bottle of Bacardi, and a highball glass of ice, setting them on the floor just inside the gate.

"Thank you, Corbin," she said. "That's very sweet of you."

He drew up a chair and sat with his elbows on his knees. She drew up a small stepladder from the corner and sat facing him, sliding an ice cube back and forth on her bruised collarbone.

"Shay says she intends to kill you," he said. "I believe her."

"It's the only way to keep you away from my family with any blessed assurance," said Shay. "Do the deed and let Rita clean up. A page from your book."

She opened a bottle of Everclear, dribbled a little swirl on the floor inside the iron fencing, struck a kitchen match and dropped it. Blue flame sprang up, licked swiftly around the spiral and sizzled out.

"I don't want to be involved in that," said Corbin. "I'd rather leave you here for the authorities to deal with."

"Since you destroyed all my files," said Shay, "Corbin's suggestion is that you tell me on camera about each of the men involved." She poured the rest of the Everclear over Myrtle's displaced wig and orange kimono.

"How you connected with them…" She smashed another bottle against the booth.

"How they died…" She broke two bottles inside the iron bars.

"And how you bled their assets."

One after another, she smashed the remaining bottles of Everclear against the iron bars, against the wall over the booths and the exposed beams above the lockup. Mab leaned forward and covered her head with her arms as glass and 190 proof alcohol rained down on her, but she didn't make a sound or change the expression on her face. Shay placed the kitchen matches on the table next to her camera.

"Short version," said Shay. "Based on the quality of the footage, either I'll hand you over to the police tomorrow morning, or I'll strike a match, walk out the door and watch you burn to death from the comfort of my beach house."

"Either way," Mab said, "you're making the assumption that you'll walk out of here, Shay. There's a difference between deductive reasoning and jumping to conclusions. Basically the difference between a journalist and a muckraker, isn't it?"

"Come downstage a squinch, if you would, please." Shay stepped out of her sandals and sat up on the table in a half lotus, taking the camera in her hands. "Speak up. The storm noise is a little problematic. Corbin, hit that light over the back door, please? Excellent. Thank you, baby."

Mab shrugged one shoulder and mixed herself a moderate rum and Coke.

Shay turned on the camera and said, "Let's start with your name. "

"You'll have better luck if you start with a pack of cigarettes."

"You're sitting in sixteen gallons of accelerant, asking for a smoke?"

"That's how I live," she said. "Obviously, I intend to be careful. As should you."

"Your name, please," said Shay. "And your rank."

"You're making another assumption, Shay. I will say that if I was in the Navy, I'd have done better than Petty Officer Third Class," she added with a pointed glance at Corbin. "Pure laziness on your part, Corbin. Or was it your drinking problem?"

"Run your game on me if you want," he shrugged. "Shay's the one with the matches."

"We've been calling you Queen Mab," said Shay. "Like Watts did. Or did he call you Louisa? Or 321Boom, Chatty Bang Bang, SinSinasty, Octopussy..."

"Chatty Bang Bang is a tranny from Chicago," said Mab, "and her thing is straight-up extortion. Runs the money through bogus leases on junked vehicles. How you missed that paper trail is beyond me, Shay."

"Let's go with Mab for now," said Shay. "I'd rather talk about Billy."

"Billy who?"

"William Roosevelt Ostermann, the owner of this bar. He's lying dead under my deck."

"I'd say you has some 'splaining to do."

Shay set down the camera and picked up the matches.

"Fine, fine," said Mab. "What about him?"

"Corbin saw you shoot him in the neck. He can testify to that and to seeing you with Eldridge Watts, whom you killed in New Orleans on August 29, 2005, during Hurricane Katrina."

"It's not my fault he got slobbering drunk and lost his balance when he shot his load," Mab protested. "That was an accident."

"You accidentally gave him Seconal?" said Shay, taking up the camera again.

"Watts was a monkey-spanking cyber-letch, who sent me a phony picture on the internet, intending to deceive me into a compromising situation. I had every right to defend myself."

"So you took that cinderblock from the hydroponics bed and dropped it on his face in self-defense. Because he presented such a threat with his obviously broken legs. Actually, I was thinking it had something to do with the fact that he didn't have a pregnant wife, like Guy and those others. I've seen all the crime scene photos, and this was by far the most violent. You didn't even care about his money. You couldn't get what you needed from Watts because no one loved him enough. He didn't have enough to lose. The aftermath just wasn't what it ought to be."

"Assumptions, assumptions, assumptions."

"I have photo evidence that he wasn't dead after he fell. He dragged himself several feet through the mud."

Mab came to the gate and said, "Had. You *had* photo evidence."

"Which you eliminated from Alberto Sykes' computer after you killed him and from my computer after you broke into my house."

"Detective Sykes' death was ruled a suicide. Check it out."

"Is that his service revolver in my camera bag?"

"How do I know what you have in your camera bag?"

"Did you kill anyone while you were in North Carolina?"

"Oh, I never went to North Carolina," she said. "I gave the card to some meth girl at the bus depot. Just to keep your little fingers busy. I knew from the beginning Ophelia was a cocktease."

"From the beginning? How?" Corbin sat forward on his chair.

"It should have been obvious to you, Corbin."

"I was limited by bandwidth and model access."

"Right." She batted her eyes. "You're usually so adept at recognizing a cocktease."

"How are you extrapolating these conclusions?" he pressed. "Ivan, Ophelia, now Rita—you were looking at the same range of data as everyone who got it wrong."

"I've developed a new computer model, Corbin. Superior to anything in use."

"Superior how?"

"It goes beyond the data, looks at who she is. You get lost inside the calculations, Corbin, locked inside your own head. The storm's out there," she said, sweeping a graceful arm toward the pier. "I'm asking her what she wants, what she needs. Is she really about to come, or is she faking it? It's there in the satellite images. I know you see it. That little shrug of her shoulder."

"Yes, when it's happening, but how did you predict it forty-eight hours in advance?" Corbin asked. "Rotation? Velocity? Interaction with temperature fluctuations?"

"Interaction with everything," she said, freshening her rum and Coke. "You look at the sky and see all this depth, but you look at a map and see flat. You look at a clock and see linear. You think ideology is one thing and methodology another, when in reality there's no line of demarcation, no condom, no firewall between right and wrong, up and down, above, below, within, without, male, female. Gulf of Mexico or a mud puddle. Wife or one night stand. All dimensions, all velocities, all natures. All of which is to say," she smiled patiently, "you don't know a cocktease when you see one, because you're all about the cock, which is limited to a few inches, and she's all about the tease, which is infinite."

"Meteorology isn't subject to that sort of dogma," he said. "It's a physical science."

"But the diversions and perversions of a storm transcend physical dimension. Global warming is about time, not temperature, Corbin. Its physics are affected by metaphysical factors—greed, compassion, vision. Not just the beat of a butterfly wing, but the essence of the butterfly's intention. Factors that are not three or even four dimensional."

"But now you're talking about chaos theory."

"No. Chaos and inconstancy are two different things, and constant inconstancy can be vectored. When you look into the eye of a storm and understand this, you'll know everything, Corbin. The chemistry, the connectivity. You'll see it."

"I call BS on all of that," said Corbin. "You can't base a predictive computer model on non-quantifiable factors."

She leaned toward him and whispered with a soft breath of Bacardi, "I'll show you."

Corbin drew back, hating the pull inside his chest, the drag of her light perfume on his intense curiosity.

"Corbin?" Shay touched his shoulder. "I think we're losing the pier."

Outside, the long train of halogen bulbs snaked to one side, snaked back.

"What..." Corbin walked toward the back door. "No way. The hurricane won't make landfall until daybreak. Those pilings should last through the first couple feeder bands at least. They should easily withstand—"

The pier lights winked out, and the windows went black. A wrenching metallic whine rose through the storm din. The next volley of lightning exposed bright, jittery images of the wallowing wood and tilted beams. There was another metallic keen from the front of the bar. A battering flight of planks and benches from the boardwalk drummed into the thunder as the porch wrenched away from the base of the building. The doors skewed and shuddered. Steady lightning illuminated a broken park bench, then nothing but driving rain.

"Awesome." Shay made a helpless gesture toward the slinging waves.

"Structural failure like that takes wind speeds in excess of 130," said Corbin. "This is nothing approaching that. That boardwalk isn't even taking the brunt of the tidal surge yet."

"You made an assumption, Corbin." Mab was back up on the soda pallet, spanning her hand across the porthole. "I, on the other hand, watched the bartender drill the pilings this morning while I played with Shay's Barbies."

Shay stood at the bar with her palms on the glass-smooth mahogany. For as many years as she could remember, Billy had kept a photograph of the two of them above the cash register. They were eight or nine in the picture. He was menacing her with a blue crab. She was in full scream, hands out in front of her purple Barbie tankini. The photograph was gone now. He'd taken it with him, knowing he wouldn't be back. Between quick images, unwelcome realization seeped in. Billy bounding up the riprap to the road. His certain payday. The late departure. He needed everyone to be gone so he could accomplish his project unseen.

"But you killed him before he was done," said Shay.

"How many pilings are still good?" Corbin asked.

"There's the big question," said Mab. "Will it tip just a little or go completely in the drink? If two pilings are drilled, and the top wind speed is, oh, say, 85 miles per hour, we'd be just fine. If eight pilings were drilled and we're hit with a gust of 125, not so much. Do the math, Corbin. The tidal surge will only get higher, the debris heavier." Mab came close to the iron bars. "I've been monitoring your email, Corbin. You've formed quite an attachment to the concept of this little bun in the oven. You really want to rely on the assumption that we'll still be here when the sun comes up? Please, tell me you're not relying on her to do the maternal thing. Think about the baby, Corbin. If you don't take her out of here right now—"

"That's enough," he said.

Corbin paced while Shay bagged her camera and tapped a ginger ale. He poured himself a shot of Jim Beam and leaned on the bar next to her.

"He was down under the boardwalk when I got here yesterday," said Shay.

"At what time?"

"About ten-thirty in the morning. So figure he did that first, then the pier. He wouldn't have had time—"

"You don't know that he did it that way."

"But he did a lot of other stuff too, carted all that junk from his place, set up those boats, the junk cars, created that whole tableau in the liquor lockup. Corbin, there's no way he could have gotten it all done. I think the bar pilings are good."

"Shay, that conclusion is based on nothing but wishful thinking."

"Maybe," she had to admit. "You should go. I'll stay here with her."

"That's not happening," he said flatly.

"She knows exactly how this is going to play out, and she wants us to leave. So that's not happening either. If we leave her here alone, she'll get out. I know it."

"If this building shows any sign of compromise, Shay, I'm going out that door, and you're coming with me," said Corbin. She started to say something, but he covered her hand with his. "I don't want to be a thug, but that's how it is."

He walked the perimeter of the barroom and, at eight-foot intervals, stretched out on the floor, one ear to the boards, the other covered with a cupped hand, trying to hear if there was a difference in the moaning of the structure from one point to another. He strained to see out the dark windows, trying to get some read on wind speed and water depth.

"If we have to swim," he told Shay, "swim across the current. It's only fifteen feet to the shore, only about ten feet deep. The surf will push us to the seawall."

"That's what I'm afraid of."

"Try to hit the riprap feet first. Get hold of something as the water pulls back, then haul ass up that wall before the next wave." He squeezed her shoulder. "It's nothing. Six or eight feet. We'll be okay."

He checked the fuel in the generator and decided they should prepare for loss of power in about two hours. Shay lit candles on a few tables well away from the Everclear and sat at the end of the bar, as far away from the liquor lockup as she could sit, braiding a chain of leftover zip ties Billy had left scattered there after he secured the park benches out on the pier. For whatever reason. For Shay's benefit. Or to mock her. It felt like payback now. There was an ironic sort of justice in it.

The graph-paper square from the makeshift envelope still lay on the bar, and seeing her name in Corbin's cramped penmanship, Shay brushed away the ash and asked, "What's this?"

"It's a probability and consequence web," said Corbin. "A risk assessment tool. That's how I process options and formulate recommendations for my clients."

Shay looked closer, turned it sideways. "Long version?"

Corbin put the zip ties in his pocket, clearing the bar between them and unfolded the large sheet of graph paper.

"We can't control the future," he said, fitting the torn corner in place, "but using available data, we can predict that if X happens, possible results are X1, X2, et cetera, and subsequently, the probable results of X1 will be X1a, X1b and so on. The computer model I designed is specific to weather, but you can apply the same basic principles to pretty much anything."

He sat on the barstool next to hers, using a swizzle stick as a pointer.

"Start with core volition B: Baby. I've compiled stats on how the baby would impact and be impacted by various probabilities and sub-probabilities, vectoring out with pink numbers for a girl causality flow, blue for boy. I tweaked to reflect factors that remove us from general population data: finances and education on the plus side, and on the negative, certain personality traits and genetic diseases—breast cancer in my family, Alzheimer's in yours—things of that nature. Following?"

"So far," said Shay.

"Birth and nursing—that's you, obviously. I'll balance with primary responsibility for diapers, bath, and other basic maintenance. We distribute the rest equitably. Developmental play, reading, diction and language, social skills, humanities, discipline. Neither of us misses more work than the other, neither family bogarts the baby on holidays, birthdays, et cetera."

Shay nodded. "Keep talking."

"Secondary volition: Marriage, vector M in green, solves more problems than it creates, I think, generally proving out better than vector JC: Joint Custody in purple. Vector M1: we both relocate to Houston. M2 parallels the JC vector in that you relocate to New York, I stay in New Orleans, and the kid commutes quarterly or biannually. This inset lays out statistical effect of dual household via standardized psychological and academic testing. Here's a breakdown of SAT scores by school district in each metroplex, magnet schools, availability of arts and enrichment programs, and statistics for cancer clusters and environment-influenced childhood asthma. Houston ozone levels suck. Houston is basically tied with LA for worst air quality in the US, but New Orleans has some serious environmental issues now, so I hate to admit it, but New York comes out ahead here. In red are the social and academic influencers: Gymboree, piano lessons, summer camp, Scouts, et cetera. Also stats on depression and suicide among teens and voter turnout in the age 18-to-21 demographic."

"Why are there two college funds?" Shay indicated an inset on the M2 track.

"One's for Baby T," said Corbin. "Hopefully, they'll be close. I want to make sure Baby T can afford to go to the same school, if he wants to.

If you start our kid's fund with an initial 25K drop, I'll start Baby T's fund with the 25K Guy and Bonnie paid me for the house."

"Oh, Corbin…"

Shay looked up at him, emotion welling in her eyes. He was grateful when she blinked it away and tapped M1(7)d.

"Dog? How big is this dog?"

"Contingent on the kid. Not some little kick-dog, though."

Shay smoothed her hands over the intricate atlas of possibility outlined in Corbin's small, square handwriting. "You certainly have thought of everything."

"No," said Corbin. "Hell, no. There's a huge realm of unknowns. People die and disappoint. Hurricanes happen. Some crazy asshole comes along to blow your head off or fly a plane into a building. There's crucible stuff like cancer and loss and failure."

"Good things happen, too," she reminded him. "You stumble on a book that expands your mind or travel to a place that expands your soul. Someone inspires you."

"Or kicks your ass."

"Either way," said Shay, "you change."

"Right. Every time you make a choice, it's an entirely new trajectory. You wake up every morning in a whole new geopolitical jet stream, but at the end of the day, that core volition exists, and you make the next choice accordingly. Risk assessment is what I do, Shay, and I'm showing you solid, research-based evidence that you are not better off on your own. Ma femme, I swear, whatever comes, we'll find a way through it."

With the winded look of a man who'd just climbed over a wall, Corbin folded the graph paper and tucked it in a side pocket on her camera bag.

"My recommendation," he said, "is that we lock in on the M1 track and make it legal ASAP. The Houston courthouse won't be functional tomorrow, but I'm betting you have at least one judge on your payroll. Or we can find some kind of clergy."

"Corbin, you don't just elope with someone who stands to inherit several billion dollars."

"That's why we need to get it done before the Hoovestahl TransGlobal legal department descends on me en masse. My attorney has worked up an ironclad, one-page pre-nup."

"No offense," said Shay, "but your attorney doesn't stand a chick-pea's chance on a railroad track."

"There's nothing to fight over, Shay. If we divorce, I pay child support. If you die, I get zero. If I die, my estate goes in trust for the kid. Both families are guaranteed visitation."

"Maybe, but if we do this…" She tried to keep the cod liver oil out of her tone. "We'd be married."

"It's the only way to address the Char piece," said Corbin, "but frankly the legal and social ramifications are secondary to—"

A tortured bray came up from the floor joists.

"Oh, God!" Shay gripped the bar rail. "Did you feel that?"

Corbin nodded, and Shay uttered a small cry when they felt it again. The building shifted enough that Corbin's shot glass slid several inches down the bar.

"That's it. We're out of here." Corbin grabbed Shay's camera bag and looped it across his body. "Right now, Shay. We're not negotiating this."

She looked up at him, eyes wide, hands out to the side as if she were trying to steady herself on a tightrope.

"It's too late," she whispered, just before she disappeared.

GALVESTON

SATURDAY MORNING
SEPTEMBER 24

```
** WTUS84 KHGX 240554 ***

HLSHGX

GMZ330-335-350-355-370-375-

TXZ163-164-176>179-195>200-210>214-226-

227-235>238-241000-


HURRICANE LOCAL STATEMENT ... CORRECTION TO TIME

NATIONAL WEATHER SERVICE HOUSTON/GALVESTON TX

1205 AM CDT SAT SEP 24 2005

...RITA A CATEGORY 3 HURRICANE AND WILL MAKE LANDFALL
NEAR THE TEXAS AND LOUISIANA LINE BETWEEN 3 AM TO 5 AM...
MAXIMUM SUSTAINED WINDS NEAR 120 MPH...WITH HIGHER GUSTS.
... THOSE THAT HAVE NOT EVACUATED SHOULD REMAIN IN PLACE.

$$
```

Shay opened her eyes and saw fire. Candles plus Everclear. Flammable plus stupid. The bar keeled on its last true pilings, raked at a 45-degree angle like a piano lid, front doors swinging wide, showing roiling clouds and lightning. Most of the liquor lockup wallowed down in the tidal surge. Outside the wire mesh windows, battering waves rose and fell. Shay lay on her back on the iron gate, her face as close to the ceiling beams as it would be to a coffin lid. She felt a lukewarm slosh of seawater wash over her. She tried to get up, but a fist in her hair jerked her head back with a hard clang on the iron bars. The blow rang like a church bell in her skull. Searing pain cut through a blossom of warmth on the back of her head. A smooth, strong arm snaked around her neck. Shay tucked her chin down and sank her teeth into it. Talons gripped her shoulders, forcing her down into the salt water. By the time Mab dragged her back up, gagging and thrashing, Corbin had appeared high above them at the far end of the mahogany bar.

"Get down here and open this gate, Corbin," Mab howled with the wind. "I am not playing with you. Open this gate or she's dead!"

"No, Corbin! Get out!" Shay bucked and struggled. "Baby, go! Get out!"

He slid down the steep floor, controlling his rapid descent with footholds and handholds on the cubbies where dishtowels and shot glasses used to be. He had Namma's gun in his hand, and he pointed it toward the liquor lockup.

"Let her go, or I will shoot," Corbin bellowed.

"Go ahead," Mab bellowed back. "Try to hit me without blowing her head off."

"I will shoot!"

"Bullshit! Unlock the gate or she dies right now."

Shay felt a quick, deep slash across her breast. Before she could scream, her head was plunged underwater. When Mab dragged her up, Shay felt hot blood on her chest and the cool edge of a broken bottle against her cheekbone.

"Next is her face. Then her throat." Mab ratcheted back on Shay's neck, spitting, treading the choppy water. "Run the probabilities, Corbin. The only way she gets out of here alive—"

The structure lurched again. Cupboards and coolers swung open behind the bar, raining down shot glasses and bar snacks. The cash register hung itself briefly on its power cord, then let go and hit the iron bars, exploding in a burst of plastic bits, bar chips, and nickels. Corbin slid down the wooden floor, and Namma's gun disappeared through a gaping crack between the boards.

The next wave forced salt water into Shay's mouth and nose and left Mab with nothing to breathe between the iron fence and the thrashing surface. She pushed her frantic face through the bars, grasping for an inch of air like Ms. Martineau's doomed Sweet Bay. Shay groped for something—anything with which to push Mab's head under. She felt another cold stroke from her temple to the corner of her mouth. Warm blood filled her ear, and Mab's voice bubbled through it.

"Corbin! Open it! Open the goddamn gate or this bitch is dead!"

Another wave waterboarded them, and they struggled for breath, cheek to cheek. When Shay could see again, Corbin was standing over her, one foot on the windowsill, the other wedged against the side of the gate by her hip, the wall behind him crawling with flames. She saw the TARDIS in his hand.

"Corbin, no!" Shay screamed.

Corbin tossed the keys in a silvery arc over her head, and Mab lunged for them, but they entered the water just past her fingertips. She sucked in a rasping gulp of air and dove down into the gloom and matted cardboard.

The moment Mab's arm left Shay's neck, Corbin seized the front of her bloodied bra, dragging her up, over to the tangled mountain of tables and chairs that had log-jammed at the submerged back door. She clutched and scrambled, but it was impossible to gain a meaningful purchase. The collection of spindly legs, broken backs, and empty boxes gave way beneath them. Every time Shay stumbled, the water clouded red around her.

Corbin managed to get one hand on the splintered boat nailed to the wall and hauled Shay up to the fishing nets and beach trophies. Together they scaled the steep incline of the floor, using the ramshackle installation like a rock face. Shay grabbed the naked baby doll and hoisted herself forward to a wig head, reached for a toilet seat and used that to grab onto a fraternity hazing paddle. Grasping each found treasure, she felt Billy's hand on the hammer and nails.

They made their way to the tee-shirt kiosk that formed a bridge to the front door. Corbin helped Shay clamber onto what was now the bow of a sinking ship, heaving himself onto the slanted door jamb after her. Shay peered down into the abyss beyond the dance floor, looking for signs of life in the smoke and sea. Waves peaked below their feet, then dropped down into darkness. Spray scoured upwards, burning their skin, stinging their eyes.

Straddling the edge of the uprooted floor, Shay stared at the blood on her shirt. Saltwater scalded her breast and cheek. Beneath a numb skullcap at the back of her head, bursts of bright, silvery pain floated on a swale of dizzy blackness.

"Corbin," she said thickly. "I don't feel right."

"No, you're good. You're okay. Shay, look at me." He snapped his fingers in front of her vacant eyes. "Shay? Stay with me."

She cleared a little. Nodded numbly. Was pretty sure she said, "Okay."

He tore the front of her shirt open and brushed watery blood from the deep laceration, exposing stratified skin and fatty tissue. Cupping her hand over it, Shay tried to press the edges together, but blood oozed between her fingers. Corbin pulled off his shirt and tied the sleeves tight around her. He separated her sticky hair from the wound on her face, tore a strip from the shirttail and wadded it against her cheek.

"Does it look very bad?" Shay asked.

He nodded. "Shay, we have to get to the Hummer, okay?"

She looked across the impossible expanse of bad luck and janky motorboat debris.

"It was just a sordid little story," she said. "To show I could cover something grittier than a pancake breakfast."

Corbin shook his head. "What? I can't hear you."

Shay pointed to the piano-keyed remains of the boardwalk. "I can't do it."

"Yes, you can, ma femme. I got you. We'll be okay."

Corbin tasted storm and blood on her mouth when he kissed her. He took a heavy plastic zip tie from his pocket, looped it through the little chain she'd made, and cinched it around his wrist. He slipped a loose tie through the last link to form makeshift handcuffs.

"Shay, give me your hand."

"No. Veto. I can't swim if you tie my arm."

"I'm not letting you go in on your own." Corbin cinched the second tie on her wrist. "We're both strong swimmers. We'll find a stride that works between us. And when we get to that wall, we're gonna haul ass, right?"

"Right." Shay nodded, and her brain sloshed like a dry martini inside her skull.

"Next wave. Big breath. As you jump. Not before."

"Corbin?" Shay said something he couldn't hear.

He leaned in and called, "What?"

"I said, M2." She pulled him closer and shouted over the wind. "I would like to do M2. If we're not dead."

"Okay. That works."

"You wouldn't rather be dead, would you?"

"No," he laughed, and even in the moment he knew this was how they would survive each other. Come hell or high water, he'd keep her bound to him, and she'd make him laugh. They'd find their stride.

"Deep breath," he shouted. "Across the current. Haul ass. That's the plan."

The edge of the plastic zip tie chafed the heel of Shay's hand as he dragged her to her feet and steadied her in the angled doorway.

"Ready?" he called, latching his arms around her waist.

"No!"

But he was gone, and she was gone with him. What was left of the world she knew was lost in the spray behind her. Shay found one deep inhale, then the Gulf rose up and took her like a freight train. As they crashed through the solid barrier of surf, she was torn from his arms and felt the distinct, sickening snap of her wrist. Agony javelined up her arm, and her precious breath wrenched out of her in a bubbled cry. Seawater burned through her sinuses as she plunged into the underworld.

In the salt belly of the surge, there was quiet.

Shay felt no panic. She felt, in fact, an awareness of not panicking and a vague sense of wonder about that. Chaos and calm became one, and while her mind's response to that was slow, her body told her to stop struggling, and she stopped in a warm, weightless place, where there was nothing but Corbin's body connected to hers, righting her, orienting her in the tumbling dark. Her feet found sand, and that made sense, so she pushed off hard, and so did he. Every time Corbin dragged her broken arm forward, Shay felt another swift spear of agony, but she followed the pull of his stroke to the top of the towering waves, then fought the bucking surface for short, precious gasps of air and brief, rocking glimpses of the burning building.

The unforgiving riprap wall rushed at her.

For a moment, Shay was back in the howling blackness of the insurance office with Corbin's body against her back, then in the big bed at the beach house, hearing his voice across the room.

Then she was a little girl, snuggled next to her father under the thrumming blades of a helicopter.

Then she was in a still white womb. She smelled alcohol and latex, felt the sickening drag and sting of a suture in the side of her face. Corbin nuzzled her salty mermaid hair and sang softly in her ear.

"C'est la petite poule blanche, qui a pondu dans la branche, un petit coco pour mon bébé faire dodo... dodiché, dodiché, dodiché, dodicho..."

The lullaby smelled like rain.

Shay heard distant thunder and then nothing.

HOUSTON

TUESDAY AFTERNOON
SEPTEMBER 27

STAFF REPORT FOR REP. CHARLES MELANCON

U.S. HOUSE OF REPRESENTATIVES

Hurricane Katrina Document Analysis: The Emails of Michael Brown

On September 27, 2005, Michael Brown appeared before the House select committee to defend his response to Hurricane Katrina. At the hearing, Mr. Brown testified that "FEMA pushed forward with everything that it had, every team, every asset that we had, in order to help what we saw as being a potentially catastrophic disaster." …Despite the requests of Reps. Melancon and Davis, the select committee has not received any of the relevant emails and communications involving Homeland Security Secretary Michael Chertoff, Defense Secretary Donald Rumsfeld, Army Corps of Engineers Commander Carl Strock, Health and Human Services Secretary Michael Leavitt, and White House chief of staff Andrew Card. The continued failure of Administration officials to comply with these document requests will impede congressional oversight of the federal response to Hurricane Katrina.

Three days after he lumbered up the riprap with the dead weight of Shay's body under his arm, Corbin lay on her hospital bed, one eye on the select committee hearings, the other on his laptop. A tropical depression spawned by a fleet-footed African easterly was getting up some convection through the Lesser Antilles, dumping buckets on St. Kitts, but Corbin was hopeful that wind shear in the region would keep it from organizing any serious spin until he was back in his office in New Orleans.

As the hearing droned on, Michael Brown, who'd tendered his resignation two weeks earlier, was willing to concede that he'd made two mistakes.

"First, I failed initially to set up a series of regular briefings to the media about what FEMA was doing throughout the Gulf Coast region... Second, I very strongly personally regret that I was unable to persuade Governor Blanco and Mayor Nagin to sit down, get over their differences, and work together. I just couldn't pull that off."

"Geezes, dog. Seriously?"

Corbin rolled off the bed and went looking for Shay, who had less talent for being a hospital patient than she did for singing. He found her in the hallway, pacing with her IV pole, engaged in animated dialogue on her cell phone.

"It's not happening, Renny. I'll license the footage with my boilerplate agreement, but I'm not going on camera. Because I don't work for you anymore. And because I'd be the Beauty Queen With the Slashed Face. That kind of subtitle lingers like stink on roadkill."

With her good arm, Shay shifted an ice pack from the raw track of stitches on her swollen blue cheek to a horseshoe of sutures around the hematoma on the back of her head. She looked battered and sewn together, but there was a ready, tensile beauty about her, a core strength that made Corbin proud of her and more than a little turned on.

"Anyway, I'm booked," she said, "I got married this morning, and he's—no, seriously. The hurricane guy. Paleoclimatologist. But he's leaving Monday, so I need to slot him in for the rest of the week. So to speak."

"Babe, you're supposed to be lying down," said Corbin.

Shay pointed her broken wing toward her father, who was over by the coffee machine, digging through his pockets for correct change. Corbin approached Shay's father, circumspect but friendly, and plugged in quarters for two coffees.

"Obliged," Hoovestahl said grudgingly.

"I want to thank you, sir. For coming with the helicopter."

"That's my little girl. I'm her father. There's not a goddamn thing between Heaven and Hell I wouldn't do to protect her. Something you better consider on your way back to Louisiana." Hoovestahl sipped his coffee, then cast the cup in the trash. "I don't expect our paths to cross again."

Corbin cleared his throat. "Actually, sir…funny thing about that…"

At the far end of the hall, Shay couldn't hear what Corbin was saying, but she heard her father's response.

"We'll see about that, you side-winding liberal son of a bitch!"

She was horrified to see tears in his eyes as he strode toward her.

"Daddy…"

"Do not open your mouth."

He grimly took her into his big arms, hugging her hard, pressing kisses to the crown of her head.

"Mr. Hoovestahl," said Corbin, "I genuinely hope—"

"I expect to see that so-called pre-nup on my desk in one hour."

"Yes, sir."

Hoovestahl stalked off. Corbin closed the door and pulled Shay next to him on the hospital bed.

"How'd your mom take it?" he asked.

"She heard two words—*married* and *baby*—followed by an angel choir. Presenting it to them as a done deal made it a lot easier. Thank you for that."

"Thank you for doing it on the roof instead of in the chapel."

"Have we heard from the coroner? Were they able to get Billy?"

"They said…" Corbin faltered. "Shay, you saw how violent that surge was. The torso was mostly intact, but the head and—"

"Stop." She pushed her fingertips against her pounding headache.

"I'm sorry, babe." Corbin pulled her close and stroked her neck. "They found a woman's body about a mile up the beach from the bar. They want me to come and take a look."

"Corbin, be careful what you say. If she did work for TransGlobal—"

"I'm not discussing that right now," he said. "I'm already uncomfortable with the flabby police report. The lawyers got here before the obstetrician."

"That's my life. You knew what you were getting into."

"So did you."

He settled his arm behind her shoulders and clicked to a local news report tallying the damages from Hurricane Rita. In Louisiana, Cameron Parish was all but demolished. Creole, Grand Chenier, Holly Beach. All gone. In Texas, the wind in the Golden Triangle took a hellacious number of trees, but the levees at Port Arthur stood up to the tidal surge, and that was a victory. Only seven people died as a direct result of the massive storm; well over a hundred were killed in the evacuation, which was now being touted as the most massive evacuation effort in US history—and the most utterly bollixed.

"Which one of us gets to say 'told ya so'?" asked Shay.

"If people had followed the evacuation plan zone by zone, as instructed by officials—"

"Before Katrina, you were telling people to disregard the official call. You can't have it both ways, Corbin. Ultimately, you have to respect people's right to make their own decisions. Tale of two cities," she added philosophically. "One embraced denial, the other embraced fear."

"People embraced bullcrap," said Corbin. "They embraced Oprah. All that crap about the Superdome."

"Don't blame Oprah for that. Fox and all the majors were already running with it. The mayor and the chief of police sat there on her show, saying 'little babies were getting raped' by roving gangs and marauders. Why would she doubt the mayor and the chief of police? That's the horse's mouth, Corbin. She would have been utterly remiss to not put that on the air."

"So, when the media can't trust government and the public can't trust the media, who's left?"

"Bill Nye," Shay said. "And if you want to get these issues out there, do it now. Rita's TVQ won't last. Hurricanes as a trending topic—the dog's been walked."

Corbin knew she was right. With several weeks to go, the 2005 hurricane season was already the most ruinous on record with almost 4,000 deaths and over $150 billion in damages. But folks up north were over it. Celebs had done their due diligence on behalf of New Orleans. The advent of instant ten-dollar text donations had salved the national conscience, so there'd be little danger, Corbin figured, of voters being stricken by the need to look past their bumper stickers. Mass audience perception would return to normal: the majority of America was just a grassy median strip between LA and New York; north of Chicago was a cow pasture called The Heartland, south of Chicago was a trailer park full of inbreeders eating Popeye's chicken.

"Maybe we should do M 1.5," said Shay. "You in New Orleans and me in Houston."

"Sure. I could do a satellite office here."

She took the graph paper from the pocket of her robe. It was smeary and warped from being wet and dried out, dog-eared from being folded and unfolded. Beyond the fine blue lines, a third dimension unfolded, a fourth even, encompassing the constructs of time and love. The future remained a mystic, wild parabola, but here was a map, coded in true colors with kindness, forgiveness, and forbearance built in.

"Corbin." Shay held it up to the light, seeing what she'd seen in the bar, but not quite able to wrap her pounding head around it. "Isn't this a predictive model based on non-quantifiable factors?"

"No, it's…" He tried to mentally step back, extrapolating the parallels to the parallels. "Holy hell. I see what you mean."

"Maybe she was telling the truth."

"If she was able to create a functioning model—"

"It would be worth millions."

"More important, it could save a lot of lives."

"Right." Shay ducked her chin sheepishly. "That's what I meant."

"If it exists," he said, "I'd sure like to get my hands on it."

Shay smiled a painfully off-kilter smile. "I bet I could help you with that."

"I bet you could." He nosed her cheek, avoiding the stitches.

"Can it wait till tomorrow?"

"Tomorrow's good, ma femme." Corbin hoped it sounded like a term of endearment instead of the way it felt—my woman, my wife—protective and proprietary in a way Shay wouldn't like. He settled his hand on her midsection, and she closed her eyes, breathing deeply against his white shirt.

Joie de vivre moved through him like a Gulf breeze.

Working as a volunteer in the wake of Hurricane Katrina, I witnessed the heroic efforts of the American Red Cross and have been making an automatic monthly donation ever since. Throughout the world, when natural disaster strikes, the American Red Cross is there with compassionate, urgently needed, agenda-free relief. They're among the first to arrive and the last to leave, and they need you to go there with them. Thank you for your generosity.

Email to and from FEMA director Michael Brown has been edited for length in only a few cases for this book; spelling, content, and details are unchanged and appear in full as sent and received, as expurgated by government censors. The Center for Public Integrity obtained the documents on May 5, 2006, pursuant to a request filed under the Freedom of Information Act. The emails cover the period from Aug. 26 to Sept. 8, 2005, and, as of this writing, can be found in their entirety at publicintegrity.org. "Hurricane Katrina Document Analysis: The E-mails of Michael Brown" staff report from the office of Rep. Charles Melancon, US House of Representatives, can be found in its entirety at http://i.a.cnn.net/cnn/2005/images/11/03/brown.emails.analysis.pdf

Weather forecasts and warnings are the real thing and can be found in their entirety at http://weather.unisys.com/hurricane/archive. Some have been edited here for length and to facilitate formatting. I encourage you to visit the website and view these forecasts as they were authored by the dedicated scientists who study this astonishing force of nature. There is a fascinating elegance about the full forecasts that couldn't be captured here.

FEMA's press release re the Hurricane Pam computer simulation can be found in its entirety at https://biotech.law.lsu.edu/katrina/hpdc/docs/20040723_Hurr_Pam_exercise.pdf. Hurricane Pam provided a wealth of knowledge about exactly what would happen when a Cat 3 hurricane struck New Orleans. Why so little was done with this information remains a mystery to many, including me.

Articles from the *Times-Picayune* have been edited for length: Copyright 2005, The Times-Picayune Publishing Corporation. All Rights Reserved. Used by NewsBank with Permission. The *Times-Picayune* was a tremendous research resource for me throughout this project. Special thanks to their excellent library staff.

SPECIAL THANKS

Hurricane specialist Dr. Jack Beven and physician/activist Dr. Wendy Harpham, MD for expert advice; Fred Ramey, Joanna Weiss, Colleen Thompson, Barbara Taylor Sissel, and the Midwives for reading early drafts of the manuscript; Aaron Sorkin for invaluable feedback on dialogue and plotting; Jerusha Rodgers for developmental and editorial assist; Gary Rodgers for listening to me talk through it for five years; and to our wonderful neighbors, George and Toni Willi, who supplied us with a lifeline to their generator, which allowed me to keep writing after Hurricanes Rita and Ike. Most important, huge gratitude and respect to the many survivors and volunteers who shared their stories with me during the terrible summer of 2005. It was a privilege to sit with you, hear you, bring you water, and welcome you back into the sun.

ACKNOWLEDGMENTS

In 2022, I independently republished six books from my backlist:

Crazy for Trying: 25th Anniversary Author's Cut

The Hurricane Lover: 10th Anniversary Edition

Bald in the Land of Big Hair: 20th Anniversary Ebook

Sugarland

Kill Smartie Breedlove

Boxing the Octopus: The Worst Way to Become an Almost Famous Author & the Best Advice I Got While Doing It

This wouldn't have been possible without the stellar team assembled by Reading List Editorial. Special thanks to project manager Salvatore Borriello for his patience, wisdom, and industry expertise; to Lindsey Alexander for her keen insight and enormous kindness; to Kapo Ng for the brilliant reimagining of the cover designs; and to Sharon, Lauren, and the team at BookSavvy PR for busting out the hustle. My assistant Patty Lewis Lott is the divine sparkplug that powers this whole rodeo, and my agent Cindi Davis-Andress continues to work miracles on my behalf—two life-changing partnerships for which I'm grateful every day.

Made in the USA
Middletown, DE
31 March 2022

63432866R00201